# *Pricking of My Thumbs*

## Charles McRaven

## A Wings ePress, Inc.
### Adventure Novel

# *Wings ePress, Inc.*

Edited by: Jeanne Smith
Copy Edited by: Brian Hatfield
Executive Editor: Jeanne Smith
Cover Artist: Trisha FitzGerald-Jung
Images: Rachel Claire from Pexels and
susanne906 from Pixabay

*All rights reserved*



Wings ePress Books
www.wingsepress.com

Copyright © 2021 by: Charles McRaven
ISBN-13: 978-1-61309-527-0
ISBN-10: 1-61309-527-9

Published In the United States Of America

Wings ePress Inc.
3000 N. Rock Road
Newton, KS  67114

# Dedication

All the good women, including my daughters, who have
worked with me in construction.

* * *

PRICKING OF MY THUMBS
(or is that just splinters?)

*By the pricking of my thumbs*
*Something wicked this way comes*
—Macbeth

# One

People ask me all the time what it's like, being a woman in construction work. Well, mostly it's the shits.

You know, the chauvinist shits who just know you can't possibly do 'their' jobs as well as they can, who expect you just to run errands and make the coffee. Every time. They're always hinting you should really be a secretary, or turning tricks, or just go stick your feet under some guy's table. They speed up when you're around, and want you to ask them how to do everything. Then roll their eyes if you do. If one happens to be the boss, he'll find obscure reasons to pay you less than the guys.

Then there are the dumb shits, the ones who won't admit you know more than they do and are always proving it.

There are the Romeo shits, who never pass up the chance to play grab-ass and can't *believe* you're not dying to tumble into bed with them. Their permanent expression around you is a 'king leer.' And when you walk away, you hear "Mm-mm, like two pigs in a gunnysack fight."

My favorites are the don't-give-a-shits, who just do their damn work and leave you alone to do yours. They're the guys who keep duckbill-cap folks like me from just taking the job and shoving it.

So that's about it. I'm not bitter, though: learned to roll with it early on. The pay's usually okay, compared with working in a shoe store or waiting tables, both of which I've done. And I was okay with it all, till the bullets started zinging on this one job.

You don't get rich pounding nails, but it's a living. A high-class hooker probably makes more, but hey, that'd really waste my comparative lit degree. Speaking of which, I foolishly applied for an editing job with a publisher once. They wanted me to type the rejection slips. For minimum wage.

And make the coffee.

Stereotyping is alive and braying, believe it. I'm 5'7" and wiry; I work out a lot and my grip has made grown men cry, but nobody sees me as being able to handle a Skilsaw, a *man's* tool. My hair's in the shortest ponytail that'll go through the back of my duckbill cap, and my boobs aren't big enough to get caught in a radial-arm saw. And I don't really give a damn whether I fulfill somebody's preconception of a carpenter. I can do the job; just get outta my way, dude.

My dad was always building things, more so after Mom's death, and could never get big brother Bert to help for long, so I was it. From age ten on. Child Welfare would have a spotted cow over that one.

Bottom line is, I can swing a hammer, and I can figure stairs and cabinets better than most men. And after seven years at it, not counting the growing-up stuff, I'm fast. Dad always told me there's good and then there's fast, but damn few good *and* fast, so don't settle for less than that. Didn't, and eventually scored it, despite envious put-downs from the aforementioned shits.

So I found myself in central Virginia this late summer, after good buddy Phil's scheme for high-end kitchen remodels dried up in Pennsylvania with the building recession.

Although we'd never been a couple, Phil and I'd sort of dried up, too, along with any savings I'd put into the business. Compound miter saws and planers ain't cheap.

And there I was, burning the last tank of overpriced gas in Hosmer, my Dodge Dakota, looking for work and not having the slightest inkling I'd soon be hiding, running for my sweet little life. Yeah, not really the job description...not supposed to include blood.

Construction can be sketchy, with enough downtime to let you travel around to places you always wanted to see, but there's this annoying thing of running out of dollars that goes with it. And face it, we're all itinerants at heart. Get to the end of a particularly great project, and we're apt to be off again instead of staying around for the next, boring one.

So Hosmer (that's out of Conan Doyle, if you wondered) let me know we should settle for a bit if I expected him to continue to function, and if Cyrano and I were going to eat. Cyrano's my dog: big sweet hound, mostly black, with one ear that wants to stand up. Somewhere in his family tree a traveling Doberman must've done more than just mark his territory, because you don't lay a paw on Wesley (that's me) unless you're prepared to lose a major part of it. He wandered up to my campsite in the Rockies, half-grown and half-starved two years ago and has never gotten past being grateful for my bagels, bacon grease and love.

Protective Phil had done some canine training once in his checkered past as a policeman. Never knew how such an easy-going guy did that for a living. Anyway, he worried about my defending myself against the weirdos of the world, so he proceeded to teach my more or less gentle dog to attack, and not necessarily just on command. Got so he or anybody else could brandish a toy gun at me or just say something in an angry tone, and only the padding let him keep the wrist or other select parts of his anatomy till I called him off. I thought that was overkill (literally), but hell, you never know...

I hadn't known anything for sure about Charlottesville, Virginia, except for vague mentions of it as one of the top places in the country to live, and that could have been in my subconscious (Maybe see how much they lied?). I rolled into a campground to sleep in the camper shell on Hosmer, did some laundry, counted my shrinking money. Okay, eat for maybe a week. Sack of dog food (small sack). Maybe I wouldn't have to hock my tools this time; you don't get a construction job without tools.

Even when things are slow, somebody's always building something somewhere. And there's never been a contractor who didn't wish for another good carpenter, whether he could afford me or not.

Employment office is a waste of time, and the good jobs never get in the paper. I cruised the hills out these skinny roads from town where they apparently didn't believe in shoulders, and yeah, there was some action. After all, some people seem to be recession-proof, and this looked like that kind of town. I skipped the look-alike pattern house jobs because those contractors always bid cheap and squeeze the grunts at the bottom so they get their profit anyway. I wanted upscale, maybe gated communities if I could get in to talk to the honchos.

"Hi. The lady out front said you weren't hiring carpenters, but I'm good and I'm fast and I know you got deadlines to meet and I know you don't have any money tree that just keeps shedding dollars for half-ass workers, and I need a job."

The specimen behind the desk in the office trailer looked me over like a side of beef—they always do—and sighed.

"Affirmative action: I hate it. How do I know you can even drive a nail, sweetie?" He had these little pig eyes squeezed back in a red face. Beer gut. Why do builders *always* have beer guts?

"Tool belt's worn through and my Skilsaw's got a hundred thousand miles on it. I can match any man you got on framing, trim, roofing, cabinets, and I bet I'm faster."

"Well, you talk a good fight, anyway. Now just suppose I *did* need somebody, what kinda dollars we lookin' at?"

I'd seen that the construction trucks were new. The scaffolding shone in fresh paint. The office was neat, even relatively grit-free. The secretary had been efficient. These were million-dollar houses going up...

"Twenty to start, twenty-five after you see what I can do, couple weeks in."

"*What?*" He almost succeeded in heaving his lard ass up in insult. "My best guys don't make that. And you're a *girl*."

*Oh, wow: observant. Now just what had given me away?*

"Yeah, last time I checked. What'd *you* have in mind?"

"You really wanta know?" settling the pounds back with the expected leer. He was checking out my small but perfect boobs like that was all there was to me. *Oh, hell.*

"Dollars. Per hour." *You slob.* His eyes came back up.

"Fifteen, tops. And I really don't need anybody right now. Coupla weeks, who knows? Turnover." He spread his beefy hands.

"Then you don't need me. I paid my dues a long time ago. Got the best references in the States. Thanks for your time. *Sweetie.*" I turned and left. Threw the secretary a glance of commiseration.

"Well, Cyrano, this place sucks, anyway," I rubbed his head. "Gates probably to keep 'em in, not out."

Followed a twisty road up into the hills, and sure enough, came to a (real) timberframe going up. Great view, out over the distant town toward the Blue Ridge. Some neat work, too, with guys using adzes and broadaxes, drilling and pegging mortised timbers together. My idea of high-level carpentry. Almost.

I hit the foreman up.

Knew he was the foreman, 'cause he had the biggest gut, was talking on a cell phone, and had one foot on the doorsill of his pickup truck. Waited politely till he ended the call, meanwhile appraising my bod. They all do that, so no big deal.

"Help you, little lady?"

Now that term wears the biggest sexist label there is. Big gut might just as well have said 'no females need apply,' but I never learn.

"I'm a top carpenter, done timberframe, and I can cut out a mortise as well as your best guy. Need a job."

"I'm my best guy, and you're puttin' me on. Surprised you even know what a mortise is, or do you, really?"

"Why would you be surprised? Yeah, I can do it, whether you've got a two thousand dollar mortising machine or I hafta do it by hand. Told you I'm a top carpenter."

"Okay, smart-ass, what's that tool my man's using over there?"

"That's a broadaxe, my kinda tool, and he's hewing an oak beam to the line. Left-handed, too." Smug smile...couldn't help it.

"Okay, so what'd you do, see a picture of one in a book?" The expected leer.

"No, I've actually forged a couple in my dad's blacksmith shop. Better design than that one, which I'm guessing you found in a junkshop. Got mine right in my truck, if you wanta see." I was getting tired of this. Guy wasn't gonna listen to anything I said. He rolled his eyes.

"Hey, Willie, this *girl* had th' nerve to claim she *made* her own broadaxe. Better'n yours, too. Ever hear ennything so funny?" Guffaw. Aforementioned Willie straightened up his Ichabod Crane frame, raked me with his bulging eyes.

"No shit. Okay, Wonder Woman, how'd you grab this axe, even if it ain't as good as th' one you just dreamed up?" He actually tossed me that seven pound axe, which looks a lot like a medieval headsman's tool...easy to imagine dried blood on the blade. Caught it one-handed, trying to make it look easy.

"No way, this's a left-handed axe; I'm right-handed. Cut my leg off. Got another one?" To the boss.

"Nah, an' you're wastin' our time here with your fairy tales. Why'n't you go apply for a secretary's job. Bet you *can* type, make coffee." Poking Willie in the ribs with an elbow like a ham.

"Your loss, dudes." I turned to leave. "And that third bent's racked about an inch. Somebody bend your framing square?" I stepped to my truck as they were staring at the bent, which is an assembled pair of posts, girt and principal rafters, with angled knee braces. It *was* off square.

Then I reached into the camper cap, pulled out my very own broadaxe. I *had* forged a conventional one, but Dad convinced me I should do another, one of those extremely rare goosewing axes. Which go for around seven hundred dollars in antiques shops.

Both sets of eyes swiveled back to me as I held this beauty up, with its proper right-handed handle, and got bigger. Most broadaxes can be handled from either end of the eye, with the wood bent to accommodate righties or lefties. Goosewing's custom-forged and you can't change it around. Despite their cluelessness, those dudes could probably shave with mine: dull tools can getcha hurt.

Stowed the axe, climbed into Hosmer. Cyrano looked about to launch himself at all that beef fat out there with its mouth hanging open, so I cranked, eased away. Did *not* give them the finger.

Sometimes I'm almost a lady.

Dry all that day, work-wise. We went back to the campground, since I had it for the week, and I thumbed a phone book. Lots of builders, but most were probably hurting, with the economy the way it was. Couple caught my eye: historic restoration, National Register work. Yeah. Dad had been a history freak, done a few of the old-style log cabins for friends, helped restore old plantation houses, churches. Funny really, because he was mostly a diesel mechanic, the job he'd always fall back on when things got dry.

Anyway, I did know how to cut a mortise and tenon and peg a joint, which was a lot more fun than nailing up plywood, so why not? Get past the chauvinist layer, I might score. I wrote down some names and numbers.

Then I took Cyrano for a long run up in some high hills. The map said these were the Ragged Mountains, and I remembered Poe's sinister short story. Well, there were McMansions on the slopes now, so the place didn't look creepy, just cheapened. And any ghosties and ghoulies and long-legged beasties would have Cyrano to deal with, even if I couldn't outrun them.

It was down a side road I saw the construction sign, and it was one of those outfits I'd written down. Okay, I'd crash this one tomorrow for sure. But maybe take a look now, if I didn't get run off. I'd actually driven by a country club enclave that had a sign prohibiting runners beyond the punch-coded gate. *Yeah, I might have a bomb stuffed down my sports bra.*

The house was a tall two-story with arched, mullioned dormers, some clapboard siding missing to show hewn timberframe beam work behind the scaffolding. Late light reflected off hand-blown window glass. The grounds were overgrown, but there were old gardens and mossy brick paths and elegant little outbuildings with slate roofs.

I was in love. What a house! Well, it was a little spooky, I guess, but it still grabbed me. Looking back later on the bloodshed, maybe I shoulda passed. *No, gotta work here, or find some way to steal it.* Cyrano, unimpressed, chased a rabbit on the way back, but I called him in.

"We're not that hungry, boy. Yet." *Okay: MacDonnell Restorations. I'm on it. Bet that house has ghosties. Let's see, be way pre-Civil War.* Older style than those back home around Atlanta since Sherman. Shenandoah Valley's where the Union troops burned everything, not here. Probably some elegant old widows right here they left alone. I could almost picture it: "Miss Abigail, they's *Yankees* at th' gate. Whut we gon' *do?*"

"Why, invite the gentlemen in for tea and cakes, Mandy, of course."

Cyrano cocked his head at me. He's sure I'm a little crazy. But hey, I'm the best he's got, right? And can he help it if his lady's a habitual reader, and has an imagination? *Suck it up, dawg.*

~ * ~

I didn't hit the pickup that came slewing out of the long drive to that house next morning, but I had to do some evasive tactics to keep from it. The guy was all over the road, gunning the F-150 with the fat tires and the gun rack like something was after him. Ghosties in the daytime? I hoped not. Or maybe friendly ones.

Casper, sure.

The dust hadn't settled yet from the spun-out gravel when I eased Hosmer in beside a middle-aged guy in jeans and a toolbelt. He had reddish hair with some gray in it, massive forearms, and a set of piercing blue eyes. No beer gut. *Hallelujah.* And right then, those weren't laugh wrinkles I was seeing. I noted only three other vehicles on the job (wow, small elite crew, *yes!*), and he was standing next to a big diesel pickup that said MacDonnell on its side. And the dude didn't look at all scary.

"Mr. MacDonnell?" I guessed, as my work boots found the ground. Hadda be. The eyes hadn't left the road behind me, but now they moved to me. And did *not* travel over my bod. *Well.*

"Yeah. Whattya want?" He was pissed. Or maybe just *still* pissed.

"Well, I wanted to talk to you, but now I'm afraid you might bite me. Wanta kick my truck instead?"

"Okay, okay." The face lost its damn-your-eyes look, and a grin threatened it. "Sorry. I just had to fire the best joiner in the business. Don't take it personally." *Joiner. Wow.* "What can I do for you, Ms...?"

"Wesley Whitestone." I extended a hand, knowing he'd feel the calluses. You don't get calluses sitting on your ass. "I won't try to tell you *I'm* the best joiner in the world, but I'm good, and I'm fast, but not sloppy. And I need a job that's not all Sheetrock and plywood." My grip was firm and dry. So was his. I kept the eyes on his...so that blue was penetrating? My hazels could bore holes in steel.

"Well, Wesley. *Wesley?* Dad wanted a boy, did he?" Not unkindly. But how many times had I heard that one*? But okay, this guy's almost another generation: cut him some slack.*

"Oh, he already had a boy, but he wanted a *real* boy. We not only did timberframe restorations, we made our own tools in his blacksmith shop."

"Really? You actually know how to temper steel?"

"Really. Dad forged me a corner chisel when I was twelve, then got me to forge him one just like it."

"I'm impressed." He seemed to be searching for the next thing to say, and I could see it coming: tough girl, so was I or wasn't I? And did *she* come with the package? No, I wasn't, but neither was I about to enlighten him. Let him deal with it. "I, uh...well, you already know I need another man...ah, joiner, carpenter...whatever. You...got any family?" *Now where did that come from?* Oh. Family. Translates as Significant Other, of either gender. But okay, I did need the job...

"Just me and my dog. Thought I'd met the right dude up in Pittsburgh, but it didn't happen." I shrugged. Actually, I'd known all along Phil wasn't anywhere near the right man for Wesley, but it made me sound normal, which might be important to this guy.

"You're not from there."

"No, Georgia. Got the South in my mouth, I know." That old line got a real chuckle. I *said* he was the wrong generation.

"Okay, tell me what you've done. And references, too. But just let me get my boys moving first."

The *boys* started with a specimen my age, late twenties, with long sideburns, dark Velcro hair and a little go-to-hell mustache, who checked me out big time. I thought about shaking it a little for him, but he was such a waste: rural Virginia's answer to Romeo. Then there was a worried older man who kept checking out the sky like Chicken Little. And a kid maybe twenty with hair that stood up like a fright wig and a face about two feet long. *Gotta be the helper.*

I checked the house out more while MacDonnell jumpstarted the crew, who were bracing up and cutting out termite-eaten beams at the back of the building where it was close to the ground. Nasty work, but necessary if you're gonna do a restoration right. Just cover that stuff up and it'd always come back to haunt you. These guys were doing it right. High-dollar right, too. This was definitely where I wanted to park my well-shaped little ass.

I said I loved this house. It hadn't been lived in for a while, and probably had been bought by some of the new money in town. Well, they'd drop a bunch of green here: cracked plaster, sloping floors, dentil cornice moulding rotted away up there. Guess those genteel little old ladies hadn't had the bucks to fight the dry rot.

Now, could the new owner just possibly be a sincere young millionaire who'd never found love? A successful but lonely writer maybe, inspired by old Virginia? A sensitive type who'd invite a girl to share drives in his prewar Jaguar SS-100 roadster?

More likely a fast-talking not-so-good old boy down from Chicago who'd made his pile in dubious development, complete with peroxide trophy wife, looking at early retirement away from the enemies he'd made. Like a specimen my crew had worked for in Dallas. Used car sales manager, the kind of dude you wouldn't trust with money for a sandwich...

"Okay, what do they call you, Miss Wesley? By the way, I'm Craig."

Did I say this guy had a really smooth voice, from way down deep inside? Maybe a preacher on the side? Liked his accent, too.

"Wes is okay. I kinda like it when people hear it and look around for some guy. So you own the business?"

"Oh, yeah. And you're looking at most of it. Got a lady in the office part-time, but it's over my garage. Some equipment there: shop, tractor, dump truck. Went bigger once, and almost lost my shirt. Had to spend all my time managing, and that's not the reason I do this work."

So, craftsman, for sure. Talk about worn-out tool belt: his really did have holes. But also these great chisels with handles of glowing wood, an old rosewood bevel gauge and a brass-fitted folding rule with the numbers almost rubbed off. Hammer his grandfather could've left him. Tools you wanted to stroke.

"Well, back to what you asked me before, what'd your last guy do before he apparently blew it, and I'll tell you if I can handle that."

"Oh, well like I said, master joiner. Bad to lose him; the owners liked him a lot, but...well, he could do anything wooden on this house you see needs doing. Can you?" He watched me as I took in the visible coming-apart stuff.

"Not shape the moulding, of course, unless you've got the shaper in your shop. But the beam repair? Sure. Rotten floor joists I can see, and yeah, that. Siding: no-brainer. Standing-seam roof: no problem. Love finish work, cabinets. And I can take out old trim and never leave a mark."

"You said you were fast. Clyde wasn't fast, he was just damn good, when he was sober. Now, I don't kid myself a top replacement is just gonna drop down out of the sky the minute I need it, so persuade me. How'd you handle this bad knee brace?"

Yeah, the one the termites had found about a hundred years ago. Okay, so it was exam time.

"Well, since it won't show, you could just cut the tenons and lag-bolt in a 45-cut replacement. But I gotta tell you, I wouldn't want to do that, unless you're strapped for money and need it quick and dirty. I'd drill out the pegs, pull the tenons for patterns by cutting the bad brace, save what's good of it to recycle for something small like stair spindles, then find heartpine to match. Lengthen the one mortise and slide the new piece in, peg it, and block the long mortise space so the brace doesn't slip if the peg goes, in the next two hundred years." I was using my hands a lot to show him. Hoped I'd made my point.

"Uh-*huh*. And how long would that take you, say?"

"It's a four-by-six full. If you had a piece of that, I'd do it in half an hour. More if I had to rip a big piece down. Got a beam saw?"

"Yeah, I do. Say an hour, then. Okay, and what would you expect to earn, for that caliber work?

"Twenty-five an hour." I didn't hesitate. "If I make you more, I want more. I'm no rookie." I put the eyes on his again.

"Um. Maybe." He was thinking it over, and this time he did let his gaze wander over me. Mind was actually on dollars, though, I could tell. Used to it anyway, and hell, it doesn't take any layers off.

So I checked him out some more, too: not a bad-looking old guy; sorta craggy face, just a little over medium height, tight abs under a fading tee shirt. But of course he'd be taken...the hot ones always are.

I decided to play games, too.

"Of course, your wife might be like some women and not want a girl on the job, but I know you're not the kinda guy would have that hang-up." I hoped.

"Now that wouldn't be a problem, since she left five years ago." The crags changed into a rueful grin.

"Let me guess: right about the time you almost got wiped out." No-brainer. A lotta women jump ship when the bucks dry up. Men too, probably. I thought of *David Copperfield*: 'Outgo exceeds income: disaster.' Or words to that effect.

"Close. There was more to it than that, but that's history now."

"Didn't mean to pry. My tools are in the truck, if you can use me. And I gotta say, I want to hug this house."

"Get splinters if you do, but I know what you mean. I get a high off jobs like this, termites and all." Then: "When *could* you start?"

"It's nine in the morning…how about now? Oh, I guess you do want to call these references."

"I will, yes. Been bit by that dog before. But if we do this, it's no booze, no drugs, be on time and don't quit early. I pay straight time if you want extra hours, and time-and-a-half if I need you more than forty. I pay every week, and I'm Class A—worker's comp, insurance— all the fringes." He paused, envisioning what it *would* be like to have a woman on the job, I guess.

"Oh, and you'd have to keep the boys from wasting time trash-talking you. Don, for sure. He'd hit on you first thing." *Thaing:* like back home.

"I can handle it. Don's the poor man's Clark Gable, of course."

"Yeah. Bob's the older guy and Henry's the helper. You'd probably tongue-tie him if you said good morning."

"Okay. So when do I check back?" I was calculating whether I could stretch the dollars till the first payday. My radar told me I had the job in the bag. Alky old Clyde wasn't coming back, I knew.

"Tomorrow, eight sharp. Come on out. You wouldn't give me these references if they were a problem, but…"

"Hey, if I had the bad luck to be the boss, I'd want an FBI background check. Terrorist carpenters under every bed."

I got into Hosmer, waved, drove away. Out of sight, I pulled over, gave Cyrano a hug. "We're in, dawg. Now let's go find a cave somewhere we can turn into a home."

# Two

The new job should have been all joy. Craig was a workhorse, and he knew his restoration work. Bob the family man was a sweetie, sort of fatherly, but he'd never work up to be a lead man. Don was a type, so predictable, his moves so obvious, I could grin through it okay. Henry thought I had something to do with putting the moon in place. Everybody knew his job, and did it.

And well, I liked working for Craig a lot. Maybe forty, lean as leather, he really should have been in cowboy boots and a Stetson, selling cancerous cigarettes. He set a pace, between hassling with inspectors, subcontractors, the architect, who did mostly leave us alone, and the owners.

But something wasn't right. Had to be the owners: everything else was cool. Balding lawyer from Baltimore in his late fifties I instantly disliked, and his trophy wife, whom I'd pegged as a total ditz. A Mimi, for sure. No, turned out to be a Gwen. And he was J. Barker Webb, if you can believe that. Did his friends call him Bark? Looked like his bite would be worse. But they had the bucks, no doubt. Craig wasn't cutting corners, and the project was, like I said before, top dollar.

And I just couldn't help wondering where all that green had come from. Maybe I'm just suspicious. Probably envious, too. If I had that kind of bucks, I'd make 'em an offer for this place they couldn't refuse.

So no, maybe not the owners. The house itself? No way...echoes of old romances and maybe some shadows: Poe all over. Maybe some Faulkner, too. Eudora Welty yeah, a few states removed. And I'd take it, ghoulies and all. *Well, just enjoy it girl; job will last through winter, when we'll be inside out of the weather.* Spring would be another year, another set of possibles.

And I'd be twenty-nine. But I'd have saved some bucks by then, if I wanted to move on. Or stay, maybe try to buy a little place in the mountains, settle in. This wasn't the worst country I'd found myself in. And those mountains, the Blue Ridge and beyond, hid some incredible little creeks and hollows, I'd found, a lot like the country north of Atlanta, close to where I'd grown up.

I'd managed to rent the top part of a cottage fairly close in by going into my forbidden cash stash, which I never, ever raided. And starve or not, I'd put those bucks back from my first paycheck.

My housemate of the moment was Sarah Wainright, a grad student at the University of Virginia doing her thesis in psych on women's dreams. Better-looking than me, cloud of dark hair, maturity level about fifteen. She did the bar circuit, too, and brought guys home (lookit me: I'm all grown up), but they had the lower level of the little house, and only Cyrano could hear them misbehaving.

About guys, now. The Don had given up on me by the second week, being a little intimidated by me 'cause I was better than he was. Shallow, with a bottomless ego, which he fed with waitresses and wide-eyed freshman girls at the university. Probably never caught on they giggled about their townie and compared notes.

But okay, I was ready for Mr. Right, if he should come riding up on his white horse (I'd been away from horses too long). And he didn't have to be a *Matthew McConaughey*, exactly. Hey, I'd never win a beauty contest, even if my bod isn't that bad. But I wanted sincere. I said that before. And no, not a nerd. My accountant brother Bert is a nerd. Been dating the same weird girl for eight years. I suspect they only converse in deductibles.

No, not like bro.

I'd liked uncomplicated former partner Phil Bartlett well enough, but it just hadn't been there. Figured it was best not to let him know where I was now, because (no conceit) he'd had a case on me. Did call his creep brother's girlfriend, Cheryl, because I'd liked her. Told her not to clue Phil in...you know, burned bridges. Didn't normally like to do that, but sometimes it's the right thing. Cheryl and I had a couple good phone visits over the next few months. She always wanted to know if I'd met The Man yet. Nah, and I was beginning to think I was in the wrong trade for that. My chosen occupation apparently doesn't attract Galahads.

About Phil, too, thereby hung an unfortunate tale. His folks, (whom I liked better than him) had scraped up and advanced him a hundred grand to help launch the business: truck, advertising, shop equipment.

Only it'd somehow disappeared before we could invest a cent. We'd all been devastated, Phil and I, his strange brother Sid, the parents. No trace of the cash, ever.

But enough about him; let's talk about me. I really didn't need to define myself in terms of some male. I was me, no apologies. And okay, I got horny sometimes. And I got lonely, too (not anyway the same). But I wasn't about to insult myself with a Don. Cold shower time. Or maybe give in and do a harmless date with one of housemate's friends from the university. Young professors, research dudes who'd never been outside in the real world.

"There's this man you gotta meet," Sarah'd told me. "He's a lit associate prof, and I just *know* you two would click."

"So why's he single, assuming he has the expected number of body parts, is more or less sane, and not too repulsive?"

"Oh, he's been married. Twice I think, but apparently just hasn't found his real soulmate yet."

"Or was more likely too blind to see it when he did. I dunno, girl, sounds like a chronic loser to me."

"You're so cynical. That tells me you have something deeply buried inside you that really needs working out. Why not just give him a chance? Oh, you'll *love* his name: Reginald. Reggie Warfield." She almost danced.

"Um. Gotta be from an old line of rich Warfields, right? Just at the U. to occupy his time. Drives a neurotic sportscar. Gambles in Monaco in summers." I was thinking of a young Daddy Warbucks in *Annie* gone bad. "Am I close?"

"Could be. Find out. Friend of Greg's, and you know Greg's got family money."

"No, I don't remember a Greg. I thought it was Wally."

"Wally was...well, just so *last century*, Wes. Greg's really it; I just feel it." *Yeah, and next week it'll be Alphonse, or Big John. But whatthehell...* "Anyway, we're going to hear Wolf Blues at Corbin's tomorrow night, and I—well, I just hinted you might come along. Reggie's eager to meet you."

Oboy, a blind date. Talk about last century. But Sarah really wanted this to happen, make her day, I guess. So okay, I'd bite the bullet and we'd do it, sort of against my better judgement. Maybe it'd beat curling up with my collection of *Classic Southern Short Stories*. Again.

We did it. And Wolf Blues turned out to be a great group; every note was really worth the rest of it.

The rest of it wasn't.

Reggie, the musical-wives lit-mouth, started spouting the romantic poets as soon as I'd shaken his hand. He gave me a firm grip, honest brown eyes boring into mine in what was supposed to dissolve me, I'm sure. Didn't. Then later, Yeats, who happens to be my favorite. (Who clued him in?)

"...Brown hair across the mouth blown..." And that, not Reggie, did touch me, a little. I got the picture I was supposed to get: dreamy place, breeze, undone hair wantonly adrift. But my hair's too short, and this was so obviously this guy's line of the moment. If I'd known chemistry, it'd have been something about oil and water dancing in a daring non-mix, breathlessly awaiting the catalyst.

Bullshit, in other words.

And it got worse. I'll admit Reggie the Regressed was a hunk, in that spoiled-pretty-boy way aging frat boys have. But he was so transparently predatory. I guess I was supposed to be flattered he wanted for the moment to add me to his list. Yeah, a girl *carpenter*, he could boast, and with these neat little boobs. Sarah almost forgot her Greg, watching Reggie's moves. Wishing she were me?

*Be my guest, girl.*

I tuned him out, soaking up Wolf's stuff, music that made me feel more alone, which I was, with Reggie there. I even quit smiling and nodding. Didn't even hear his murmured proposition as we were getting our jackets.

"Well?" He was finally getting frustrated.

"Well, thanks, Reggie. Great blues, but..." *Okay, you want Yeats:* "'I have drunk ale in the country of the young and I weep because I know all things now...' We're just not the right two people, okay? Sorry."

I thought he was going to pout.

"Bye, Reggie."

The workouts at the gym could get my mind on other things. The best, though, were the long runs up in those blue-tinged hills with my best friend Cyrano. Sometimes we'd do three, four miles or more out and back, in the crisping fall mornings, before the sun burned hot through early haze. I almost said to hell with guys, those times.

There was lots to do here besides the bar scene: music venues from bluegrass to classical. Theater groups out the ears here and over in the Valley. I could get to like this place, maybe. And there *were* men who were not awful. Had to be, somewhere. But mostly freshly divorced and bleeding, and too many weirdos and way too many mama's boys, each of whom wanted another mother to tell him how gifted he was.

My mom had died of cancer before I'd gotten to know her well, which can't sound forlorn enough. At four, she was to me cool hands on my hot face, soft words of encouragement, a taken-for-granted, loving presence. I wasn't aware of the months of wasting away, of her sad, lingering goodbye, until later.

So Dad became all of it, for me: had to. Bert was enough older we didn't seem like siblings, and we were totally unalike. But looking back, I really had all a girl needs, I guess. Certainly no other regrets, for my part.

But hey, maybe now I really was looking for a substitute dad myself. Sarah thought so. Sarah the Shrink. I did miss him terribly though: the great times building, fixing things together, the campouts, the ballgames. My dad was a helluva guy. Heart attack out of nowhere my senior year at U. of Georgia. He didn't get to see his girl graduate, and it hurt me enough for both of us. And no, the hurt hadn't gone away.

So except for stodgy Bert the Numerals, who stayed planted in Atlanta, I was alone. But lotsa people were, in this world, and they coped. I guess they did. I had, even if I did often feel like maybe Ben Franklin's half a pair of scissors. And yeah, sometimes I did want to start screaming, or throw a roaring drunk, or start an eye-gouging fight with the next self-satisfied slug I met. But I rarely lost it, really.

I *could* lose myself a whole lonely weekend in Yeats, in tragic Ireland amid the Gaelic ghosts and the old dreams. Or I could decipher Faulkner for days, and discover more every time, maybe more even than he felt, pouring that love song of his roiling South into page upon rambling page.

And I had been able to share some things with some men. Just not enough. Not the magic combo: Shakespeare and blacksmithing. Whitewater, Keats and horses; Huxley and walls that were plumb.

Did The Man even exist? Probably not. But 'a (woman's) reach should exceed her grasp,' right? Browning would've understood.

Compromise: always that. So no white horse. No craggy countenance wreathed in Scottish rolled Rs, with ruined castles in the background. No white-sailed sloop out of Newport with cocktails at five. Hey, I'm a *carpenter;* my dad was a diesel mechanic. I've got calluses on my hands and on my manners.

But, other side of the coin, Dad may've never read Joyce Carole Oates, but he could still appreciate fine craftsmanship, or art, or music, and so can I. We weren't totally culture-deprived.

So, would Mr. R. wheel up on a Harley? No, not a Harley. I'd hold out for a vintage Stearman biplane, even if I couldn't have Yeats with it. Compromise: the word wasn't the same turn-off now it had been.

Not quite.

~ * ~

I did get a call from Nil Phil up in Pittsburgh. Just checking in, he said, but I knew he hadn't gotten completely over our non-romance yet. I'd tried to make it clear back when I'd left, that no, I wasn't turned off by him, but neither was I turned on (definite requirement). He'd argued that time would change that, but I knew if the chemistry's not there, it just ain't there. I liked Phil okay, and we'd been friends, sure, but as far as I was concerned, more like brother and sister. Well, not like me and my brother Numbers Bert, who I always suspected was from another planet.

"Great to hear from you, guy. Yeah, I'm okay. Got a pretty good job for a while here in Virginia." I didn't tell him where.

"You always wanted to go back south," he mused.

"In my blood, I guess. How're your folks?" Small talk, because I really didn't have anything to say to good old Phil.

"Oh, they're okay...still broken up about the money. Sid still thinks he should have been the one to get it, and of course he's still burned that it disappeared."

"I can imagine. So were you, and so was I. But I dunno, with the economy like it is, whether we could have made a go of the business or not. Cycles, you know. We could have expanded like you wanted to, and most likely lost it all."

"We lost it all anyway. So now we'll never know what we could have done. Together." *Oh, there it was again.*

"Well, I hope the s.o.b. who took it chokes on every last dollar. You didn't deserve that, Phil, whether we'd have made it work or not." No, he really didn't, but I didn't want to listen to him wallow in regrets. Changed the subject. "You met Miss Right yet?" I'd encouraged him to date.

"You were Miss Right, Wes."

"That woulda been nice, guy, but it just wasn't meant to happen. Hey, give my best to Sid and Cheryl and the folks, and let's keep in touch, y'hear?"

We said our goodbyes.

~ * ~

Craig MacDonnell liked the new girl okay. He sort of wished she were a little older, and maybe they could have a relationship. But he'd seen too many middle-aged women who'd toughed it out in the man's world of building, and that'd hardened them. Wesley had a freshness about her he liked...not all armored up yet. But it was obvious she could take care of herself. Had to laugh, the way she'd handled Don the wannabe ladies' man.

He reflected yet again on how fast the years had piled up on him. Here he was halfway through life or more, totally out of touch with that girl's generation, finding himself in a social world of ex-wives with kids, the few times he'd tried the dating scene. Seemed everybody had a lotta baggage, which he guessed he did, too.

Nothing wrong with doing the solo thing for a while longer, though. Got lonely, but a lot of the time he'd been married he'd felt lonely, too. *No, don't go there. Over and done with, and a good thing, too.*

Five years, though. Didn't seem that long. He still sometimes opened his door at the end of the day, half-expecting to see her, feet propped in front of the TV, maybe still in a bathrobe at six at night, drink in hand, eyes red.

Cost a lot, getting out of that marriage. Blind to get into it in the first place. His brother had warned him off that woman, the way older brothers sometimes do.

"I listen to too many victims of train-wreck marriages in my congregation, Craig. Each one thinks I oughta side with him/her against the other, and it'll all be better. Preacher can't do that; my job's to try to knit it back together if that can happen. If it can't, divorce is the last resort.

"But I don't wanta see you get off on the wrong foot to begin with. I know you're tired of the engineering, wanta go back to building, but how's she gonna take that? Marrying a successful dude on the way up, then having to cope with downtime, no-work cycles? Hey, it's your life, bro, but step back a little, can you?"

But he hadn't listened. He loved his brother, but he guessed looking back there'd been some of that little-brother resentment in the equation. They didn't think alike either, and he'd been so sure things would work with the young daughter of that back-to-the-earth couple. She'd sure known what it was to build, farm, share.

*Well, seemed like a good idea at the time.* Shame hindsight was so clear. Didn't make it all any better, though. Still building the business back from ruin, five years after the home-grown meltdown.

~ * ~

The face in my mirror was a...strong face. Yeah, that. Hazel eyes were okay. Mouth, chin, nose not bad, but it didn't really add up to pretty. Not the first face the boys asked to the prom. No, more like the one after the homecoming queen had turned them down. Except for guys like Phil, maybe.

*Ah, to hell with it. Wouldn't want a man who's after just a pretty face. Shallow men are for shallow girls. But is that a wrinkle? Laugh wrinkle, gotta be. Gone, if the light's just right. Cyrano, snuggle up, guy. Mama loves you, you ugly thing. You'd resent a man anyway, wouldn't you? Thought you'd mangle the Don that time he slipped up and put a hand on me. You sure know a loser when you see one.*

Don. Maybe he was what was phony about this job. Drove that expensive muscle car with the petroleum appetite. Bootlegging on the side? Running drugs? Nah, not bright enough for that. And Craig was sharp; he'd spot the first buy. Don and Gwen should run off together. What a soap opera that'd be.

*I'm rambling. Old people ramble. I'm not old, just lonely.*

*Craig's a lonely old guy, too. The boys say he doesn't date much. Seems like a sensitive one. Got a college degree in something, surely engineering. I could maybe see a thing there, if there were a party, or something. Not one-on-one. No, that'd be the father image, I'm sure. Big mistake. Screw myself out of a good job, too, making it with the boss, even if I could. Dumb, and yeah, dumber.*

~ * ~

The work on the great old house kept being good. Surprises, like a signed beam, maybe by the joiner who'd done it. Date wasn't readable, beyond an October, 17...but Craig had narrowed the construction years down to a few: forged nails, blunt-tipped screws, split heartpine lath under the horsehair plaster. He knew this kinda stuff, and it was fun hearing him speculate.

And he was the one who spotted it first, for the very reason he'd been at this kind of work so long. Fireplace against an interior wall, with shallow cabinets either side. Only, in the room behind, its wall stood out more. Henry had made a run to the building supply store, and Don and Bob were out replacing siding. Craig called me over from where I was taking out warped baseboard to get the pattern for a replacement.

"See this?" he pointed, the blue eyes hiding something. Looked like a kid who'd just discovered where Mom had hidden the cookies.

"Yeah. Thick wall, sure, but there are these niches here to take up the space."

"But they don't go all the way to the chimney on this side, see? Hollow back there. Some of these old places had secret hideaways, Wes. Maybe escape routes."

"You mean for smuggling runaway slaves?"

"Or protection from Indians, in the real old ones. This's not that old though, around 1790. No, it could be a hiding place or some way to let a lover sneak in, maybe, or say the original owner was into something not quite legal, needed to get out while everybody was sure he was in."

"Oh boy, you got an imagination. If this were England, it could be a priest hole," I told him. "You know, where the closet Catholics hid them from the vigilantes under Henry the Eighth."

"I remember something about that, I think. But this is just Virginia, not that kinda witch hunt." He laughed.

"True. And finding secret passageways is something out of Nancy Drew. I'd say it was a builder's mistake, got covered up." But I didn't really want to believe that. Hey, Poe's *Cask of Amontillado*, right?

"There'd be the same built-out space in the basement, maybe to lead into an exit of sorts. Wanta make a friendly bet on that?" He was teasing me.

"Do I get half the gold stash when we find it?"

"About that...I have never found more than a stray copper penny in these old houses. Tools left on ledges, yeah, plastered over. Diary once, what the mice hadn't chewed. Part of a Bible, old combs, buttons. No cash."

"Use a metal detector?"

"Don did, couple times, but there's so many old nails, pieces of horseshoes, rusted chain links, the thing went crazy. And he'd dig some, on his own time, but it was a bust.

"So, are we both too cool to go down and measure the chimney base?" A challenge in those blue eyes.

"Your nickel? Hey, it all pays the same."

"Oh, okay. Call it a work break. You don't cut me any slack, carpenter."

"Joiner, remember?" I liked teasing him, too.

We measured the chimney plus the distance to the first wall recess, and it left a possible twenty-inch difference. So, Craig explained as we went down the creaky old basement steps, the brick chimney base would equal that total, but if his guess were right, not all that would be chimney.

We were like two kids on an adventure, with flashlights, because no electricity worked down there yet. It was more of a root cellar actually, dirt floor that hadn't stayed dry, decayed bits of board around, rats' nests, stuff thrown down. Last owners probably scared to trust the stairs, the bottom step of which was rotted away. Picture of the old ladies again, trembling at what might be lurking.

"Okay, Sherlock—pardon me—*Mister* Sherlock, which side? I'm turned around."

"Here. Hold this end." He climbed over a broken table, shone his light on the tape measure. "Aha." Hand in that cookie jar.

"So you're saying this brick wall is hollow, maybe only one brick thick?"

"Yeah, and if we took out a brick, we could see in."

"Better idea, boss. There'd have to be a way to get inside up above somewhere, right? Let's look for that: secret panel, code words, hidden lever, incantations."

"You're fun."

"And we're both crazy. You read the *Hardy Boys*?"

"Didn't everybody?"

"Wanta tell the crew?"

"Not on your life. Don would blab it all over town, and there'd be a line of gun-rack fat-tired pickups here by tonight, guys with pickaxes."

"You're fun, too."

But there was no secret panel on the main floor or in the bedroom above. Solid plaster above wainscoting, and none of it removable without wrecking it. So, one-time access just closed up?

"Oh, sure," Craig slapped his forehead. "The attic. Of course."

"Of course?"

"Yeah. Come on...there'll be a trapdoor next to the narrowed-down chimney." He was as excited as a kid on his first date...*Hey, Mary Jane, let's us go look for skeletons in haunted houses.*

And under three broken chairs there was a place where several of the attic floorboards ended those same twenty inches from the chimney, and those that butted them didn't match in width. But there were hand-forged nails holding the boards down.

"Do we try to pry it up? No handle or anything. Not that I can see, anyway."

"Maybe not. Make noise. Maybe later. And maybe I'm wrong, anyway."

But something else was not right here, for me. Or maybe I just wanted there to be more to the puzzle. Anyway...

"If the trapdoor had been nailed shut that long ago with these forged nails, close to the time the house was built, there'd be pry marks where it'd been opened. There aren't. So, never used? Or just fake nails? Heads only, to divert suspicion?" He nodded, started to slip one of those cherished chisels into the crack.

"Here, you'll break that handle." I passed him the thin little flat bar I use to pry moulding. He grinned and got to work moving chair pieces. The trapdoor, because that's what it was all right, came up grudgingly, but that was just from the tight fit, not nailed through. Hey, a couple hundred years, it liked being where it was.

We shone light down a long, long shaft, with iron spikes sticking out of the chimney brick...hand-holds. Lots of cobwebs. Badass spiders, for sure.

"After you," I pointed.

"No, we've been gone too long. The guys'll think we're up to something." Grin again.

"Oh, yeah. Don'll think I've lured you off to seduce you." My turn to grin. "His thought processes are one-track." I kept my eyes on the trapdoor we were replacing, so that wouldn't embarrass him.

"Yeah. So this should be a nighttime thing. Nobody here..." A pause. "Wanta do it?" Another challenge.

"What, you expect me, a young, innocent girl, to crawl down a shaft full of black widow spiders to discover old bones or something else gross that'd give me nightmares for the rest of my life? You're a sadist, boss." Trying to suppress another grin.

Failed.

"Don't give me that crap. You'll be in that hole before I get up the stairs."

"But I'll bring a broom to fend off the cobwebs and intimidate any ghouls we find."

We got back down to the main floor to find Don the Uncool looking for us, suspicion all over that one-track face.

"Been making out," I told him, and went back to taking off baseboard.

"Boss?" His mouth was open. But then it was usually open.

"Been making out, like the lady says. Whattya need?" Hey, the boss was cool, you may have noticed.

Don, looking from one to the other of us, that one-way-street mind of his trying to take that in. Then finally: "Boy, you had me goin' there, you two. Oh, this major post out here, it's loose at the bottom. S'posed to be load-bearing, you know. Other stuff holding the wall up, way things have settled, I guess. I said just shim it an' forget it, but Bob wants you to see it." They went out, and I chuckled.

*Yeah, making out, I guess.* One thing Craig was, he was hands-off. I was getting the idea he was going out of his way to keep everything all Miss Manners proper. I'd had my butt palmed on so many jobs I'd almost quit the trade. But hey, not like it was gonna get rubbed off. Got past the prude thing years ago, even if I did still whack hands when they needed it. Sometimes with a hammer in my own hand, too.

# Three

So that night after good dark, I met Craig at the job to go adventuring. Kind of neat, actually, doing kid stuff with a 40-year-old. Sort of thing that let me forget our age difference. We left Cyrano outside as designated watchdog, and used the flashlights so the neighbors, who were pretty far away anyway, wouldn't wonder. Maybe they'd report strange lights moving: aliens, real ghost stuff.

The place *was* creepy at night, and it was easy to imagine things going bump behind you. But hey, I was with a tough guy and a semi-homicidal dog I was sure could sense hostile presences. Not to worry; just enjoy.

Craig had thought to bring a long rope, which we tied around the chimney where it stepped in, and a compass and a hundred-foot tape measure.

"No telling where the tunnel, if there is one, comes out," he pointed out. "And if some of the spikes are rusted through, we'd be stuck." Okay, made sense. "I'll go first...doubt if you could catch me if *I* fell."

"Then you get the broom, and I won't fall unless one of these rusty spikes pulls out."

None did, as we inched down. Old wrought iron, which doesn't rust as badly as modern steel. It did occur to me that this was absolute madness, like going into an abandoned mineshaft that could collapse any second. No, that'd be when we got to the supposed tunnel. And how long would it be before anyone found what was left of us? Didn't wanta dwell on that one. Maybe I'd just wait at the bottom, pretending I could pull Craig out with the rope if he got overpowered by falling dirt or a vampire convention.

The lath-and-plaster sides of our shaft became all brick, so we were in the basement, finally. And yeah, Craig was gone, the rope trailing back below me.

"Hold on, boss. You wanta have all the fun?" My voice sounded strange, boxed-in, but his was hollower.

"Tunnel, all right. Arched brick, so it should hold up. Just getting the direction." I told him to tie the rope around himself anyway, still with that feeling we shouldn't both get beyond the point of no return.

I get those feelings, and sometimes ignore them at my peril: bad and worse memories. Experience.

"Won't need that. It's sound, and not like a cave where we could get lost."

"Humor me. Pretend there're gas pockets or something up ahead, or dragons I can drag you away from."

"Mother hen."

"Enjoy it while you can." But there wasn't much rope left, so scratch that. "Okay, whenever you're ready then, Jules Verne, since your nerve apparently hasn't failed you." The grin. Nice grin, really. Not a Don leer at all. Good, Don would attack me in a place like this, and then I'd have to cripple him.

The floor was dirt, a little damp, with just enough slope down to drain. We were going what would be right from the front of the house and curving back a little. So following the hill, I guessed, around and maybe toward a sort of ravine I remembered, that had an ancient iron footbridge over it.

The first hundred feet. Then the second. Then, maybe sixty feet on, an iron door. Actually. Dungeon? Treasure room? We both grinned like fools. Craig was searching for a way to open it.

"Looks like hinges at the top, Wes. Should be a handle down here, then." It was partly submerged in dirt, but yeah, a handle. Like a lever, out sideways. Very rusty.

We scraped dirt away, pushed on it. It didn't move. Craig stood on it, and it creaked once, then froze up again. He bent, got both hands on it, and pulled. It creaked again, back into place. He stood on it again, and it went further this time. Up again. Down some more, and finally it freed up from whatever held it.

"Doorstops inside," I pointed, "so it swings out." I pushed. Nothing.

"Maybe both of us," and he braced alongside me. "On three."

Nothing. Not a creak. Maybe led to outside, and there'd be dirt washed up behind it…old leaves, sticks, grass?

"Need a battering ram, I guess." I saw absolutely nothing to hit that door with.

"Back up to it, and let's stomp it together," he suggested. So, two heavy construction boots once, twice, six times. Another creak. More hits, and we could see a crack opening.

"Where's the crowbar when a girl needs it?" I lamented. But with enough pushing and some prying with the broom handle, we got the thing open. Shone our lights in. No, out. Fresh air, warmer than this earth temperature.

We were under the ravine footbridge all right, and an identical iron panel, which this door turned out to be, seemed to be holding the other end of the bridge up. Another door? And where'd it lead?

"Oh, clever, boss. These don't hold up anything, but who'd think to open one?" He was out, and examining the other iron panel.

"Okay, this one doesn't open. Yeah, clever. So all we get is out of the house, or in, for whatever reason. And I'd say this ravine goes up into the woods and then it's to anywhere you needed to go."

"So, no gold, no skeletons, no dragons. Darn, I was hoping for at least a convention of ghosts."

"No snakes, either. Be grateful."

"Oh, I am. And yeah, even one ghoul probably would've wiped me out."

He looked around, shrugged. We agreed to go back overland, and pushed the door shut, latched it with the barely-visible outside handle, which we covered with dead leaves.

"What do we tell a neighbor we're doing, out with a broom?" I giggled.

"Maybe compulsive woods-cleaning?" Chuckle.

"Or we chased a bear?"

"Or we took it away from a passing witch?" Silly talk that had us both laughing. This *was* fun.

We went back up to the attic, pulled the rope up, replaced the trapdoor, piled the chair pieces back. Craig checked his watch.

"Boy, that didn't take long. Only nine. Well, it was great while it lasted, joiner..." His voice trailed off.

And whatthehell, it was Friday.

"So, wanta go for a beer, contractor, or is that fraternizing?"

"No, 'cause isn't fraternizing just between men? And yes, let's do, since all I'd do otherwise is stay home and paint my toenails."

"You're fun *and* you're crazy."

We went to an upscale place, despite our work clothes, where we were more apt to run into Sarah and her current diversion than Don and something in leather. There was a jazz trio who were good, and this was okay. I could handle this. And of course, I felt closer to this hunk after our pointless sleuthing. We ordered imported beer. It came complete with frosted mugs.

"So, I'm gonna pry shamelessly. Tell me about you, outside of bashing old houses and hiring terrific girl construction workers." I had absolutely *no* shame.

"That'd make this a date, wouldn't it?" Blue twinkle.

"First date, safe ground. *Boss.*" I said I liked to tease him.

"Okay then, we take turns. I'm from one county south of here. Went to Virginia Tech in engineering. Didn't like it, with everything going to computers. Don't like computers, which I know is weird. Married a woman who turned out to like spending money and collecting other men. Took a big ego hit on that one." Couple of pain lines around his eyes: he still hurt. Chased them away with that grin. "Your turn."

"Um. Degree in comparative lit, of all things. Dad was my best buddy after Mom died. He and I built things. Did a lotta stuff together, which I miss a bunch. Couple of not-even-near-misses with guys, on settling down. I like having my own options instead of somebody else's. Your turn." We ordered another beer each.

"Well, I started liking old houses way back, so later got into fixing broken ones. Made a lot less money than in engineering, but made up for it by working harder. I guess I'm to blame a lot for not being home more for Valencia."

*"Valencia?* Daughter of sixties hippies, right?"

"Oh yeah. Never had anything growing up, so wanted it all. Saw this up-and-coming engineer, I guess, as the ticket out and up. Not." Tilting his mug at me: "Next."

"Okay, you already know I've knocked around the country a lot from the references I gave you. Seen a lotta great places, met some solid folks, some of the other kind, got a headful of good memories. I read, I work out, run, have a thing for horses. I like myself okay, and my life. Dunno where I'm headed, but keeping on, enjoying it all meantime. Like it here so far, and may just settle someplace like this if that happens. If not, the road's still there, and it can get habit-forming." *Yeah, Jack Kerouac.* Shrug. "I guess I'm a pretty uncomplicated case, really."

"Well, I guess I'm a typical engineer type: sort of methodical, not too curious about the rest of the world. Never traveled much, don't know what I've missed. But I appreciate good things a lot. Suddenly finding myself forty years old, which is still a surprise. Last time I looked, I was twenty-two." He thought a minute. "Maybe Nelson County, Virginia sums it up it best." He was selling himself short there, but yeah, I'd heard that county didn't have but one oversize village, and the inevitable junk on the one highway through it. Like that made it backwoods? Or maybe real America.

After some more catching-up, we fell silent, listening to a silver-haired genius on the trumpet improvise. This beat hell out of curling up with Cyrano, this sharing. So the guy was what, twelve years older than I was? *Still human, girl.* And not a predator, or my radar wasn't working at all.

And when a nice guy doesn't push, that should set off red flags. He's either sincere or practiced enough to pull off a score before a girl realizes it. And make her enjoy every spasm of it. Well, maybe not *red* flags. Say signals. Checking him out more out of the corner of my eye, I liked that better.

*No, put a chock in it, girl*; this was the *boss*. Keep it friendly, even if I was finding myself wondering how those muscled arms would feel around my bare-skin body. And—admit it—kind of wanting to find out. Little shiver at that thought. *Air-conditioning must be a little too high in here.*

The feeling passed, like they do if you let them, stand back and watch them dissolve back into reality. Plenty of time for whatever might happen down the road...no need to seize the moment, or this guy. *Too old, anyway, remember?*

"Been great." We were at my truck, and I squeezed his hand while getting in just fast enough, but not like an escape. Result of practice, that move is. Forestalls any fumbling, but doesn't turn the guy off. Little promise, maybe a tiny tease.

"Yeah. See you on the job." His grin, like he really wasn't spending the weekend alone, puttering around waiting for Monday and the work that was his life. And maybe he wasn't. I didn't know *everything*. I stifled an urge to race after him.

~ * ~

Sarah and Greg were smoking weed at home, and the burned-rope smell drifted up. She'd hinted that he was into some heavier stuff, which excited her, but no details. Sarah liked to try everything once, or she felt she was missing out. Now there's a mature philosophy of life for you.

I knew I wasn't missing anything when it came to the chemicals. Dad had given me good advice early on: most of alcohol and drugs is social. Get away from others you'd share with, and see how empty it all is. That's the real deal, not the "yeah, baby, I'm with you" group dependency thing.

Get Sarah off away from people, though, she'd wither in a day. What would she have to analyze? Trees and rocks don't give you much to ponder. I'd observed early on that psych majors have some real issues; that's why they're psych majors. But no pointing fingers, here. Live and let...self-destruct.

~ * ~

Got another call from the Phil, late at night when I was prone to get a touch of the blues. I almost welcomed the ring of the phone till I found out who it was. This time he didn't push the old flame bit, though. Something else on his mind.

"Wes, Sid and I've been over that whole thing about the money, for maybe the thousandth time, and I wanted to check with you again, see if you might've had any other ideas. You remember anything else? I mean, you were there and all..."

Oboy. Where the hell was this going? Yeah, we'd shared the apartment, even though I'd insisted on hands-off. Buddies, Phil and me, and it had to stay that way. And yeah, for some stupid reason he hadn't put the cashier's check in the bank right away. I never understood that whole bit. Who goes around with that much money stashed somewhere in his apartment? I mean, a cashier's check is just like cash: anybody can endorse it, with minimal I.D. Might as well carry the bills around in a briefcase, right? Nobody does that.

Well, maybe a drug dealer or a politician.

"Gee, Phil, nothing's come up, no. Like you, I've gone over everything I can remember, and probably as many times as you have. It was wherever you kept it, then it just wasn't. I remember trying again to talk you into getting it into the bank that Thursday..."

"Yeah, and you'd finally convinced me. But it was gone Friday morning when I went to get it. That's the way I remember it, too. But was it really still *there* Thursday? We didn't check, did we?"

"Not 'we,' Phil. I never knew where you stashed it. And I don't know when you checked last. Wish I had: that'd maybe narrow it down to that night. But we were there, straight through after work.

We ordered in pizza, remember? Sid and Cheryl were there, too." Yeah, it'd been the four of us. And after the others had left, that's when I got onto him again about that hunk of figurative green right there with us.

"Well, Sid's been after me a lot on it, is all. And the folks...hard thing to get over, even after all this time."

"Hey, nobody's rich enough just to blow off a hundred Gs, and I know your parents had to scratch hard for that. And you and I'd already put our own money in. Rotten thing, no matter how you look at it."

"For sure. Well, how's work?"

"It's okay. Should go on through the winter. Then I'll probably get on the road again. Overdue in Atlanta to do my sisterly duty visiting Bert. See what's happening down there, I guess. After that, who knows? Might be something good going on there, and I'll stay near home for a while."

"Think any more about going back around that place in Missouri, looking up that guy I remember, Glenn?"

"Nah, he was about to leave the country after that Dear John bit from his girlfriend, and my memories of that hand-to-mouth time aren't that good." Glenn Armitage and I'd worked together some out there. He'd remembered Phil from somewhere, which is sort of what had landed me in Pittsburgh, though years later.

"You oughta settle down, Wes." Sure, and I didn't need a crystal ball to know where *this* was heading. Yeah, next he'd suggest that things had to be better in Pittsburgh by the time my job was over here, and why didn't we plan...*Oh, just put a sock in it, Phil. Does the roof have to fall in on you?*

"Someday, yeah. Just not ready, yet, gotta spend more time, go see more places, I guess. Follow the road, let it all play out the way it's supposed to." *Enough of this.* "Well, you take care, guy." We punched off.

Well. Yeah, I could see Serpentine Sid the big brother (actually, he was smaller) ragging about that money, since he hadn't been that subtle about resenting the folks putting it up for Phil instead of him. Of course, Sid wasn't trying to launch a business, take an entrepreneurial risk...just not his style, I guess. Seemed perfectly happy punching computers all day long.

Sid Bartlett: I'd never understood what his girlfriend Cheryl saw in that guy, unless maybe he had a wart in the right place. She was a sweetie, sharp, good looking, and we'd been close. I could've seen her and Sincere Phil as a couple, but hey, who knows what clicks between two people? Or doesn't click. One thing I had observed about Sid was, he could talk people into things.

I suppose bullshit is a gift.

~ * ~

J. Barker Webb considered this old plantation house the perfect place for him and Gwen to settle into. She could have her horses, get into whatever social things were going, and he could practice law in nearby Charlottesville conveniently. And his other interests could be neatly kept out of sight there. Who the hell would ever suspect anything shady at a fine old place at the end of a long drive? Like everywhere, he figured there was a social level that just didn't get bothered by nosy people.

Privacy, that's what his money was buying. And it was a hell of a lot cheaper, long run, than in Baltimore. Country retreat: what every harried executive type longed for. *And we've got it, finally. Kids grown, Gwen and I can hole up here without intrusion.*

But there was a detail he had to correct. That contractor MacDonnell had fired Clyde Kelly. His business, of course, and yeah, the guy did drink too much. But Clyde could have his uses. Have to keep him close some other way, then, get a few more good men together, too, now that this was to be their base of operations.

~ * ~

Cyrano and I went camping up in the Virginia mountains one fall weekend, among red leaf carpets and swift water over boulders under an impossibly blue sky. We hiked some trails and watched migrating hawks from a lookout. Not in a hurry about anything, just sat and felt the sun and the slight wind. Lost back there beyond the end of things, totally cut off from any form of civilization, with nothing but a dim woods road to lead us back, whenever we decided to take it.

Then I followed a trail down a spring branch that got bigger as it dropped. I set up my little backpack tent close to that stream where I would hear it even asleep. My very favorite sound: water over stone.

A guy camped downstream smelled my coffee and paid us a visit. Mike something, good-looking in an outdoorsy way. He was a geologist, he told me, working for a coal company further south. And he guessed this camping out got in the blood, since he spent most of his time out pecking on rocks just like these. Mike was a couple of years out of college, maybe twenty-five, and what you'd have to call clean-cut. He had a sort of chiseled face (like a rock?), wide smile. Uncomplicated, that's what I'd have concluded, if I were judging.

Mike of the Rocks thought my name was neat. His word: neat. And sure, it *is* neat. I wondered what he'd be like when he grew up. Probably trade his bachelor apartment for a brick rancher with an equally uncomplicated wife who was...well, *neat*. But for now, we sipped my coffee and let the air thicken toward dark, made inconsequential talk and watched the campfire flames dance.

And it all got sort of dreamy after our shared freeze-dried dinners and unhurried camp chores. The Subject never even came up in our quiet talk: no awkward suggesting, ritual leading-up-to, no questions asked or needed. Hey, I was a grown-up woman, and I didn't have to answer to anybody. Couldn't understand why images of Craig kept pushing into my head, though, which I stubbornly pushed right back.

The feel of our bodies together was as natural as coming home, and as gentle as if between old lovers. Maybe Mike was already grown up that way.

After he'd slipped out and I'd slept in next morning, I didn't expect to see his tent, and I didn't. Reflected briefly that neither of us knew how to find the other, and that was okay. The creek water was beyond icy, but pure. And I felt cleansed, too, like the amber air, the sky beyond clinging leaves, the crystal stream. Nature having its ancient way...a man and a woman, all the baggage of civilization (uncomplicated) stripped away.

Literally.

Of course, we hadn't been complete fools: no STDs; we'd seen to that, at least. We *did* have to live in this century, after all. So I guess anyway you looked at it, we'd just sort of used each other, Mike Whatsis and I, and what was so bad about that? Need. Need was natural, yeah. And I didn't care what anyone else thought about my private life. *Besides, you'll never know about it, Craig MacDonnell, so stay out of my mind. Boss.*

*Oh, and I hope you're smiling, Mystery Mike, on your way back south, because I'm smiling, too.*

# Four

It was a couple weeks later, another Friday afternoon. Craig said he was really pleased at the progress we'd made, and invited us all for a beer. Not an upscale place this time, but a grubby, down-by-the-river joint where a lot of construction types went, judging from the pickups with company names on them. And inside were the duckbill caps with Cat and John Deere on them, and the sunburned, sawdusty good old boys, who're the same from one end of this old world to the other. The Jims and the Mikes and the Johns and the Rays, each with his background, his own story to tell: all different but all the same, too.

The five of us got a table meant for four midgets, and Craig waved to some other builder beer-guts. The girl who came over had been poured into her jeans several pounds ago, and chewed gum, but she lit Don up like a sudden idea.

"Hello, Tiffany Babe. When're you gonna let me take you away from all this?" *Gag. Retch.*

"Oh Donnie, you're all talk. C'n I getchall?"

"Just try me. Pitcher, boss?" Craig looked at me, remembering that imported stuff we were drinking before.

"Okay by me. You guys?" to Bob and Henry, who nodded.

The place was close and noisy, so even with it chilly outside, the draft was good. We'd been doing some detailed work all week, and it felt great to relax with each other. Tight crew like this is rare: always one horse's ass in everyone. Well, Don could qualify on that, but he was harmless.

A dude came over I didn't know, but everybody else did.

"Clyde," Craig scored a chair from the next table. "Sit with us, man."

"Hey, Craig, Donnie, guys. Who's this?" nodding at me. He was stocky, maybe thirty-five, but with a whiskey nose and watery eyes that you could say were blue. Patriotic eyes, my dad would have called them.

"Wes Whitestone, this's Clyde Kelly, master joiner. Wes is on the crew now."

"My replacement?" Almost a leer, but not mean.

"From what I've heard and seen of your work, Clyde, nobody could replace you. You're good." About a 50% smile for him, which, first impression, was more than he deserved.

I didn't like him.

"Well now. I'm with this lady already. *Boss...*"

"Now Clyde..."

"No," he waved a hand. "No hard feelin's, now. I'da been you, I'd run me off *and* kicked my ass that time. So how's the job goin'?"

"Good. A little ahead right now, even with all that termitey wood we had early on. The Webbs paying okay, so yeah, it's good. What you got goin'?"

"Oh, I'm seein' th' day comin' I'll need to get into...somethin' else, really. Lookin' at a couple business deals."

"No," Bob protested. "Hey, you're one of th' best, Clyde." Glance at me. "Don't get outta th' trade, now." Henry took his eyes off me too, to join that sentiment.

"Well, get careless 'n cut my hand off, one a these days. Naw, I'm doin' some cabinets on my own till I see which way to jump. Don't hafta answer to ennybody much."

"We miss you, buddy," Henry said, bumping him good-naturedly on the shoulder.

"Yeah, well, movin' forward all th' time, I guess." Then to me, "Like to come out an' see this'n's work, Craig."

"Sure, any time. Both the Webbs really liked your stuff, Clyde, but they like Wes's too."

*Now there it came, again.* Something just wasn't right and this time it was about the Clyde. Maybe just a little too folksy? Something. Beneath the good-old-boy patter there was...almost another personality, you might say...or what? You got the idea this guy had an agenda. Deviousness? My radar didn't tell me just what. The talk went on, the firing smoothed over as well as a thing like that ever can be. Clyde kept darting those bloodshot eyes around the room like he was looking for someone, or hoping to avoid someone. Druggie? Or just a drunk.

"Well, good t'see you all again." *Not y'all.* "Coulda stayed sober, I'd still be one of you. Take care now, an' keep all yer fingers." I expected him to lurch away. Didn't.

So that was Clyde, the best in the business. Basket case now. Wonder Craig kept him on as long as he did. Well, the boss was easy-going, and loyalty seemed to be a big part of this crew.

Nice, that part.

~ * ~

*So old Craig's found a woman to replace me. And seems she's good at the work. Well, guess it was stupid, getting myself fired. Still, I think I can weasel my way back in with the Webbs if I work it right.* Clyde remembered Gwen Webb had liked him, even flirting a little when they'd go over plans. Or maybe he'd imagined that.

The truth was, Clyde didn't have any other carpentry work lined up, and that didn't worry him much. He had other things to do, to plan. Working with his hands had always been something he liked to do, and he'd become good at it. But that wasn't where his head was, or where he got his dollars.

He would go out to the Webb place though, cultivate the owners some, see where that led. He wanted to stay close to that family for more reasons than piling up sawdust.

*Wesley Whitestone. Foxy thing, and I can tell you and Craig have at least the start of something going. Well, Craig's a good man, even if he did fire my ass. And like I said, I guess I deserved it. Gotta keep the lid on the drinking. What I've got going won't hold together if I overdo that.*

He called a number he knew well. The man on the other end of the line had jumped him bad for losing the Webb job, but he'd cooled down since. "Just find a way to get in on what they've got going, Kelly. If what I hear is right, we could get ourselves into big money with this guy."

*Yeah, pay dirt. I happen to know there's a lotta cash goes through Webb's hands, and I—we—want in on that in the worst way.* So, he'd make that visit, check out Miss Wesley's work, but be sure to find some time with the Webbs, or at least Gwen. She always got what she wanted from the old man and if she wanted Clyde, she'd be sure he was back, one way or another.

~ * ~

Okay, I did renege just a little and actually go out for a cool one with Craig a couple times. We were polite and didn't ravish each other, and it looked as if we could become good friends. That's rare for me. Guys either seem to turn me off, or maybe they click, at least at first. My *friends* are girls, it's that simple. Well, there was old Phil the Pill, but he hadn't wanted to do the just-friends thing.

But Craig and I did like each other's company, and in any other situation it could go further. Maybe after this job was over, less complicated. Or if I moved on...No, that'd be a silly, long-distance thing.

And Sarah hadn't given up on me yet. She seemed to be settling in with Greg the Loser, and kept wanting me along with whomever. And the 'whoms' weren't all as bad as Don or Reggie, but...*forgettable* says it best.

I really didn't like being around Greg that much. No, I didn't like being around him at all. Seemed he was stoned a lot of the time, and I suspected he was using some of that hard stuff regularly. Not a good influence on our Sarah, who was maybe sampling some herself. Seemed to be floating a lot.

Traveling around, you run into the drug thing even if you try to avoid it. It's like tobacco: kids want to try it, show how cool they are. And all of it hooks you, both chemically and psychologically. So even if Dad's isolation test is valid at the outset, once you're addicted, playing the Lone Ranger doesn't help.

Another thing about the Greg: he always seemed to have money to spend and his job wasn't that good. Family money, Sarah had said. He was a research lab assistant in the biology department of the university and his work depended on grants. Sarah had told me there were months at a time he wasn't working, so it didn't take a rocket scientist to figure the bucks were coming from *somewhere*. I really didn't want to know from where.

But I didn't want to move out, either. Charlottesville was high-rent, and our cottage was a good deal. Didn't want to blow my dollars on a whole house of my own, and a lotta folks didn't want dogs. Phil the Pal and I'd shared that apartment in Pennsylvania, but I was off that kind of arrangement. At least till Mr. Right came riding up on his white mechanical bull or whatever. And it didn't look as if that were about to happen on a construction job.

~ * ~

Clyde did visit the job site once, when the owners were there. And it was a little weird, I thought, his managing to spend time with Barker Webb. And what I heard of an exchange between Webb and Craig about that, after Clyde left.

"...wish you'd kept Clyde on," I picked up, from where I was re-hanging a paneled door we'd restored.

"Drunk one time too many," Craig told him. "He'd have hurt himself bad or somebody else. No, I can't have that on a job."

"Oh, I understand. And you're doing well without him. Too bad he can't keep it under control any more...Gwen liked him, is all..."

Okay, so he did good work. But really, what else had been to like about the guy? I was as good, and I'd shown I was faster, and I wasn't a drunk. And Gwen, the ex-cheerleader, had wanted to keep him? What, he have a wart, too? But of course, he'd been male, and that had to be better, right?

I ran the screws home in the door hinges and set the stops tight. Great old wooden box lock I'd rebuilt and adjusted just right. Had to forge a new catch, too. *Match that now, Shifty Clyde.*

My metal skills were handy on that job. I could heat the iron with an acetylene torch and hammer what we needed on a piece of railroad iron, so no big equipment outlay for forge and anvil. And we needed everything from shutter dogs to replacement H and L hinges, and I was *the man.*

Well…

I had developed a real dislike for the owners. Oh, Gwen was just the usual ditz, but J. Barker gave me the crawls. Sure, he wanted all our work done exactly right, was willing to pay for it and I was glad for that. So was Craig. But shady? I expected to find moss growing on his north side. And a certain condescension that was a lot like a fungus, or an oily rag coming in under the door. And we all know lawyers make lots of money, but this place was a couple hundred acres and we were talking millions to buy it in the first place, and a bunch more when everything was finished.

There was his Ferrari, which you could hear half a mile away, and homecoming queen Gwen's high-dollar Mercedes. And now there was a farm manager, no less, *three* new tractors in the equipment shed, and rumored thoroughbreds on the way.

Now, I'm not knocking anybody's living the American Dream, but the man had an air of throwing dollars around like there was plenty more, not to worry. Nouveau, in spades. Rumor was they supported their grown kids' lavish lifestyles, too, which I guess you would expect. Son Jerry had a Beamer Z3 he wedged himself into, and no trace of a job, lived downtown somewhere, while Samantha the daughter was trying to be an actress in New York, among a couple million other hopefuls. That couldn't be cheap. I often wondered how much of that city's economy was fed by the bottomless contributions of disappointed non-stars.

But was I just envious? Probably. If Dad could have, and had set me up like that, I'd probably have been totally worthless, too.

Good part was, the Webbs left us mostly alone to do our job, once they saw how good we were. They lived in a country club lease temporarily, and apparently found enough to fill their days that we saw them only about once a week. Never the daughter, and only a few times the fat frat boy son. Craig dealt with them, and I tried to keep busy and out of the way when they bobbed up.

The weeks passed, the work was still good, and by midwinter we were on the home stretch with that great house. There was plaster repair, which none of us did, but the sub was good. And paint, and final cabinetry. Floors had been leveled, sanded, flat-varnished, and covered with red resin paper to protect them till final waxing. Heating system was on, and the dreary, wet days outside failed to depress us. We were a good crew on a good job with a good boss, and we could stand the owners. It just wasn't supposed to get any better than this, despite my lingering unease with things.

~ * ~

My overhearing Sarah and Greg was a fluke. Cyrano and I had been out for a run despite the weather, so we didn't drive up in Hosmer. Their door had been cracked just a sliver when we reached the stairs. Other fluke...I'd shut the front door quietly, I guess.

"*Got* to pay the guy." Greg, frantic. "These boys don't cut you any slack..."

"Oh honey, how'd you get in so deep? And no, you know I don't have any cash. I'm on loans, here..."

"...guy Vince is a mean bastard. He's new, and he's out to prove himself to the others..."

I tried not to listen. But they'd hear us on the creaky stairs. I stepped back quietly, opened the front door again, called to Cyrano, who was already inside, and shut the door with a thump. Headed upstairs. Quiet now, behind their door.

Vince: out of a gangster movie, that name. And maybe our boy Greg just owed too much on his car, or...no, this Vince was out to prove himself? And the others? Didn't want to know. Did *not* have *any* curiosity about this. Sarah's life was hers to blow, and Greg's situation was way outside my universe. And that was just the place I wanted—intended—to keep it.

Forgeddaboudit.

And I did, grilling some fish Craig had given me. Seems he was a fishing Nazi; had to be, to go in winter with his fly rod and waders. Brr. Glad he hadn't asked me along. I could see it in June, maybe. But yeah, with hushpuppies, real Georgia food. Maybe some turnip greens...no, they'd be from Mexico or someplace, but I guessed I could pretend.

Shoulda invited Craig over for this, but we were still not into going to each other's place. I'd been out to his, but just for a quick load of lumber from his private stash. Great hideaway in the woods (no surprise), but no time to snoop. So hadn't done the tour, although now I could see that, and maybe soon.

We hadn't had another soul-baring session, but Bob, who'd been with Craig the longest, had told me again he dated some, but not seriously. Still scorched from the trauma of the thing with the ex, I was reasonably sure. And old Bob was just playing harmless matchmaker, I guessed. A lotta people seem to think that's their good-deed duty: hook up any oddies, whether they want it or not.

Oh hell, the truth was, I had this recurring thing in my head about that substitute father role. And okay, maybe if Craig'd pushed, I'd have swept that under the rug, but he hadn't. So every time I'd done the math, it had come up wrong: *I'm twenty-eight; he's forty.* Whole different generation, whole different value system, likes, hang-ups. He just didn't seem to be totally into the 21st century. But maybe that wasn't all bad...

And whenever I remembered that casual campout sex with Mike of the Woods, I found myself measuring it up against Craig, and not liking it a lot. Now *that* comparison had to be a father fixation, I was certain. Hey, I didn't have to answer to *anybody* for my choices. I said that. And Craig sure as hell didn't have to, either.

So forget that. *Here, have a hushpuppy, Cyrano. No, trout have bones in them. Don't want my best guy choking: I'd really be lost.*

I punched up the phone.

"Hey, if you'd get your ass over here, you could help me eat all this fish. Or am I too late to feed the provider?"

"Actually, I was just considering which can to open. Sure it's okay?"

"Should have invited you before. Shame has forced me. They're *your* fish."

So okay: that was finally done. Just had to remember not to rip his clothes off as he came through the door. No, we were *friends*. Remember?

Somehow Craig and I got onto the Greg thing, and drugs, and even Clyde, whose current (shady?) occupation we speculated about. And yeah, we knew there was a lot of it going on there. And other arms-length subjects like that, so we were okay all evening. Cyrano liked Craig, who of course didn't make any threatening moves, so he didn't rip him apart. He even let him tickle his tummy, which was my special treatment.

It occurred to me as we gave each other a quick goodnight peck, that this was the way a relationship should really progress, anyway. To hell with that whole now-generation package. You know, do it right: meet a guy, get to know him a little at a time, do things together, even have mixed feelings sometimes as one little step at a time, the blocks built toward what was really right.

Or not. But certainly, the whole jump-into-bed pattern hadn't worked for me. And I got the feeling it hadn't for Craig, either. So if friends it was to be, okay. If more, why sure, despite the math.

Numbers had never been my strong suit anyway.

# Five

Greg Bunche (I'd started referring to him as a buncha trouble) finally had it all worked out, but he'd need help. Not much—he'd take all the risk—but for a few critical minutes. Of course, he couldn't tell Sarah the details. None of it, really.

"All I need is for you to give me a ride to my car at the garage. I've got one stop to make, then you drop me off, okay?"

"Sure, but there's this one detail, lover. You know I don't have a car."

"Borrow one. Hey, you know that recliner we looked at? Borrow Wes's truck and we can get it afterwards."

"But you said it was too expensive."

"Been thinking about that. I can swing it."

"But all that money you owe...we can't buy anything..."

"Got it all taken care of, trust me. No, that recliner will be my gift to my special lady, okay?"

Sarah asked me that night if she could borrow Hosmer. Could she drive a stick shift? Sure, she said, so I called Craig to bum a ride to work next day, for woman and dog. He seemed glad I asked.

I had my toolbelt, Skilsaw and drill when he rolled up in his pickup. I left the keys with a sleepy Sarah and we headed for the job.

"How's Sarah doing with her research?"

"Seems okay. Spends a lotta time with her current guy, Loser Greg, but hey, maybe they're actually studying."

"What is it, dreams, you said?"

"*Women's* dreams. Didn't realize we had our exclusive brand, but maybe so. She's worked on me, of course, but her theories seem pretty far out."

"Like what?"

"Well, she's convinced I'm on a constant search for a substitute for my dad, which I suppose I can buy. But she tries to twist every dream, or fragment of one I remember, to fit that premise."

"So if maybe you dream of going fishing, she thinks you have a hole in it where your dad should be?" The fish expert, yeah. But I *had* enjoyed that, not so much the fishing as just being with Dad.

"Close. My dreams are pretty basic: I'm running, which I do a lot, you know, or I'm with Cyrano and we're exploring. I don't see much father-fixation there. Once I dreamed I was under my truck fixing something, and she interpreted that as a desire to be ravished by it. Can you imagine? A *truck?* We shared a laugh over that one. Cyrano licked my face. He thought it was pretty funny, too."

What I didn't tell Craig—had never told Sarah or anyone else— was that I did get these...messages, I guess you'd call them, and they might come from dreams. No, I didn't get revelations in the dreams themselves, or sit bolt upright at some shocking, save-the-world insight. I'd just wake up in the morning sometimes with the certainty that this or that thing was the right thing to do, or not to do.

Maybe other people had those experiences too, but nobody'd ever told me he had. So I just accepted it as part of the Wesley makeup, weird or not. Sometimes I'd be 'told' to head for a specific place in my wanderings, but I explained that by reflecting that I'd probably had that place on a mental list anyway.

But every time I'd ignored one of those directives, I'd regretted it, one way or another. You know, land a job with a nasty boss, have to live in a roach chateau, or just hate the location in general. Flip side, following the lead, I'd made some great friends, or discovered out-of-this-world places, or just had experiences to treasure. So, was Somebody directing me? Didn't seem logical, since I wasn't into religion as such. Or even that hooked up any other way spiritually.

Now I didn't confuse this with my built-in spot-a-clod radar, which was the result of experience and scars. No, that might have made me a little cynical, but it didn't come from any mysterious source. It wasn't infallible either, as my checkered past relationships proved.

But the messages didn't always relate to places; often just courses of action: get out of this job before that shaky roof the boss won't fix right collapses. Dump this guy before he turns homicidal. Go to Arizona because there's this girl who's just lost her husband in that crazy war and needs a best friend. And I did, and he had, and she did. Creepy maybe, but good, bottom line.

Well, one thing I've learned is that nobody's average, dig deep enough. We've all got quirks and so maybe mine is getting pushes in the right direction from...who then, Dad? Maybe Mom, who I barely remember? Or am I just getting little insights in those moments between sleep and waking, which I read somewhere are our most receptive (vulnerable?) times.

~ * ~

Greg's ingenious plan for extricating himself from his major debt was, on the surface, simple: he'd rob a bank. Not easy, with today's security systems, but of course he'd worked out the details. And yes, it was a monster risk, but he had to get the money to the guy named Vince, tonight. And Greg knew the people further up the chain had surely given that guy his orders. He'd been able to stall Vince's predecessor, but that was then; this was now, and time had run out.

So, keep Sarah completely in the dark: the less she knew the safer she and he, would be. Drop him off, pick him up, drop him at his car...home free. And Vince would have the money, and he'd have his life back.

*Shouldn't have skimmed those deliveries. Should not have taken their money. But who could know a bunch of crack-heads would keep that tight a count? Hey, just a couple hundred here and there. And not like they'd earned it, right? All drug money, all illegal.*

But apparently those guys expected some twisted sort of honor among thieves, and they'd found out to the penny how much he'd lifted. Like a damn business, this was, with bean counters. He drew on the weed and giggled at the image of a sallow-faced old guy in a green eyeshade punching up figures, like in a bank or somewhere.

Yeah, bank. Right after lunch, when nobody much in, gone back to work. Branch didn't have a guard, depended on the security system. All of which was electronic. Maybe a backup, but should be time, in the confusion. And there *would* be confusion.

This was exciting. Hit the system with a simple plan, get free again. Then maybe disappear. Or not. Done right, he could thumb his nose at them all, go on with the routine. But yeah, in a rut here. Pay Vince's people, keep a good stash, do a fade-out.

Would miss Sarah a little, but hey, there'd be a Sarah in any town, any place he wanted to be. Didn't have to build his life around any girl. Lotsa lonely women, and he was doing them a favor, wasn't he? Being there for them for a while. Boy Scout, yeah. Giggle, again.

The stuff he was smoking as they drove wasn't top-grade, but it was clearing his mind. He thought back to his first contact. He'd asked about the hard stuff, and the old guy—Peebles had been his name—had assured him, "Anybody has the green, he can get you the white. All you need is the cash."

Yeah, the stuff was everywhere, coming up from Florida in students' cars, in over-the-road trucks, innocuous shipments, many small, some big, but all adding up to a tremendous flow, with a corresponding avalanche of cash changing hands. Easy cash, but with that temptation to skim a little more...

Sarah stopped the Dakota beside the abandoned service station, her mind on the interview ahead. Just half an hour away, but Greg had said he'd be quick. She hardly noticed as he took the two sets of tire chains he'd put in the back of the truck. He disappeared behind the building. *Now, if this woman's dreams can substantiate the premise...*

Greg waited while a white van passed, then after a quick look around, heaved the bunched chain up toward the overhead electric wires. He'd read of a man stranded on the Alaskan Highway, faced with freezing to death, shorting out the power lines like this. Repair crew had found him in time.

The first chains hung over the top wire, but didn't reach the lower one. Nothing happened. His hands were sweating, even in the chill. *Okay, again. Concentrate. Sort of like making a basket.* He let fly.

This time there was a blinding flash and loud pop. Fire shot out like monster fireworks, but he didn't wait.

Sprinting toward the bank, he pulled a ski mask over his face. Just like in the movies. He couldn't restrain a giggle. What a high! He shoved the glass door open and pulled the fake gun out. The lights were out, and it took a second to get it all clear: startled clerks, eyes wide at the sight of his gun.

"*Nobody moves!* No pushing buttons. Get the cash now! Into this sack. You and you!" to a frightened girl, who couldn't have been eighteen, and an older woman. Their hands shook as they grabbed bills. He scanned the others: another older woman, a round guy in a suit, frozen, scared. The woman and the girl were scooping cash. Lots of beautiful cash.

"Now down on the floor! All of you! Nobody moves, or you all die." This was so *easy*. They were scared shitless of a toy gun.

Funny, really *funny*.

He was aware of lights coming on, fluorescents blinking. *Backup generator. Took long enough...cheap system.* He pushed the door open, checking the street. Pocketed the gun, walked a few steps, pulled the mask off, clutched the paper bag to him, and ran around the corner.

Sarah was writing in a notebook, already having forgotten that bright flash. He got in naturally, forcing himself not to hurry.

"Turn here now. Up this street." Away from the bank, which he was sure would be swarming with cops in minutes. He looked back, caught a glimpse of a shape at the glass bank door. *Damn.* But it was okay…all they'd see was a truck turning at a normal pace.

But what the bank manager also saw was part of the receding vanity license plate: HO…some other letters. Might not be important, a blue pickup in a town full of pickups, but it was all he had.

And all he could tell the policemen who responded to his call.

"I'm detective Nate Peterson, and this is patrolman Roger Morris. Got video?" the tall plainclothes one asked.

"Maybe some. The backup didn't kick in till he was almost out the door. Happened really fast: lights out, and boom, he was in and out in what seemed like only a few seconds. Don't know how he got the electricity off." The guy was still shaking. "Never been in a robbery before." He mopped his face with a handkerchief.

"Know how much he got?"

"Counting, now. Lot of customers at lunchtime. Maybe a few thousand. Most of our cash is put into the vault several times a day."

"Okay. Let's see what's on your surveillance camera."

The video had recorded routine business until 1:15 p.m. when it went blank. Jerky images followed, then steadied as the generator power had come on. A medium-height man in a ski mask, jacket and jeans was turned away, opening the bank door. He started off, shoving his gun into a pocket and walking away, the sack of money tight to his body. Not another soul in sight.

"Not much. The angle of the glass door distorts him once he's through it. Okay, you said only a blue truck, license what, again?"

"HO was all I could get. Out of state, though. Thought I saw that… tapered symbol." The man made a shape. "The one Pennsylvania has."

"Keystone. That's good. Anything else?"

"The pickup had one of those camper caps on it," the young clerk offered. But that was all Peterson could learn. Probably just a passerby, not hurrying, the manager'd said, but he'd get on it anyway…

Greg Bunche had picked up his car, then met Sarah at the furniture store after her interview, where they'd bought the recliner. He'd been disappointed that the pile of bills hadn't added up to more, but was sure he needed to go through with the purchase to keep his story tight. Not that the robbery could ever be traced to him.

~ * ~

At day's end, Craig and I drove up to my house to find a police car there, and this lanky specimen in plainclothes and a uniformed cop poking around my pickup. I hoped Sarah hadn't done a hit-and-run or something. Stepped on the clutch instead of the brake? I said she was a ditz.

"Oh, that's Nate," Craig said. "Now what's this about?" He slid out. "Hey, guy, what's happening? Been a while." Extending his hand.

"It has, Craig. You know Roger Morris? And who's this?"

"My new right hand. Wesley Whitestone, Nate Peterson. We go a long way back."

"Glad to meet you, Nate." I gripped his hand. "My truck been misbehaving?" I was checking it for dings, or worse.

"Could be. You two been at work, I'd say."

"Yeah, the sawdust gives us away, doesn't it?" Craig admitted.

"All day?" It wasn't an accusation, but this was going somewhere, all right. Didn't have to use my radar to pick up on that.

"Sure. Finishing a job out southwest in the county. What's wrong?"

"Well, we've got ourselves a bank job, and what *could* be a coincidence. Manager saw a pickup, first license letters HO, Pennsylvania, and we traced it with the DMV up there. Description fits, but of course that doesn't mean any connection. We're just following up. So the truck's been here all day?"

"No, my housemate borrowed it to haul some furniture. She should be home. Got the downstairs part of the house."

"I'll want to talk to her, then. Again, probably nothing, since the robber was a man, but anything'll help."

Peterson was easy-going, not like the other cop, who kept fingering his gun and eyeing me, alternately watching my maniacal dog. Open and shut for him, probably: vehicle seen at a robbed bank, my truck, ergo, I was the perp. Only question for him would be, where had I stashed the cash?

Sarah confirmed her use of Hosmer, which incidentally was my customized license plate. Peterson asked her the relevant time.

"Let's see, it was just after a one-thirty appointment. About two-thirty. We went to Gordon's to buy the chair. On sale."

"We?"

"My boyfriend and I. He met me there, came back and we unloaded it here."

The detective got Greg's stats. The questions went on a few minutes more there in the entryway. Cyrano was nosing around the other cop outside, who was trying to decide whether to pet him or shoot him. *Sure: accessory, Sherlock.* I called him over…not everyone is a dog lover.

"Need us any more, Nate?" Craig asked.

"Not that I can see, but let me have your phone number, Ms. Whitestone, just in case." I gave him my cell number, called Cyrano away a second time from impending homicide.

"I like your dog," Peterson said. "Not all hound, is he?"

"Some Doberman, I think. Wants to chase rabbits and mangle anybody looks too hard at me at the same time. Conflicting loyalties." Something was nagging at my memory.

"Okay," Craig said. "Good to see you again, Nate. And I'll see you on the job in the morning, Wes." He left. I let Cyrano in, started to pull my boots off. No, there was something…

I opened the door again. Peterson was scanning his notes.

"Detective, I just thought of something. Come in out of the cold a minute?" He nodded to Roger the top gun, who'd taken sanctuary in the squad car, now that all perceived danger from girl carpenters and vicious dogs was past.

"Remember something helpful?" He scratched Cyrano's ears, obviously a dog guy, 'cause he let him do it.

"Yes. Now, I don't want to get Sarah into trouble, but neither do I want her druggie boyfriend using my truck to rob a bank and get *me* in trouble." And I told him what I'd heard about Greg's desperate need for cash. "He was sure some guy named Vince would come after him big time if he couldn't pay. He was scared, said something about this Vince wanting to prove himself to the higher-ups. Weird." His eyes had flickered at the name Vince, I swear it. Now, what was that?

"I see. Do you know this Vince, by any chance?"

"No". I watched for something else, but he changed the subject.

"Well, this may help. So you're a carpenter, too?"

"Craig calls us joiners when we're on timberframe work. Next one's a log cabin. Maybe we'll be loggers there."

"He's a great guy. We went to school together. You're not from Pennsylvania."

"Georgia. Been working my way around. Lucked into Craig's job. Yeah, we get along." I wanted to ask this old friend about the ex-wife, but that wasn't my business, was it?

"Okay, thanks Ms. Whitestone. Timing doesn't seem right, but you're covered no matter what. And let me hear if you run across anything." He gave me his card.

~ * ~

"What you brought us was way too little cash, Greg boy," the man called Vince informed him. "You've held out fourteen G's, and we counted eight and change. We need the rest. Now."

"I thought...I was sure there'd be more. But yeah, I can get the rest. Just need a little time, is all. I can..."

"No, I don't believe you, smart guy. Now I heard about that bank job today, and here you come with about what they lost. Okay, but you can't pull another one like that, and they're prob'ly about a half-inch offa your ass right now. So yeah, we'll credit the eight you gave us, but the boss's gotta decide what happens next."

They were in Vince's pickup truck, parked at a shopping center behind a wall of parked cars. He used his cell.

"Yeah, it's me. Our man Greg says he can get the rest, but he's got no plan for it. Told him that won't cut it. What's your call, boss?"

He listened. Greg was sweating. "No, I'd say he's dry, but you tell me, and it's done." He listened some more. "Okay then," and he punched off.

"What'd he say?"

"Said give you another chance, which I don't agree with. You're a crack-head shit, Bunche, and you messed with the wrong dudes. But the boss's the boss, so I'll take you back to your car." He looked around. "The long way, so nobody notices us."

Greg was so relieved he thanked Vince twice, planning, searching for another way to get the rest of the money. Maybe borrow some here, some there. Six thousand: not that much, really. Sell the car...No, owed too much on it. Try the parents again. *Got to. Sarah's got nothing...* He didn't notice they'd turned down a gravel track off the highway.

"Okay, guy. Boss says you got a little punishment comin', for not payin' on time. Gotta walk home." Vince's hand was in his jacket pocket.

"But it's two-three miles out. Can't you...?"

"Out, dude, before I forget my orders." Vince's tone had never been friendly, and it was decidedly less so, now.

"But...Okay, *okay*. I'm outta here. And I'll have the rest..."

The man called Vince waited till Greg's feet were on the ground, then shot him twice, so he fell away from the truck. He reached, pulled the door shut, then drove away.

~ * ~

"He's skipped, looks like," the stakeout officer called in at midnight. "Called the girlfriend, who says she hasn't seen him. Want me to stay?" Nate Peterson had had a long day. And this was a long shot, but after what that girl carpenter had told him...

"Switch off with Anderson and go home, Bill. Either of you get anything, call me at home." It just wasn't right, this guy disappearing just at the wrong time. And a druggie, the girl'd said. Needed quick cash...

He put the wheels in motion for an APB on the car: red Nissan sports job. Computer cross-checking in Richmond got the plate numbers, so maybe…Or just as likely Bunche would reel in from a late night somewhere. In which case, they'd have him anyway. He closed up, went home.

Back on the job the next day, Peterson got the word: car empty at a shopping center parking lot. Okay, so the bird had flown. *So he's our guy then.*

But a scant half-hour later, the call from a farmer on his way to town: body by the roadside. Farmer hadn't touched anything, so no I.D.

Peterson and Morris drove to the scene, and yeah, it was Greg Bunche. Had been. Everything still on him. Everything but the missing cash.

The detective called me at work to let me know the news.

"Looks like you were right, Ms. Whitestone. The drug connection fit, but the timing was still off for the bank thing. So I spent some more time with Sarah Wainright, and she remembered dropping Bunche off for just the time he needed to hit the bank."

"You think she was in on it?" Why was he telling *me* this?

"Not really. Just gut feeling…even with the shock, she isn't acting guilty. What we need is something—anything-—to tie into a drug ring. Money's gone, of course, so why waste Bunche? Unless it was plain robbery, and it doesn't look like it. Anything more at all you can tell me? Even if it doesn't seem connected, I need it."

I racked the brain, but nothing came. Oh, Clod Clyde had said he was looking at other ways to make a living, but…

"Longest of long shots, Detective, and just a gut feeling of mine, too. Guy worked for Craig told us he was looking at another line of work. Absolutely nothing definite, but the shifty eyes, nervousness sort of got to me, and I thought drugs, first thing. And it might've been that I just didn't like the guy, so don't take it too seriously, but you said you wanted everything. Oh, Craig's here. Why don't you see if he knows something about Clyde Kelly that'd help?" I took the phone to the boss.

"No way, Nate," I heard him say. "Harmless drunk, if there ever was one. But hey, go check him out. Did say he was thinking of quitting the trade, but we all say that one time or another." So the boss was giving Loser Clyde a clean bill of health. Hey, none of my business, any of this.

We got back to work. And later Craig heard from Peterson that our Clyde had a tight alibi for the time Greg had died, was actually with J. Barker Webb, no less. The wife'd liked him, after all. And damn, his alibi was he'd been going over some plans for more construction work the Webbs wanted done.

"Now, why wouldn't they hire us for that? We're here. We're good; we're fast. We do guest houses, stables. Don't we?"

"You never know, Wes. People try to hire the contractor's help on the side, figure to beat the overhead that way. Can't tell you how many times owners have hit on my guys to moonlight, cash under the table. I'm Class A, with all the expenses that go with it. Carpenter working out of his truck charges less, keeps all the money. No records, no taxes. I'd say that's Clyde's current M.O."

"Chickenshit," I almost spat. Told you I didn't like the guy.

"You're loyal, Wes. Lotta guys aren't."

~ * ~

Sarah was pretty broken up over Greg's death, so I spent as much time with her as I could. She'd convinced herself he'd been the right guy for her, despite his obvious flaws. But as callous as it may sound, I was mostly relieved for her. I mean, what's to like about a dude who's on drugs in the first place? Then apparently gets in on dealing the stuff, too, and is dense enough to skim cash from the worst guys alive to tangle with. *Then* he robs a bank, and according to Sarah, for too little to pay them back.

Worse than dumb.

No, I just couldn't see the redeeming side of the late Buncha Screwups. I wondered how hard Sarah had worked to justify the relationship in the first place. Some of the others I'd seen her with weren't saints either...but on a scale, Greg'd seemed a step down.

Not being into psychology myself, I wasn't prepared to say she'd just been overly grateful for the attention. Hey, she was a nice-looking girl, just not grown up yet. And attention from a chronic loser? Spare me that sad song.

But I was there for her, and I did make myself listen as she spilled it about how he'd been on the point of a major change, and that they'd made plans for a life together. I'd never sensed any ambition at all in the guy, but hadn't looked very hard. Maybe he'd been the one who'd been grateful for *her* attention.

Kind of like a pair of waifs who ain't got much but cling together against the trauma of having to get up every morning. *Oh, we ain't got a barrel of money...* Love that song. Anyway, I was pretty sure she'd get over him soon enough and that seemed to be what was happening, next few weeks.

# Six

The Webbs had hired a horse guy to go with the horticulturist who was planting stuff all over, clearing brush with his crew. And Roy the Horse was a real turn-on. He was thirty-three, had trained and shown horses all over. Even doubled for a famous actor in a popular movie, since the star couldn't ride. If you looked close at a couple action scenes, you could tell it was Roy, not the other famous heartthrob doing all that expert riding.

"But I didn't get the girl," he complained to me one lunch break as I was admiring the horses. The Webbs weren't strictly going for thoroughbreds; they had a couple that weren't so high-strung and expensive. One, a roan gelding named Walker, liked me from the first. Hell, he even liked Cyrano in a symbiotic sort of way.

And I liked Walker. Got to visiting him as often as I could, take him a piece of apple or sugar lump. I've had the little-girl thing for horses since I can remember, and got the chance out in Texas a couple years back to indulge it. Gotta get a place someday and at least one beast.

Guy I hung with out there a while (for some reason) used to tease me about horses. Said it was psychological.

"Women just naturally want a big hairy animal between their legs."

That guy was *such* a loser.

But one time Gwen Webb saw me stroking Walker, and asked me if I rode. I told her I'd survived about as long as I could without it. So she said well, go ahead and ride Walker if I wanted. Her kids didn't do horses, and J. Barker was hooked on the showy thoroughbreds. She liked the other non-aristocrat, a gentle mare named Daisy.

"And say, why don't we ride together some weekend?" She hadn't really met many people she liked since they'd moved here from Baltimore, she said, and she'd like the company. Okay, slumming with the help. Didn't take offense, being absolutely non-class conscious, and would've taken her up on it if it'd included cleaning horse shit off her riding boots.

So we did that, and I began to see more to this woman than the airhead she'd seemed at first. Despite the distinct impression she left that she was, indeed, slumming. She talked about what she'd wanted to do—be an architect—when she was young like me, with the whole world ahead of her.

"But then I met Jay, and all that went out the door. Now I feel like window dressing, you know? Oh, he's let me design and remodel places we've owned, but he's really just humoring me. If I were your age and single, I'd make my way to the top...I know I would."

And on and on. She wasn't boring, just bored. And all the bucks rolling in had to dull the pain more than a little, poor thing.

"Did you study architecture, Wes? I mean, here you are, doing this exciting work with Craig, which I do like a lot, and you must've had training."

"Afraid not the academic kind. I studied comparative literature for some obscure reason. But yeah, Dad and I built stuff from the time I could lift a hammer and hit my thumb. He was a real craftsman. I feel I learned from the best."

So we rode their acres, and a lot of other acres, too, on adjoining farms and old plantations where Gwen had permission. I got to liking this country better the more I saw of it. Rounded fields where ghosts had probably fought in the Revolution, big trees that were maybe there at the time. Hidden little glades with maples and sweet springs of crystal water. And yeah, I could actually get to liking Gwen, too, in reasonable doses. Most of the time, she was a lot more human than I'd figured.

You know: stereotypes.

And there was Roy, the horse god. He divided his time and talents among several spreads, so he wasn't here perking my hormones every day. Had a helper who mucked out and fed the menagerie; he just did the training and working-out and made the decisions. And my interest in the horses apparently told him I wasn't a total loss, so he started getting friendly. Gwen approved. Said a girl could do a lot worse…Roy would be a big man in the equine world before long. Sly wink.

Okay, Wesley the carpenter—joiner—and Roy the horse hunk? That could work. He hadn't done college, but it seemed that being around all the local richies and some not-so-local notables had let some cool rub off on him. And damn, he was *so* handsome. Tom Cruise, eat your heart out. Probably had girls hanging off him like a wide receiver, when he wasn't wading in horse manure. After all, where else could a horse groupie feed her habit and get laid at the same time?

Okay, I was well aware that everyone sort of cuts good-looking people a lot of slack. Gotta be something more there, surely. Isn't there? Couldn't there be? No? But…Anyway, in the final analysis, I'm like just about everybody else. I'd rather make it with gorgeous than ugly. And who wouldn't? I've been told it doesn't make any difference with the lights out, but you don't wanta puke either, next morning.

Now, I knew guys like Roy were too good to be true. And I also knew, despite the fact that I'm damn sharp, I don't look like the drop-dead model types guys like that wanta be seen with. Not *that* skinny, for sure. But, bottom line, I said okay, why not?

So when Roy Rogers Cool casually asked me out, I just as casually said yes.

He drove a big 4-wheel drive diesel truck, which I liked. Gear, saddles in the extended cab behind us, smell like a stable, seductive engine throb that said muscle. He pulled horse trailers to shows regularly, he explained, and didn't see the point of a car, which was really pretty helpless, as he put it. *Yeah, get stuck in the horse shit.*

Hey, I was a truck girl.

But *all* this guy could talk was horses. And after dinner out and a good bluegrass band, his mind was still on horses. And when he finally got around to making his move on me, I got the distinct feeling I was…incidental, I guess you'd say. A convenience? A body? Horse substitute?

Roy wasn't exactly predatory, which I'd expected; he just didn't seem quite to be of the same species as girls. I'd envisioned chills and tingles when he ran his fingers over me, but what I felt was more like hooves. And I remembered a similar experience with another horse-king, back in Texas. One that I also hadn't let happen.

Damn, are *all* the men here from another planet? I'd wanted to—looked forward to—shamelessly getting into this young Marlboro Man's bed, but *this?* This was turning into a plastic imitation. Not like reality at all. Not like…well, not like the mature, gentle, thoughtful man a girl wants to give herself to.

I even found myself comparing Roy to my boss, Craig the Scarred, Craig the older-but-wiser, Craig, the kind of guy I knew wouldn't love casually. And I even flashed on Mike of the Granola, but like I said, was sort of ashamed of that, now. Was I finally getting some maturity? Could be.

"But…but Roy's so *sexy!*" my propelling inner voice cried. "So picture-*perfect.*" Hey, you only go around once in this life, right?

Grab it, girl.

I took his hand out of my blouse. What was he planning? In his *truck?* On the damn *saddles?* Looked him in the eye, that bad habit I have.

"Wrong time, wrong place, wrong two people," I told him.

"Oh, sorry. I thought you…I guess I dunno what I thought, Wes. Well yeah, it *is* late. Gotta get an early start for a horse show tomorrow, anyway. Sorry."

And that was, by God, that.

At home, I felt relieved, more than anything else. But just where had that about Craig come from? We had no hold on each other. My sex life was mine, and nobody else's, dammit. Just what had triggered *that* comparison?

~ * ~

Clyde Kelly had done it, and neatly. Slipped back onto the Webb place, contracted for more construction work. Found a couple guys for a crew. He'd be close to all those dollars, and it looked like he'd get his share, all right. The son, Jerry, didn't like him, maybe didn't trust him yet, but that'd change after they'd worked together for a while. Clyde could ingratiate himself with anybody when he really wanted to.

It gave him a degree of satisfaction to be working there after MacDonnell had fired him. He'd cut the drinking and was doing a helluva job on his own, right under his ex-boss's nose. Snippy Wesley didn't like him, it was plain, but who gave a damn? She could do her thing and he could do his. Only she'd be gone soon, and he'd still be in, even after the building stuff was done.

Wesley. Okay, so she was as good as he was, but how the *hell* had she gotten so fast at it? Rule One was that you hadda go slow and careful, especially on restoration work: duplicating, matching, doing precision work. Well, he guessed no matter how good you were, there was always somebody better out there somewhere. Longest shot that she'd be here, right in his face, though.

*Well, Miss Priss, I won't be doing this work long. Got a lot more going for me, while you'll still be driving nails.*

~ * ~

Gwen Webb and I hadn't become best friends or anything, but she did ask me to go with her to choose lighting fixtures, carpet, plumbing styles. We had about the same tastes, and it was fun spending somebody else's money. And I was on the clock, too. I reminded her of that, but she just waved it off.

"Not real money, Wes, just lawyer's fees." Both of us laughed.

So, with those final items installed, the crew got onto the punch-list: all those things you forget to do, the things the owner notices that your eyes just slipped right over. That always takes about three times as long as you figure on, but are the most important: visible, and the first things non-carpenters notice.

So with that done, too, this job was finally over, and I hated to leave it. Loved that house. Have to find a way to buy one myself someday. Rob a bank? That reminded me: the murder part of that Bunche case was still unsolved, just before spring.

And there was this idea that I could move on, bucks saved, a breaking-off point before the crew got onto that log cabin restoration. Cabin, yeah...half a million, and with a timberframe addition.

To die for.

And there were these three things holding me: the Webbs wanted to throw a party in a couple weeks for everyone who'd worked on the job, including Roy the Horse, the stable boy, John the horticulturist, Clyde, the crew of us, and assorted significant others. Hey, we weren't society, but Gwen wasn't that pretentious really, when you got to know her.

Number two was, I liked the crew (even Don, grudgingly), liked the work, liked the town and the area. Better than any place I'd been. Maybe try to save for that rundown historic treasure even. Yeah, by the time I was maybe fifty.

But face it, girl, Craig MacDonnell was the prime attraction. Last day on the job, he finally asked me on a real date. Maybe figured it wasn't strictly fraternizing now? Who knew? Anyway, dinner at his place, some good blues CDs, the works. I didn't think I'd told him I had a thing for the blues, so did he just sense that?

Now, what girl in her right *mind* turns down a craggy, gentle guy who's not *that* old, got a lot to share. And yes, sexy. As in strong hands, tight abs, a little mystery about him. And been in my mind for months, apparently.

Not yes, but hellyes. And I hadn't needed any other-world directive to guide me to that decision.

His place was out on a road northwest of town, past the high-dollar McMansions, but before the double-wides and rundown farmhouses. With luck, he told me, urban sprawl wouldn't engulf his fifteen acres in his lifetime. And no, he didn't have kids to leave it to. Valencia the Wife hadn't even wanted to *hear* about kids.

Well.

Inside, his house was all heavy beams and stone and glass that looked out on big trees and a small creek I hadn't noticed the one time I'd been there. The floors were scarred recycled heartpine (what else?) and all the wood cried out to be stroked.

I did that. Repeatedly. The countertops in the kitchen were aged copper with a marble cutting block inset.

"Nice patina," my fingers on that, too.

"Spilled tabasco sauce does that, in time." Grin. Nice grin. (I've said that.)

"To inject a jarring note, didn't Valencia treasure this house?"

"Hated it. Wanted white Formica and everything painted. Said she'd had old stuff in the commune growing up, and damned if she'd put up with it here."

The place was so masculine. I could see places it could use a woman's touch, but not—God forbid—the wrong woman. The furniture was a mix of rare but simple antiques—the kind that have 'sold' signs on them in the shops—and handmade newer stuff. I guessed rightly these were Craig's work: tight mortises, wood rubbed to a glow.

Loved.

I confess to a feeling of almost being home there: man's place sure, but hadn't Craig said I was his right-hand man? So my plumbing was different (thank God); that didn't mean I couldn't become as much a fixture here as Craggy Craig. But I said *almost*, and underneath my awe and being overwhelmed by all this, I was really just floating around. A spectator, blown away yes, but almost afraid to touch anything. Well, not *quite* afraid. But something needed resolving...

Too cold to grill outside, but the man did steaks in the broiler, and big baked potatoes.

The veggies were frozen, of course, but hey, fresh would be perfection. And who does perfection? I jumped on the salad, finding all sorts of goodies to throw into it. I'm no *cordon bleu* chef, but I don't starve, either. And Craig or somebody had stocked his kitchen right. Hmm, probably—certainly?—another girlfriend. *But I'm not in that category, first date and all.*

Well, technically first date...

Cyrano was luxuriating on a deep rug before a good fire in a gigantic stone fireplace. He'd checked the place out, then given me a long, accusing look. Like why didn't *we* live in a place like this? *Well, tell you what, dawg, you help me make the dollars to pay for it, we'll do it.* Anybody can be a critic. Not for the first time, a picture came of him with a toolbelt on, carrying a two-by-four in his mouth, and it made me smile.

The blues emanated softly from an expensive setup: lonely guitar, mellow sax, muted trumpet, soft bass, and lingering keyboard notes. A blues hater would've melted. We had a glass of good wine apiece while things finished cooking, and the boss gave me the tour. Up in a loft was a big, pencil-post bed in a room the size of my whole apartment. Glass looked out over the brook to outdoor-lit, massive granite outcrops with stone-walled paths that led to certain surprises, adventure.

And you could go out on a deck, among the tree branches, still bare now, and cold. But nine months of the year, it'd be heaven. There were other rooms, too, but with absolutely no shame, I stayed fixed on that paradise bedroom.

Still floating, through a meal I should remember forever. Still with my feet not on the floor, still a woman-shaped question unanswered, unasked. We sat on a couch before that fire, my bare feet rubbing Cyrano's tummy, Craig very, very real and warm beside me.

And I saw the months we'd worked together as anticipation, taken all together. Oh, denial, too. Holding off, buddy-buddy, arms-length immersion in that great work we'd done side by side. Anticipation: subconscious savoring of what surely was to come.

Had to come.

Those side-tracks, sure: Wilderness Mike, the Sarah-induced talking university heads, Roy the Mistake. Don...no, not Don. And all the time, this terrific man in my head, invited or not, always there.

We picked up the verbal discovering, exploring, that we'd left off that other night—too long ago—after the tunnel adventure. Which we'd never told anyone about, and probably wouldn't: their house, our secret. We laughed about that now.

I found out more about this man: his growing up, his family. Aging parents in Florida, brother Alan, a country minister on the old family place next county with a wife and clutch of teenagers. He wanted me to go meet them soon.

And some of his dreams. Like mine, a bunch of those dreams had been put away, his to fit Very Blind Valencia's needs. But he'd chucked the engineering career, built this place.

You can't wall in *all* of you.

I told him about Dad, and we were both reminded of a sixties song about a brave little orphan girl who's determined to make it, no matter the odds. But I hadn't been an abandoned child; I was twenty-one when my best friend died. Maybe not all the way out of the nest, though. No, I hadn't disappeared, but the nest had...

It got late, and that anticipation, that tingling that had grown in me like fire, like fear, like...destiny? was about to burst inside me. And what was in *his* head? Surely this wasn't all one-sided. What had gone wrong with my radar? I was shy, suddenly. Not before Craig, but before this sweet other presence that was building in the air, in this place, in this fragment of time out of all time: mine.

Ours.

*Okay, girl. Okay. Time to do this...Or not. Can I walk out that door? Oh hell, I'm confused, disoriented. Where's my control? Why can't I look into those bottomless blue eyes, face this...this...Because I'll drown. Fire, fear, what I was born for...No, dammit, I'm in control here...*

I managed to drill my eyes into his, in that damnable stony stare of mine that said do it or die, shit-head. I couldn't stand this anymore.

And Craig MacDonnell laughed. He put his finger to the side of my grim mouth and tugged it upward in a lopsided smile.

"Do you bite?" The eyes merry, but deep, like I said.

For answer I pulled him to me, eyes on his, our mouths drawing closer. Closer...Then I twisted, got my teeth in his neck and marked him.

"Hey!" I drew back, hit him with a cushion, jumped up. He started to rise, but I was on him like a second skin, kissing him, tickling him, straddling him, rolling him off onto the floor. Our laughter is all that saved him from Cyrano's jaws. We rolled all over that floor, cackling like fools. I felt his teeth in my neck, too. I got my tongue in his ear, and he grabbed a handful of my ass.

Finally, gasping, giggling, we rolled apart. I petted Cyrano to reassure him, and started to pull Craig toward the stairs. But he did a quick dodge, and had me lifted in his arms, foot on the step. We never took our eyes off each other all the way up. He set me on the big bed, then stepped back.

"No." I slid off, took his hand, led him toward the bathroom. I've got a thing about showers. I made my hands move like molasses in January, unbuttoning, loosening. Wasn't easy: I wanted to rip his shirt off, see the buttons fly. His fingers were working, too, on the soft shirt I wore, which slid off, faint as slight breeze in leaves. I slipped my fingers into the mat of reddish hair on his chest as he reached around me. The singing I was hearing wasn't the blues, it was one with the tingling where his fingers loosed my bra, one with the heat of his skin on mine.

Water streaming in the shower, and the two of us sluiced, kissing, exploring. And oh God, he was soaping my breasts. I caught my breath, thrilled to my toes. This wasn't like anything I'd ever experienced, not even in fantasy. We were out of the shower then, wet and slippery and hugging and laughing. And then on that incredible bed and he was kissing me all over, sending chills like heat lightning, drying me and moistening my skin at the same time with his tongue. Then he was kissing my stomach, the inside of my thighs, and omigod, omigod, that wasn't all he was kissing...

Craig knew how to pace us, knew how to build this (nothing wrong with *his* radar). Until, sensing where I was, we joined, and soared together.

I will *never* forget that night, even after I'm dead. There were little words, caresses, assurances, murmurings. Even, finally, the sweetest sleep.

~ * ~

Awakening first, I watched Craig's face in the growing light. It was not so angular, relaxed like that: almost boyish, in sleep. A damn good face. I kissed it softly.

His eyes opened slowly, the blue deepening as he came awake. He touched my face, and I knew I belonged to him. All the other experiences I'd stumbled into, through, looked back on, good and bad, and some totally indifferent: all preparation for this...this awakening to the real thing. This man—all man—with so much to him, so much depth, so much of what had to be untapped love.

But dammit, he belonged to me, too. To hell with any others who might be in his life: I was staking my territory.

We had a leisurely breakfast: leftover steak and eggs and yes, grits. Hey, I'm from Georgia, where you can order a martini with grits on the side. Could it get any better than this? And why would it?

Any ideas I'd had about moving on were way back on the shelf. Or maybe not even on the shelf. All the places I hadn't been yet didn't matter any anymore. This looked a lot like home to Wesley.

# Seven

So we started on the cabin job, and the boss and I started to become a couple, out in the open and no games. We didn't make any long-term plans, just enjoyed hell out of each other and really got to know our hang-ups, likes, fears. I began to see him as a rock I could anchor to. *And yeah, just let it happen, girl;* this was life, right here.

Wallow in it.

We got down to visit the brother Alan and family, and I got the feeling this country of ours was in pretty good hands with people like that in it. Alan was the stereotype minister: studious, sincere, kind. Wife Ellen was quick and insightful, and instantly likeable. Selena and Jason and the irrepressible twins, Morgan and Tegwin, were every combination of the parents, with a lot of individuality thrown in. I *said* great family.

And it was in that couple of weeks that I began to realize this was for sure the place I wanted to stay. And not just because of Craig, although he was most of it. There was something about this part of Virginia that brought a lot of the idealized South into focus for me, a Southerner to begin with.

Not so much the old-plantation colonial mystique, and certainly not the later cotton economy of further south and west. No, more like a composite of Pocahontas and Thomas Jefferson and Robert E. Lee and tall Georgian houses and warm, red brick and old, old ways of doing things that had an air of the sacred about them. I remembered a quote from Benet: "In Richmond, the trees in the streets are old trees that remember your grandfather's name."

It all added up to my wanting to become a part of all this. And that terrific house of Craig's might be a different, modern version of what I was trying to identify, but it was definitely a vital part of it all. Hey, this was the 21<sup>st</sup> century, like it or not.

~ * ~

Now, I can't tell you why I awoke with this subtle feeling that the Webbs' housewarming party was gonna be a disaster, but I did. Maybe it was the old negativity re J. Barker. Maybe I felt subconsciously that, okay, I was finished there, and better to leave it at that. I do remember trying to ignore the...what, warning? And managed to.

Gwen had said it was to be semi-casual. I wore one of my few dresses, one with some frills up top. Hell, I'm no Dolly Parton; I need all the help I can get. And medium heels. Didn't want to trip and fall out like a drunk. Craig picked me up, wearing a corduroy sport coat and slacks. Give him a cancerous pipe, he'd look like a college professor.

Well, a college professor with calluses.

The hostess welcomed us like rich relatives, and even J. Barker unbent long enough to give me a perfunctory hug. Didn't make me like him any better. The crew were there, with wife and girlfriends. Henry was with a teenager with a space between her front teeth, and both were self-conscious. Craig and I made it a point to spend time with them. Bob's wife looked as if she might have left the water running at home, but she thawed out after a bit. And Don, God's gift to the gum-chewing set, had on his arm a tipsy sorority girl, slumming—well, not exactly—with her townie, and loving it.

I scoped out the others as they arrived: the Webbs' puffy Beamer son Jerry, with a cheerleader type. Roy with a redhead who looked like...well, a horse, what else? Long face, loud, rangy. *Good for you,*

*Roy Boy.* There were some others: grounds crew, some guys we'd just seen in passing Clyde had on the other building projects, girls and older women, looking uncomfortable in all the glitz.

And surprise: the Webbs' daughter Samantha, down from New York and her non-acting career. She was pretty, in a way that was the opposite of Jerry's coarseness, with her mother's ash-blonde hair and just enough of J. Barker to give her face a sort of hard look. I made one of my instant-impression assessments: *predator.* Just what had decided her to deign to gift us with her presence, I didn't have a clue. Probably doing her daughterly duty...see the folks and collect more money. Her greeting to us was about as sincere as her makeup, but she raked Craig with those eyes. Was I jealous?

And Clyde himself. Sober. The Webbs had told us they'd insisted on Clyde's going to AA twice a week if he aimed to draw a paycheck there, and apparently it was taking. But I didn't like the smug look on his face: he was still working there, and we weren't: yah na na na na na. *Oh, screw you, Clyde the Clod. And whatever you rode in on, including the girl you couldn't find to bring here. Somehow I doubt if you'll make it with Samantha.*

It was a good party, anyway. A foursome was doing bluegrass and folk stuff on guitar, standup bass, banjo, mandolin and reedy voices, but the harmony was tight. Craig and I danced some for the first time, and he was smooth. How could he not be? Webb Senior kept finding a corner to talk with Clyde or Jerry, and Gwen flitted around, determined not to let things lag. She danced with any man who paused long enough, including Craig. I wasn't jealous. Hey, I even danced with Dipshit Don.

Couldn't help noticing how Samantha Webb was hitting the alcohol, but I guessed she could hold it okay. And how she zeroed in on Hunk Roy from the moment she laid eyes on him. I felt sorry for the horsey date, but figured she was probably used to it, if she'd known him for any length of time. I reflected that a woman would have to be really blind or really a doormat to have any sort of relationship with the Roys of this world.

It wasn't long before the girl, who probably wished she were out on a horse somewhere, assuaged her loneliness with booze, too, trying not to notice that she'd been shot down. Gwen saw the situation, but could spread herself only so thin, tending to this motley crowd.

Craig and I wandered around, checking out the house with all the Webbs' stuff in it. A computer room you could probably launch missiles from. A gun collection with everything from a Revolutionary War Brown Bess musket to a deadly black Glock automatic, and everything in between. We learned that everybody in the family spent some time at a firing range.

*Whatever gets your cookies off.*

But after a while, this soap opera started getting stuffy. It was the first day of my period, and the wine punch hadn't helped, maybe because I'd sampled it first, before the *hors d'oeuvres* could insulate my stomach. Anyway, I wanted some air. Craig was at the moment knee-deep into talking shop with the rest of the crew (he was a *man*, after all), so I slipped out the back.

It wasn't that cold…one of those freak days in early March that lied about real spring. I made my way to the stables to visit with my man Walker, get a little horse smell on me. Passed close to Roy's big truck, and heard gasps from inside. Windows all steamed up. *Okay, so yeah, on the saddles, I guess.*

Made a discreet detour to allow this little drama to continue as it would. Maybe shoulda invited Roy's date to visit the horses with me. Couldn't help thinking what a slob he was, walking out on her in front of everybody to go make out in his truck with the first pretty face he saw. Grateful that my common sense or whatever it'd been, had rescued me from that disaster.

Stopped at the outside freeze-proof faucet at the horse barn to splash water on my hot face. Then went to see Walker. He was in the last stall, and someone had piled square bales of hay in half the passageway. I went around, and he nickered a greeting.

"Not tonight, dear," I teased him. "Got a date with another man. Sorry." I let him nibble sugar lumps out of my hand. Loved that soft muzzle. *Got to get me that horse, that place. Unless Craig and I…*

*No, too soon. Let it happen like it's meant to, girl. And enjoy the hell out of it, meantime.*

They slipped in so I only heard the door at the front click shut. Glow from a very dim bulb showed J. Barker and Clyde talking low. I started to clear my throat, say something to Walker, announce my presence.

I didn't. *Something weird, here.* I strained to listen, hidden back there.

"...all there?" Webb. There was an honest-to-God briefcase, just like in the movies.

"Yeah, counted it. All hundreds. Jerry said twenties would be too bulky."

"Okay. Now there're way too many bodies around tonight, so let's just slip this in here somewhere till it thins out. People going to cars and all. Oh, any more word on the Bunche thing? I've been outta town, you know."

"Not a peep, boss. Cold trail, like I said. We're clean. That guy Peterson is an amateur anyway, and he's got nothin' to tie us to that."

"Don't ever underestimate the cops, Clyde. That's how careless people get caught. Now, I gotta show my face in the house. You, too. Have some fun tonight, guy. You been doing good work: get some R and R."

"Nah, all th' women taken, unless Donnie passes out on his girl."

"Hey, grab Wesley. Nothing serious with her and Craig, I'm sure...he won't mind."

"Like to. That woman thinks she's so hot."

"You know what they say: give the mean ones a good screwing, they'll follow you around like puppies."

*What?* I thought I'd retch, right there. *Assholes.*

"I wish. Yeah, I'll put this under here, then. Jerry said the delivery went smooth. Guys liked the stuff."

"My boy's a smooth operator, if a little impulsive. You keep up the good work, Clyde my man, you'll move up, too."

"Sure, boss. See you up at the house."

I was sweating nails back there. Fear of discovery first, then yeah, what had to be a drug deal. So *this* was where the Webber got his cash. And Clyde, his new business. And Webb Junior. *Wow*. And oboy, the late Buncha Trouble Greg, who'd really gotten his ass in a crack with these guys. Oboy, information overload. Which I definitely hadn't wanted any fragment of.

I patted Walker a last time with a hand that trembled, slipped up toward the door. I'd just glimpsed the hiding place, under saddle blankets. I listened: no sound outside. I hesitated only a beat, then pulled the case out. Simple lock. I found a worn hoof pick and tried the lock. It popped: cheap. Inside were hundreds, lots of them, banded about that many each. Ten grand to a bundle, then. And lotsa bundles. I eyed this stash. Some of this, I could be in Paris, overnight...

*No, don't touch it, girl; it's poison.* Besides, I never really wanted to go to Paris: all those snotty Frenchmen.

I re-locked the case, stuffed it back under, slipped back out the rear door, out of sight and sound, and waited a long time, heart thumping. Then I moved out.

I was halfway back to the house, when someone grabbed my arm from behind.

"The hell you doin' out here, woman?" Jerry the Grub's voice.

"What? Oh, Jerry. Been visiting my favorite horse for the last time, what else?"

"You been back there a while...didn't see you go in."

"That's because I went in the back door, close to where I threw up in the bushes. Too much wine too soon, I guess." I sounded cool, I hoped. This guy emanated evil.

"Oh, can't hold your liquor, huh?" He laughed, not a pleasant laugh. "Well, I'm gonna take you to Dad...let him decide."

"Webb? Why? He doesn't care if I give his horse sugar. Neither does your mom." Jerry wasn't sure of anything, I could tell. But, impress the father; take no chances. I thought of the late Greg. "But yeah, let's go see him. Hey, I got nothing to hide, except you're right: never could hold the booze."

"Just act normal then. And just so you know, I got a gun on you."

*Oh, shit.*

"Good for you. I'm all for the Second Amendment. More people should carry...crime goes down."

"No shit." He let me in the back way. Seeing Clyde, he asked about his father.

"He's in the computer room, I think. Showing off the new setup." He eyed me, but I brushed past him, into the crowd.

Jerry didn't know what to do next. He started to reach, haul me away, but I spoke to Gwen first.

"Lady, I'm sick. Just blew lunch out back. Could I lie down for a few minutes? Don't know if I overdid the wine punch or I'm coming down with something." I tried to catch Craig's eyes. No luck.

"Sure, honey. You just go up to my room. Here, I'll go with you. Hope you're not getting the flu."

"Hey, Craig," I called, "I'm going up top for a bit. Got the blahs." I pointed to the ceiling, bored my eyes into his. Jerry was almost against and behind me, and that gun shit had me scared. I jerked my eyes toward that grubworm twice, not sure if Craig was getting it.

"You okay?" he came toward me.

"Will be in a little. Mr. Webb wants to see me when I won't throw up on him again. I'm hoping the high altitude will help." I rolled my eyes upward. *Get It, Craig. Get it.*

Jerry was sticking to me as I started off. His mother moved up again.

"I'm going with her, Jerry," she said. "Your girl's getting lonely over there. You go on, now."

We mounted the stairs, Gwen clucking over me and my holding onto the rail, shaking a little. I'd grabbed my purse, which had very little in it but keys and my cell phone.

"I'm PMS too, Gwen. That's gotta be part of it."

"You poor thing. Thank God I'm finally past that. Here we go." Then: "What did Jerry want?"

Okay: to tell or not to tell? No-brainer: he was her son. And she wasn't my friend, maybe in up to her sweet ass with the drug thing. She couldn't be *that* blind. Or innocent, probably: Jerry *had* left me in her care...

"Oh, I spent a few minutes in the stable with Walker after I tossed my cookies outside, and he saw me. Thinks I'm a horse thief, I guess." I popped a quick glance: Craig was watching me from below as we went down the hall, out of sight. Inside, I washed my face at the vanity I'd installed a few weeks ago in her bathroom, rinsed out my mouth. She puttered around helpfully, but I could sense her mind working: If Jerry had brought me to Mr. W, there was a reason. She'd find out asap, I knew. Then what?

I wasn't about to stick around to find out. I slipped my shoes off, lay down, shuddered, thanked her.

"I'll be okay in a few, Gwen. Thanks loads. I'm sure it's the punch, on top of the rest...empty stomach. Never could hold my liquor."

"Just relax, honey. I'll check on you when I can get away." And she was gone, determined hostess.

I was up at the latch click, ear at the door. I heard her go down the hall, and risked a crack in the door. She was dropping from sight down the staircase.

I raised one of her windows. Let 'em think I'd done a human fly thing out and down. Then, shoes in hand, I slipped out, closed the door, slid down to the end of the hall to the attic stairs, behind their little door.

Cloak and dagger stuff, for sure. But the Webbs and Clyde wouldn't take the chance I didn't hear something. These guys just didn't *take* chances with their operations. *So I'm outta here, like a ghost.*

There was an old dresser over the trapdoor, barely visible from a dim window, and I shoved it quietly, I hoped, aside. *Okay, what do I have to open this thing?* Only a nail clipper and my stubby fingers. I got the lid up a crack, dug my work-split nails in, lifted it. Went down the iron spikes, cursing my dress and the heels. Let the door down. Wished for a way to lock it. Wasn't one.

Dark as a sack of cats in here. Absolutely *no* light. *Okay, don't panic; not like you're gonna get lost.* I even managed to pull spider webs off my face without screaming. Just.

I half expected to hear feet pounding on stairs as I went down, inches away from all that partying humanity I could hear. Nothing yet. I kept going. No rope this time, just these rusty spikes. *Damn dress.* I was shaking. Deep breath. *Don't make a mistake.* I felt the wall: still wood, lath, backside of plaster. Could hear some of the merriment through the wall, dimly. *Come on, basement.* Okay, bricks. Not far, now. I might survive if I fell. Yes! Dirt underfoot. Tried not to think about creepies or ghouls; moved out, hand against the wall.

~ * ~

Inside the house, Craig saw Jerry and J. Barker Webb in tense conversation. They were joined by Gwen, then Clyde. Craig didn't know what this was all about, but it looked serious. Maybe he could get up to talk to Wes, find out...

Just then, Clyde and Webb Senior started for the stairs. Craig saw the bulge in Clyde's jacket pocket. Jerry went toward the back door. Gwen smiled brightly at someone, and steered people toward the parlor dance floor. Craig watched the men on the stairs out of sight, moved closer.

"Gone!" he heard faintly. "Bitch is gone!"

"Don't panic. Nowhere to go. Window...no, surely not, too high..." The voices faded. There was the sound of another door opening, then another.

*Okay, she's made it,* Craig breathed. *And I'm outta here. But just what in hell's going down? She's onto something, and they're onto her.*

He slipped out the front door, caught a glimpse of Jerry circling the house. Looking up at the second story windows. *Keep looking, guy.*

While this was going on, I was moving cautiously, my mind busy, trying to remember how the iron door opened. And assuming I *could* get it open, what then? Would Craig figure it out, join me?

He'd have to, eventually. Unless he thought the bad guys had caught me, made me disappear. *No, don't think that way.* Wishing to *God* I had a flashlight. No, it'd be okay; I was past the worst part.

But, wait! When Jerry didn't find me, he'd go up to the attic. And Clyde...no chance *he* wouldn't find the trapdoor. Time. I needed time, but just maybe I had enough.

I thought about calling Nate Peterson on my cell. Had his card in my purse...no light to see it by. I tried the glow from the cell—wasn't up to date with the searchlight model, but couldn't make it out the tiny number. Okay, call information. I punched numbers. Long wait. *I don't have time for this.* Finally. Gave his name, but didn't know the address. Damn.

"We have a Nathan Peterson on Commerce Street. Seems to be the only one in town. Would that be it?"

"I think so. Let me have the number, please." Wait some more, then the recorded voice, with the number. I memorized it. Punched it up. Got a recording. But it was his voice, I thought.

"Nate. Wes Whitestone. Overheard some bad stuff at Webb's place." Quick directions. "Big bucks, drugs, link to Bunche. Craig and I are trying to get away now. Party going on. Your call." He had my cell number and caller I.D. I was sure.

I moved out. Would he get the message in time? Then I called 911. Maybe shoulda tried that first, talked to a human. Shouldn't matter for Craig and me, but if he wanted to make a bust...

"Yeah. Listen closely. This is not a crank call. I've left a message for Detective Nate Peterson at his home, but he might not get it." I gave the Webb address again. "There's a drug ring here, and I'm in hiding...they're after me. My name's Wesley Whitestone. Peterson needs to know this. I'll try to escape."

"Ma'am, are you in danger there now?"

"Yeah, guy with a gun was after me, but I'm okay for now. If the police can raid this place, they'll get a big-time drug dealer and some of his men. Okay?"

"We're on it. Trying to locate Peterson as we speak. Can you give me any other details?"

"Well, I saw a lot of cash, overheard some about the deal. Also some about the Bunche killing a few months back. These are the bad guys, no doubt."

The voice seemed to believe me, and that was a relief: sounded like something out of a bad movie. Damsel marooned, bad guys closing in, hero clueless somewhere else, no possible way...You get the picture.

I'd been feeling my way along during this, moving slow, but covering ground. Underground. Spidery, scary, ghoulish nightmare scared-of-the-dark-and-what-might-be-hiding-in-it.

Ah, the door. Now where was that damn handle? Okay, I felt it. Now, Craig had stood on it the other time. Rusted back, now? Hoped not. Had to come down hard on it.

Nothing. Oh, damn. *Okay, jump on it, and I'll fall on my ass.* But nothing else for it. Balanced best I could...

Just then the handle creaked, moved. *Yes! Craig's out there.* I pushed down, too, and the lever moved, released. I put my hands on the door and pushed. It swung open with the same protest of months before.

A light shone in my face.

"Hey, don't blind me. Dark in there...my pupils are the size of saucers."

But it wasn't Craig whose voice I heard.

# Eight

"Out, bitch!"

Now, who the *hell?* I strained, shaded my eyes, stumbled out. The door closed behind me, and the light shifted from my face.

Jerry Webb, the Slug, again. And he had the gun in his other hand. Nasty-looking automatic. And he wasn't alone. Craig sat, back against the other bridge support, blood running down his face, dazed. So he *had* come for me, but yeah, Jerry'd maybe followed him, slammed him.

"Now, we're gonna go see Dad. Find out what you two got goin', and who you've talked to. *Up!*" he motioned to Craig, who staggered to his feet. "Now, I dunno how in hell you got here, bitch, but I'll find out. I'll find out everything."

We were working our way out of the ravine toward the house. *Oboy, now's the time for the cavalry to come charging in.* There was no way in hell they were going to let us go. Poor Craig, conked on the head. If he and I could jump this guy, we could...*Oh, no*: another light coming.

"That you, Jerry?" Clyde's voice. *Damn.*

"Yeah, got the woman. Followed MacDonnell to a damn *tunnel.* Dunno how..."

"I found where it starts, up in the attic. So you got both of 'em?" He shone the light on us. Craig bloody, unsteady. Me, dress torn, dirt-streaked: two real prizes.

"Yeah, while you were wastin' time in the house."

"Okay, then. Mr. W will wanta do some serious talkin', here."

"Don't I know it. Good thing I was on it...they'd've been long gone." Jerry Webb obviously was not wild about having Clyde in his territory.

They took us to the stable, with the house still full of people. Jerry went for J. Barker. I kept my eyes away from the hiding place.

"Just what the hell's going on here, Clyde?" Craig demanded.

"Talkin' to th' wrong man, boss. Mr. W's calling th' shots."

*Chickenshit!*

Okay, if Nate got my message, or the 911 people got things moving, the longer we could wait, the more likely he—they'd—come. Or not. Hoped those people didn't want more intel before they moved. Might call back. *Ouch.* Clyde would grab the phone, surely...I got an idea. Slipped my hand into my purse, hoping Clyde wouldn't see. Felt for the redial button on my phone, punched it, coughing a little to mask the faint beeps.

The Webbs returned, Jerry puffed up at having caught us, J. Barker looking...resigned, I guess you'd call it. A walking sigh.

"You people have put me in a very awkward position," he began.

"How so?" Craig asked. "You hired us to do a job, we did it, everybody's happy. End of story, except now I've got a bloody knot on my head and the king of headaches, and I'm naturally a little curious about why."

"Jerry got carried away there. Sorry about that. But he thought Wesley might possibly have overheard some...sensitive information, and brought her to see me." He gave us a smarmy smile. *Hamlet: Smile and smile, and be a villain.* "Maybe nothing, but then she disappears. And through a secret passageway in my own damn house that nobody told me about. And you go to meet her at the outlet. People with nothing to hide don't run, MacDonnell, so now it looks like Jerry was right."

"I ran because Jerry pulled a gun on me, Mr. Webb. For no reason other than I came to say goodbye to the horse I've been riding. I figured he was drunk or had gone over the edge, and that scared me."

"You used a *gun*, Jerry? Was that necessary?"

"Maybe not, Dad. Just afraid she'd make a break for it." He shrugged.

"And the passageway. Why wasn't I told about that?" to Craig.

"We discovered that, but knew if word got out while we were working here, treasure-hunters would swarm the place. Nobody here to keep them away till you moved in. This is our last time here, so tonight was to be the time to let you in on the surprise. Maybe an escape route for runaway slaves, maybe some other mystery. Figured you'd want to keep it quiet, too."

"That should have been my decision, though, not yours. But as I said, now things have...well, they've escalated, you see. Jerry's clubbed you, and we have the two of you who may think you know something damaging to us." Despite the coolness, his bald head was glistening. "Now, if we let you go, with our apologies, that should be the end of it. But if you *were* to tell something to someone else...you see where this leaves me? Put yourselves in my shoes, here. I'm just not sure it's worth the risk."

Jerry Webb was getting red in the face. I was feeling Craig and I were hanging in a balance, and about to tip.

And not the right way.

"Tell me again, Jerry, where you found Wesley."

"Comin' out of this stable, back door, like I said."

"When, exactly? Just after Clyde and I were in here going over those guest house plans?"

*Yeah, sure.*

"Oh, no. Good bit after. Maybe ten, fifteen minutes."

"And you say, Wesley, you were back with the horse?"

"I'd gotten nauseated, maybe the wine punch on an empty stomach. Needed air. Threw up outside in the bushes. Heard the horses here, and needed to get my head clear before I went back in. Washed my face at the outside tap—you can see the wet place there—

came in the back door, spent a minute with Walker. Going back to the house, not like I had anything to hide, and Jerry nabbed me."

"I see. So, did anybody see you leave the house?"

"Maybe. Somebody was in the downstairs bathroom, so I went on out the back door. Wasn't hiding."

"But then you went through the secret passage. Why?"

"Hey, I wanted to avoid Jerry there, with his trigger finger. He scared hell out of me, pulling a gun for no reason. I tipped Craig to meet me earlier."

"That doesn't sound logical. You went with Gwen to her room to lie down, then you disappeared. No. And this is, as I said, awkward..."

"Dammit, Dad, if she heard *anything* about me wastin' Bunche, the money, we're in deep shit. We..." Webb angrily cut him off.

"*You talk too damn much, Jerry!* Now they *have* heard too much. And you've just slammed the door on any options we might have had." He turned to us. "So now you know about the late Mr. Bunche and his unfortunate end. Sorry about this, now..."

"What in hell are you all talking about?" Craig was still in the dark or a good actor. "Who's this Bunche, and what's he got to do with anything?"

"Won't work, MacDonnell," Jerry snarled. "She knows about Bunche, so you would too, then the cops would..."

"*Damn* your big mouth, Jerry!" his father roared. "All right... you've done it. So now *you* handle it. And do it right, for Godssake. Go with him, Clyde. And I don't want to know where and I don't want to know how. But it better be clean. Maybe a car wreck. Figure it out. That's what I pay you for."

"You mean kill 'em both?" Clyde asked. *Was he that dense?*

"Oh God, you're green. Of course, I mean kill them both! And I'll take this now." He pulled the briefcase from its place under the blankets and stalked out. Jerry didn't look a bit chastened, if maybe Clyde did.

Craig looked at me, a look full of pain, and I knew he'd suspected something like this all along. So now, having discovered each other (right under our noses), we were about to lose each other to a drug dealer and a gifted carpenter gone bad. Damn.

We were going for a ride, just like in the B movies.

And I remembered that slight warning from that morning just as I'd come awake: *Ides of March, Wesley.* Damn me for not listening.

I also remembered something I'd read: *don't ever get in the car with the bad guy, or you're already dead.* Forget grabbing the wheel, crashing the car and miraculously walking away. Just *don't* get in the car.

The car in question was a Suburban tank the Webbs owned, and we were pushed toward it. Okay, chance a run? No, enough light from the house and gardens, we'd be easy targets. And oboy, I realized, one of us runs, the other gets it. No, stick together. Two heads supposed to be better, but against two *guns?*

And where was Nate Peterson? And that cavalry? Nowhere. They were nowhere. These two hadn't taken my purse, so small it couldn't have held a weapon. Just held my phone. How much of what was said got through? Any of it? Would the 911 boys and Nate Peterson even hear any of it? Maybe not.

Looked like this was to be the end game.

We got into the car and Craig's truck. *Okay, all over, now.* Jerry drove the Suburban with me beside him, Clyde in the truck with Craig. I guessed we were going to be in a wreck, or maybe robbed and shot. Whatever: it was going to happen.

But just how in *hell* had I gone from harmless girl carpenter to drug lord victim so quickly?

We eased out the long drive, that route Cyrano and I'd taken months ago that started all this. To the paved road. We were nearly a quarter mile along when we met three police cars, rocketing toward the Webb place.

"What the hell?" Jerry slowed, craned to see them turn into the Webb drive. "How did...*you bitch!* You called the cops! Hadda be you...you're gonna *die,* bitch. Right *here* if it wasn't for th' blood. But you're both history! Why, you…" He was so wired, I was afraid he'd do it anyway.

"Take it easy, Jerry," I tried to calm him. "The cops won't find shit. Mr. W's cool…nothin' there. They'll never find a trace of anything. And even if we did call the cops, it won't help us a bit. We're *history*, right?"

"You're damn right about that. Okay. Just pisses me so *bad*… when'd you do it, bitch? Back in the tunnel? Cell phone?"

"Y'know, I'm getting really tired of your calling me 'bitch,' Webb. So it makes you feel like a big man? So okay, you'll do what you gotta do anyway, but just put a sock in it now, okay?" *He* was pissed? I was ready to snatch that wheel, and to hell with it.

"You don't talk to *me* that way!" He swung a backhand, but I got both arms up first. It only made the car swerve.

"Go ahead: run off the road, kill us both, damn you!"

He calmed suddenly.

"Oh, so that's it? Tryin' to shake me up. Won't work. *Bitch*. I got it under control, see. And we're almost there. Nice quiet place for a robbery. Too bad you two hadda resist." Nasty laugh. Nasty man.

Nasty, nasty situation…

It was a turnout on a high hill, with a view of the town, lights jewelling the night. Yeah, just the deserted place for lovers to be ambushed. Surprised nobody else was up there.

We pulled over, Clyde behind us. Jerry pushed me out, got out on my side. Afraid I'd run? He had his gun on me. And Clyde had a gun on Craig.

"Now, Clyde, way I've set it up, they're stopped here in th' truck. Guys slip up on 'em, jump 'em, rob 'em, shoot 'em. Simple."

"I guess. Hey, I never wasted anybody before. Your call."

"Damn right it is. Now, botha you, in th' truck. We'll put the keys in after, Clyde."

Then his ugly face got even uglier, in the reflected lights from the car. That could mean he was getting an idea, if that ever happened with him.

"Y'know, we oughta do him first, then both rape her. Whattya think?" It was light enough for me to see the leer. Nasty didn't say it.

And they'd have to kill me first.

"Take some time. Somebody'd come by."

"Yeah, guess yer right. So, in th' truck. Now!"

I caught a glimpse of Craig, shielded by my body, reaching through the still-open door under the truck seat: he wasn't going down without a fight. Could I grab something out of the truck bed, too? No time. Maybe a rock off the road? Nothing I could see. Craig was shifting his weight, maybe something lethal in his hand? Couldn't tell. Suicide move...didn't matter, now...But I stepped aside, gave him room.

"Okay, that's enough, Jerry," from Clyde.

"Whattya mean 'enough'?" He half-turned.

"I mean you're under arrest for murder, attempted murder and a whole lotta other stuff we got on you. Set the gun down, easy."

*"Why, you..."* He was stunned. So were we. Clyde was a *cop?* Clyde the drunk? The drug-deal *Clyde?* I registered that his gun hand was steady, rock-like.

Jerry wasn't having any of this. He turned slowly toward Clyde, the gun hidden, but ready. Then he jerked it around, just as Craig swung, chopping down on the gun arm with a crowbar, hard. If it didn't break, with that sound it should have. The gun flew. Jerry howled, clutching with his good hand, went to his knees.

"Thanks, boss. I might've had to waste him. Here, hold this," handing him his own gun. And Clyde produced a pair of cuffs, slammed Jerry facedown, snapped them on amid a storm of obscenities. Then he read the guy his Miranda rights, punctuated by his groans and yes, crying.

"We've been after these guys a long time," Clyde explained, to our open mouths and all the questions bubbling up...

*Wait a minute: how could this be? All that time working for Craig? That good a carpenter? And all along...*

"One of you ride with us?" he asked. "And yeah, maybe drive, too. This snake might get ideas."

"I'll do it," Craig offered. "And wouldn't that just make my day?" Jerry was all cussed out, whimpering over his ruined arm. They got him into the Suburban, which Craig drove.

So we caravanned into town, my mind churning, driving that great throbbing diesel of Craig's. Clyde the alky? All a pretense?

No way.

But we did the jail thing, with Jerry bitching all the way, and yeah, hurting bad. We waited while Clyde did whatever paperwork he had to. Told the fuzz there to get a medic for the slug's arm. Then we both pumped him with questions.

"How did you pull that off, Clyde? The bloodshot eyes, the staggers. You're an actor." I was all admiration. This slob I'd so disliked had put on armor, if maybe stained a little.

"Rubbed stuff in my eyes. Burned like hell. Hey, let's go grab a beer somewhere. Let me check in with Nate first, though." He punched numbers.

"Clyde here. How'd it go down?" He listened. "Oh, shit. Really? And he's gone? Yeah, forgot to tell you about the escape passage, but...Okay, he must've found a car somewhere. Damn. And he'll have the cash, of course." He listened some more, then punched off.

Looked like his dog had just died.

"Webb. Slipped out the tunnel. And he'll have contacts everywhere. Probably disappear, leave it all. No telling how much he's got stashed."

"Wow," Craig said. "But right now, I'm worried he knows where to find us, and what he or his buddies will do next."

"Probably nothing just yet...too busy getting away. Well. Blew it, after all this." He was less than overjoyed.

He told us how he'd been a carpenter before taking law enforcement courses in college, joining the force in another state. Then the DEA thing.

"Got to be a stranger for an operation like this, and construction types bein' itinerant, that worked."

"Okay," I agreed, "so you're a real actor. But you had Webb there in the stable, money in hand. Why go any further with it?" That was only my first question.

"Didn't have enough of the goods on him yet. No drugs, for one thing: Jerry'd handled that part. And had to have witnesses. So when I played dumb in the stable later, I got him to order the kill. And I got

Jerry to claim the hit on Bunche. And I also got it on the record." He held up a tiny digital recorder. Cute thing, and apparently it recorded okay through clothes.

Craig beat me to the next one.

"So why'd you do the drunk act, get me to fire you, Clyde?"

"Well, I kind of shot myself in the foot there, boss. I'd figured the best way to get inside the Webb ring was to become the kind of loser they'd recruit: weak enough to be pliable but not so dumb I couldn't be of value to them. And of course, that tack got me in trouble with you on the job. Guess I overdid it a little.

"But, funny thing, the firing didn't seem to hurt me with them. Actually let me get closer to Webb, if not to Jerry…sympathy thing, I guess. And Gwen liked me, for some reason, even if Jerry didn't. Got Barker to call me for the other construction stuff. You ever read Henry Fourth, Part One, Wes?"

"Sure. So you were doing the Prince Hal thing, playing the loser to make the comeback play better? Seems to have worked. Webb was so self-righteous about reclaiming you from ruin."

"And making me go to AA, that was a hoot. When I was supposedly there, I was working my butt off at my real job."

"Okay, you pulled it off. But here's another one: Sarah told me Greg Bunche was gonna have to pay off a guy named Vince, or the guy would likely kill him. Then Jerry claims *he* did Greg. What was with that?"

"That was our boy Jerry, who thought it'd be cute to call himself Vince—real gangster name—and divert suspicion. Told me he did it—bragged about it—used a different gun, and again mouthed off in the stable, you heard."

So now Craig and I had this drug lord lawyer on our case, highly pissed that his boy would probably fry. He'd find out quick we were the ones who'd caught the kid. And he already knew we'd helped bring down this part of his operation: no more historic house and land with horses. The Ferrari just history, country club and the other trimmings, all gone. No way ever for him to show up here again.

My man was thinking the same thing: how do you hide from the guys who never play by the rules? Hey, I could maybe do a fade here, like always, but Craig had a life, a going business, that great place.

And no way was I ready to walk out of that life, either.

"It sucks that Webb got away," Clyde was saying. "He'll stay disappeared, leave Gwen to dump it all. We got her, but nothing'll stick there except confiscating everything we can. Then he'll put it all back together somewhere else, but not soon. And meantime, like you said…"

"Meantime, Craig and I are not his favorite people."

"No, and there are way too many ways the bad guys can hit from far enough away we don't catch them."

"So," Craig turned up palms, "what's your advice?"

"You're tight with Peterson, so let's get our heads together with him and find a plan, tomorrow—today, now. But Webb's sharp, and we won't underestimate him. If he's gonna try to take you out, he might not wait till we can get you protected. Catch us off-guard. So let's take a little evasive action right now."

I'd been thinking: my place wasn't safe, and neither was Craig's. So okay, Webb couldn't know yet about Jerry, but he'd know one of us had blown the whistle. And no, he wouldn't know about Clyde the Narc yet either, unless he'd bugged him some way. Still left him with us as targets, though, and yeah, catch us off-guard.

Like right now…I checked the plate glass of the café.

"Let's go somewhere dark and safe, Craig, I'm seeing ghoulies."

"Yeah, me too. What action you got in mind, Clyde?"

"You've got that brother down in Nelson County. If you could set something up through him…"

"No, Webb can find that out in a heartbeat."

"Okay: Saturday. What'll happen with the crew Monday?"

"Ouch. They'll need me. New cabin job. And no, they can find that too…" Thinking.

"Wes, you have any desperate escape ideas?"

"No safe house? Or is that only in the movies?"

"Afraid not on this one. Distant relatives?"

"Brother in Atlanta. But again, Webb and his network."

"Right. So you've both gotta disappear big time. Craig, I hate it, but damn, looks like you've gotta shut down. Lay the guys off. I could say I'd run things for you for a while, but real soon I'm gonna have cross-hairs on me, too. I'll have to pack up and relocate quick, myself. Damn it!" He wasn't over losing Webb.

And Craig was seeing his business—profession, life's work—going all to hell. And that great place. How could he—we—go back there, with half the drug nasties in the world after us? Answer was, we couldn't. *Damn* Barker Webb! How could my just petting a horse turn everything to shit like this?

I watched this great guy I loved sort of slump at the shoulders as it all hit him and sank in, those lines in his face subtly deepening, and I moved to put an arm around him. Clyde was talking.

"...outta here, now. Webb'll still think you're both dead in your truck somewhere, so we got a window while he tries to contact Jerry. But he'll know something's wrong with that...guy's not dumb. And yeah, me too. My phone will probably ring any minute now. I'll try to get our guys to trace it, if I can keep him on long enough."

Clyde made another call, probably to some subterranean vault where computer nerds who never saw daylight clustered around futuristic cyber-toys. Surely that high-tech. But then, no safe house? Oh right, this wasn't fiction.

"Can you guys cash out quick? Right now? Get travel money? Monday'll be too late," he asked us.

"ATM's the only thing. If their organization's on the ball, I guess they can trace credit cards. Any paper."

"Wouldn't chance it. *Damn* my big mouth about that escape passage. Guess I was playin' the part too well."

"Okay, people." I was suddenly all business; self-preservation had kicked in. "We can do wire transfers from anywhere, then run. And we and our dollars don't hafta stay in the same spot. I'm gonna say we've got time—barely time—to pack and git. I'd like to say Webb and the slimeballs have enough to do without picking on us, but too chancy. Craig, we're gonna hafta do some truck-trading like today, and then just vanish. That is, if you're with me…"

He kissed me, cutting me off, and yeah, kissed off a big part of his life, too. He was on board, and that made something good well up inside me.

Whatta man.

# Nine

So, rolling stones now. We picked up my stuff and Cyrano without waking Sarah, then drove to Craig's place. Just as a precaution, Clyde and another cop followed us. But nobody ambushed us either place. We threw the basics into both trucks, shut off water and power, poured antifreeze into drain traps, locked toolsheds and the house. Craig worked fast, and I knew it was to keep from registering all he was losing.

And whoa, I was losing it too, wasn't I? All this...

*No, get the hell outta here...we got each other.*

We said goodbye to Clyde, and with the pre-spring sky graying into dawn, we caravanned west over the Blue Ridge, and on into West Virginia. We stopped for lunch, where Craig called the lady who worked for him part-time, and regretfully laid her off, with a bonus we'd send. Told her to contact the crew, pay everybody with pre-signed checks we'd left, then the cabin owners...no explanations, just that we were gone. Damn. I'd met her once, and both of us were sorry about this. I reflected that good old Bob wouldn't have been able to take over the job, and sure not Don.

What a waste.

Okay, now we were just two anonymous people in pickup trucks. Craig had taken the magnetic company signs off his, and only our license plates could give us away. Mine was still Pennsylvania, and we talked about that.

"We'll need an address to register another vehicle," Craig pointed out.

"Yeah, and with our trucks gone from Virginia, the goons'll know we drove away, as opposed to flying or Amtrak. So let's get farther from home before we slow down to trade. What's invisible?"

"White van, no doubt of it. And we can fit our stuff in. You okay with ditching your Dakota?"

"No, or seeing you leave your home and career, either, not to mention your great truck. But if we're gonna fade, let's do it right. Can you deal with your place any reasonable way?"

"Brother should be able to handle it okay. Sell it, I guess, and figure how to get the bucks later. I can trust my lawyer on that, too, another old friend. Gonna have to get used to travelin' light..."

"Craig, I'm so damn sorry I got us into this."

He cut me off with a kiss again. Nice. Okay, no recriminations. I could handle that. But something else...

"Where do you wanta settle? Or do you? I've been all over, but you choose."

"Haven't traveled much, really. Oregon, maybe? Montana? And we'll have to make a living somewhere..."

"Always construction work, I've found, but you won't wanta do cardboard houses. New England, maybe? Lots of timberframe restoration there."

"Too cold. You been to Texas?"

"Oh, yeah. Mountains in part of it. Coast is nice, between hurricanes. If cold is out, so is Montana, Colorado, places like that."

Now, I wasn't just waking up at the moment, but with the lack of sleep and all the excitement, I guess I was what, off-balance? No, just receptive. And I knew right then where we were supposed to go.

"Oh, Arkansas has mountains, too, a lot like Virginia, and cheaper."

"Let's do it. Say trade trucks in Ohio then, get an address we can put on paperwork and stuff, then drop on south. Okay?"

"Sure. What about names, now that we're on the Evil Empire's Most Wanted list?"

"Damn! Hadn't thought about that. Need new social security cards, too? Drivers' licenses?"

"Hey, I don't like this any better'n you. But half-ass won't cut it. There'll be a forger somewhere, with all the illegal aliens around."

"People disappear all the time, so we should be able to. If we don't use credit cards or write checks..."

"Computers make it tough, but it isn't the law that's after us, and how hard will Spider Webb work on this? I hate the thought of always having to look over my shoulder, but we're in it, guy. Deep."

"So let's enjoy it." He grinned for the first time since Friday night at the party. Damn, I loved this man. And was that just last night? Couldn't have been. Must've been some sort of time warp, right?

"And we've got a better way here, Wes. I'll call Nate Peterson. He can fix the I.D. things for us, I'm sure."

"Okay. But I'm thinking, with the connections the druggies have, could they get into police files? I mean, Nate's gotta involve others if he's gonna get us fake stuff."

"So okay...let's tell him to let the trail stop in Ohio, then. Not that I don't trust Nate, but you're right. Hey, I don't know much about computer hacking, but I doubt any place is safe, the trolls spend enough money."

~ * ~

We rented a cottage in Circleville, south of Columbus, Ohio, and I put an ad in a local bargain sheet for my truck Hosmer. We had the address, so when we bought the big white Ford van, it was all legal. And now, thanks to Nate Peterson, we were Leila and David Cameron: Lee and Dave. Hafta get used to that name now...guy yelled for me to dodge a falling beam, I wanted to know it was me before, not after.

We'd agreed on the married couple story, to help forestall raised eyebrows and the otherwise inevitable hittin'-on-Wes, wherever we landed. Yeah, and maybe hittin'-on-Craig, too—who knew?

Craig got a good trade. After all, his was a truck to die for: extended cab, air, diesel, all the goodies. But the ¾-ton van was okay for now. We got it registered and insured, and our stuff loaded in.

I'd set a decent price on my Dakota and hadn't budged. The buyer paid, and we went to the bank for the cash before I'd give him the title. Cyrano and I said goodbye to our friend and often home, but we weren't losing nearly as much as Craig.

Could live with it, I decided.

~ * ~

I got yet another call on my cell phone from Phil the Pittsburgh Pal, but he wasn't as nice as in the past. And he got right to it.

"Wes, I need to come see you, talk about stuff. You still in Virginia?"

"No, finished up there. Actually, I'm on the road , Phil. Heading out at the moment; not sure just where I'll land." *Now just what is this?*

"Well, Sid and I've sort of been checking off things that might've happened to that money, Wes, and what's the old saying? 'When you've eliminated all the other possibilities, the one left has to be it, no matter how weird'?"

"Something like that. I think it's from Sherlock Holmes, Conan Doyle. So what's the verdict?" I didn't like where this was going.

"Well, *you* were the only other one close. You were living right there, had a key. And much as I can't believe you'd ever even think about..."

"Hold it, Phil. You're saying you think *I* had anything to do with that? Is *that* what you're saying?"

"Well, not really. But there's nothing else that explains it. I just wanta talk to you about it, go over the whole thing again."

"Listen, guy." I was highly pissed at this. "I was on board with you all the way, on *your* project. You know I put what money I had into getting us set up for the business: I didn't hold back. How in the *hell* could you even imagine I'd screw you over that way? That's so *insulting.*"

"Hey, I didn't say..."

"The hell you didn't. Whose idea is this, Phil? Sid's? Who's got you thinking this way? Do your folks think I stole their money?"

"Oh, no. They always thought the world of you, Wes. It's just..."

"Now, you listen. I'm sorry as hell something happened to that cashier's check I nagged at you to put in the bank where it'd be safe. You didn't do it, and somebody, someway, got hold of it, must've cashed it. Now, for the *last* time, I'm telling you I had nothing to do with that, and I think you damn well know it. And you also know I live cheap, got no aspirations that include big bucks. I didn't even ask for the money back I put into the business. And I don't ever want to hear another *word* about all this. *Goodbye*, Phil."

"Wow, that sounded serious," Craig reacted.

"Yeah, rotten thing all the way, and now the poor guy's started thinking I'm the villain in the piece." I told him the particulars.

"Sounds to me like the brother's the one he should be looking at, if he resented the parents' giving the money to Phil."

"I've thought of that a bunch of times, but the two of them are so close, I never wanted to insult him or his folks with the idea. Anyway, the thing for me to do is erase Phil from my memory. Maybe it's time for me to get another cell phone, another number."

That little episode rankled, but there were other, more immediate details to attend to. Before leaving town, we went before a lawyer Nate's connections knew, maybe a couple times removed, and gave sworn depositions to be used in the Jerry case. Nate had explained that the court would have to recognize that, as hunted fugitives, we couldn't show up to testify. Not that our account would be needed, but just in case.

Then we hit the road again, blowing off the rest of our rent on the cottage.

~ * ~

Gwen Webb had known Jay would have to get away any way he could as soon as they'd seen the flashing blue lights. All they'd had before was Jerry's suspicions about Wesley and maybe Craig, but there had to be something more to this. Her husband didn't have time to give her any instructions; he was off up the stairs to the getaway he'd just told her about, with nothing but a gun and a briefcase.

So the party went all to hell, with cops everywhere, looking for Jay and Jerry. Yeah, and Clyde, too. She didn't know where those two were; Jay must've sent them on some errand. Jerry's girl was pretty much out of it, having drunk too much while her boyfriend ran around doing whatever it was he'd done instead of paying attention to her.

She'd decided it was vital to get daughter Samantha out of town as quietly as possible, too, and had sent her off with Bob and his wife in the crowd leaving. With whispered instructions to get the hell back to New York before the cops made any connection, along with a sizeable check, which she told her to cash asap.

And now Gwen was under constant surveillance, obviously the best link the cops had to her husband. Soon enough, they told her about Jerry and how Clyde had infiltrated the organization. She was understandably furious. All this they'd built, bought, going down the tubes. *Damn that traitor Clyde!* And whatever Wesley and Craig had found out must've been a part of it. Damn them, too.

No word from Jay, who'd certainly gotten away clean. Security was now the tightest here, so she didn't know how he'd get word to her. No way was safe, with all the electronic stuff they had today. *Just have to sit tight and wait about that,* she guessed. Didn't like that idea. No, not at all.

But what could she do? The narcs were freezing everything; how'd they expect her to live? Well, they obviously didn't give a shit. She'd claimed zero knowledge of any illicit activity that might have been going on, and there was absolutely nothing they could get on her, as long as she stuck to that story. They'd interrogated her over and over, and she'd just played dumb, given them a brick wall.

But now something had to change. She couldn't go on living in this expensive place, and with Samantha expecting regular checks to keep her alive in New York. The girl wouldn't admit her aspirations in acting weren't going anywhere. She'd go into one of her rages if you even brought it up. Strange, those. Ever since she was little, and no one could reason with her. Just have to let them blow over.

Well. Gwen would have to come up with something, that was all. Later, she was sure she could contact the right people in Baltimore to get back with Jay.

So now it was all about getting away from there. And she couldn't take a damn thing with her, other than what she could cram into her bag. No car, no possessions, just her body. Well, by God, if that was what it was going to have to be, she could and would do it.

They hadn't locked her up, under the circumstances, and of course couldn't confine her to her house. So they'd tailed her tight wherever she'd gone—grocery store, druggist, everywhere. They were like glue, hoping in their dumb way she'd lead them straight to Jay. He'd always said don't underestimate the cops, but actually had a low opinion of their methods, and maybe he'd been right.

*So just have to give them the slip.*

The first step had been to trim her hair short, which wasn't that much different from its usual length. Damn long hair had always gotten in the way, so she'd gone for the mommy cut anyway when the kids were small. That'd make this a little easier.

She drove out the long driveway for what she knew was the last time, with a lot of regrets. Thought briefly of racing off from the follow car, but knew there'd be a roadblock ahead, and she didn't need the added suspicion.

This was supposed to be the last place for Jay and her: no more mobility, moving from one upscale place to another upper-scale one. This was to have been it, and they'd done it right. Now it was gone, and who knew whether they'd be able to do this or anything approaching it again. Somewhere else. Somewhere safe.

If such a place existed.

Damn, that made her see red. Raging, bitter, bloody red.

*But got to focus, tend to the problem at hand.* She went to a favorite exclusive women's shop in the biggest shopping mall near town, noting that usual unmarked car following. *All right boys, you're gonna get a surprise if this comes off, and catch hell for it from your boss.*

She parked, clicked the lock remote, and walked. She'd miss that car, with all its goodies, but not to think about that now. Cars were replaceable. But Jay must've been boiling over having to leave that Ferrari. Good riddance...that thing would've given them away at the North Pole.

One of the tails stayed near her car, watching. The other followed her into the store, not even trying to be inconspicuous.

She tried on two dresses, with the aim of boring the cop, who was watching from a discreet distance, out of his mind. Each time she came out of the changing booth, shaking her head at the clerk.

"Just let me browse a little, Natalie," she requested. The girl agreed, left her alone.

Near a display of wigs and falls, she waited till the cop turned his head to check out a girl walking by, did a quick glance around, two steps, and grabbed a wig off its stand, crammed it into her bag, and casually strolled back into view. They'd have surveillance cameras, she knew, but in a small shop like this, probably no one was monitoring all the time. Still, she'd have to work fast.

She headed for the restrooms, and once inside, locked herself into a stall. She changed into another outfit from home she'd stowed in the big bag, shoes and all, then fitted the wig as best she could. When she heard the last woman leave the restroom, she peeked out, then stood in front of a mirror and adjusted the thing.

It wasn't a really good fit, and it was medium brown, but it hid her short straw-blonde hair completely. Okay, now some appropriate makeup. *God, this isn't my color at all, but let's hope that tail on me isn't up on women's styles.* Then a pair of glasses, a scarf, and whothehell could that woman be? *I hope.*

She called a cab on her cell, to pick her up in front of a tire store further down the mall. They'd probably pick up on that, with all their tech stuff, but maybe she'd have time.

She walked out nonchalantly, hoping the bag wouldn't give her away. What man noticed a woman's handbag? *Find out real soon.*

She left the store, went far from her car, slipped between others down toward the tire store. *Just get your ass here on time,* she willed the cab, putting cars and distance between her and the store she'd left.

It was just pulling in as she stepped out from in front of the door of the tire store.

"Where to, ma'am?"

"They won't have my tires on for a while, so take me to the other mall on up the highway, the one with the Starbucks."

"Sure thing. These guys do all our tires for us. They'll take good care of you."

"Great. Didn't pass inspection...didn't know they were that worn. My husband's supposed to take care of stuff like that. Just didn't happen." She looked back, caught a glimpse of one of the tails walking rapidly toward the tire store, scanning everywhere. So they'd figured it out already. Maybe not as dumb as she'd thought. *But too late, sucker: the woman you're looking for doesn't exist anymore.*

The cab driver dropped her off, she went inside the coffee shop and immediately called another cab from a different company, using the shop's landline phone. Tried very hard not to keep checking for the cops this time. Of course, if they'd picked up on the cab, they could find out where it'd taken her. Matter of time, then.

Sneaked a look, finally. Nothing suspicious. Yet. *Come on, come on.* It was cool, but she was perspiring. Patted her forehead with a tissue. *Gotta keep calm.*

When this cab arrived, she directed the driver to a house in an obscure subdivision. An equally obscure man lived there, a link in J. Barker Webb's chain. An elderly, anonymous-looking individual anyone would assume was a bookkeeper or maybe a shoe-store clerk, thick-lens glasses and all.

She didn't let herself look behind her once on the trip, although her nerves were on high alert. *If they catch me, they still won't have shit.* Of course, then they'd know she was no innocent bystander, either. Well, they knew that anyway, by now. But it was worth this or whatever other chances she'd have to take, to get the hell outta Dodge, get onto finding herself a life again.

She was able to arrange for an anonymous-looking Honda, which she assured the owner would be returned to him very soon. He knew to believe her, but a sizeable cash payment accompanied the deal, anyway. She drove away north, as certain as she could be, given today's sophisticated tracking technology, that she could still get back among friends undetected, if she could just make it to Baltimore. And now she felt sure that was going to happen.

*Just don't get cocky.*

She went over a list of connections, none of whom would know where Jay was, of course. He'd cover his tracks too well. But someone *would* know someone else who just might work that connection. She glanced at the rearview mirror, smiled, exhilarated.

*And screw you, Clyde Kelly.*

# Ten

Arkansas is a state sort of square, cut northeast and southwest by hills that flatten out into Mississippi and Red River delta on one side and grow mountains on the other. I'd nearly starved in the north part once: greatest scenery this side of the Rockies, but dead economy there.

So we found Russellville...with a college, enough industry, and close to some of those terrific mountains to the north. Not Rockies big, but accessible, with clear creeks and old cabins and still a crossroads store, sometimes. And yeah, there were river valley farms closer, with horses, if it could come to that.

We wouldn't both get hired at the same place, so Craig went job-stalking first, while I tried to civilize a hillside fixer-upper out in the country with cheap rent. It was perched, with an outside stairway that creaked, over an unfinished walkout basement. With—get this—a *trapdoor* in the floor opening down to inside stairs. We both grinned when we saw it. Escape route again? Who knew?

He'd have to settle for a job with fewer dollars than he was worth, with no work history he could give, but hey, our expenses were down. Dog food, people food, rent, gas. I was used to that. And I'd find something, too, if it was just temp stuff.

Not to worry. We'd live; we were invisible.

Weather was about what we'd left in Virginia, spring being just a little later here. Still cool, but the cottage had a cast-iron woodstove, and the owner said we could cut dead wood off the acres he also owned around us. His place on the farm was a quarter mile away, so we were pretty private. We liked that.

Taking stock, we had our hand tools, clothes, and a few extras: Craig's chainsaw, axe, fly rod and vest, the few kitchen things of mine, books, tent, stuff. And his double-barrel antique shotgun and a working replica of a Colt .44 caliber that weighed about a ton. So okay, we'd have firepower without having to go through a dead-end background check or the black market for any new artillery.

Hoped we wouldn't need it.

This going from upstanding citizens to hunted refugees took some getting used to, I can tell you. We had suitably worn replacement social security cards and drivers' licenses, but no work references, no histories. Have to create those, so this was gonna be home till that could happen.

We guessed we could manage with that, too. And it wasn't but a few days later that Craig landed a job with a custom furniture maker, nice tight work he could enjoy. At home, I painted, hammered, fixed for a couple weeks, not bored at all. At night my man came home wood-scented and happy, for a guy who'd left everything behind. Well, everything but me, and he was okay with that. Better than okay, and I was set to do my woman thing to make damn sure he stayed that way.

As the weather warmed, on weekends we explored the mountains north of us, Cyrano terrorizing squirrels and rabbits and romping like a puppy. The Ozarks weren't really mountains, more of a high plateau cut up by deep rivers and creeks, but you could've fooled me. Smoky blue ridges layering off into infinity, bluffs of red and yellow sandstone sheer into deep, green pools of whitewater streams. Gravel bars to camp on, with green-leafing canopies dappling sunlight. All cozy in the tent at night, with rippling water over stone, and nobody near. That was the best part: we coulda been Adam and Eve.

And maybe First Dog, yeah.

We followed old logging roads and deserted creek-ford tracks, parking the van and playing pioneer on foot. Places only hard-core hunters went, and didn't tell anybody else about.

I also took this opportunity to find out more about my man Craig's (Dave's) likes and dislikes. I've said I'm an insatiable reader, and that's something I wanted to share with him. Engineer, and that's a real stereotype. I once knew a guy in college who combined that in a double-major with philosophy, but that was a rarity. Most engineers I'd known were almost monosyllabic.

So I introduced him to Yeats, figuring why not? Start at the top. And he didn't just endure it, but started really to get into those yearning, grab-your-heart lines. It got so he wanted to read aloud to me, and the guy was a natural at dramatizing the right words, evoking the images. With the predictable result that he could melt me with a phrase. He hadn't done drama at all, but he could've stepped into any actor's shoes. God, had I found the Renaissance Man, or what?

And to hell with the white horse bit.

~ * ~

During those first weeks, Number One Dog and I'd hike the woods and old fields near home, smelling the new earth, feeling the spring-promises on soft breezes. Tiny bluets peeked up, and little yellow flowers I didn't recognize smiled at us. Looking back, it was a suspended, floating time, so serene, so free, so fragile I knew it would have to end.

Everything ends.

This time it was simply my need to get busy again. My hands just had to be working; I had to be accomplishing things. Gotta admit, I did think about getting pregnant and submerging myself in domestic bliss, but that didn't look like the answer, just yet. Craig woulda gone for it, I think, but no, not yet. Things needed a kind of closure, maybe. A period, before really starting the next sentence.

I liked our landlord and his wife. George and Shirley Connaly were salt-of-the-earth, late fifties, kids grown and fled. Couple of times I walked over and helped him weld broken machinery, fix farm equipment. Shirley'd feed me and talk about quilting and canning and kids, a cigarette dangling from her lip. Always had strands of her graying hair plastered to her forehead, red hands busy, jeans and shirt stuffed with her pounds. Straight-talking, earnest, knew bullshit when she heard it. Not-too-vague hints that Craig—Dave— and I should have kids, too.

"They're a shitload of trouble, but y'gotta love ever' minnit y'got 'em. Lonely now, nobody but George to fight with."

Both of them worked all the time in that trapped cycle of farm chores that never takes a day off. George was long and leathery— reminded me of an older, sun-baked Nate Peterson—with a beaked nose that got there way ahead of the rest of him. He stooped a little, like he expected every doorway to get him across the eyebrows. Hard hands that made fists that could probably drive a fencepost unaided, or coax a hairspring into place in a gold railroad watch.

They'd built our house for the eldest daughter Dorie, who'd occupied it briefly with her first husband, Arlie. I got to hear a lot about Arlie, and how he hadn't been good enough for their daughter. *Sure, no bias there or anything.* Okay, never met her, but she'd play hell ever living up to her mom.

George thought I was a genius after I located the trouble with his asthmatic Farmall C tractor—leaking intake manifold gasket. He'd had that antique for about a hundred years, and vowed he'd restore it completely. Someday.

I'd told him I was looking for a job, when he mentioned a welding shop he'd heard needed help. And he knew the owner.

"Yer very good, Lee. Know y'been workin' construction, but weldin' pays good. Now, you tell ole Bill Dobbs I seen what y'done here, an' I b'lieve he'll hire yuh. If y'don't mind workin' 'mongst rough ole boys." He grinned, spat tobacco juice.

I told him I'd never worked with any other kind of ole boys.

Talked it over with Craig, who said why not, if I wanted to try it.

"May depend on what I find there," I mused. "I like a good crew to work with, but leering big-guts'll put me off. I'm picky...that's why I went to work for you."

"I'm picky too...why I hired you." Grin, kiss. Damn man, couldn't keep my hands off him. Didn't try.

"Tell ole Bill when he leaves home..." I was humming the old song on the way to the welding shop after dropping Craig off. Didn't know what to expect—maybe a Rosie the Riveter thing, but I was cool with that. Not starving, not desperate, just needed to be hittin' it somewhere.

Dobbs was George's age: a blocky, red-faced guy who was like a bulldozer on steroids. Hands that'd hide a dinner plate each, and a crewcut. I liked him right off. *Yeah, and stick your father-image stuff, Sarah the Shrink.*

"George says you c'n weld. Y'done tig, mig, stainless, cast iron, carbon steel, acetylene?" First words out of his mouth.

"Yes, but I'm weaker on cast iron. I can braze, or pre-heat small pieces, but if you do cracked engine blocks, I wanta hide an' watch you do it."

"Guess so. Nah, too big a deal, with all the slow heat-up an' cool-down after. What'd you do, take a course in tech school?"

"No, Dad let me play with his toys at home. I'm actually more of a blacksmith, but nothing scares me."

"Horse shoein'?"

"Like horses a lot, but don't trust myself there. No, carbon steel hardening and tempering, forge welding, beatin' the hell out of hot iron."

"Don't say? Maybe y'could teach me some of that."

"I dunno, you might not be strong enough." Grin. I even poked a finger into one of those massive arms.

"Gittin' old, all right," after a chuckle. "Why'n't you come over here, tell me what rod you'd use on this I-beam."

"D.C.? Okay, a 7018 Fleetweld 5/32, at 135 amps so I don't burn through."

"Think that'd penetrate enough?"

"If I don't get in a hurry. Keep the rod moving slow, preheat to both sides. Or I could go to 145 if you're in a hurry."

"Show me."

I did. Moved the rod tip faster at the higher amperage so it wouldn't burn through, and it did the job. Lose concentration, and you had a hole to fill, a little at a time. So, speed could waste time, in the end.

"Aluminum?"

"Don't think you'd wanta hear me cuss when it all fell through. Hey, I'm no expert, but I can pull my own weight."

"I'd say so. What're you worth?"

"Tell the truth, I'm out of my territory here. Why don't we say you pay me the same's a guy doing the same work?"

He didn't even have to think. "Just don't tell him, okay? I think you might do." He offered me a giant hand. Mine still had calluses, and he caught that.

Then I met the crew. Irvin Akers was older than Dobbs, a lean black man with a huge smile, married to a nurse. Luther Martin (really) was round, maybe thirty-two, three, and hummed a lot.

"I see your service truck's not here. So, one more guy? The red car over there?"

"Yeah, that's Dirty John Black. Neat freak. Impresses the customers, though. 'Bout your age. Be back soon. So, when can you start?"

"Tomorrow okay? Need to get myself some wheels. My man's on four-tens, so he'll need the van."

"Sure. Seven to three-thirty. But don't go to a dealer for a car. Here's the local trader: prices better. What're you lookin' for?"

"Always had a truck, but we've got the van. Maybe just a car, but I'm big on four-wheel drive. Jeep, maybe."

"They go high around here, lotta hunters. Y'won't want a gas guzzler. How 'bout one of those little foreign SUVs?"

"No, Dad always bought American, and I'm warped that way, too. But hey, you got work to do, Mr. Dobbs. I can find some wreck…"

"Don't wanta see you get burned. Do that enough around here. And I'm Bill and you're Lee. Oh, here's a small-engine Ranger four-wheel drive. Be okay if you don't need horsepower."

"Sure, had one of those once. Say, can I borrow this? I'll check this one out, and if it's been rode hard and put away wet, I'll look some more. And thanks for the job, Bill."

The boys gave me thumbs up as I left. I waved.

# Eleven

I found this not-so-used Jeep Patriot SUV. Woman thought she'd wanted the stick shift, but got tired clutching in stop-and-go traffic. A little pricey, but the good gas mileage with the little 2,000 cc. engine should even that out. Craig and I could go up in the mountains on the non-roads in it, and...

*Hey, I should include him in this, shouldn't I?* I meant, would my guy get bent if I left him out? About that, now...

I called him at work.

"Okay if I buy myself some wheels? Got the welding job."

"You know it's okay. What is it?"

"Jeep SUV. S'posed to get thirty m.p.g if I drive it barefoot. It'll get us up into those mountains."

"Go for it. Got enough cash?"

"Think so, we're still haggling. Okay, be by at six for you."

So I was mobile again and employed. Felt good. Some of the... tentative aspect of our lives was sliding off now. Maybe put roots down here?

Wait and see.

~ * ~

Bill Dobbs was a good boss. He moved fast, got a lot of fine work done. Likewise Irvin, the fatherly guy with the white teeth. Steady, both of them. Luther and John were average at their jobs; the blimp was a little sloppy but okay. D.J.'s wife must've steam-cleaned him at home, he was that neat. Took time to set up everything just so, then went at the work like he was gonna kill it.

They all treated me like a welder, not like a woman, and I figured that was because I wasn't single, far as they knew. Therefore not available? Who knows what goes through the male mind? Luther was the only one of them unmarried. He got flustered easily when we talked; probably post-adolescent complex, but okay, really.

They were good guys. Enough so that Craig and I spent some weekend time with them, one or two at a time. Irvin was a fisherman, and showed us where the good creeks were. His wife Lou was a helluva cook. Bill liked fooling with old cars, and I could enjoy a Saturday afternoon with him among his relics. No kids, just him and wife Beth, who sold real estate. She and landlady Shirley liked to bowl, and both of them were good.

Luther had probably been odd man out all his life, but people liked him so he always fit in. Lived in a 'burb house his parents had left him and played banjo some with a scratch bluegrass band. The other guys said he was good.

Now Dirty John was a piece of work, like I said. But okay, all of us have our quirks, and being tidy can't be all bad. But when we met his wife, Aggie, at a company beer-and-catfish fry (Irvin had caught the fish) we knew she was on something. Wasn't drinking much, but she was laughing too loud, fidgeting, popping up unexpectedly everywhere. Craig and I exchanged glances and rolled eyes. This one would have needle marks on her, for sure.

Now, if you'd asked me, I'd have picked northwest Arkansas as the *last* place a druggie would surface, despite the movie *Winter's Bone*. But Aggie didn't have that Arkansas accent, and yeah, neither did John. So from where? Didn't matter, of course; everybody's gotta be from somewhere. But okay, I'm nosy. I asked.

"Oh, we're originally from Maryland. Wanted someplace… quieter. Right, John?"

Then I noticed she'd almost never opened her mouth without checking in with husband first. Weird. Okay, just one of those insecure girls who has to get Daddy's approval to sneeze. And so John was surrogate Daddy. Not the first time *that's* happened. Hey, Sarah the not-so-Subtle you know, with her theories about me.

And just maybe that had something to do with my holding off (or was I?) with my man Craig. *Oh shit, forget the psych stuff, girl: don't make life more complicated than it already is.* But I couldn't seem to stop speculating about the others.

John the Clean might be this domineering fascist too, making poor little Aggie his slave…no, there I went again with the armchair stuff. Trying to make a modern-day Gothic novel out of a welder and his bride? *For Petesake, Wes—Leila.* And Maryland…might just as well be the moon.

One thing I'd noticed out here: everybody was not all tuned in and rabid about politics and the state of the world and the economy the way they were back East. I mean, you could start an eye-gouging fight in parts of Virginia just by admitting you were blue, or red, in the wrong crowd. Here they'd just grin and offer you another beer.

Luther got out his banjo that night and we sang along. Even danced some, on Bill's deck: basic two-step stuff, but hey, I like to shake my bootie, so we improvised. Craig was a helluva dancer, I'd already discovered, and he was with me. Aggie shrieked and clapped, then cut her shaky eyes toward John to make sure that was okay.

Then Boss Bill the Bear danced with me, and I got the idea he could toss me up like a baton and spin me. Craig danced with Beth—hostess, after all—who couldn't keep off his toes. John and Aggie just watched. Maybe they were afraid she'd fall on her ass. Or that the Clean One would smudge himself somewhere.

We were having fun. Luther was sweating, fingers flying on the banjo neck and notes tumbling out like a sack of bright, spilled crystals. Then Irvin guided his Lou onto the floor, a quiet, elegant lady who'd been helping Beth all evening. Okay, nice looking reserved couple; maybe Luther could play a waltz.

But he didn't. I don't know what those sounds were, but that beat would make a dead man stomp. And reserved Irvin and his equally reserved Lou proceeded to tear the place apart. The rest of us just stared while those two welded themselves together like Siamese twins, spun out, meshed, shook, twisted, jumped. Wow. I wanted to crawl into a hole. Hey, they were thirty years older than me, and would put any of those TV dance contestants in the shade.

I couldn't stop talking about those great people on the way home, and had to reflect on the stereotypes people where I come from have of black folks. Only word for Irvin and shy Lou was *class*.

I did feel for Addled Aggie, who'd obviously been driven to whatever controlled substance, by either her insecurity or a sadistic Germless John. She was only about twenty, and something was proving just too much for her to handle.

Not my problem, by any stretch. So I tried to put her out of my head, get on with things. But Craig had picked up on her too, sensitive guy that he was. He suggested I spend some time with her: big sister. Okay, maybe. Not to poke my nose in, but yeah, when I could get around to it.

~ * ~

Welding is fascinating work, believe it or not. You get so focused on getting that bead of molten steel to penetrate just right, the metal to flow the way it's supposed to. Then there's the finished product: a useful whole you synthesized from random pieces, and it's a hoot. Time slides by too, and it's lunchtime, then quitting time. And my neat little Patriot whisking me off home in time to create my man some culinary monstrosity. Or he'd bring home barbecue or some other no-work entrée. I liked my job.

I liked my life.

I called Aggie to see if we could do lunch. She could. Bill didn't care what time we left...just get the jobs done. I told the John his bride and I were plotting. Caught him off-guard for a second, but then he grinned, flicking imaginary dust off his sleeve.

"Sure. She hasn't made friends here like in Baltimore. But she'll need money. Take her this ten." Wow. So he controlled even her lunch money? Hey, she worked at a florist's...but didn't even get to keep loose change? *Pig. Male-control-freak pig.* Super neat, but still a pig.

And *Baltimore?* Oh, no way any connection. No, no way in hell.

I picked Aggie up and we went to this Mom and Pop place where they didn't deep-fry everything. Craig and I avoided fast food, and had scouted town for places that didn't poison you with unpronounceable additives.

Aggie was as nervous as at the fish fry. She had this thing of twisting her hair and darting her eyes around. Drive you bonkers to watch her.

"Hey girl, relax. Far as I know, the terrorists don't know this place exists." Nervous laugh, and she let go the mangled hair, kind of a wheat color, short.

"It's just...I quit smoking, see, and...should have done it a long time ago. John's been after me to...Anyway, I'll get past it, I guess. But God, do I want one right now."

"Oh. Tried the nicotine patch, or the pills?"

"John didn't want me to. Said cold turkey was the only way. He's really been sweet about it...the habit, and now the...nerves and all." Fingers back in the hair, eyes flicking for Mr. Bad.

We ate semi-Southern, which was as close to Georgia as I'd get here. Not real South. I remembered a lot of these mountain Arkies fought for the Union in the war that matters the most to us unreconstructeds. But Mom, the cook, roasted things and I loved her for it.

"John says you miss Baltimore," I tried as a subject.

"Did he? Yeah, I guess. Friends there, family, contacts. You know anybody there, Lee?" Oh yeah, I was still Leila...

"Only people were a couple moved down to Virginia, I think. Lawyer and wife." No way in hell, big as Baltimore was, she'd know the Barker Webbs. And I didn't want too many folks knowing about our immediate past, even Agitated Aggie. But she wanted to talk, and I guess that's what I was there for.

"John said David did carpentry."

"Old houses, yeah. And Ohio's full of 'em. Lots more history back East, like Maryland, Virginia. Not like all the recent stuff here in Arkansas."

"John likes everything new and white." (Yeah, he would.) "I couldn't bring an antique anywhere near home." Rueful laugh.

*Even if he gave you the bucks.* Well, she was unwinding a little, anyway. Guessed living with a machine like him'd make anybody nervous.

But I suspected more than a kid trying to kick the nicotine habit. She didn't, for one thing, seem to crave a smoke after lunch, when tobacco junkies need it most. Okay, pry a little. Hey, I'm a nosy bitch.

"Like to quit early," I yawned. "Get home and sneak a joint before Dave gets home." Watching out of the corner of my eye for a reaction. I got it, or part of one.

"You do weed? I mean, you seem so...straight and all."

"Dave's the straight one. But no, I wouldn't even know where Mary Jane lives around here. Anyway, they'll probably legalize it after I'm too old to give a shit." We left the restaurant.

"Hey, I've enjoyed it, Aggie," as I pulled to the curb at the florist's. "Maybe we can sneak off again sometime, see a raunchy movie or something without the guys."

"I'd sure like that. Thanks, Lee." A real smile.

Okay, so next I was supposed to get word someway of a source for pot, or maybe she'd have some next time?

Or not. Didn't matter. Just being nosy. And I hoped the Nazi she was married to wouldn't grill her too much about our color-outside-the-lines lunch.

"How's Aggie?" the Clean One asked, first thing.

"She survived. No, really, we're gonna start our own new political party, us wives. Flowers and steel. Like it?"

"Are you ever serious, Lee? What've you planted in my innocent wife's head?"

"Tried to get her onto grits and black-eyed peas. Didn't work. But she's a good kid, John Boy. Handling the smoking thing well, considering..." *Watch, again.*

"The...oh, yeah. Yeah, I'm proud of her for that."

So, were they both using? Either he wasn't, or was controlling the intake enough he could hide it. Probably that.

Didn't matter. Not at all. I'm for freedom of choice in just about everything: alcohol, drugs, sex. Sure. Although any one of them can getcha killed, you get in with the wrong crowd.

~ * ~

Samantha Webb hadn't been happy at her parents' getting raided, or her brother's being thrown in jail. But what really burned her was that the checks had stopped coming. So Dad was on the run; he'd surely managed to grab a load of cash on the way out. And Mom was holed up in Baltimore, ferreting out where her husband was, and literally broke.

New York hadn't treated the girl well. Not only because there were many thousands of other theater hopefuls clogging the system, but because everyone seemed to resent her forcefulness. She'd always known what she wanted, be it designer clothes, another girl's boyfriend or a sportscar, and she'd gone after it. Her father had encouraged her, admiring her spirit and take-no-prisoners style. But it seemed pushing her way to the top wasn't going to happen here, as it had in their part of Baltimore growing up. Here you had to be just another face in the crowd until by some miracle the law of averages got to you.

If you hadn't died first.

She'd done experimental theater, community theater, benefits, all the non-paying efforts that were supposed to get you exposure so the big guys could discover you.

Hadn't happened. And unfortunately or not, she'd made enemies along the way among the other girls who didn't have the balls to make it in the first place. So who gave a damn about them anyway.

But now her situation was serious. Dad had always seen the necessity of her hanging in there till the big break, if Mom did not-so-subtly hint that she should just grab herself a young exec. That solution was worthless, with the number of hungry women in this town going after anything male.

Gwen had been in contact with her daughter, but hadn't been able to send money. Said she'd just have to find work till they got together again and into something stable. *Yeah, thanks, Mom.* Not easy, that, with that same competition going. And her roommate was poorer than she was. But yeah, she knew Dad wouldn't forget her. There'd be money just as soon as he could get his hands on it.

*But damn that snake, Clyde Kelly. Yeah, and the carpenter couple, too.* The folks had set it all up just right: semi-retirement in the horse country, away from old enmities, with a good income and who cared where it came from? They'd kept her and Jerry up in style, and now, thanks to those people's meddling, he was inside, with a good chance at life with no parole. His fault really, wasting that guy like the dumb-ass he was, but he'd pulled it off till they'd soured it.

And she was broke in the most expensive place in the world. But surely there should be some way to even that score at least. But okay, Dad would be onto that, too. *Just get me some cash first, then maybe there'll be some way I can help.*

~ * ~

So summer wore away, with our exploring the mountains and Craig teaching me to play with a dumb bit of fluff on a hook at the end of a line. He caught bass; I caught sunfish about as big as a business card. We made a few casual friends outside work, which was good, since his boss was a superstud bachelor. I didn't want my partner straying into that scene.

Aggie did for a fact share a little grass with me one Saturday morning when the guys were off fishing in Irvin's boat on the Arkansas River lake. We got pleasantly stoned, giggled a lot, and then she started prying into my life.

*Okay, go easy, here...*

"Rollin' stone, girl, till I met David. Knocked around, dog an' me, all over...work awhile, move on. Not much fun."

"But you were...*free.*" Wistful, that.

"Yeah, but honey, sleepin' with a dog don't cut it, believe me."

She howled so hard I wondered if Dirty John could be a real dog in bed. And of course, that picture got me tickled, too.

Now, I don't smoke pot as a rule; don't smoke anything... Dad's counseling. But hey, I guess this was maybe asserting my independence? Craig wouldn't approve, and that might have a little to do with it? Or just a couple gals acting out.

Whatever.

But I gotta admit to a little amateur sleuthing here, too. So no way would Aggie and Antiseptic John know the Webbs in metro Baltimore, but the drug scene? Now you're narrowing the field, right? Oh, sure: territory, turf, gangs. But those guys know each other, surely. And while I didn't expect Insecure Aggie in Russellville, Arkansas to tip me to the current whereabouts of on-the-run J. Barker, late of Albemarle County, Virginia, a little information-fishing couldn't hurt. Or could it?

*Maybe better leave this alone...*

But sure enough, little Aggie was feeling so grateful for my attention to her, she confided in me. A little. After all, could I be a narc? No way.

"If you ever wanta try something a little more...fun, Lee..." She let it trail off, not sure how much to let slip.

"Um?" Let her tell it, if she were going to.

"Oh, nothing. Just...Forget it. No, it's nothing."

"Hey, whatever." *Anybody has the green, he can get you the white...*"Only, if it's kinky group sex, I'm out."

"Oh, it's not *that*," and here came the giggles again. "I wouldn't do *that*."

"'S okay, girl. I don't pry. Your call." *Don't push.*

"It's just...well, let's just forget it."

"Sure. And I'm up for most anything else, from bobbing for apples to rolling shitheads' yards." Giggles again, both of us.

~ * ~

"I know it's outta the realm of the possible," I admitted to Craig, "but think: if there were some remote way we could locate the Webb and get him iced down, we wouldn't have to look over our shoulders ever again. Even go home." It was late, and we had our bellies full of hushpuppies with the fish he'd caught. Deepest South food. And I wanted to get this out before our thoughts and emotions naturally turned to other pleasant things.

"That'd be great, but talk about long shots..."

"I know. Just thought I'd pry a little with Aggie. Maybe find out who her pusher is. And we're David and Leila, remember? In Arkansas. No way can anything come back on us."

"Yeah, I guess. And I oughta check in with Nate, see how that stands. Be nice if they've nailed him already."

"Don't bet the farm on it: crooked lawyer, drug lord, with all the technology dirty money can buy."

We used cell phones to contact anyone back in Virginia, figuring that was safe. After that last call from Failure Phil, I'd dumped mine and bought another upscale one with more gadgets than I could figure out. I guessed, if our flight pattern ever got too techno, we'd buy cheap ones and throw them away after one use: cloak and dagger stuff. I put my ear close to the phone when Nate came on. Craig smelled good.

"Hey, guy. Dave from Ohio. How's the web-site going?" Code talk: I loved it. Surely hacker-proof.

"Still not final, I'm afraid. No help from the wife...she bailed on the deal. First phase solid, though. Let you hear if there's a break. Give Lee my love." Punched off. Yeah, I'd heard you hadda keep it short.

"Okay. Cop talk, you heard. So nothing on Webb Sr., Jerry's going down, and that's good, but Gwen's disappeared. Now, how'd they let her get away? Surely the best way to get to Webb."

"Dunno, but I'll bet this isn't the first time they've lost the gendarmes. Gwen's sharper than you'd think." I remembered that about her thwarted architecture career. A cool one: maybe something as simple as in a door and out an open window. How good could small-town detectives be? Well, I guessed Nate Peterson was on top of things, but whoever'd been watching Gwen Baby probably weren't rocket scientists.

"So," Craig went on, "they're probably setting up again somewhere, maybe having a place in the country restored again. Or not. Maybe doing the polar opposite. Webb's sharp too, and count on him doing the least expected thing. New names though, histories. Just not with Jerry Boy this time, who was really a liability."

"For sure. So whattya think then, do I back off Aggie, or play amateur sleuth and try to find a connection?"

"Well, like you said, we're David and Leila now, halfway across the country. Can't hurt, I guess, but just don't make her suspicious. And do be careful. Anything to it, it'd backfire right on us."

"Yeah, and I've been thinking: if Aggie's on the hard stuff, and maybe John, too, how're they financing it? He's a welder, makes what I do...she's in a flower shop. Drugs ain't cheap, so they gotta be dealing, too."

"Hmm. College town and all. Kids on dad's allowance, away from home for the first time, playing 'look what I've found.' Yeah, I guess that's likely. No place seems safe from those people."

"What scares me is the networking they can do now with the Internet, hacking into everything. Territory can be as big as they want. Clear to here." I was picturing this big spider web of a thing, with little people out in the boonies getting losers hooked, connected to bigger distributors. Then, way in the middle, like giant evil arachnids, guys like J. Barker Webb running it all, getting richer.

And other guys like Clyde Kelly infiltrating the organization, nailing links in the chain, but never getting it all. Must be frustrating as hell. Made you think those no-laws people who wanted to legalize it all might just have a point. No, the do-right machinery that was in place to hunt druggies represented thousands of precious jobs in our tangled economy. Jerk those away, the Dow would probably tank.

And in a big-money enterprise like we were faced with, little fish like repulsive Jerry Webb were as replaceable as light bulbs. He was dimmer than a light bulb, but you get the picture.

So I decided better leave this alone...safer. Aggie could let something slip to a higher-up, and we didn't need that kind of attention, no matter our fake names. And she just could be what she appeared to be: an insecure child bride with a domineering husband. Pretty common thing, I'd say.

Well, enough about other people's troubles. We put all that aside, like we'd been doing our best to manage. Didn't help our fugitive status to dwell on the bad stuff too much. Try to keep it upbeat. This wasn't a bad life, long as it could continue. And if we didn't rock the boat, we saw no reason it couldn't.

And right at that moment, in that bed, in the outback of Arkansas, there were other things pressing between us. Literally.

# Twelve

Northeast a state and a half away from that part of Arkansas, a man in his late fifties was showing a photograph to two other men. One was a Norse crewcut ex-Marine type, early thirties. The other looked like you couldn't get him clean with a wire brush and pressure-washer. Black, oily hair, blue chin, ill-fitting, off-the-rack dark suit.

The picture showed a group of construction workers posing in front of a neat, tall plantation house with dormer windows and new paint. There was a young man with a wild shock of hair, an older, worried-looking man, another maybe thirty, with a Clark Gable mustache and a cocky grin.

Then there was the obvious foreman, about forty, with reddish hair tinged with gray. And beside him stood a girl with short ponytail through the back slot of a duckbill cap, her hand on the arm of the foreman. All wore tool belts.

"These two," the man indicated the girl and foreman. "They're gone months ago, probably with police help. No way to know where they'll turn up, but they will, eventually. Carpenters, high-end restorations. Now what I want is this picture out in the field. Way out. To *everybody*."

"Any names?" the crewcut asked. The other guy was checking out the girl in the picture. Saucy, go-to-hell look. Totally different from the women he came in contact with: junkies, alkies, shopworn broads who hung around servicing the guys with the bucks.

"Names won't mean anything anymore. You know that."

"So, okay," the grease-laden one asked, his eyes still on the girl in the picture, "what's th' bottom line, boss?"

"My boy's inside: life without parole. These two did it. And I'm having to start over, at my age. Can't practice law, got next to nothing." Then he dropped the big one. "And the girl got her hands on half a million of my money, which I didn't even know was missing until after everything went all to hell. So what'd you do, Karl, if it was you?"

"Off 'em. Prob'ly already spent the money." No hesitation.

"How about you, Denny?"

"Yeah, sounds right. But sure work 'em over first, try to find whatever's left of the cash. Anything else t'go on?" There was a touch of something wild in his eyes, something not quite in control. Maybe too heavy on the steroids.

"Not much. The guy's place for sale in Virginia...dead-end with the lawyer handling it. They won't go back, and if they do, we've got people there. I've been trying to get somebody inside with the cops there too, but not yet. And it'll probably be the Feds, anyway.

"Guy's ordinary, country accent, but he's a traitor. Oh, the woman's from Georgia, drawls. And she's got a smart mouth on her."

*Yeah, bitchy. Like to get some of that,* Karl fantasized.

And with that, J. Barker Webb, now known as one Parker Goode, burning with the need for revenge, sent his men out onto the lines of the drug web. He went over that last night in Virginia again. *Girl must've seen the briefcase, raided it before Jerry caught her. Had to've stashed it in their truck. Or maybe it was Clyde. He said he'd counted it, and like a fool I believed him.*

*Damn them all.*

It was surprisingly easy to scan the picture, upload it onto a computer, and send it out along the long tentacles of the Webb organization. It was in the hands of the various dealers in a big part of the country in minutes.

~ * ~

I didn't push it with Aggie Black. Just stayed friendly, tried to put a little starch in her spine. Didn't want to provoke Mean John, so kept it light. She wasn't that bad, if she could grow up before the stuff she was on could kill her. Little like a stray dog you couldn't turn away, even if it was a bit mangy.

On a more pleasant subject, Craig and I'd talked just a little about the marriage thing, without his exactly asking me. I could tell he knew I'd need that to be a 50-50 discussion, and I guessed I did. Woulda been nice if he *had* come home with flowers and a ring, but well, I wasn't ready for that yet, and he could tell.

And a refusal or a put-off? Damage.

Really, I wanted the hunted-man syndrome gone before we made it permanent. Okay, so it was already permanent, we both knew that. But buy a great place, start having kids maybe, become two other people—not yet.

Meanwhile, we hiked those terrific Ozark mountains miles to the north, fished clear streams to die for, camped in wilderness, let Cyrano think he was king of the woods. Only thing missing from any plan to disappear further into this up-country paradise would be a way to make a decent living.

There were roads being bulldozed into impossible sites for richies from Dallas and St. Louis and Des Moines to build monstrosities above the rivers. But their money didn't go far for the local economy: usually out-of-state builders and ego-ridden architects eager to make their statements and get into *Architectural Digest*. Those nature-hugging transplants were actually slowly destroying the very things they'd come here for.

We weren't sure this was where we wanted to be permanently, either. I could tell Craig missed Virginia. There were no plantation houses here, no echoes of antebellum life, no *Gone With The Wind* nostalgia at all. This was pioneer country of log cabins and steep, rocky corn patches you could fall out of, and a legacy of hunters and trappers. And yeah, moonshine stills up hollers you didn't go into.

I missed Georgia some, too, but after bumming around these years, I could settle anywhere, I figured. Maybe back in Virginia, sure, if the badasses could ever be banished. Did not wanta have to deal with the reconstituted Webbers paying us a social call.

I could imagine Nate Peterson chafing at the dead-end of that case, up against drug-lord-financed super-technology and a no-doubt oiled network.

And what about old Clyde? Probably undercover again somewhere, inserting self into some perilous chain of scumbags. Clyde was slick; it'd be his kinda guy who'd blow the lid off operations like those. I often wondered how far an agent would have to go to get the goods he needed. Hafta get his hands dirty, sure. Maybe eliminate competition. Kill? Oh, yeah, he'd have blasted Jerry that time if Craig hadn't smashed his arm first.

The thought blighted my sunshiny mood.

~ * ~

Craig had volunteered to shop for groceries that after-work day in August. I was grateful, and climbed the steps to the little house wearily. Dirty John, the Clean and I had been out with the service truck all day, welding on some earthmoving equipment. Heavy stuff, and we'd had to jack some pieces together with a hydraulic ram so we could align it to do the welding.

I was worn out, and my work boots weighed a ton. Took a long shower to get the rust and welding-flux particles off me and out of my hair—occupational hazard for welders—then stretched out on the recliner in a bathrobe. Nothing on under. I liked to surprise Craig that way. The AC droned in its window, successfully lulling me toward sleep.

I don't know if Cyrano heard it first, or if his lurching up added to my registering the squeak of the outside stairs. His ears don't stand up all the way—too floppy—but he was all bristles. A low growl started in his throat. The squeaking stopped.

Craig? No, the dog knew his step, and no sound of an engine. It was still light outside, but yeah, time for him to be home. I stood quietly, slipped to the door on my bare feet. Slid the lock shut, listening, hand on Cyrano's head. Okay: basement door locked, and it was metal. This one could be broken in, though, if the dude beyond it were determined. I tiptoed to the shotgun leaning against a wall. Snaps from movies: you blasted the baddy through the door and he flew off into space in pieces.

Could I do it? Who *was* that outside? Fear of overreacting, blowing away a friend, an innocent.

Just then a foot slammed against the door, which shuddered. I pointed the shotgun. Cocked one barrel. Cyrano barked, which the intruder ignored. That meant he was dead serious about all this. Another kick, and wood splintered. A hand reached in for the lock.

My dog was on that hand like on a bone. Man's scream from outside. He got what was left of his hand loose, then another hand started shoving a gun through, accompanied by cursing. Before he could shoot, I aimed over Cyrano and blasted a hole in the general direction of the door, which took out part of the wall, nowhere near what I'd aimed at. The hand disappeared, feet thudded on the stairs. Almost had to pick myself up from the floor, with the recoil. And the roar had shaken the little house.

Now I did hear an engine, and whoever was on the stairs ran the rest of the way down. Cyrano let out a couple more barks that shook the house again. I held the dog, cracked the door to see a guy in jeans and a black tee shirt disappearing into trees. Holding a very bloody hand.

Craig stopped the van and opened the driver's door. It was on the house side, so he was shielded. But on the stairs, he'd be a clear target.

"*Stay down!*" I called.

"What? What's wrong?"

"Just stay there! Guy beyond you in the woods with a gun, tried to break in! Keep on this side of the van. I'll open the basement door."

He turned to look, of course, but through the windows of the two doors, that made him a little harder to see, anyway. Then he ducked down. I lifted the trapdoor and clambered down the ladder-like steps, unlocked the metal basement door. He rushed in.

"What the hell, Wes? A guy with a *gun?*"

"Oh, yeah. Was on the stairs when we heard him, then started kicking in the door. Cyrano and I didn't let him. He ran when I blasted the wall and you drove up. Didn't hit him, but he'll have only part of a hand, now."

"What'd he look like?"

"Moving fast. Medium, all the way. Crewcut light hair, jeans, black tee shirt. Muscles. Not young, not old. Never saw him before, I'm sure." I was shaking a little. "Now, just what could this mean? Here, and now?"

"Could be a random break-in thing. Maybe just hoping for an empty house..."

"My car's here. That kinda says there's a warm body inside."

"Coulda hit you for the keys, then on foot."

"Daylight. Course if he was wired on something..."

"Okay, let's think a minute. Can we afford to assume this is just a failed break-in? And that he's scared off for good?"

"What's to keep him from coming back?"

"Right. Okay, switch gears, then. Worst case: he knows who we are and knew you were alone. Maybe didn't know about the dog, but that wasn't stopping him. Who wants to get to you...us?"

"Barker Webb, whose rotten life we helped ruin, that's who."

"In which case, this guy'll be back, surely with reinforcements. He'll have left his car hidden—knew the way. If that's it, we don't have any time."

"The cops?"

"On what grounds? No, if we're blown here, we've gotta move, Wes. Cops couldn't protect us."

Just disappear? Leave this place *right now?* Our jobs, everything? Seemed a little extreme, until, as Craig already had, I considered the alternative. But for Webb to find us *here?* How? Then

I remembered Anxious Aggie and The John, from Baltimore, and the obvious drug thing. Network like Webb surely had, he could send word to the ends of the world. And to his goons.

It took us only frantic minutes for me to get dressed, to pile stuff in both vehicles through the basement, staying on the house side, and to say goodbye to the place.

"Go first, Wes. I'm guessing he—they—will expect us to run. If anyone follows you, I'll follow *him* with this." He hefted the double-barrel shotgun.

"Okay. Gimme the pistol, then. Don't wanta get jumped at a stoplight. Oh, just as an afterthought, where we goin', guy?"

"Oh, gosh. Just outta here for now. To I-40 West, I guess, then maybe north. We'll stop where there're people, and figure something."

We rolled out. I kept thinking, of course, that this was so unlikely, the Webb connection. Just some random...then a red car pulled out from a farm lane right on my tail. Right where it'd have been left by the dude sneaking up to break into the house. And I thought I knew that car.

I floored it. Then I fumbled my cell and speed-dialed Craig.

"Bogey's onto me."

"I see him. I'm gaining...hang on."

"Don't want him blasting me." I was getting chills up my spine. Checked the mirror. Was that...? The driver...looked like...

"No. Oh, hell...okay, I'm on his ass, Wes. Now touch your brake for just a second, right before that curve coming up, then punch it."

A plan...yeah, we needed that. That *was* John Black. And yeah, the crewcut with the artillery. I was waiting for the shots, the shattered windows. The shattered *me*. I touched the brake pedal lightly, then stomped the accel to the metal.

Craig saw the red car's brake lights come on as the driver instinctively hit them when he saw mine come on, and he wheeled the big van out, shooting alongside. He saw the other driver was John Black. Before the passenger could aim a gun left-handed past him, Craig wrenched the wheel, shoving the big three-quarter ton loaded rig into the car with a crash of complaining metal.

Its right tires dropped three inches off the edge of the blacktop onto the eroded shoulder as the driver tried to hold against the van. The gunner couldn't get a shot past him, struggling with the wheel. Then the car reached a rise over a culvert at a wash, no concrete guard over it, so the right wheels went off into air. The right side of the car dropped into space as Craig wrenched the van back onto the road into the bend to the left.

Blur of red. The car started its roll, airborne, the right front touching down, then cartwheeled, slammed into an oak tree, top first, at about sixty miles an hour. Doors flew open, airbags exploded. The car wrapped itself around the big tree with its underside out, wheels spinning, and stuck there. Small limbs rained down.

Both of us stopped. Craig had the shotgun aimed. Forget airbags protecting them: there wasn't room left from that crushed-in top for two hands, palms together. A lot of blood around, but no explosion. Yet.

Things had flown out the doors. A gun. Maps. Pieces of car, and other pieces I didn't want to think about. *Try not to gag.*

"Let's roll, girl. I'll call nine-one-one...one-car crash. We need to be gone. Now!"

"Yeah. And wasn't that...?"

"John Black. Other one had to be the housebreaker. We'll stop where US 71 goes north. Now, before anybody comes."

I got my tight little ass into my Jeep and outta there.

~ * ~

I can't claim I was cool and calm about seeing two people smashed flat. One of them I'd worked with just a couple hours before, after all. But there was relief, too, as if a little of the apprehension that'd marked our days was gone. Not like we were in the clear, no, but even with the need to pull up stakes, no goodbyes, no traces, at least we were *doing* something. *Yeah, running again.* I'd Miss Big Bill, Irvin, Luther, and our landlords a lot. But our hides were top priority. Had to be.

If Craig was having misgivings about shoving those two cretins off into pancake land, he wasn't showing it. Simple self-preservation: guy trying to get a bead on you after kicking in your door, you didn't stop to have a beer with him and talk things over.

And that little episode let us know just how serious the Webbmeister was about all of this. Somehow, Wes and Craig, by any other names, were in the cross-hairs.

*But Dirty John Black. Now how the hell…?* So, just like I'd thought we could maybe track back to Webb, he must've tracked us some way. Longest of long shots, but send what, information everywhere their empire reached? *Okay,* maybe he even had a picture from somewhere. So, hundreds—thousands?—of eyes out for us. All the way to little Aggie and Mr. Not-So-Clean, yeah.

And Baltimore. Not that distant a connection after all.

We sat in a restaurant off US 71 headed toward Fayetteville and Missouri. Still shaking some. Pushing food down that wasn't quite ready to go there. Figuring it out. Or trying to.

The van had red paint streaked down its right side and some major gouges. Need to lose it, soon's we could. Dump it? Sell it? The cops didn't want us for anything, so…Or did they? They'd see the white paint on what was left of that car, get to doing their detecting thing, surely.

"Gotta dump the van," Craig's mind was paralleling mine. "Let's cram everything into the Jeep if it'll go, maybe hafta burn the rest."

Damn. We'd put several thou into that van, and not like we had a lotta cash on us to travel on. Had to be a better way…

"Okay, we abandon it, we lose. They trace it to Lee and David. We sell it for what we can get, they trace it to Lee and David. So let's sell it for what we can. Oh, can Nate get us more new I.D.?"

"Hope so. I'll call…No, it's late there. Do it in the morning. And yeah, we hole up in Fayetteville a few days, like in Ohio. Give Nate what we can about the druggies, which isn't much, though."

"I'm guessing Baltimore's the hub, but the Webb won't be that obvious. Wish we could've learned something from Late John. Suppose the narcs could sweat Aggie?"

"Maybe. But she'll disappear. Yeah, I better go ahead and get Nate out of bed about her now."

He punched numbers on my new phone. Hour later there, but he got him. Craig filled him in. Where to find Aggie. The possible photograph, all we had. Not code talk: too vague, and this phone had to be clean. Didn't it?

"Go on to Joplin, though, man, up in Missouri. We can connect with you better there. Call you later tomorrow with details. And you two watch your backs. Don't know how many are out there."

*Oh, great.* Somehow I'd hoped it was only Webb and a couple others. And they were two down, now. Three, with Jerry the Slug out.

Would that realization cause them to back off, cut their losses? Or just make them more determined? Didn't know that one, and boy, were the stakes high now, with the bodies starting to pile up.

Anger, though. John the Dirty and I'd hit the job hard all day, side by co-worker side, and then he'd brought a hit man out to do us. Big time chickenshit. So maybe after our working together for months, he couldn't do it himself...still almost made it happen. And sweet Aggie would probably have pulled the trigger herself, if the crewcut badass hadn't shown up to do it. Things sure as hell weren't what they seemed. Yeats again: *My rhymes more than their rhyming tell.*

We stayed in a motel in the mountains and drove on up to Joplin next morning. Got our money transferred to a bank there. That was risky, we knew, but hadda have the bucks, and we took it all in cash. Then we found a body shop guy who paid us about half what the van was worth. He planned to do the metal work and paint, then resell it. Best we could do. The essentials fit into the Jeep if we didn't breathe deep, and we gave the rest to the Salvation Army.

Nate arranged a second set of I.D. papers. He reported that the narcs had caught Aggie Black packing. They'd gone with a warrant, and seized a real stash there. So they'd try to squeeze information out of her, hope it'd lead them to the top. Doubtful, but that's the naïve thought I'd had, too.

We were now Crane Lewis and Jean Dodson. I'd wanted the single thing again for a coupla reasons. First, like I said, I wasn't ready for actual marriage yet, even to this great guy. And second, in a twisted way, when I *was* ready, I wanted to do it right. Real names and all, out in the open. Sloppier to do if you're already supposedly there: keep the names the same and all.

Just not neat.

# Thirteen

"So, Jeannie, where d'you want to go this time?" *Oh, have to get used to the new name. Again.*

I'd asked myself that same question, of course, and had expected some sort of direction from my private inner guide, but nothing'd come. Maybe this running and hiding stress was numbing my receptors. Didn't like that thought much. Didn't like any of this. But we had to land somewhere.

"Got a coupla friends east of here I helped put up a cabin a few years ago. They almost never use it anymore...kids never liked it and grown now. Back in the boonies. No electricity, no plumbing, on a nice creek, National Forest Wilderness area next to it, thousands of acres of woods. You up for going to ground for a bit?"

"You're talking smoky kerosene lamps and carrying wood and water, aren't you? Could get old."

"Yeah, probably wanta leave before winter. Get snowed in on that non-road. Which wouldn't be bad, except we'd hafta get out to work somewhere."

"Oh, that. Well, let's do it for a while. Winter comes, there won't be construction work, though." He was right. I'd had to wait tables over the cold months more than once. Well, do it again if I had to...

We looked up my friends, Trish and Tom Mallory in Springfield, to see about the cabin. Sure, we could use it. They'd been part of a group of friends some years back who'd divided up a big piece of land, and some of them had built getaways. Trish and Tom were artists: he a teacher and she in commercial stuff. They'd wanted the cabin for a place to escape to with their then-teenage kids. Trish now had granny glasses and was seeing their kids leaving home, and Tom was the stereotype artist: focused, sometimes in another world, just taught classes to support his sculpture habit. They were as glad to see us as if years hadn't gone by.

"We'd want to rent it, maybe for several months," I explained. "See if we wanta stay in the area. I know Branson's still booming, at least in the summer, so we just might, if things work out."

"Say," Tom had an idea. "We're thinking of building a summer house up in Michigan. You wanta buy the creek place? We built it mostly for a place to go with the kids, but they went with us what, Trish, only a half-dozen times?"

"Buy it?" Umm. Hadn't thought of that. But no bucks for it, unless Craig's place in Virginia sold. I threw him a look. He shrugged. I knew they had about twenty acres. Good a place as any to stay disappeared; I couldn't think of any way the Weird Webb could get to us there.

"Hey, maybe. Can we do a month-to-month rent, see where this might go?"

They were okay with that. Craig was Crane to them, but of course I was still Wes. Shouldn't matter: no drug ring there, even if it surely was rampant twenty miles away in Branson, with all the music venues and outside-the-lines influence.

It was 60 miles south, off crooked Highway 160 east out of Forsyth. A half mile of ledgerock limestone and scrub cedars down to the cabin, which sat in dense cover. Below it was more woods, then a grown-up field and the clear creek I remembered. Some smallmouth bass in it, I told Craig, and a bigger creek maybe another half mile on down. He liked that. Sure, bigger bass, or does it work that way?

Water would be a hassle. The creek was 200 yards down, and you don't drink creek water anymore, what with cow piss upstream. The Mallorys had arranged for water in containers from an older couple who had the land above them. They'd stop on the way in and fill up at their well for the weekends they'd stayed. I knew the Macks there, liked them a lot, and had helped with their livestock. Might work.

We stopped and visited with them a while, glad to see them and they were glad to see us. It'd been too long, and I remembered how much time I'd spent with them before.

Anyway, the cabin looked like it had always been there. It was old oak logs, moved from a remote ridge in Arkansas and reconstructed here. Glenn Armitage, the guy I'd worked with around here, was friends with the Mallorys, so we had been in on the house-raising, and they'd hired us for the finishing.

"Wow," Craig took in the cedar porch posts, the close-laid stone foundation, the chimney, the aged logs, the hand-forged hinges. I took some pride in it all, having done a lot of this very work with my own skilled little hands.

You parked and walked the last hundred feet to the high porch, and unless you knew the cabin was there, it was hidden. I liked that, too. We'd be about as invisible as two people could get.

We let Cyrano stake this new territory, and laid out provisions. Water in two five-gallon containers, non-perishables to go into the mouse-proof enameled cabinets. Partial loft above had a ladder to it, and a rail to keep sleepwalkers corralled up there instead of down face-first eating the floor.

Privy out back, which in spite of my back-to-the-earth bent, I didn't like. But we could scrub up in the creek for another month or so till it got icy, and it was very private. After that, it'd be hauling water to heat in a zinc washtub. Maybe we could rig a shower of sorts. Hell, we were builders, weren't we? And the pioneers had managed. Forever. So maybe they didn't smell good, so what?

We tramped the property lines, which went to the creek on two sides where it made a sharp bend. Across the road in, there was a sixty-foot cliff down to woods and the water. I showed Craig how you could step off into the top of a tall oak that grew close, then climb down. Good swimming hole there, and those bass you could see under ledges on the other side. Glenn and I'd hit the creek a lot that summer we'd done the cabin, and this was lots closer than hiking down, across the creek, then up it.

I could tell he was thinking this would be a helluva place to own, even as a weekend hideaway. The necessities, wood and water, would be a grind, but who needed electricity? Cell phones worked, thanks to a new tower up the hill on a high peak (called a knob, there) above the highway. And of course, we'd both used generators on jobsites for years.

"What about a well and septic system?" I read his thoughts.

"Could get a drill rig to the upper part, okay. Hafta rent a backhoe for the septic. Find a place where there's enough soil to perc over the ledge rock." That was okay...we both did backhoe.

And of course, you could still buy those gas refrigerators for a price, and a gas water heater, stove... maybe we *would* make a deal with the Mallorys.

"Need a water storage tank uphill, though," Craig went on. "Use a generator to pump it full, then gravity. Bury it so it doesn't freeze. Yeah, we could do it."

"And if we do, we should, before winter."

"So, I'll call Alan and see if there's any hope for the house sale. If not, we tough it out for as long as you want to."

Hey, I'd live in a cave with this man. But the work situation was a real factor. I remembered the Macks telling me they'd driven out every day for many years to jobs, till their retirement. Get old, that.

~ * ~

Karl Kramer reported in to his boss Barker Webb, that his partner, Denny of the crewcut, along with a minor guy, John Black out in Arkansas, had managed to get themselves wasted. And that the couple Webb wanted had disappeared again.

"Car wreck. Accident, cops are sayin', but we both know that's bullshit. Pair of marks don't just fade the same night our guys get wiped without a connection."

"Damn. Those two are getting expensive. Anything else?"

"Narcs got Black's woman with a good stash. Word is she's sayin' it was all Johnny. They'll try to pump her, but they got no case. He's dead...she'll walk."

"But they'll watch her. There goes that branch, for now. Do we need her back in Baltimore?"

"Nah, got too many already."

"Then let her dangle. She doesn't know enough to hurt us. Has no idea where we are now, either."

"Not unless one of the middle guys tells her."

"And that won't happen. Oh, keep sending the pictures out, Karl. It worked once. It'll work again."

*Yeah, and I wanta be the one gets to that girl first.*

~ * ~

Craig's brother'd had a lowball offer on the house, we learned, which he knew we wouldn't want to take, so hadn't called. Craig agreed; we weren't in a hurry, if we could rough it. And the bad guys couldn't know which way we'd jumped, so we felt pretty safe with the status quo. Besides, we both hoped we could go back there someday.

I spent some time up the hill with Kelcy Mack, canning and freezing vegetables from their great garden while Craig looked for work. Good PR, and I said I liked her a lot. She had white hair and granny glasses, too, a sunburned face and hands harder than mine. She and Charlie would live there, she told me, till they carted them off feet first. Kids and grandkids all gone off to St. Louis and Kansas City, and didn't visit often. They ran cows on fields up there and on one long one down on their part of the creek. I liked the sound of the cattle, and the fuzzy new calves would break your heart.

It was Kelcy who told me my old carpenter buddy Glenn was still around. Glenn Armitage. Gee, I'd thought he'd headed west. I owed him for finding the Mallory job for us that time I'd been penniless in Harrison, some miles southwest in Arkansas.

"Oh, he wanted to leave," Kelcy told me, "but you know the old saying: once you drink Ozark branch water, you'll always come back. And here *you* are, too."

Glenn's significant other had dumped him, and he'd been bummed with this country—or maybe with everything. Anyway, he was a good guy. Be nice to look him up, Craig—*Crane*—and me, for a beer sometime. Kelcy said he was still doing construction at the resorts and music venues in Branson. But I knew that unless things had changed, that'd dry up in the winter.

Craig didn't find any work at first, so we spent some quality time hiking and fishing. I never got past the frustration of hooking tree limbs behind me, or snagging roots underwater and losing flies. Hey, some of us aren't destined to be Izaak Walton, okay?

I snared some books from the library in county seat Forsyth, and we read to each other by lamplight. Now that very soon becomes the stuff memories are made of: soft light, sounds of cicadas outside, the occasional hoot of an owl. Craig's low voice, with just enough Virginia in it to knock the edges off the words. He liked to compliment me, too, on what he called my kissing the vowels. I get dreamy, remembering.

He kept finding cheap short-term work he was way overqualified for.

"I did hear of something neat, though, if it happens. Some lawyer wants to restore—duplicate, really—a big Victorian house up a little creek north of Branson some famous artist had a hundred years ago. I'll track down the architect, see if something's there."

"Sounds fun. Forsyth's closer, though. Kelcy tells me the restaurants will stay open through October. Guess I'll see about that."

"A real waste of your talents, my dear, not to mention your college degree. Maybe you should teach."

"Redneck kids fine literature? Nah. Besides, I didn't take all those required education courses: child psych, public school art, theory of this and that." There was a small college nearby, but they'd want a PhD. And a transcript in my real name. "Let's see if the Victorian thing gets going and maybe we can go as a team."

Turned out it did, but no, *we* couldn't: my plumbing wasn't right (thank God again). Craig got on as a lead man, but the contractor didn't even want to talk to me. Chauvinism alive and strutting, even though I was used to it (still pissed me off). The job would be under roof and dried in before the cold weather, so it'd go on through the winter. Okay for my breadwinner, even with the long drive, 'cause the bucks were good.

Then I got this idea: why not talk the Mallorys into springing for the well and septic at the cabin? Be worth a lot more when they did sell it, to us or somebody else. Give it a try. I could dig the hole for the tank and do the trenches. And Craig did plumbing. Hated it, but he'd done it when necessary. Even had a license, from back when he was starting his business and had to do a lot of everything himself.

"How much would that cost?" the Mallorys' obvious question, and yeah, always the hardest one to answer in construction of any kind.

"If we get a good water flow in a couple hundred feet, about ten grand total, with the generator for the pump and the septic. But then you'd want to build on a bathroom, too. And some kind of real kitchen."

"Um, we hadn't planned to spend any more on the cabin, Wes, with the other place in the works."

Okay, no job there. And—reality popping its ugly head up—when the road out of there got icy, Craig couldn't even get out to work. Unless we left the Jeep a half mile up on the highway and hiked. Maybe we oughta count on moving on before winter, after all. Except I liked it there, and where else would we find winter work anyway? Always a hassle in our chosen field.

This was all a real bummer, having to run from Virginia and Craig's business, his great house, contacts, all because we stumbled across a crooked lawyer/drug lord. Yeah, who now wanted to blow us away. Well, maybe if we *could* tough the winter out, things'd cool down by spring.

But what, then? Go back to Virginia and take our chances? Never know when some goon might off us? (I could picture some—any—ordinary guy in any ordinary situation, like just walking toward us on a sidewalk, suddenly pulling a gun and blasting us.)

Didn't like that picture.

So, tread water, I guessed, till something changed in the equation. Wasn't change the only constant in life? Dumb precept. No help at all.

~ * ~

Samantha Webb had just about starved on what she'd made waiting tables. The tips were all that'd saved her, along with the sale of some of her jewelry. But thank God, or whoever, the parents had managed to find each other again through whatever grapevine Dad had going, and the money was coming in again. They hadn't told her where they were, fearing the cops would track her down and squeeze her.

Oddly enough, those guys hadn't even come after her, although that'd seemed like a logical course. Jerry'd always said how dumb the police were, and maybe he'd been right. Lotta good it'd done him, though, the way things turned out.

But it didn't really matter. Dad at least was willing to keep her there till things happened for her. And yeah, maybe she'd have to give up the idea of an acting career, like most of the others she knew. So okay, she was starting to look a little more seriously at the men she met, though most of them in the theater were either gay or broke. Creative, fun, but broke. Maybe she'd have to go back to Baltimore and start looking up old boyfriends to see which ones had made it big.

But not yet. No, if the parents were okay with her staying the course, that's what she'd do. For a while longer, anyway. And if they got themselves new identities and a new place, maybe it'd be somewhere she could join them, have a little family life again. Couldn't be all bad; with Jerry gone for good, they'd certainly appreciate her more.

~ * ~

In Pittsburgh, the carpenter Phil had finally agreed with his brother that Wesley Whitestone had to be the one who'd stolen the money meant for the ill-fated remodel business.

"She was here all the time," Sid had said so many times. "Had a key, could have come back any time you were gone, ransacked the place. I know you don't wanta believe it, but she shot you down, bro. All of us, really."

"Doesn't seem to be any other explanation. But she put her own money into the business, Sid. She wasn't a gold digger."

"Maybe just to fool you. And it wasn't that much, you remember. Anyway, the hundred Gs disappears, then she disappears. Open and shut."

"Maybe. But nothing we can do about it. No telling where she is. Months ago was going west, all I know..."

"So she *told* you. You know any of her family? Friends? Anybody she'd go to, or who'd know where she is?"

"Already called her brother in Atlanta. She hasn't been in touch with him. Never close, those two, anyway, she said."

"How about places she worked? You said she had all those references...maybe she's checked in with some of those."

"Only one I remember was that guy Glenn out in Missouri she worked with that time, friend of a friend. And he's supposed to've gone out to the Coast after his girlfriend dumped him. I dunno, Sid, you may be right about Wes, and I suppose you are, but it's just a dead end, seems like."

~ * ~

Things just weren't happening, as far as work went for me. This late, the people who had those seasonal jobs weren't about to let them go, since they'd dry up in a couple months anyway. So unless I got lucky and somebody else didn't, I couldn't get his or her job.

So I continued to hike a whole lot of National Forest non-trails with my wilderness partner, who thought this was the way to live. He could track all sorts of creatures I wasn't even aware existed, chase anything that'd run from him, bark as loud and long as he wanted without my shushing him, and lie on the floor and do absolutely nothing after a day of it. Craig was bringing home the figurative bacon, and said don't sweat the job thing, but I was getting antsy, as usual.

One pastime we took up was target shooting. Craig said that, since we were on the run and didn't know when the next crisis might arise, I should know how to shoot. Somehow, that was something Dad and I'd never done.

We told the Macks we'd be banging away some, so they wouldn't think we had a young war going down there. Or that we'd been making moonshine and were being raided by revenuers. They were cool with that, since Charlie kept a shotgun handy: the deer ate their garden; they ate the deer.

"Shotgun's only good up close," Craig pointed out. "It'll blow a hole in anything within a hundred, hundred-fifty feet, you saw in Russellville, but then the pellets lose force, spread out wider. Good for bird hunting, squirrels, small game, and you're more apt to hit the target with the wide pattern." He showed me how to hold it without blasting my shoulder off, hard against it to absorb the shock. I cut down on a paper plate tacked to a stump and actually hit it. Well, part of it. And up close, yes, I knew what it'd do: let a lot of daylight into just about anything that got in front of you.

Back further, I could see what he meant. We were shooting #4 shot, which he said was for geese or turkeys or medium-size predators. This time a few pellets hit the plate, but they just left individual holes, not massive destruction. He explained that with bigger buckshot, for deer, bears or deranged humans, even one of the swarm of lead balls flying out there could kill whatever or whomever it hit.

This gun wasn't my thing. We tried that giant revolver, and I felt like Wyatt Earp. How the hell did those guys ever whip that thing out of its holster and destroy each other with any kind of speed? Or was that just Hollywood? Maybe just plastic guns? I needed both hands just to hold it up and keep it from tearing my thumbs off with the recoil. Craig showed me how most shooters shoved the gun forward as they pulled the trigger to offset some of that. That action messed up my aim big time.

I realized why the two-handed stance, feet braced apart like in the action TV shows, was the preferred way to commit mayhem with a pistol. That is, if one had the leisure for it. (Hold it right there, Abdul, while I get set to blast your ass off). When surprised and having no time for the subtleties, it seemed you just pointed and triggered and hoped Abdul wasn't faster than you were.

I also realized that the preferred nine-millimeter automatics you read about and saw in those movies were probably a helluva lot more efficient than this cannon. Hey, this technology was 175 years out of date. Colorful, but clumsy. At least for me. Craig had practiced, and he could look almost like a Western sheriff keeping the peace (Drop it, Deadwood, or I'll ventilate yore black heart). I figured I'd just have to trust vicious Cyrano to protect me if and when the crunch came.

I did help Charlie Mack with haying and wood-cutting, but just as a neighborly thing to do. He was such a neat old guy: slow about everything he did, but got a huge amount of work done by the end of the day. Had these bushy eyebrows and deep-set brown eyes that twinkled a lot. Veins on his hands and arms that stood out, and lines like canyons in his face. Charlie loved a good joke, and was always passing them along. Some of them were clean, and all of them were funny. He and Kelcy were right up there with my favorite people in the world.

And I would ride with Craig to work, then drive over to Branson or haunt Forsyth in search of a job, but like I said, no luck. Springfield was a big town, and sure, we coulda both found jobs there, but that'd sorta be beside the point. We liked it on the creek, and wanted to stay.

# Fourteen

"Ever see these people?" the man from St. Louis asked the Branson guitar player, Derek. He scanned the photograph quickly; he was trying to get this difficult run just right, but this morning's hangover was making him fuzzy. Had to get it together before the dumb tourists got thick out there for the first set.

"Nope. Who're they?" He hoped the man would go away, but didn't want to blow him off: one of the movers. But he ran his fingers over the strings once anyway.

"Couple the big boss wants. These two on the end. Dunno the background, but he's hot to find 'em. Word I got was that he's sent these pictures out along every branch, all over."

"Must want 'em bad. They don't look like your typical junkies'd owe him money." The two were clearly construction workers, ordinary every way you cut it.

"Yeah, bad. So you get this one. Ask around, dig some. And just consider it part of your job, okay?"

That rankled Derek. Here these guys from uptown were, pushing the troops around, with their curt orders, like they didn't even need them, when they'd have nothing without the bodies in the field.

"So what's in it for me?" He'd never liked this particular middleman…give a punk like that a little authority, and he started throwing his weight around. Just like in business, which Derek hated just about more than anything. Business, that squeezed the little guy at the bottom while the fat cats at the top got all the gravy.

"Put it this way, shithead: you get your ass in gear, do like I say, and maybe I *won't* feed your eyeballs to the crows." He pulled a knife and a deadly blade flicked out. He reached, hooked a guitar string, jerked hard, and severed it with an electrified twang.

"Hey! What the…"

"So I'm gonna tell the boss you were just thrilled at your new assignment, right? Couldn't *wait* to start showing this pix around, asking. Doing your damn job. Ain't that the case, guitar man? I c'n tell him that, can't I?" The eyes were mean, the mouth twisted. The knife was just inches from Derek's eyes. Out of the corner of which he could see that nobody was around. Nobody. He gulped. His hands shook.

"Yeah, you got it, guy. I'm on it. Yeah, you c'n tell him…yeah." He was sweating.

The knife clicked shut.

"I knew I could count on you, Derek. You're the soul of cooperation, an' that's what I like about you. Oh, an' we ain't got a lotta time, th' boss says. He wants these two like yesterday."

~ * ~

Since Kelcy'd told me about Glenn Armitage, I'd had one of my insistent alerts: we shouldn't look him up. Now, that didn't make a damn bit of sense, and I attributed the warning to the uncertainty, anxiety, a too-cautious reaction to recent events. Hell, Glenn had been a good friend who'd actually rescued me from near bottoming-out that time. Sure we'd get together with him.

So we did, and a girl he'd met since he hadn't gone west. Reenie was an upbeat dynamo who did things with computers at the hospital in Branson, Glenn told us while we waited for her at a restaurant. He'd changed little in four years, still into outdoor stuff, working enough to support his kayaking and camping habits. Didn't really like the commercial construction he was doing, but he could take it. I wondered if he'd ever outgrow his wilderness streak. Probably not.

Reenie breezed in, all blue eyes and blonde-ness, energy and suntan, gave Glenn a hug, then registered Craig and me.

"Hey, people, I'm Reenie Wilkes, this incredibly lucky man's dream. You're Wes and Crane, right? You look familiar, some way. Ever been to Chicago?" All in one breath.

"Only through there on the way to someplace else," Craig told her, "but if we'd known you were there, we'd have stopped." That grin. Was I gonna hafta start keeping tabs on my hunk?

"Oh, smooth man. You in politics?"

"Not yet, but maybe that's next."

I liked her: brash. Pulled you in. I guessed former homecoming queen, but how bad is that, really? And Glenn obviously adored her. Maybe it'd last, this time. The girlfriend I remembered had come from money and, as it turned out, was only experimenting with the simple life. Got tired of his round-the-clock outdoors existence. Went off with more money: a young financial tycoon. To a demanding career as a trophy wife, I guessed. Nasty job, but well, somebody's gotta do it, right?

Reenie was tall like Glenn, and it was soon clear she could handle her own kayak or climbing rope. Like to have her on my construction crew. It took us about five minutes to become best friends, and my radar said yeah, that was the way to go. She'd done the knocking-around-the-country bit, too, but loved these mountains. And planned to stay till they dragged her away. Another Kelcy Mack in the making.

She should be so lucky.

We had a great dinner, then went to a decent music show by one of those semi-retired performers who'd put in a few token appearances here every season to keep her name before at least part of the public. Good singer still, but when her grandson joined her onstage, you noticed the wrinkles.

Glenn and Reenie both fished, so Craig invited them to the creek. Water low this late in the season, but he knew the bass would hide under the ledges and come out for the right fly at the right time for the right angler. Not me. Just not the right stuff.

It was on that visit the following Sunday that things started falling apart. Again. They drove down in Glenn's vintage Land Rover, and Reenie seemed even perkier than her usual bubbling over. She loved the hideaway cabin, and of course knew by then I'd worked on it with Glenn.

"Get me a piece of ground, you can build me one just like it. Won't even want a road in…hike into a dark hollow somewhere nobody can ever find it. My idea of heaven." She gave Glenn an elbow in the ribs, and he got this foolish grin on.

We took beer and food in an ice chest to the creek and started enjoying the day. There was a place just below a rapid that had these huge boulders up out of the water you could wade to. Moss on top, the perfect place to stretch out and watch birds gliding, or shut your eyes and hear bees humming nectar into their socks. The sound of that crystal water would put a dedicated insomniac out.

Reenie's bright laugh floated off up the bluff across the wide creek. I told her we used to go further back up across the old field and shout insults, which would come back to us as echoes. So, of course we had to do that today, and it gave us all the giggles. We'd hurl jibes at our least favorite movie stars and politicians, and most of the time agreed on just who those were…fun.

"Hey," she raised a finger later in the day. "I was sure I knew you two. Or I should say a guy I know does."

"Yeah? Who's that?"

"Oh, friend of a friend, really. Name's Derek Sigel. Guy out at the theme park. Had this picture of you on some construction job…"

Picture. Oboy: I'm going into shock. Another tentacle of the Webb ring? Hadda be.

"Small world," Craig put in. "Don't recognize the name, though." He sent me a glance, wanted to know more. "Where'd he say he knew us from?"

"Dunno that. Just was asking around. Must've worked with you on a project somewhere? He couldn't seem to remember your names, though."

"Could be. He in construction?"

"Well no, he's in a band. From St. Louis, I think. They do atmosphere stuff during the season at the theme park. But he knew you were carpenters."

Damn. How big *was* the Webb web? This was not a coincidence. From St. Louis. Could that be where J. Barker was holed up? Good a place as any, I guessed. And close enough to have a pipeline right to Branson. My face must've registered my concern.

"Rackin' the brain, Wes? I guess you guys must work with a bunch of people all over the country, right?"

"Oh, yeah. But guy in a band? Maybe does carpentry on the side..."

"Could be. Dunno many musicians who can support their habit without a day job."

Habit. Yeah, easy a drug connection. I was getting the picture, literally: send out enough photographs like that, however he'd come by them, and law of averages, somebody sometime would surely recognize us. *Oh, damn.* I shot Craig a look. He rolled his eyes, shrugged.

We managed a good time that day, anyway. But both of us knew Reenie or somebody else who'd seen us would sooner or later let it slip who and where we were, in complete innocence. Or not. The Webb probably had a price on our heads by then, and where there's honey, there're flies. Big, nasty green flies that materialize out of nowhere soon's they smell whatever's rotten. And no, we couldn't confide in anybody. Being hunted had to keep on being lonely business.

But yeah, no need to panic yet. Enjoy the day, which could be our last here. I showed them the now-only-trickling waterfalls up a side branch, the view up a steep trail on a point of land above where that brook came into the main creek. Wave after blue wave of hills off to what must be the end of the world. Other sights, of which this place had plenty. And of course, that step off the bluff into space to land in the oak tree. That was the *piece d'resistance*, and we did it about a dozen times each, laughing like fools.

"Just gotta avoid that logical first limb...it's dead. Been meaning to cut it off, but we don't do this every day." Charlie Mack had originally shown me the place. He'd gone that way to tend his cows when he was younger. Saved him driving down, fording the creek twice to get to his bottom-land field. And that was just the kind of thing he and Kelcy'd loved, stepping into space, shinnying down six stories.

No fish that day, even with the oncoming dark, when Craig said fish come out to bite flies. Not. But we grilled steaks on the gravel bar and produced some acceptable off-key campfire singing. Along with dips in the creek by starlight that night. I hadn't gone skinny-dipping in years, and was afraid Craig might not go for it. Wrong. Turned out he was up for anything I was. Reenie's shrieks echoed off the bluff, and probably scared hell out of all the wildlife for miles.

During all this fun, I was trying not to think we'd have to blow town again, just as we were getting to enjoy this place, the people, what coulda been a life. Stuff like that kept creeping into my head, spoiling our time. I hoped our acting job was convincing, all the way to grinning like fools and waving goodbye to them, late. Didn't breathe easy till we saw the Rover's taillights disappear around a bend.

"Well, guy, do we evaporate now, or chance a few more days here? No doubt the Webb has some picture of us he's sent out on the territory, and we've probably been seen up close by about five thousand people since we came here."

"Easy that. No, we can't push our luck. But I will go to the job tomorrow, collect my pay. You be ready by early afternoon, okay? I'll leave at noon, tell 'em there's a crisis back home, wherever the hell that is now." He was pissed, but no more than I was. When would these bastards give up? How many more neat places would we have to leave before we could disappear completely? Find a life somewhere, even if it was in what, Ecuador? Nah, didn't know Spanish, and neither did Craig. Or maybe it was Portuguese? Didn't matter.

Only good part of it was, we wouldn't have to fight this icy road in winter. But that wasn't a lot of consolation.

# Fifteen

The stereotype wise-guy Karl called his boss in St. Louis. He'd heard from the music dude in Branson, who it seemed knew everybody there. No, he hadn't exactly seen the couple himself, but two storekeepers remembered them clearly. That was enough, he and Webb—Parker Goode—agreed. It was time for him to go hunting.

"Just ask around, Karl. Locate them. We can get you backup when you find them. Don't want to lose another good man. And try hard to find that money."

"Hell, boss, I can handle it myself." Karl thought of himself as a pro, and had the record to prove it. The higher-ups wanted something fixed, he was the man.

"Listen: MacDonnell broke Jerry's arm that time when he had a gun on him, and we don't know just how he took out Denny and John Black, but he did."

Karl was sure he could take two rube carpenters, but he agreed, mostly to get the boss to drop it. Hell, they'd just been lucky so far. And luck wouldn't protect them from a pro. Do the dude first, then take his time with that tight-looking piece. She'd cough up the money all right, too, after he'd worked her over enough.

~ * ~

Didn't take me long to put our stuff in boxes next morning after Craig left. We'd hardly unpacked. And there wasn't that much.

He'd been worried about leaving me alone for the few hours, but I reminded him of my attack dog and the fact that it'd be hard for the average vehicle to get down here. And I hadn't had any more warnings from my special angel or whatever. That might sound odd, but no, there was nothing predictable about that particular phenomenon.

"Oh, yeah. But keep the pistol close just in case, okay?" He'd kissed me then, and not just a quick peck. I was reminded that all this was, by damn, worth it. So we hadda run again. No matter, long as we had each other.

Yeah, my man and my dog: the necessities.

~ * ~

The gray car eased over the rocky non-road alongside a field where an old farmer was on a tractor raking hay. Then past a rough little farmhouse with a white-haired woman hanging clothes. She looked his way. *Damn,* Karl thought, *this's beyond th' boonies. Prob'ly the only car gone by in a month, way that old woman stared. An' no wonder, bad as this excuse for a road is.*

He checked the photograph again. *Foxy bitch.* One of the reasons he'd wanted to come on down here was the hope she'd be alone. The word he'd gotten from the music guy and his connections was that MacDonnell was working on a construction job under another name, but the girl wasn't. So maybe, if she was there, before the guy came home, he could have a little time with her. *Yeah, quality time.* That thought put a leer on his face.

*Shit. Gonna bottom out here, get stuck. Pull over and park it. Slip on down...can't be much further, if that old coot at the highway was right. Damn guitar player wouldn't come: tourist gig. Well, don't need the chickenshit, and yeah, it'll be sweeter this way...*

~ * ~

My cell rang. I'd gone down into the sunlight of the old field to get a shirt off the line I'd washed out in a big pan. Loved the smell the sun gave clothes.

"Wes? It's Kelcy. Gray car just drove down. Creepy looking dude inside. Thought you oughta know."

Omigod. *Omigod!*

"Thanks, Kelcy. One guy?"

"Yes. Won't make it far on this road. Watch yourself, okay?"

"Sure. Prob'ly just lost."

No, he wasn't lost. I punched off, started back toward the cabin. Gun was inside, of course. In the damn cabinet. Cyrano was nosing around after something somewhere down on the creek, hadn't been able to warn me. Nothing had warned me: no premonition, no guardian angel. Only that thing about avoiding Glenn...

And suddenly a big guy in a white shirt and suit pants materialized beyond the house, just a few feet past. I wouldn't make it up the steps. *How'd he get here so fast?*

I calculated: house, pistol were out. *What?* He was pretty close, on the path. And he'd seen me. Could pull a gun and hit me from there, no doubt. I'd have to play it cool.

And hope.

"Hey," I called, "how you doin'?" As friendly as I could manage. *Got to get inside, get to that gun.*

"Okay, but I guess I'm lost. Heard this was th' way to the creek." Yeah, she looked good, out here in these damn woods. Clean, natural, sort of, no bleached hair, makeup. *Yeah, clean...*

Just then Cyrano ran up, and I called him to me. Didn't want him getting shot if he sensed danger. Go for the guy's gun and die: he wasn't *that* well-trained.

"My dog's a little hyper. Better tie him up...he's bad to jump up on people. But yes, the creek's on down. You a fisherman?" Dumb question: this guy'd never seen a live fish; he was the stereotype hit-man, out of his element here. I could be wrong, but I knew I wasn't.

"Nah, just out sightseein'. Didn't expect it to be so rough. Hadda leave my car up where the road got bad. Say, could I get a drink of water? Hot out here."

Okay, I could get into the house, but he'd be right on me. Not a good choice, but neither was this. He could waste me and my dog in a flash out here.

"Sure, come on in. I'm Jean Dodson. My guy Crane'll be back soon...he's off this afternoon." *Stall for time, any way I have to.* And just maybe he hadn't found out my real name.

*Nah, he won't be here, bitch. He'll come at the end of th' day, and that'll give us time for just about everything...*

"I'm Karl Kramer. Down from St. Louis to meet some suits out at the theme park on a deal. Got here early, and heard at this little store this creek was a great place. Get away from business for a while." *Keep it friendly; make sure she doesn't grab any hardware.*

We were inside. No chance to go for the cabinet. I took cold water out of the ice chest, poured us both a glass. Maybe throw it in his face, get a few seconds. But what, then? *No, keep playing for time.* I glanced at my watch. *Not long, now.* Craig would be here, and that oughta distract him maybe enough...

"So you're what, part of the entertainment stuff out at the park? They got great music out there."

"Not exactly, but yeah, we're into all sorts of things." He was checking the place out, looking for anything dangerous. I sensed he was about to push it.

And he did. He set the glass down, smiled this crooked, ugly face-twister, and everything changed.

"Okay, girl. You might as well know I'm here for *you*, if you ain't guessed it yet, and I think you have. So let's just stop playin' games." He took out a picture of the construction crew in front of the Webb house and plopped it onto the work table. Craig and me, grinning. So any doubts I might've had were dashed. *But keep on with it, girl. And the only thing you've got to work with here is your ass...*

"Okay, no games, Karl. And what I said about Crane coming home? Not true. He works till four-thirty. So we've got us some time. Tell me what you've got in mind." I ran my eyes over him, the way I hoped a horny groupie might.

God, he was ugly.

"That's better. An' what I got in mind? I think you know th' answer to that. I think maybe that's why you tied your big dog outside. I know your guy's a lot older'n you, and I also think you're th' kind of woman would appreciate a real special time for a change. Am I right?" Leer. Ugly leer.

*Okay, don't let it show how repulsive this bastard is. Play along till...*

"Y'know, Karl, you're one of those rare guys can read a woman right. But there's something I gotta know first, if you'll tell me. Why is Webb so hot to get to us? I mean, only thing I did was go out to his stable to see a horse, back in Virginia, and all this firepower he pulls? Just whatthehell's all this about?"

"Like you didn't know? Playing dumb? Well, half a million might sound like chickenshit change to you, woman, but my boss, he don't forget a thing like that. And whatever's left of it, I want it, y'know? But we'll get to that later, you'n me. Won't we?"

"Half a million?" I was understandably shocked. "You think we'd be living in this hole if we had that kinda green? Hell, we only got a beat-up Jeep, Karl, and I don't get to go anywhere. Washing things like this shirt by hand? We don't know a damn thing about any half million bucks."

"So you say. But like *I* said, we can work on that later, after you'n me have ourselves a little fun. Right?"

"Okay, right." *Shift back into the role, here.* "And you got no idea how clueless most men are, and don't give a shit what we women really need." I raked him with my eyes, smiled. But just how seductive can a girl look when she's scared shitless and about to puke on top of it?

~ * ~

But he smelled a rat, being one. Wasn't buying it. And sure enough, he reacted just the way a guy like that would.

*Whoa, this is goin' too easy. Watch it, here: she's tryin' to pull somethin'.* He reached, grabbed the girl's wrist, shoved her against the wall, turned aside so she couldn't get a knee into his groin. She didn't resist. Her eyes had just gone wide...had he read her wrong? *No, be sure.*

He slapped her, ripped her shirt half off. She didn't fight back then, either.

"Hey, you don't hafta get rough, Karl. Whatthehell? I'm not givin' you any shit, man." *You son of a bitch! That'll cost you big time. And damn, did that hurt.* But I wasn't going to let him see that. No tears, no weakness...

"Just makin' sure you don't. I can waste you in a heartbeat, bitch." He took a very large and very sinister gun out of the belt at his back, waved it. "Now, get over to that couch."

"Hey, there's a bed up in the loft. If we're gonna do this, let's do it right..."

"Nah, get trapped up there. I wanta keep my eyes open. Now!"

"You really don't get it, do you, Karl. Hey, I'm *glad* you're here. What? You think I *like* it out here in the boonies? I want outta here in the worst way...no electricity, no plumbin', no car. No *life*. Okay, you got your orders, whatever they are, I can see that. So whattya expect, me to fight a big man with a gun? That'd be dumb as hell, and I'm not that dumb.

"Now, if you and me can talk, maybe work something out between us, I got no problem with a little roll in the hay. I been putting up with second-class sex too long." (Sorry, Craig). I looked him up and down again. "Or maybe you're not the man you look like?" *Prick this prick's pride.*

"Now that sure as hell ain't th' problem. So, you wanna do it right? I'll show you *right,* bitch." He laid the gun on the table, but within easy reach, loosened his belt. Eyes hungry.

I slipped the rest of my shirt off. He slid one pants leg down, then bent, kicked off his loafer, but had his eye on his gun. I reached back as if to unsnap my bra, never taking my eyes off him. Trying to look sexy, which was one helluva stretch, just then, my face still burning. I switched to the metal button on my jeans instead, tugged at it like it was tight. He kicked off the other shoe, slid the leg free, balanced on the other foot.

*Now!*

I hurled the glass of water in his face, hard, knocking his gun off the table in my haste, and shot out that back door like the proverbial arrow.

He roared, sputtered. Cyrano barked.

I ran.

Bolted for the bluff, dodging. Behind me, too soon, a shot, wild, loud. Then there was scrub cedar between us. If I could get down the magic tree, I could maybe lose him. Damn, it was further than I'd remembered...

I lunged into space, caught the right limb. Avoid the bad one, but get *down* this mother...

I could hear that he was somehow above me already. Wow, he was fast for a city slob. I was screened in leaves, moving as fast as I dared. Six stories of nothing below me...

He stuck the gun in his belt, hesitated only an instant, seeing the way, then stepped out, reaching.

The dead limb snapped.

*"Holy shiiit!"* he screamed, and crashed past me, arms flailing. Caught on his side for an instant on another limb, screamed again. Hadda crush ribs. Fell right through that one, breaking smaller limbs below.

When he hit the rocks at the bottom, it was a smash, a crunch. I peered down in the silence. Head at a crazy angle, pouring blood and some awful blue stuff. Gun ten feet away. Heads don't turn that way on live people. Owls, maybe. Wave of nausea. *Oh, shit, girl, don't pass out up here.*

I climbed down, stepped around the mess, got the gun. No, he wouldn't move...half his head was almost gone. I'd have puked for sure this time if I hadn't been so scared. And angry.

"Good enough for you, *bastard.*" Then I thought of something. Went through his pockets, with the gun on him, just to make sure. St. Louis I.D. Probably fake? The picture of us, which I kept. I wiped off any of my prints on the rest, pressed his fingers on stuff, his hand onto the gun all over. I was so focused I forgot to lose it.

I punched Craig's number.

"Get your sweet ass home, *now*, love. We got another body, and I want us gone before we call the cops."

"A...*body?* What...?"

"Not now. Everything's cool, including him. You'll pass his car on the road down. He was alone. Another of Webb's."

"I'm outta here. Damn, I *knew* I should have…"

"*Not now!* Just get here, before I lose it." Actually, I was still icy calm. Didn't know how long that'd last, though.

I did know Kelcy would worry. And want to call somebody when she knew. Okay, hike up, stall her. I climbed the tree, trying not to think of falling on that pile of shit down there. Found my dog waiting faithfully at the cabin, again thankful he hadn't been there to try to protect me and get shot.

Reflected as I put the clean shirt on: guy wasn't too sharp. So he gets me. What then? Wait for Craig to come home? The Macks would check in, for sure. But no, I guessed citizens where he was from didn't get involved.

I got this picture of Charlie Mack riding hell for leather down on his tractor, shotgun loaded. I loved those people.

At their place, a little out of breath, told Kelcy the guy'd wandered past, down to the creek, and I'd gotten shaky, wanted company.

"But I heard a shot."

"Yeah, that's what spooked me. Shooting at snakes, maybe. Dumb tourist, I guess. Didn't wanta be down there with him.

"Oh, and Crane just called. He got word his mom's had a stroke back in Virginia. He's coming home now; we'll hafta go on back there, take care of her."

"Oh, we'd hoped you'd stay this time, Wes, since Crane found that job. He's such a nice guy."

"Guess we won't this time. Get some cash, we'd like to buy Trish and Tom out, come back. You know, that Ozarks branch water." I hugged her.

I was saying goodbye to Charlie when I heard the Jeep coming. Hugged him too, ran out and waved Craig down.

"You okay?" He was checking me out all over.

"Relatively, yeah. Okay, just room to get past the evil one's car. His I.D.'s St. Louis, so I'm guessing, with the music guy's connection, that's where the Webb monster is now."

"Could be. So okay, how'd you do it? The hit guy?"

He had a strong arm around me, guiding the Jeep over the ledges. And I was beginning to feel a reaction setting in, now that it was all past. *Not yet, girl: just hold it together.*

"Didn't, really. He'd made a move on me, sure you wouldn't be here. I got his eye off me, bolted out the door. He tried to follow me off the bluff, and the bad limb broke. The *he* broke. Bad." Picture of the remains again. *Stay down, stomach.*

I gave him more details while we put the stuff in the Jeep. *Déjà vu* once more. Showed him the picture of us grinning on the Virginia job. And I told him about the suspected half million.

"Wow! So that's why they haven't given up on us, Wes. The guy give you any specifics?"

"No, just that it was missing, and that the Webber thinks we have it. So okay, they won't give up then, no matter how far we run or where we hide. I've heard guys like that can get past anything but betrayal and missing cash. You know, the Godfather thing. Business."

"Nasty business, yeah. So did the Webb just make up that to tell his goons we'd robbed him, or do you suppose somebody else snatched it?"

"Doesn't make a particle of difference, since the hit team's after us. I remember there was a lot of green in that briefcase...pretty full. I'd say somebody else scored the bucks before Webb took it. We know now it wasn't Clyde. My guess is Jerry, but stealing from his own father? Coulda also been Samantha, I guess, same deal, or any of the drug chain. We don't know who was in on it."

"Yeah, all that cash is probably always a temptation for anybody who's got a finger in the pie. But like you said, whoever took it, we're suspects number one and two."

We drove out, waving to Charlie on his tractor. God, I'd miss those two. And this place. The creek, the cabin.

Even those fish that didn't want to get caught.

Once on the highway, we called 911 to report a missing person. No details, other than that a tourist must've wandered off, disappeared. Then, on that snaky Highway 160 east, we called Nate Peterson. Again.

"Webb's guys found us again, Nate," Craig told him. "Another one gone, fell off a cliff here out of Forsyth, Missouri. I.D. St. Louis, Karl Kramer, and we know another St. Louis guy's showing this picture of us, the crew from back on the Webb job, asking around. Might wanta get the narcs homed in there."

"Roger that. Sorry it happened again, but that picture'll be poison. Lotta drugs among the drifters around Branson, so it's not a stretch, there. Know where you'll go next?"

"With fall coming, construction'll be tough. We'll find us a hole somewhere, I guess. Like to come home, but know we can't, yet. Hope that'll change soon." Craig was not a happy camper. Neither was Cyrano, and I sure as hell wasn't.

Home, yeah. *Some* home, somewhere. But Virginia not safe yet. Good guys hafta ice the Webb first. Gwen too, probably, only how to do any of that?

Nate told us Clyde would head to St. Louis, undercover. Right outta a secret agent movie, that. Well, he was good; maybe he and somebody's army could do the job. Shades of Jason Bourne.

So again, what was next for us? I didn't have a clue, cruising east through that great country we had to leave, but seemed Craig had a plan. I was glad. The events of the last couple hours had about unnerved me. Take a while for the image of that broken piece of garbage to fade from my mind. So a few miles down the highway, he let me in on what had been going around in his mind.

"Wes girl, I'm gonna be an engineer again. Be easier to stay hidden."

"You hated that."

"I know, but we've just been lucky so far finding work. Without references or a following, construction will let us starve."

Didn't I know it.

"But you also hate computers. All of it's probably that, now."

"Oh, right. Well, there's maybe a place for a grunt the computer nerds turn their calculations over to. Somebody's gotta do the actual work." He didn't sound hopeful, but yeah, I doubted that anyone would make the connection: construction type lost in some high-rise among the other semi-white collars.

But I didn't want my man dreading going to work every morning. To do what? Be a machinist? Go around like a messenger boy with somebody else's drawings of bolts and wires for future power plants? Once you've been a free agent, so to speak, you're never really time-clock material again. And Craig had been the boss: hadda be worse. But that wasn't what was bothering me. Learning about that picture of us out there, yeah, and the maybe-fictitious 500 Gs, had changed the whole equation.

"No matter what we do this side of maybe Iceland, we're still targets for any of Webb's druggies armed with our picture, man of mine. No matter what our jobs are or where we land, we're not out of that spider's reach." It was almost a wail, and it signaled the first time I'd let this shit really get to me.

Think about it: it was only luck that'd saved us both times. If the crewcut clod in Arkansas or Dirty John had acted a few seconds earlier, he could've shot me easily from behind. Or put a slug into a tire and I'd probably have careened off the road instead of them. And Greasy Karl, if his I.D. name were right, just happened to be macho enough to try to do the Tarzan thing and break that strategic limb, and his head. Third time could be the biggie for us both.

I didn't want there to be a third time. We had to do something else till the wheels of the law crunched J. Barker Webb and company.

So I brainstormed our situation as the miles unrolled under the Jeep's wheels. And then I got an idea of my very own. Hey, it happens, even when I don't get the mysterious picture, or whatever it is.

And I sorta wondered why I hadn't thought of this one before. Just too wound up in basic survival, I guessed. You don't think clearly when you're frantically searching for a hole to crawl into and pull it in after you.

"Okay, love," I put it to Craig, who'd been silently acknowledging the futility of his latest scheme, "we do disguises. These guys don't know us. They've probably only got the one photo—you remember Gwen's taking it that time. So I become a blonde or a redhead with colored contacts, let my hair grow, and stay away from construction and welding…"

"And I shave my head and develop a smirk and become an insurance salesman? I don't think so."

"Maybe not that. But okay, for starters, what ideal situation would you really want to have if you could? If you had every choice in the world, no strings or crazed druggies in the picture?"

"Umm. Become a recluse up some dark hollow like Reenie said, grow a long beard, never change clothes, and go fly fishing every day."

"Besides that."

"Wes, you know I'd really like just to go on back to Virginia and pick up my—our—old life, do work we love, have the house we love. Each other we love. Out in the open, like normal people."

"And wouldn't I love that, too. But that'd be suicide, and neither of us is ready for that, yet. Gotta be crazier than we are for that move. So let's give it a different shot: do light disguises in another place, somewhere we can find work. I think our current I.D.s will be okay, far enough away, and we're probably not in anybody's database that way.

"The picture won't do any maniacs any good, and there'll be nothing else they can go on. We'll be safe, until maybe Clyde and the good guys can get to the Webb. I'm hoping, with all the legal wheels turning, that'll happen."

"I guess so, eventually. Okay, yeah, let's give that a shot. But I'm afraid too many people know our current aliases. I'll get Nate to do us another makeover. Damn, I hate this, Wes! When are we gonna get to be normal again?"

"Wish I knew. Guess we'll just hafta grab whatever life we can as wanted fugitives. And speaking of grabbing, and being wanted, we've gotta keep this whole pile of crap from making us weird with each other, love." I snuggled up to him, and felt that strong, protective arm around me. To hell with the Webb.

"So where?" his eyes on the highway unrolling before us. Yeah, the open road, to anywhere we wanted to go, as long as it had anonymity and some kind of work that wouldn't drive us the rest of the way insane.

"Well, Kentucky's coming up. Let's just start looking for any kind of work we can stand for a while, preferably someplace small and logically out of the drug trade, if there is such a place, and land there."

So we had to collect new names again, plus the basic paperwork, and were going to have to get used to being who we weren't, again.

*Damn, this stuff's getting old.*

Couldn't take the slightest chance, with these guys. As I'd observed, with enough dirty money, the evil Spider Webber Man could buy enough technology to spot a Crane Lewis and Jean Dodson no matter how far outback we'd managed to squirrel ourselves away to.

Yeah, somebody'd always have a computer, and the Internet reached everywhere: even into our socks, probably.

# Sixteen

It'd been a real bummer ever since grad school. No job, and the degree hadn't earned her squat. And playing around with drugs with Greg had been a big mistake. You thought you could just do a little here and there, then leave it alone, walk away. But it was everywhere: at the university, in town, around every corner was a contact, and all you had to have was the cash.

Yeah, cash. Waiting tables didn't bring in much, unless you got into a high-dollar place, and the competition was high for those. Who'd think there were so many educated women out there having to sling hash after all that work to try to get above that? Well, most of them grabbed a guy with a career, and just shoved any ambitions they might've had under the table. Glad for the little they had.

Not her. She'd worked her butt off to get where she was and wouldn't keep wasting it just surviving. Besides, who the hell was out there for her? Mama's boys, ego-ridden professors between marriages. Wesley'd been right about them: a waste of time. Sarah wondered where she was. Had blown town over that bust when they got the bastard who killed Greg. She could maybe find out from MacDonnell's family in the next county.

But that wouldn't get her any closer to out of here. Needed a stake, something big to spring her someplace new, where the job market wasn't a closed society. And she'd stay the hell away from anything that even suggested drugs.

*That reminds me: that guy Greg knew, who's got that picture of Wes and Craig and the crew.* Somebody was looking for them in a big way, and it wasn't the cops. Maybe that Webb guy they never caught. She reasoned he had to be a big man in the business, to have had all that money. His kid was just a little fish, but the cops'd had a lot of stuff on him about the drug chain. Yeah, so that'd be Webb, out for revenge, probably. Nasty people. But they sure had their hands in a huge flow of money. There ought to be a way to get her fingers on just a little of that.

*No, Greg tried that, and look what it got him: dead.* But she had to admit it: that guy really wasn't all that sharp after all. Now she just wondered if a smart girl couldn't find a way to pick up a few dollars without getting drawn into the sewer. *Gotta be some way...*

~ * ~

We crossed the big river at Paducah, stayed over, did some critical shopping before we moved out again. Only now I was a blonde with blue contacts named Chelsea Cameron, and Craig (Carson Boyle) had a head of distinguished white hair and plans to grow a goatee as soon as nature complied. And I swear, the reflections in plate glass windows were of two total strangers, if you hadn't known.

We sort of angled our way across and up through the state, casually checking out towns on the way. Rest stop time, we'd get off the highway and scout around for things like interesting construction happening. Lunch, we stretched it, asking the locals. Always a few duckbills at out-of-the-way cafes, who knew all the dirt.

Not much luck, unless we wanted to try for some commercial job in one of the towns, which we didn't see many of either. Then something that'd been tugging at my mind decided us to head north through Frankfort. Maybe just that I was tired of the big road. Anyway, we got into that big triangle made by Louisville, Lexington, and Cincinnati, more off the beaten-down path. We still hoped for something interesting, since we'd probably be there awhile.

Best not to be miserable at work...make us mean and nasty.

It was just outside a little county seat town called Owenton that we saw this big tractor-trailer with oak cabin logs on it, all tagged and coded. The truck was stopped at a roadside lunch place, so we wheeled in. Craig ran a critical eye over the logs.

"Nice," he said, and I could see they were. Long, big, which meant a pretty substantial job, unless somebody was planning just to put up a barn. But these weren't barn logs, with nice beaded ceiling joists and a staircase as part of the load.

We were admiring the logs when the driver came out, complete with toothpick, beard, and yes, a beer gut. I left the pitch up to Craig, being a little out of my depth. I mean, I'd done logs, sure, but probably didn't possess the repertoire of bullshit he had. And of course, being a man in redneck country would get you further.

He didn't disappoint.

"These nice logs. Goin' someplace close?"

"Yeah, down th' road close t'Gratz. Lawyer got a little farm there, found this ole cabin, got it tore down, wants t'put it up on th' place. You a cabin man?"

"Oh, yeah. Done a bunch of 'em, all over. Don't reckon he'd need a little help?"

"Wal, way I heard it, he was plannin' on havin' th' hired man do most of it. Delano Highfill, fam'ly from 'round here close. Good with carpenterin', but ain't never done a cabin, he tole me. Y'might hit up th' lawyer 'bout workin' on it." The man was trying not to be too obvious about checking me out. Hey, I was now a blonde, and talk about stereotypes...

"B'lieve we will. Where c'n we catch him, reckon?" Craig was purposely slipping a little into the man's speech pattern. Dad used to call that 'hound dog talk,' and he'd told me it was worth gold in the right situation.

"Due in this ev'nin' from Cincinnati. Comes down 'bout ever' weekend, but wanted t'be here when these logs come, too. Got horses on th' place, wuz where th' ole schoolhouse burnt down. I'm headin' there now, but prob'ly be awhile 'fore he gits there. You c'n foller me if y'want to."

Now how in hell were we supposed to know where the old schoolhouse had been? Didn't matter: he did.

"So you're not gonna work on th' job yourself?"

"Me? Naw, don't know nuthin' 'bout buildin'. Tryin' t'make a livin' 'th this ole truck, if I c'n keep it t'gether long 'nuff."

"Well, we will g'on with you, then, mebbe see if y'need a hand unloadin'."

"Now that'd be fine, I reckon. Delano, he's got th' lawyer's tractor, but this here's a load, fer shore. Dunno's th' man'd pay you, though."

"Don't matter. Heard of 'n old plantation on th' river close t'Gratz, and like t' get down, see it." As far as I knew, Craig had never heard of Gratz, Kentucky, and certainly not of any plantation there.

"Oh, that'd be th' ole Brown place. Run down t' nuthin' much left, now. Buncha hippies livin' in th' ole house. Feller owns it in Louisville, keeps horses an' cows on it. Yeah, real old, that'n. S'posed to've been there 'fore th' Revolution." He swung up into his truck.

"Now just where did all that come from?" I asked, and not without admiration, when we were under way, the big rig rumbling ahead.

"Just made it up. I know this part of Kentucky was settled well before the Revolution, and the good river bottomland was taken first. Logical guess." That grin, different now with the white hair.

"Well, like Reenie said, you should maybe go into politics, with that on-demand bullshit ability."

"Gets doors open, sometimes. We'd have done better in a rusty pickup truck, and if I'd chewed tobacco, though."

"God forbid. Here I get you looking almost respectable, and that'd have blown it, big time." My turn to grin.

Delano Highfill was a piece of work. He was maybe late 30s, but looked 60. Crippled up, red whiskey face, just a tremor in his big hands. We learned he ran the place for the lawyer, Mangrum

Pierce, of Pierce & Pierce in Cincinnati. The other Pierce was an uncle, Delano told us.

We did indeed lend a hand with getting the logs off the truck and laid out on rows of concrete blocks in a logical order for reassembly. The house would go up right where the old schoolhouse had been, we learned.

Craig even spotted a place where somebody had tagged the logs in the wrong order, and got that straightened out. He'd done that so many times we didn't waste any time, and I could see both Delano and the truck driver, whose name was Bobby Dale, appreciated this. They'd never have had a prayer of finishing before dark without us; that was obvious.

So much so that when Pierce showed up later, Delano told him outright he should get us to help with the job. He and Bobby Dale bent the lawyer's ear even before he came over to meet us.

"My man here says you know a lot about putting up cabins," he greeted us. "Name's Mangrum Pierce," extending a horseman's hand. Or maybe that was just the way he was dressed: to ride.

"Carson Boyle, (I hated that name) and this's my fiancée, Chelsea Cameron. Yes, we've restored more than I can remember, all over. This one's really nice. Have a professional find it for you?"

"No, not at all," he laughed. Nice laugh. He was early 30s, chiseled features, with that unmistakable horseman air about him. "No, my girlfriend and I just stumbled on it, out looking. So I got lucky, did I?"

"You gotta know, most of these old ones have dry rot and powder-post beetles that'd make you glad to settle for termites. More than luck here, though...this one was done right in the first place."

"Supposed to be late 1700s. Possibly some records in Owenton. Shelby's really into history; she'll get to sleuthing out anything there is to find."

"Well, we're in between jobs, heading back East from one in Missouri. If you need help with this one, we'd like to talk to you about it. I'd hate to tell you how many of these I've seen that got started, then sidetracked, and went to compost."

"We can talk, sure. Of course, I'd need to see some references. Got a scrapbook of your work?"

"Wish we did. Fire in the place we were staying in Branson got the important stuff while we were gone. Bad wiring in an old lakefront place."

*Oboy, he's off again.*

"Branson. Yes, my folks took us there as kids. I remember those old fishing cabins on the water. Well, let me have some references, and then we'll talk dollars. I might not be able to afford you."

"Sure. Chelsea, why don't you write these down? Glenn Armitage in Branson, Alan MacDonnell in Virginia, Nate Peterson in Virginia, and Clyde Kelly—where is Clyde now, Chelsea? He moved somewhere after we did that cabin for him in Circleville."

"I'll get on the phone, find out where. We've got the numbers for the others, but I'm not sure of the e-mail or snail-mail addresses anymore. That okay?"

"That'll do, sure. I'll call 'em tonight. Meanwhile, if this works out, I stay in the little farmhouse down there weekends, and you could stay there, too. Water's terrible: cistern, so I bring bottled. But everything works. Shelby's got it civilized a little. She's counting on helping with the cabin here, too."

"Sounds like my kind of girl." I smiled. "You gotta know women are better'n men at things like chinking cabins: more patience." I dug an elbow into Craig's ribs.

"Oh, she's right, Mr. Pierce. That's the hardest part of a restoration, and people are forever doing it wrong, and the rain gets in and the cabin rots down. I'm okay at chinking after all these years, but Chelsea's the expert."

"Y'don't say? I never thought about that aspect of it. I know this one originally had clay chinking, over short split sections."

"And they'd have to redo it every few years. But these logs were sided over, which is why they're in such good shape."

"You can tell that?"

"Sure. See these indentations on the thicker logs? For vertical furring strips, to get the siding boards even. And here's something you don't often see: some of these logs were hewn by a left-handed man."

Now, I knew about left-handed broadaxes, but tell it from the log? That was something even I didn't know, if it was real. Hard to tell the gospel from the tall tales, I was discovering, once Craig got his yarns going.

"Come on, you can't know that." Pierce was hooked.

"Yeah, see this sloped cut? Log hewer stood on this left side, chopped down on the final pass, left this angled broadaxe mark. Now this one's right-handed, done with a right-handed axe. Probably somebody else at the house-raising, or maybe the guy was even ambidextrous."

"Yeah, Delano can use either hand. So the axes were made right and left-handed, too?"

"Not exactly. Handles curved away from the log so you wouldn't skin your knuckles. Most axes took either a right or left handle, put it in from one side of the eye or the other." He was using his hands a lot to illustrate. "Goosewing axes, the real classics—German design— were forged one way or the other, so you couldn't switch. Real rarities now…worth a fortune in antiques shops." Okay, I did know that one, since I'd forged mine. But Craig was enjoying himself. And cool lawyer Pierce was taking it all in like a trout on a dry fly.

"Well, that's a lot more than I've ever heard. Why didn't you find many left-handed hewers?"

"Old folks thought left-handed stuff was evil. You know, Satan's children. Tried to switch any kid over, and usually succeeded. Some of them developed behavior problems like stuttering because of it, though. You know, dominant side of the brain and all."

"Seems I've read something about that. Well, looks like you know your log cabins. Say we did work something out, you'd work with Delano, here. He's good at carpentry. Pretty much put that old farmhouse back together. I was going to hire just a farm helper to do the grunt work, but I'm thinking if things go better and faster, there'll be less time overall, and I might just save money."

"Now that's a rare insight, sir. Most people just look at the cost per hour, and end up years later having put money down a hole."

"Well, they teach us in law school to keep an eye out for the dollars, you know." Little tilt-head shrug. Yeah, I was thinking of J. Barker Webb, whose life was dollars. "So, you staying around close, then?"

"If you think there's a place for us here, yes, we'll grab a motel room tonight. Otherwise, we'll head on to a proposed historic project in Huntington. Woman's getting a grant of some kind there."

"Well, let me call these references. Sounds like you're the right people, but you know..."

"Sure do. When I had a big crew, I got stung more than once, not checking when I should have."

We arranged to call in late after he'd been snowed by our contacts. We were pretty sure the guys we'd named would get on board, if he even bothered to call them all. Certainly Nate would, and Alan, 'cause we'd quickly checked in with them. I was a little nervous about Craig's including Glenn, but why not? Oh, the Virginia people knew our current names, but well, Glenn knew I was Wesley...

I made a quick call, got him, and filled him in. He was cool with it, but sorry to learn we'd blown town. I told him the story about Craig's mother, and reminded him of that Ozarks branch water.

~ * ~

*They've cut me out*, Aggie Black realized. *Johnny and I were doing good work for them all this time, and they've just left me out in the cold.* She could've spilled a lot to the narcs when they had her, but she hadn't. She'd been loyal, and what did it get her? Not a damn thing, that was what. *And now I don't even have a job anymore, and no place to go.* Oh, they'd been nice enough there at the clinic, getting her off the stuff, and God, had *that* been hard. Trying to find her a place in society again, with their do-good attitudes.

*They really think we're all pieces of shit, that we're not quite human if we've been hooked.* Like no way would a social worker ever let herself get into that position. *I can tell you, honey, the right guy comes along at the right time, and bam, you're on it.*

She guessed she was lucky Johnny had wanted to marry her. Lot of girls she knew got pulled in by guys who just dumped them afterwards. But he'd been so controlling...she'd gone from being under her parents' thumb to being told everything she could and couldn't do by Johnny. She'd thought she'd scream every time he pointed out some spot of dirt or bit of dust she hadn't cleaned up yet. *He was sure crazy that way.*

But dammit, he was her man, and now he was dead. Dead with that crazy Denny who was after Lee and her guy. Never knew what they'd done, but the higher-ups wanted them bad. And that was a real shame. She'd liked Lee a lot. They'd had fun, first time since she was a kid. Lee'd cared about her, cared about people. All the guys at the welding shop liked her, too.

*God, I miss her. Miss my family, too. Maybe now that I'm dried out, I can get back to Baltimore, start over...*Would they even take her back, though? No, not a chance in hell. Her mom always suspected she was on something, and Dad just threw her out of the house over Johnny.

Well, he was dead now, and she missed him more than anything. So much it made her crazy. *I even miss him yelling at me all the time.*

If things could just go back to the way they were, she knew she could handle it. Johnny and she could maybe have got out, gone somewhere else, started over with no drugs, no connections, just the two of them out there, making it on their own. *Just him and me against the world...*

But that guy Jack who was just in here, telling her about them not wanting her to get in touch, he'd said they knew Lee's guy, that David, was the one offed Johnny and Denny. The cops said it was just an accident, but she didn't believe that. Johnny was too good a driver just to go off the road and hit a tree. Jack had said there was white paint scrapes on the car, like somebody'd run it off the road. And yeah, the van they had was white.

She guessed she couldn't blame a guy for fighting back when somebody was out to do him, though. *But if only Johnny'd left it to*

*Denny to do the job, I'd still have him...no, that's history now. I got to go on from here, any way I can.*

But she knew, soon's she was out of here, somebody'd show up with some stuff, and it'd be so easy to get back on it. *Got to fight that, if I'm going to survive.* She knew too many girls'd done that. And got so they couldn't do anything—keep a job or even take care of themselves. Be on the streets, turning tricks for the stuff. *I won't ever do that, no matter how bad it gets.*

If she could just find a way to make some quick money, she could fade out of sight, go someplace they never heard of drugs, start over, get herself a life.

Well, there was that picture they'd sent down of Lee and David. Those guys at the top must want them bad, she reasoned. *They'd pay, I bet, if I could find them...*No, Lee was her friend. But if David *had* killed Johnny...No, she'd have to be a lot worse off than she was to do something like that.

And she'd have to hook up with somebody else in the chain even to start looking for them. Get herself into another relationship with some guy a lot worse than Johnny'd been. Or even some woman, who wouldn't make demands on her. No, she wouldn't even know where to start looking for somebody like that.

*But just maybe...*

# Seventeen

So Mangrum Pierce, Esq. hired us, at a somewhat reduced rate, considering lodging was part of it. We jumped on that restoration like frogs, and worked Delano Highfill to a shadow. He had other farm responsibilities with the horses, the ubiquitous tobacco patch, and general upkeep like fences and equipment, but he was available most days almost all day.

He lived in a trailer on his father's place on the highway, alone since his last wife had left with their kid, but came early every day, and usually sober. Delano was a living country-western song, if a little out of tune.

We had the footings dug and poured, stone foundation in, and were well into setting logs by the third week. That log part goes fast, Craig told me, and I remembered from the Missouri job that he was right. Delano would suspend each log from the tractor's hydraulic bucket by a chain, and we guided it into place, thunking the corner notches together.

Where a repair was necessary, which wasn't often, we'd found a few short pieces left over from a neighbor's fallen-in log cow shed that worked. Fitting a splice or insetting a piece where we'd cut out bad wood so you could hardly see it was a joy, and our work was *so* tight. No place for modesty here...we were the best (and fast).

When we'd get to the second story, we'd have to hire a boom truck or crane, but those were the best logs, so should go together like a play set. Craig told us about chaining a beam to the tractor bucket for extra height, but pointed out that on this sloping ground, it'd be too easy to turn the tractor over. Delano said thanks but no thanks to that scheme...he'd had one of his numerous cousins squashed that way.

The house was what's called a double-pen, with 36-foot logs notched at the center for a cross partition. Each end had a fireplace cutout, and the aged limestone chimney rock was there, hauled by Bobby Dale from the original site.

I was to be in charge of the fireplaces while Craig and Delano did final carpentry, after the logs and roof were up. I'd learned stonework that time in Arkansas, working with a really fine mason who was local there. That had been the best sandstone in the world, but I could handle this okay, with some extras from out in the woods.

The farmhouse was livable, if a little creaky and leaning. We boiled the water, and bought bottled. Seems the local custom was to use those cisterns, there being a belief that with all the underground cavities in the ever-present limestone, a well would leak out all the water you found. Maybe so.

The practice was to let the rain wash off most of the bird shit on the roof, then go out in it to divert downspouts from the gutters into the cistern. A lot of folks didn't even let the roof wash off first. We applied chlorine to the water, too, but like I said, boiled it a lot for dishes and even laundry. Used the bottled for drinking and cooking. No real problem; it'd have to get a lot tougher here than that for us to complain.

September slipped away, and fall was a lot like Virginia: crimson maple leaves and skies so blue they made your eyes ache. Air turning a sort of amber, with a hint of frost to come. And we were happy: Pierce paid regularly, was continually impressed with progress and the level of our craft, and nobody knew who we really were, here. Just wasn't going to get much better than this.

And Craig and I got to talking more about our situation. Sure, the hiding part wasn't fun, but on the upside, we'd fallen into good jobs, met good people, found one place we liked a lot, even if we'd had to leave it. And the nasty guys hadn't succeeding in doing us (yet), which seemed more than just luck. I began to think maybe it was the Big Guy upstairs who was watching over us. Not much on religion, but if good things kept happening, I'd sure take a closer look at it.

~ * ~

The young woman needed money. Her man of whatever moment had always been able to turn up a little, one way or another, but now he was history. And while, sure, she had a trickle coming in from her crummy little job, that didn't cover expenses. Or a little fun stuff on the side, which she found she had to have. She'd thought she could control the need...just a sample now and then, sure, fun stuff, but it hadn't worked out that way. Where was her discipline, her will?

She was no longer the bright, savvy girl who'd always been able to call the shots. Or had that just been her own self-perception? Had she ever really been the one making the decisions? She liked to think so, anyway.

But now things were getting desperate. Now she owed money to the wrong people, and that wouldn't cut it. She felt she had a little time, if she could just come up with a way to convince them she could in fact get it. God, everybody in the world needed money; what made her think she had any special pipeline to it?

Pipeline...She remembered something. There had been word out among some people she knew that a heavy hitter, a guy up high in the trade, wanted to find two people who owed him big time. No details on why, or just what stage that was all at now. But she could ask around. You never had to go far to make a contact, and everybody knew everybody else when it came to the chemicals.

And she was pretty sure she could still get in touch with somebody who very probably knew about this couple on the run: where they were hiding, how to reach them. There just might be some way to put this together into a package that would mean the money she needed. And hey, wouldn't that be sweet, to cash in from somebody in the trade to pay off somebody else in the trade?

Yes, she could start the wheels moving in that direction.

~ * ~

Mangrum's Shelby-by-damn-Birmingham was a woman whirlwind. Ordinary brown hair, not that drop-dead gorgeous, but a ball of fire. She could hold her liquor, and sometimes even had a drink in her hand until she needed to put it down to help us place a log or nail up a brace. But once show her how something had to be done, she was on it like stink on horse manure. Irreverent, funny, energy spilling out all over you if you stood too close.

And while she was new to them, the woman loved horses. Pierce had half a dozen, mares and one stallion, plus a gelding the stallion was always running off. Big Bob was the stallion, and Thunder could outrun him, luckily.

We watched in amusement as Bob would suddenly throw up his head and charge the smaller horse, evidently not understanding that he didn't have the equipment to be competition any more. He'd whirl and be off like a shot, just snapping-teeth ahead. When they'd both gotten their speed up, Thunder would veer off a ridge and the stallion would shoot past, shaking the earth. Testosterone Bob never figured that move out.

Weekends got to be even more fun, with Shelby and Mangrum usually coming down early to help with the cabin on Fridays. Then later we'd ride, picnic, fish the river. She sang, and he played guitar. Very well, it turned out. Had wanted to be a pro musician, but realized early on he'd rather eat.

She actually owned a small but exclusive dress shop in Cincinnati where I wouldn't be able to afford even a swatch of fabric. She was just learning to ride, and both her man and I taught her some of the finer points. Craig preferred both feet on the ground, but did trail-ride with us a few times. I was sure I could win him over in time. Hell, I've said he even looked like a cowboy.

~ * ~

In St. Louis, Webb/Goode had hit a brick wall. His higher-up, a very powerful man in Miami, had reviewed his vendetta on the carpenter couple, and decided it had gone far enough. Three men from the operation were gone. Four, if you included Webb's own kid, and that was too many for a personal thing. Be different if it was *business*, he'd said, but from now on, Webb would have to keep his personal stuff out of the flow of things. Did he understand?

He guessed he'd better.

But after a few months, during which no word at all came up the chain, he got a cryptic message. Seems a woman who'd known the girl had information on the couple's current whereabouts, and was willing to talk deal. She wouldn't give her name, or the circumstances or place she'd been in contact. Simple deal: she would deliver, he would pay.

A lot.

Webb knew who'd been Whitestone's housemate in Virginia, had checked through his contacts to see if she'd heard from her. He also knew of John Black's wife in Arkansas. But he knew nothing about any other female connections the carpenters had, either before or after they'd fled. And while this might be the result of his strategy with the photograph, which had worked up to now, more likely it was somebody recent, claiming as she did to know their current hiding place.

And this might not even be a woman at all. Good way for some guy to throw him off any trail, have him checking out nonexistent connections to the girl.

Or hell, it was a narc setup. A ploy to get him out in the open. Looked at with any kind of objectivity, it stank of the cops. *So just leave it alone.* He wasn't a sucker for a setup, and this one was clumsy.

And he did leave it, week after unproductive week.

But it wouldn't leave *him* alone. Those two could be anywhere, he knew. Some place nobody with the picture had reached. Some hole somewhere so deep they were sure he'd never uncover them.

And it was working; that's what pissed him off so badly. Here he had all the state-of-the-art technology at his fingertips, all the tentacles of the organization—well, up to the boss's ultimatum—and he couldn't locate two ordinary people. Damnably frustrating.

He didn't confide in Gwen. Vowed to find a way, despite the imposed freeze, despite the dead-end he was looking at. He *would* find them.

But he would *not* step into a transparent trap set by the Feds. How stupid did they think he was?

*Of course, it could be real.* First off, the price was too high. That'd queer it if it'd come from the narcs: they'd want him to tip to it so much they'd have made it more tempting. So okay, he supposed he *could* let it go to the next stage, maybe be able to check her/him out more.

Only there wasn't a next stage. The woman had made it clear she wanted a clean deal: the marks for the bucks. All she wanted was the okay. Absolutely necessary to find out more about her. Try to smoke her out, a little. Or him. He could surely do that, but he had to have more to go on.

He sent word by the organization grapevine, gambling that the boss wouldn't learn the true nature of it. And maybe that wasn't so smart. But he emphasized that this was not to be done again: she had to contact him personally. The price—that very steep price—he tentatively agreed to. Time and place would have to be worked out later. Draw her out.

He wasn't any closer to sniffing out whether this was a trap. So the woman would call him. He knew it wouldn't be on a land line he could trace, even with the resources open to him.

Maybe just forget this; write the whole thing off.

No, dammit, these people owed him: owed him his son's smashed arm, life sentence, the loss of the entire Virginia setup, which was to have been his and Gwen's permanent home: the good life. And owed him that half million. Of course, it was Clyde Kelly he really wanted, but finding him in that Federal network would be a total impossibility. Hell, he could be behind a damn desk in Rome by now.

So, wait for word to come back. Take the next step afterwards, whatever his instinct told him. He could do that. A lot of money, yes, but he could replace money. Hadn't exactly been doing without, these past months, here in the middle of the country.

Yes, he could do that, too...

~ * ~

By Christmas, I had one fireplace working, and the house was dried in. On a cabin, that means windows, doors, outside chinking, gable siding and roof. We all celebrated the big day with a huge fire and decorated a tree there on the plywood subfloor. No heating system yet, but the subcontractor was due soon. Likewise plumbing and electrical.

We were using a long, heavy extension cord from the farmhouse, which sometimes tripped the breakers down there if we plugged in too many things at once. We'd take turns jogging down to get it back perking. But it lit up the tree that night, and my fireplace warmed that end of the place okay. We'd blocked the other fireplace hole with plywood temporarily, and the house started feeling like a house instead of a pile of logs.

Delano got drunk and repulsive at our party, kept mumbling about his ex-wives (two, or was it three?) and the kids he was missing. Mangrum said not to mind him. He always sobered up and came back to work on time. Shelby got happier, Mangrum outdid himself on the guitar, and Craig and I soaked it all in, gratefully.

We were building a nest egg, with very low expenses, and nobody was shooting at us. That can *make* you downright grateful. The job would last till mid-spring, with cabinetry and the other chimney, stairs and the thousand finishing items and punch list you tend to forget about, that make a house a house.

Yeah, it was good.

So good, I began to worry. In my experience, when things go along smoothly, you get the feeling something's gonna pop up and bite you. Just look at our recent history. And we'd been in this game of run-for-your-life long enough to make it very clear there could be no slip-ups when and if that monster did bite.

We did this great weekend in Cincinnati as Pierce's guests. Met the uncle, a raffish grab-ass who tried to get me alone, which I avoided. Hit some nice music places (no surprise), and ate some good food, all on our hosts. Pierce and Pierce were doing all right in the legal beagle business.

And while there in that big town where you could find just about everything, I decided to make a discreet purchase. Didn't tell Craig about it, partly because I felt foolish buying it. But, humor my paranoia, I guess. My secret. Any luck at all, I'd never use it. But I kept it in my jeans pocket every minute. Like a pet worry stone, I guess.

Shelby and I were having a ball on the house. I'd taught her the basics of stonework, and she'd helped me with that fireplace and chimney. I'd cut Pierce's initials and date into a round piece I mortared in, leaving the century out so folks could speculate later on the age, 100, 200 years or more back. Everyone likes a historic house to be older than it really is. (Yeah, Grandpa wuz born in that house, an' it wuz real old then). Like the loudmouth telling it really could know.

She and I talked fixtures and flooring and stair rails and closets. Then she found these glowing old walnut general store cabinets at a place in Owenton that was to be torn down. With a little fitting, they would become her kitchen woodwork. Wow, about a hundred fifty years of patina on them already. A real hoot.

I had this little worry about how much she was investing in this great place. I mean sure, she and Mangrum were tight, but I guess I was just old-fashioned enough to want to see a ring on the girl's finger. Guy like him was a catch, and well, he could stray, you know, and keep all the marbles.

I didn't bring it up, of course, but Shelby let me know in a girl-talk session that he'd already asked her the Big One, several times, and *she* was the one holding out. Wow. Now that was beyond cool. She had her independence, and damned if she'd let that evaporate until she was good and in-your-face ready. Helluva girl.

Once the cabin heating system was in and working, it got downright cozy on that job. I put the second chimney off till warmer weather since it was outside, and with the hole covered, we were able to keep out January. Subs were in and out, plumbing, running the wires for more than the one major circuit we were working with, doing their thing. The house was getting itself in shape for its next 200-plus years, there on its hilltop overlooking miles of blue-tinged Kentucky ridges.

We rode down to the Brown plantation site one of those freak warm days, all four of us. There were indeed hippie types living there, with no running water, no electricity, small dirty children tumbling happily over everything. Homespun garments of every description flapping on clotheslines, dogs yapping. Cyrano's size pre-empted any territorial crap from them, right up front.

Nobody seemed to have any means of livelihood, but there they were, about three mixed-up families of them, best I could count. I'd thought all that'd gone out with the '80s, but then every generation has to rediscover its particular brand of rebel-and-drop-out.

The old house had been magnificent, but now shutters hung crazily, roof had been patched in places and left to leak in others. No paint, few unbroken windows. Should have been at least one ghost, but I guess these denizens would just have welcomed it and offered it a toke.

Come to think of it, that's probably what they were living on... surely had a patch of weed hidden away somewhere. I'd read that the principle agricultural product in this region was marijuana. *Well, live and let live.* I did kind of wonder what kind of creatures those kids would grow up to become.

If they did manage to grow up.

~ * ~

The big break still hadn't happened for Samantha Webb. Looking back, she'd made all the right connections, done all that was possible to get her name and face out there. This party should just be the crowning event, then. Costing her a lot of money, but whatthehell was money for, if not to promote her career?

She'd talked the idea over with her parents, and while her mother hadn't been that enthusiastic, Barker Webb had said sure, go for it. Apparently, whatever he had going for them in St. Louis was bringing in the bucks. She got the idea he was doing better than ever in his new position.

Didn't want to know too much about that...not necessary.

She watched a black-and-white-dressed girl from the catering place carrying a tray. She'd been in Samantha's acting class her first year here. As far as she knew, the girl had never landed a part in anything, not even a commercial. She avoided the eyes, seeing no reason to embarrass the other non-actress. *Only difference between us is that I've got parents who support me, and she doesn't.*

*Damn, this town eats people up.* Here she'd invited everybody who mattered, some of whom actually had shown up, probably the ones with nothing else to do, and it'd probably get her zilch.

She took another drink off a passing tray, ran her eyes over the men in attendance. The usual: small-time producers only here for free food and maybe a score with one of the young hopefuls, predator agents who'd promise anything, other jaded wannabe actors, some of whom had crashed the party.

Well, at least she'd try to enjoy herself, not let Dad's money go completely to waste. The alcohol was finally creating a sort of haze she could mistake for having a good time. She took another drink.

*That curly-haired stud with the three girls around him looks hot.* Didn't know just who he was, but looked like the best thing there. *If I gotta wake up in the morning with the king of hangovers, I'd rather it be with somebody not too repulsive next to me.* She shrugged, started for the group.

~ * ~

Craig and I did keep in touch with most of the people we cared about during our exile. He called his brother regularly, both because the two of them were close, and to check on the house status. Just in case, they spoke in a kind of code I gathered went way back to when they were kids. Used cartoon character names, a generation out of date: Snuffy and Dagwood. So I guess I was Blondie, now.

No good offers on the place yet, with everything kind of slow still, but Alan was keeping an eye on things. His eldest, Selena, was a sweet kid of about sixteen, and she'd go with him to tidy the place up and shoo away the skunks and 'possums.

I called Kelcy and Charlie Mack to see how they were standing the winter, which I knew could get bitter there. They were okay, she said, but they had some news about the weirdo who'd stumbled down their road the day we left. Seems he'd managed to fall off the bluff near the Mallory cabin and splatter himself on the rocks. Speculation was he'd maybe planned something like that, as a suicide.

No, he hadn't planned it, but yeah, his mission *had* been suicidal, all right.

They had some other not-so-good news. Seems Glenn's wonder woman Reenie Wilkes had suffered some sort of breakdown, had to take a leave of absence from her job at the hospital, and gone up to Chicago to her parents' place to recover. No, didn't know if she'd dumped Glenn, but maybe so. Just left him a long, rambling note, and bam, she was outta there.

*Oh, bad.* Glenn didn't need that, again. What in the world had gone wrong, I wondered. Nerves? Not Reenie. She was so happy with who she was, so sure she'd found the right place, the right man. Pressure at work? She didn't seem the type to let that get to her. Well, you never really know what's in anybody else's head; I'd learned that for sure. I remembered how Clyde Kelly had fooled us all, with his charade. Surely Reenie wasn't an undercover cop, too.

Was she?

I didn't check in with the folks in Russellville. Just too close to the drug operation there, I was afraid. Didn't know what'd happened to Aggie, or who might let something slip. Bury that then, much as I'd have liked to talk with Bill, Irvin and Lou and the others. Be hard to explain our sudden departure, anyway. Burned that bridge, if reluctantly.

Nate Peterson had no hard news, but had heard from Clyde Kelly that their operation in St. Louis was yielding some progress, one slow step at a time. The Karl Kramer I.D. we'd given them had helped. Good. Maybe by the time we moved on from Kentucky, the monster Webb and his ilk would be smears of unpleasant history and we'd be able to pick up more of our lives again.

~ * ~

It had been a long drive, but Phil's determination to find Wesley Whitestone and somehow get that money back—or what was left of it—kept him keyed up and pushing. The anger, too, at having been so taken in. He'd been sure she'd been the right woman for him, even if she couldn't see it, and he'd let her get next to him, then rob him. *Damn fool, to trust a woman like that.* It'd taken Sid months to convince him of the truth, which he just hadn't wanted to see. But now it was all crystal clear.

Glenn Armitage had been surprisingly easy to contact, despite the rumor that he'd gone out west. Wesley had planted that one, too, come to think of it. And yes, Glenn had seen her, with some guy, not that long ago, back in Missouri. Guy's name hadn't matched, but yeah, she'd probably dumped whoever she'd run from Virginia with...

But that wasn't the best part. Glenn had actually gotten a call from her, saying she and the guy needed references for a log cabin job in Kentucky. And when the owner had called to check, he'd told Glenn approximately where the job was. Somewhere nobody'd ever heard of: Gratz, south of Cincinnati.

Small place, probably not even a village, so it shouldn't be hard to locate them. And sure enough, he was to learn that everybody knew where the Cincinnati lawyer was having that old log cabin put up again, and knew there were these two carpenters working for him. And yes, one *was* a woman.

Bingo.

Knowing ahead of time from Glenn there were the two of them to deal with, Phil had reluctantly taken the precaution of buying a gun back in Pittsburgh, going through the necessary background checks, waiting the required time. There were quicker ways for an ex-cop to get firepower, but he'd done it right. He'd been a good shot back when he was on the force, but never in this world expected to have to use this weapon. Still, he'd finally realized she was a hustler, a thief, not at all the woman he'd trusted.

And what kind of jerk would somebody like that hook up with?

Yeah, her current sucker just might well be some kind of an outlaw. So, if either one of them got rough...

# Eighteen

I can't say I had a premonition of danger that morning, but I'd been uneasy. Things just didn't come together the way they were supposed to: the pancakes I made for breakfast were leathery, the bacon soggy. Craig was helpful—he always was—but the things he did didn't seem to help my mood. I was careful not to let it communicate itself to him. Nobody likes a bitchy partner.

The thing I do remember was not wanting to go to work that day. Not sure why at the time, but this job, which we both had enjoyed so much, suddenly just didn't have any appeal for me. Weird. I was almost at the point of telling Craig I just wanted to jump in the Jeep and play hooky, maybe run up to Cincinnati, or down to Frankfort, instead of working.

And of course, he'd have let me get away with it. I suppose that realization was what made me suck it up and get on with it. Sometimes when I had the mullygrubs like that, a good hard work session took it all out of me.

*So, Wesley, go get that damn chimney flashing finished first thing, up on the ridge of the house I've been putting off: I'll have a good view from there, anyway.*

So I was up on scaffolding when the pickup drove up, but I was hidden from view. Sort of staying out of the cool breeze.

I knew that truck.

And I knew the guy who was looking the place over, taking his time getting out. And from the angle where I was, it looked like he was stuffing something lethal into his coat pocket. I ducked back.

Okay, so *this* was what was wrong. And right out of left field. But he hadn't seen me yet.

"Crane," I shinnied down the scaffolding, still out of sight. "That's that guy Phil from Pittsburgh, thinks I have his money, ex-cop. You talk to him, tell him...whatever you need to. I'm going to disappear. And maybe I'm paranoid, but he might even have a gun." I was sure it'd be serious, or I wouldn't have gotten that warning. And hell, he wouldn't have come all this way...I grabbed Cyrano's collar and we slipped inside the house.

"How the hell...okay, I'm on it." He went out to meet the man who was still checking out the house from where he'd parked beyond a stack of lumber. Okay, he thought, Wes had said the guy'd been getting obsessed about that missing money, so no telling what to expect. Maybe the worst. Surely he wouldn't get violent, but a gun? Craig let his eyes move around, looking for a weapon if necessary. There was a medium-weight cruising axe leaning against the wall, within reach...

"Hey, can we help you?" from Craig. The guy was still looking around, obviously searching for me, but couldn't see me from there. And of course, he'd never seen Craig. I moved Cyrano to the stairs and up. He was okay with that: new game with his crazy lady. I shushed him. He'd hear Phil's familiar voice, but one thing this dog did was always mind Mama, no matter what.

"I...well, I was looking for an old friend. Folks at the store on the highway said she was working on a cabin up this way. Might've got it wrong..." The guy was plainly unsure of himself.

"Could have been. I haven't been here long. There were two other people on this job before, the owner told me, left in a hurry. What's your friend's name?"

"Wesley Whitestone. Medium height, brown...oh, you say the others left?"

"What the owner said. And yeah, he did mention one was a woman. Week or so ago, now. I know Shelby, his fiancée, and they asked me to help finish it for them." Craig hadn't batted an eye when he heard my name.

"Well, I must've missed her, then. Just...thought I'd drop by, in the neighborhood..." Craig caught the Pennsylvania license on the pickup. *Yeah, neighborhood.*

"Sure. No idea where they went, and the owner said they didn't even pick up their last checks. Weird. Really left him hanging on this job. But if they do show up again, who can I tell them came by?"

"Oh, I'm Phil Bartlett. Knew her back in Pittsburgh a while back. Well, nice cabin you're working on. You do these as a specialty?" He wasn't ready to give it up and leave, it seemed, just yet. Kept glancing around, hoping to spot me. Shifting around, too, to get a better look. I edged into a far corner, keeping my dog quiet, who'd for sure heard and remembered his old trainer's voice, long before I had. *No, dammit, Cyrano, he's the enemy now.* The sound of Delano's hammer at work covered any noise we'd made, and he couldn't see me from where he was, either.

"Actually, I'm an out-of-work engineer. I'm just helping out the carpenter over there. He's the one in charge here." Delano was up on a ladder, more or less out of earshot.

I was sweating lead bullets up in that room in spite of the weather, as out of sight as I could get, breathing shallow, trying to make both of us look small. I had no idea how far Phil's obsession had pushed him, but that last time we'd talked had been scary. And if that were really a gun he had, he might go off the edge, do something really stupid. Laid back guy, but that cop background hadda mean there was something else inside him.

I could hear a little of what was being said below every time Delano's hammer stopped, and I appreciated my man's cool. *But just getthehell out of here, Phil: you're sick.* Yeah, he should go beat on his weird brother, who surely deserved it for something: probably wouldn't share comic books with him as a kid.

By that time, Suspicious Phil had almost completed a circuit of the cabin, nodded to Delano, who was doing second floor window trim. Thankfully not where he could see me inside. Craig had picked up the axe casually, going along beside him, and now shaved a stray piece of old bark off a log, as if that were important. I didn't know if the tension were building between them, but it sure as hell was up there with me. I just hoped it wouldn't come down to Craig's having to persuade the guy with that axe. *Ouch, and against a gun?* Well, he'd done it before, with a crowbar.

But Phil wasn't that positive about the situation, not getting negative feedback. Craig was being the perfect engineer/builder, polite, not the least bit suspicious.

"So. This the whole crew, then?"

"Actually, no. Another guy supposed to be here, but he's bad to drink. Probably nursing a hangover somewhere. Can't get good help for work like this, which is why they asked a computer nerd like me." He grinned in self-deprecation.

"That way all over, I guess." Then I thought I heard, "Mind if I see inside?"

*Omigod. Omigod!* This was gonna mean a disappearing act. And we couldn't manage a leap out of a second-story window. But wait, the scaffolding was outside the window at the other end. If we could just...

"Sure. A lot not finished in there, but yeah, I'll take a minute, show you around." He called up to Delano:

"We're goin' to look around inside, Del. Be up to help you set up the scaffold for that next window in just a bit." Delano just nodded, went back to hammering. Hey, that's what the guy did. And with either hand.

Okay, I could just maybe get to the other end of the house where I *might*, by some heroic effort, get woman and dog out of that window onto the scaffold, if I moved fast. Then, thank God, Craig stalled. *Love that man.*

"Oh, I heard it was the woman who did that fireplace and chimney. Not many women stonemasons, I guess."

"Yeah, Wesley did stone. Think she learned it out in Arkansas, or someplace."

"Well, we'll just hafta find somebody else to do the other one. You wouldn't happen to be a stone mason, too, would you?"

"No, carpenter. I specialize in kitchen remodels. That's what Wesley and I did when we worked together."

I was down the narrow hallway like a shadow, Cyrano sensing the situation was serious, again out of sight of Delano. Across, and had the (new, quiet) window open before they came up the temporary ramp and in the front door, still talking. So out, grab the scaffolding, haul my dog onto the walkboard. He thought that was fun, actually. I'd have to slip us back inside when they came out, and their voices let me know where they were. I had time to push the window closed before they, yeah, actually came up the stairs, looked around. *Hey, guy, I'd have appreciated your keeping that loser away from here.*

My heart was doing a tattoo up there, but the excitement was at least keeping me warm. And it didn't last long...they were back downstairs and outside again. So, back inside like a well-rehearsed escape act, I lugged and hugged my dog. If he'd let out a bark...but he hadn't. Guess he'd correctly picked up on the vibes, figured old friend Phil was now history. And yeah, not his lady's favorite dude anymore.

And then, thank God, Phil just did a final sweep of the cabin, gave up, mumbled something, and got back into his truck, cranked up and drove away. Gutless. I let the dust settle, then came down the stairs, wanting to hug Craig, too. But Delano was noticing, from the ladder at the other end of the house. Not that that should make any difference.

"Just a guy looking for a job," Craig told us. "Beginner, though. Didn't want him taking my job as helper." All three of us laughed.

But later, I just couldn't leave it alone. I knew Craig had figured Phil would get suspicious if he didn't let him inside the cabin, but damn, did that put me in a spot. So, yeah, I unloaded on him, even if I couldn't quite keep a grin off.

"Oh, I knew it'd be tough on you, but also knew you'd handle it. All he did was glance into each room, and I knew you'd think of the scaffolding." He grinned apologetically.

"And if I hadn't?"

"But you did."

"*And,* had you even remembered about my dog, trained by none other?"

"Ouch. Wow, that got past me, all right. Didn't remember he'd known Cyrano. Dumb! But how'd you keep him quiet? He had to know the guy."

"He's smarter than both of us, apparently. But hell, you did a great job, lover." And I gave him a full-body hug and a kiss designed to melt him into the floor.

Worked, too.

~ * ~

Barker Webb finally got the call, after giving up on ever hearing from the woman again. And yeah, she was definitely female, or a go-between. The whole thing of the pipeline was uncertain: too many unstable people involved, he guessed. And the feeling had never left him that this was all some Agency setup. Part of it didn't seem to fit that, though. They wouldn't have made him wait, for one thing. But neither would the woman. In his vast experience, when people wanted money, they wanted it right then. The whole thing was too confusing, but it was all he had.

And when it came time for the exchange, he'd make certain it wouldn't just be a simple hand-over. He'd been in on enough buys to ensure every possible angle was covered. So okay, if the woman was real, maybe it'd all go down as planned. If not, no Fed would ever see a trace of J. Barker Webb in person. This was the survival game, and he damn well knew how to play it and win.

~ * ~

It was February, and we'd had a few lies about warmer weather that'd let us start the other chimney. Inside work was humming, and I got to appreciate Delano Highfill's skill, when he was sober. Craig would show him once how to do something fairly tricky, like mortising in stair treads, and the man would be after it, mallet and chisel. He was indeed ambidextrous, a surprise for some reason. You get to thinking a redneck can't be as adept as somebody who's had a veneer of education, and you're wrong. The wood doesn't know the difference between a damn Ph.D. and a guy who can't spell dawg.

Mangrum Pierce had a bad habit of neglecting his law practice to come down early weekends, like I said, and so did Shelby, they were so taken with the house adventure. He could do some simple stuff, which we let him, but mostly he just wanted to be part of it all. Both of them were getting literal cabin fever with all the bad weather, and this was their escape.

Which was as it shoulda been, what the place was for. Well, few more weeks or some more surprise nice days and we'd be able to ride those horses again. And not long after that, Craig and I'd be through and out of there. To whatever was next.

~ * ~

Nate Peterson handled the usual routine police stuff with the familiarity of one who'd known this town all his life. Predictable: the robberies, the occasional shooting, now more drug-related, with the influx of Cubans and Mexicans bringing the stuff up with them.

The old place was changing, with the counter-culture downtown, the proliferation of restaurants, music venues, boutiques. The old money was still there, but mostly out of town, down those winding driveways with the imposing brick entryways and wrought-iron gates. Those great plantation houses changed hands every five years or so, when the aging execs who'd finally made their piles and could buy them died, and the wives sold out and went back to be near the grandkids. The real estate brokers and lawyers were making a bundle out of all that action.

Now and then a high roller would blow into town, and the established heads, including the force, would tune in to whatever he had going. Usually just high-level investment: buy a couple downtown buildings, spend a lot upgrading them, get them leased out, then sell out and go on to whatever those guys went on to next. Usually nothing illegal, although there was the expected rash of behind-the-scenes deception, betrayal, lust and greed by-products. Just on a bigger-dollar scale.

His job was okay most of the time. Always hurt, though, when he had to bust somebody he knew who'd gotten in too deep. All the potential out there, it was a constant temptation for the local guys to try to cash in, and get themselves burned. And right at the critical parts was when they'd too often try to pull off some sort of score to salvage it all.

He often wondered lately—and worried—about how his oldest friend Craig was faring. Still with Wesley, last he heard, using the latest set of fake names he'd managed for them. They'd found each other just before having to run, and he'd been glad for both of them. So far, they'd managed to stay ahead of that crazed Webb guy and his vendetta, but how long could their luck hold?

Well, the Feds were after that guy hard, so maybe the couple could keep up the chase till he was nailed. No word since the call from Kentucky: guy checking references. That earlier tip they'd given, he'd passed on to Clyde Kelly about the St. Louis possibility. The narcs would've been all over that, and sure, Clyde would surely let him know when something broke there.

He took a call about a break-in at some university students' apartment. Yeah, he and Morris would look into it. He punched off, glanced over papers on his desk. Business as usual. But sure would like to see his buddy again, maybe get some fishing in when—if— they came back.

~ * ~

I decided that part of Kentucky was okay, but somehow it didn't reach me the way the Arkansas and Missouri Ozarks had. The people where we were all seemed just to be sort of...well, temporary. Only a few of the ones we met owned the land they parked their trailers on. A lot were sharecropping tobacco with the few big landowners, doing that labor-intensive grind the weed required.

They borrowed money to buy worn-out cars at county and state auctions, which they never seemed to get paid for before they quit running. Then they'd rust down, decorating the front yards forever. The kids dropped out of school at alarming rates, and we knew of more than one 15-year-old girl getting married. Or starting a welfare family anyway.

This one story you wouldn't believe: Delano told us of a local kid who wasn't very bright, who'd been drawn into a tractor-stealing ring. Apparently farm tractors either don't have ignition keys, or they're all alike, or can be hot-wired. And farmers leave them in the fields a lot. Anyway, he got caught and sent up, taking the fall for the others, who must've been marginally smarter.

Well, seems he had a 14-year-old girlfriend, who promised to be faithful to him while he was inside. But she promptly married another dude. Then, when he got released early for good behavior, she divorced the husband and married him. In her eyes, that was being faithful, I guess.

And alcoholism was rampant. That county was dry, but the next one up the river wasn't, and there was this stream of pickup trucks crammed with thirsty bodies on the twisty roads every night.

Only some of which stayed on the right side of the road.

Not to put the place or the people down, but this just wasn't gonna be the part of the country for Craig and me to settle. Sure, as a weekend getaway for Cincinnati folks like Mangrum and Shelby, it was ideal. But somehow, the echoes of Crockett and Bowie and Boone had gotten lost in a culture of light-bread-and-baloney sandwiches and gasoline fumes and bad TV.

So we were glad the job was nearing its end. We'd miss our bosses, sure. Even miss Delano the Switch-Hands. And sure the horses. Hey, this *was* limestone bluegrass country, after all. Not all bad if you could tune some of it out.

~ * ~

One midweek night, we got ourselves another damn out-of-left-field surprise. Not the good kind. A car drove up to the farmhouse after work, while Craig and I were creating something nice to eat in the kitchen. Cyrano was out somewhere stalking something furry. I went to the door, and there on the porch was—surprise!—Reenie Wilkes.

I was speechless. She didn't recognize me at first, as blonde as she was, but peering closer, she made the connection.

"Damn, girl, I was sure I was in the wrong place, there for a minute. Whatthehell's with you?" No hug, no glad-to-see-you. My radar kicked in. What *was* going on here? She pushed past me roughly, slammed the door, and then without a word, damned if she didn't reach into her bag and pull a black automatic out, and wave me over to Craig, whose mouth was open.

*Holy shit!* This couldn't be happening. This could *not* be...

But it was. A crooked grin was on her face, and it made her ugly. I said she was tall, and she looked like an Amazon, with that sinister gun on us. I slipped my hand into my jeans pocket. Wished that was a gun in there.

"Reenie, what *is* this?" I managed. Things were trying to click in my head, but not coming up with whatever this meant. Sure, she'd apparently lost it back in Missouri some way, blown town...But how could I have been so wrong about this woman?

"What this is, Wesley, is part of a deal. The important part of a very high-priced deal." There was something like triumph on her face. That'd be because she'd found us. But I was still in the dark, big time.

*Oh, oh, found us...*

"What sort of deal?" Craig asked. He appeared calm, but I knew his mind was working. Maybe not on what this was all about, but on which way to jump next.

"Simply put, I deliver both of you to a man who's willing to pay me a whole lotta money for said delivery. We could get more complex, but that's the gist of it."

"Webb." I couldn't keep from blurting it.

"Webb? Who the hell is Webb? Man I'm dealing with's name is Goode. But maybe names don't mean a helluva lot in his business. Which is money, a lot of beautiful money, a bunch of which I'm gonna get."

"Reenie," I decided to give it a try, "why are you doing this? We were *friends*. This guy's a sleazeball, drug lord. He's ordered hits on us twice, for no reason other than we stumbled onto his operation. Don't get into this...it's poison."

*You seem to be forgetting the money you stole from him,* Reenie thought.

"*Why* am I doing this? Surely you can't ask anything as dumb as that." Ugly laugh. "For the *money,* duh. You think I like punching a damn computer every day of my life? There's a lot of money out there, just for the taking, *dumb-ass.*"

And for the first time, I realized Reenie was on drugs. Don't know why I hadn't spotted it earlier. The hyper bit, the too-loud laugh, gung-ho outdoor stuff. All frantic, chemical-induced. I didn't know just what reaction different substances produced, but this woman was on something, and it was making her crazy.

Craig interrupted my train-wreck of thought.

"So just what's the plan, Reenie? You said 'deliver' us, to a guy named Goode. Okay, what's that involve? You plan to herd us both off to where, St. Louis?"

"That's not something you two need to know. But yeah, you get tied up and stowed in my car, and we go for a long drive."

Sounded like she hadn't planned this part of the scheme out very well. Be pretty hard to keep the gun on both of us while she trussed us up. Hey, she was big, but not *that* damn big. Shoulda brought help, I'd have said, but of course she hadn't wanted to split the take, and big ego, probably thought she was tough enough to handle this by herself. Maybe make one of us tie the other up? Okay, loose knots, maybe. But who'd tie the other up? Craig seemed to be thinking along those same lines.

"Well, girl, you gonna shoot us if we resist?" He was still calm, reasonable, not like there was this cannon pointing at us.

"Don't think I won't. Don't really want to do that, but like I said, there's real money at stake, and I happen to need real money just now." *But the guy wants them alive, so he can sweat 'em for the missing money...*her hand was shaking. She focused on it, willed it to steady. But she was also thinking it hadn't been too smart, not bringing somebody with her. But in the real world, who's out there gonna help kidnap two people without wanting a big share of the bucks?

"Well, think about this, then," and Craig bored in on her with those intense eyes. "Whichever one of us you shoot first, the other will damn sure make you eat that gun. And real people don't just drop like on TV. They're hard as hell to kill. There's no way you can get us both, because we're not scared shitless, Reenie. We're not scared at all. We're both tough as hell and you know it. And we'll fight like tigers, even with bullets in us.

"And on top of that, we're about at the end of our rope. Nothing to lose, really. Nowhere we go can we be safe from that madman, and he's proven that three times. You shoot one of us, you'll *die*, I can guarantee it. The other of us will rip your guts out and feed your eyes to the crows, woman!"

His voice had gone hard, and I felt shivers up my back. I got a picture of the mangled Karl Kramer, and of the smashed would-be assassins in Arkansas.

I also saw the big kitchen knife Craig'd been chopping vegetables with, and that called up conjectures even bloodier. Not inches from his hand. Reenie saw it too, and her shaky eyes got big.

She licked her lips, her mind working, eyes moving. She should go for Craig first, gambling I wouldn't be able to stop her. But I was betting her deal had to be to deliver us alive: she wouldn't shoot, I felt sure, hand shaking like that.

But how many times had I been wrong?

And then the damn gun started its move toward Craig. *She was going for it!* So, dead or alive, then? Her eyes went hard. Pinpoint pupils: some brain-frying drug...

I chopped my balled fists down on her forearm with everything I had as Craig, his arm a blur, dodging aside, hit her in the stomach. She was tall and strong, but the double-strike shook her bad. Choking scream. Gun went off, blowing splinters from a hole in the floor, and she clutched her stomach, the piece flying off somewhere else. Craig was trying to grab her, hold her. Didn't want to hurt her bad. She ducked down, maybe to go for the gun again. Craig hauled her up, arms flailing, trying to get at his eyes, claw them out. She screamed again as he spun her, slammed her face-first against the wall, which shook.

"Get me some rope, Wes." Still calm, deadly. Reenie tried to kick back at him, squirming loose, yelling obscenities. She was one strong bitch.

I thought *enough of this shit*, and grabbed a chair. Swung it high, hard, broke it over her head. She morphed into a heap on the floor, and pieces of chair ricocheted off the walls. My adrenaline was screaming.

We tied her up tight, stopped some bleeding, propped her up against a wall. Craig looked a question mark at me.

"Can't exactly turn her over to the police out here, too much exposure," he worried. "What'd the charge be, and her word against ours, who'd believe us?"

"How about attempted murder?" and then I just couldn't keep a straight face. "Okay, guys, you've heard the whole thing. Clyde, if you read me, now you've got a lead on Webb."

And I took the tiny digital recorder out of my pocket that I'd turned on as soon as I'd seen the gun. I'd wanted one ever since seeing that one Clyde had at Webb's the year before. Craig's mouth came open gratifyingly. I grinned.

Reenie wasn't in any shape to appreciate the technology. And to quote Rostand's original Cyrano, that fact failed to disquiet me.

We called Nate Peterson, just to get the proper police procedure down, and to give him the tip about the not-so-good Goode guy, who had to be Webb. He said he'd get the word to Clyde, and also call the local cops here in Kentucky and set it up right, so expect them soon.

Yeah, we'd do that.

"And say, good to hear you two're still alive."

That, sure.

# Nineteen

We were back on the road again. Hated to leave the job unfinished, but didn't have any idea how much the Webbshyster knew about us from Reenie, just then. Besides, Delano could finish the carpentry, and hey, Shelby could probably do the rest of the chimney, knowing her. We called, made our apologies, gave them the bit about Craig's mother again, and said we hoped we could come back when things settled. None of us liked it, but what choice did we have?

Nate called us back to inform us he'd have yet more new I.D. for us as soon as we could pick it up, place he directed us to. Damn, I liked that guy. Taking good care of us again. Didn't know what would happen to Reenie, with what the cops had on her, and really didn't give a happy shit.

So then we picked up the same conversation we'd had coming into Kentucky those months ago. Where to go, what to do. For now, for long-term. Forever?

Craig surprised me:

"Y'know, Wes, why don't we head for Georgia? I'd like to see where you grew up, what that country's like. Gotta be a big part of who you are, which you know I love. Whattya think, girl?"

"Wow, hadn't thought of that. Sure, I do sorta miss the place—places—there. Dad actually bought a bit of land up on a terrific creek fish hide in, a spot to die for. We were gonna put up a fishing cabin soon's I graduated college, but that spring was...was..."

"Okay, you told me that's when he died. Maybe too many memories there? We don't hafta..."

"No, I do wanta go back. Besides, brother Bert sold that place before we even put in a foundation. I wanted him to, actually...not ready to deal with all that at the time, y'know. But that was just a piece of me, then. I'm okay with the old homeplace bit, the house we did live in, which he's kept and rented out. Tries to send me money from that when we touch base, and that's been good a couple times.

"Sure, let's do it. Only thing, I'd expect the Webber to've checked that area out, as a logical haven for me—us—to run to."

"But since we didn't," he reasoned, "and he's got a trail everywhere else for the past year, I don't think that's an issue. And I'm getting it from you that some of that mountainside stuff's a lot like that at that great cabin in the Ozarks. Wanta see it, see you back in it. See if that could maybe work."

So, possibly a little old shopworn homesickness deep down anyway, and sure, like my man to see more of where I'd been, who it'd made me. Actually enjoy showing him around, now that we didn't look anything like who we were. Sure nobody'd ID me even as a dumb blonde.

Yeah, we'd do it.

So south we drove, humming along in the Jeep, not worried about cash, free as two hunted fugitives could ever be, temporarily at least out from under the Webb-cloud. Good feeling. And maybe old stomping grounds would be the place we *could* put down roots.

Again, for me.

~ * ~

Some of Tennessee then, with its echoes of twangy country music and a metropolitan Nashville and not-yet-green hills and the ghosts of Civil War battles: Franklin, Chattanooga, Shiloh. Cowboy boots on non-cowboys in fat-tire trucks with stocked gunracks and grinning girls in straining Levi's.

Guessed all that wasn't that far from my own lifestyle, actually.

Then Georgia: home and not home. Memories, eight years old—yeah, it'd been that long. Longer, with college. Changes, of course: new houses, old crossroads stores gone. Everything seeming smaller, closer together. I'd heard that happened when you tried to go home again, but just eight years? Did seem like a lifetime, though.

You know, the high school non-experience, the crushes on the football studs, the hating oneself for not being popular, striving to be cool, to fit, maybe even to lead. And later, visits home from college, when all the local stuff seemed so narrow, now you were of that not-really-elite. Green, that's what you were, and yeah, not so experienced even now, even after seeing a chunk of the world with all its warts.

But nostalgia anyway, at what was and can't—shouldn't—ever be again. The old boyfriend Dad had looked sideways at and I could never again be drawn to. The silliness that's a part of what memories are, the old triumphs and defeats.

And the warmth of home, mostly Dad and me, with occasional input from strange Bert, who I guess Mom would have made more human. Yeah, if she'd been there.

Favorite restaurant, where at lunch I saw a high school classmate, 40 pounds heavier, too made up. She glanced at me, then her eyes traveled away, no clue to my new I.D. Relief then, since we'd been close for a year. Had two little kids with her, and another embattled housewife. Little pang...cute kids, a pair of girls with their lives ahead of them.

Their mother had been smart for her Roswell, Georgia background. Wondered how she was fitting in, here on the outskirts of Atlanta, which was now (and then, too) such a dynamo of the 21st century. She looked frazzled, and the kids tugged at her constantly for attention.

*Hey, girls, give Mom a break. She's carrying the suburban world on her shoulders, has to run fast to keep from drowning.*

It didn't take Craig long to start lusting after those fish he knew were just itching to bite a dry fly. Up those now-bankful creeks. Just like Dad.

*No, Sarahshrink, leave that one alone.*

We drove way up in the mountains, to creeks Dad had fished and I'd played in. Didn't go to the site of the dreamed-of cabin—not ready for that—but did discover lost hollows choked with laurel and hiding little waterfalls. More water here compared with the Ozarks, and not as huge as the intimidating Rockies, but wild land still, dirt you could get your hands into, get next to.

Too wild, in the career-necessary 21st century.

I've mentioned that I just don't get that finny obsession, so okay, I dropped my Izaak Walton off at a laurel-choked mountain path. Somewhere between the end of the road and the end of the world. I could hear rushing water, and so could Craig. Grinned like a fool and disappeared...rod, vest, floppy hat and all.

Half-second of almost-panic. But no, I wasn't so insecure as to think he'd throw me over for a smallmouth bass.

Maybe *two* smallmouth bass?

I headed for Roswell, where there were knee-keep memories, and stores. You know I travel light, but a girl's gotta give in to the urge now'n then. Cyrano and I left my man to his hooks, line and maybe even sinkers? Who knows.

Didn't worry about ghouls identifying me, blonde and ditzy as I now was (ditzy?).

~ * ~

Craig let the sound of her wheels fade, then moved noiselessly through the brush to streamside, where water pooled below boulders. Slick, dark under the clear late winter sky. *Early in the year, but fish gotta eat.* Besides, he just needed to get off by himself, even for half a day.

Away from bastards trying to kill him and Wes, away from running, hiding—well, hiding now on a clear mountain stream couldn't be all bad—and the tension. Wes could make him forget that for a while, with her irrepressible energy and her delightful smart mouth. *And omigod, that wiry body she gets all over me with. Woman can start a fire with just those eyes.*

But the shadow of the drug monsters never really left them. The fear that the next person they met could see through the disguises, would smirk and pull a gun, blow them away.

He dropped a wet fly below a big half-submerged rock, and saw the eddy spin it. But in his mind, he saw a faceless man: jeans, boots, plaid shirt—harmless construction type—walking toward them, lifting a hand in greeting. Only the hand held a gun, and it spouted a bloom of fire before he—they—could react.

*Hey, cut this out! We're okay. She's okay...got that trigger-happy dog with her. Nobody'll know her, now. And dammit, I'm fishing...*

He retrieved the fly, whipping the line in a long, curving loop behind him in the only clear space, dropped it again further downstream. Yeah, fishing, not to be sabotaged by imagining disaster behind every tree.

*Shoulda gone with her, though. Shouldna taken this break. All it'd take: one druggie recognizing her. And here where she grew up...damn fool to let her go off alone...*

A strike. Deep down, good fish. Surge of adrenaline, like always. Set the hook. Feel the life down there through line, rod, hands, arms. Arc, dip of rod tip. *Fight's on now: focus!*

The fish wanted down behind the boulder. Probably a ledge there it wanted to get under, so the edge could cut the leader. Craig pulled sideways, stepping into the water, gauging his pull, rod bent just short of the pounds-test of the leader.

The fish came, jerking, fighting, past the end of the ledge with its broken-off edge. Then it made a run downstream, and Craig gave line, letting it slip through his fingers at that apex they made, of the triangle formed by the reel and first guide. Snubbing, but only slowing the run.

He took two steps, sloshing now, the sound adding to the rush of water through the rocks. The fish turned toward the last deep water in the pool, and Craig walked in precious feet of line, using fingers and thumb, letting the slack fall out wide, sensitive to the pressure on the light leader.

The icy water found its way into his construction boots, spilling over their tops, instantly numbing feet. He thought ruefully of the time it'd take to dry them, get feeling back...

The fish jumped: a smallmouth bass, and he pulled it another foot closer before it hit water again. *Nice fish.* And yes, a fighter, making a reverse run across the pool, trying for a tree-root tangle where Craig knew he'd lose it. He tensed the rod, curving the path the bass was on, bringing it closer, off-course.

Another run: snubbed. Then another, and another. Man against game fish. Then it was close, and the man reached with his net, rod high, line wound and gripped with his left hand on the handle.

A stick cracked behind him, and he spun instinctively, dropping also into a crouch. The fish jumped a last time, feebly, but the line slacked and it shook free.

"Oh, damn, I'm sorry, man," the voice belonged to a man just parting the streamside laurels. "Clumsy. Cost you a nice fish, looks like." He was watching the surface ripples as the bass streaked away.

He wore construction boots that could have been Craig's twins, jeans, and a brown canvas coat with a fishing vest, and yes, a red plaid shirt showing at collar and cuffs. He was medium height, wore the requisite duckbill cap, maybe 30, give or take a year. Hand gripping a flyrod, though, not a gun.

All this Craig saw and processed in an instant, and he concluded it was no threat. *Paranoid, I guess. Seeing bogeys behind every bush.*

"'S okay: I was gonna catch and release" (not true). "You just startled me." He wound in line resignedly, hooked the fly to a reel crossbar.

"Din't see you. My favorite hole, an' last thing I expected: another fishin' hardcase, ahead of th' season this way." Embarrassed grin.

"I can see why: good water. Well, there'll be another hole. Wanta take upstream or down?"

"Your choice. Up's good, but there's a waterfall down a couple hundred yards. You c'n have it; deep pool below. Don't know this creek?"

"No, girlfriend told me about it, dropped me off. You're here middle of the week, too. No job?" It was a logical guess, and the young man's manner reaffirmed the construction trade.

"Not right now. Building'll maybe crank up in a few weeks agin. Been hittin' th' few places got somethin' goin', but dry now, this r'cession."

"Don't I know it. Been lookin' m'self," Craig was aware he was slipping into the slower speech of this Georgia native. Couldn't seem to help it.

"Where you from?" The inevitable question.

"Virginia, mostly. Worked all over, wherever there was buildin'. You're f'm here." Not a question.

"For sure. Folks' place just over there. Wife 'n me stayin' with 'em till things git movin' agin, or maybe longer. Mom, she's glad of it, th' baby an' all. Oh, I'm Colin." Work-hardened hand extended. "Colin MacNabb. Din't see your wheels."

"Carson Boyle." His identity of the moment. "No, woman's gone till 'round noon t'pick up few things, check out any jobs. Let me escape for a while."

Craig liked this young man immediately, although he would have expected him to be carrying a cane pole and a can of night crawler bait. *No, don't go stereotyping here...21st century.*

"Well, let's git fishin', Carson. Whyn't we hit it couple hours, then meet back here. Git a bite over't th' house, then. Reckon that'd fit with yer lady?"

"Thanks. Maybe...hafta run it by her. Be here 'round then, all right."

Craig worked his way downstream, maneuvering around boulders and through streamside brush. The promised waterfall sound reached him, and he hand-grabbed his way around and below the four-foot drop.

The pool was wide and deep, with only this faintest of paths to it. *Fisherman's paradise. Generous, letting me have it. Nice kid. Had some education, but this recession's driven a lotta people back to the farm, I guess.*

Five casts later, Craig got a strike, but didn't hook the fish. And he didn't mind a bit: the long, looping line glistened in the warming sunlight, and the sound of the water over stone let him imagine he was alone in these mountains. Alone with his supple rod and graceful line and precisely dropping fly in a realm where there was no time, no duty, no claims on him.

No people.

*Now, how could Wes not love this? Here we are, in her backyard, place to die for, and she's no fisherman. Well, prob'ly sit on that big rock and let that magic poetry wash over her, lose herself in this place more'n I am. Fishing ain't all of it.*

*Not quite.*

This time Craig didn't release the bass he caught, or the next two, thinking maybe to contribute them to the MacNabb larder if he and Wes did indeed visit. If Colin had snared a couple more, that'd be a feast.

And surely this mountain haven would be lost to, isolated from, any drug-chain bloodhounds. *Yeah, gotta be someplace safe from the Webbsters.*

~ * ~

So around noon, I eased the Jeep into this woodland turnaround to spy my man bullshitting with a guy about my age, and both of them had fish. Craig's creel showed a fishtail, and the other dude had four smallmouths on a stringer. *Outfished? Surely not...*

And wow: I *knew* this man. This was...okay, now...Colin something, from U of Georgia. Colin...

"Hey, you look like Wesley Whitestone," he called, peering, soon's I hit the ground. Damn blonde hair hadn't fooled him, maybe because I had this narrow-brim hat on. Always liked hats, and not just the duckbills.

But I was cool.

"Colin. Damn, it's been what? Ten years?"

"Nine, anyways. I courted this girl's roommate, Carson, back when we were all young and dumb."

I could see the wheels spinning in Craig's head. So no anonymity here. And he'd be Carson Boyle still, even if I was still Wesley to Colin.

Okay, didn't matter. Colin...*MacNabb* hadda be outside the drug trade. Looked like a construction grunt now, like us.

I knew he'd come to college from somewhere around here, but he'd dropped out before I'd gotten to know him well. Lack of dollars, probably. Nobody in these mountains was rich, except the Atlanta weekenders.

Colin had this open, guileless face that made you trust him, and Colleen the roommate, who I remembered was pretty sharp, had gone for it. Of course, I'd set my sights way far past these hemming-in ridgelines...test my wings. I'd been glad for them.

Didn't know what'd happened to Colleen after they'd split (reality check, maybe). Probably in an Atlanta ad agency making the bucks. Or putting her feet under a CEO's table? What'd she majored in? Who knew.

But here was Colin, quintessential country boy despite his couple years at the U, obviously not working at present, fishing middle of the week.

Like us.

Had a wedding band on (my radar at work), so little wifey maybe hitting it at an office somewhere? Or not. Truckstop waitress? Gum-chewing Cracker queen? *Now stop this, bitch, you and your Yeats and your fantasy world. Your edges are rougher than his any day.*

"Just twistin' Carson's arm, git him'n you t'come over th' house, eat with us. Colleen'd like that a bunch, see you agin."

*Not really? Redhead Colleen?* My mouth'd dropped open. But hey, why not?

Curiosity high, of course. You go to school reunions to see how much better you've done than the others. And sure, she'd majored in...International Relations, it was, wanted to work in some embassy somewhere. Probably got pushed aside by all those missionaries' kids who already knew the language. Headed back home.

Well. Married to old Colin, and here further back in the sticks than I'd been. And what were the odds? Well, names Colin and Colleen: those odds, too.

*But get real, should we fugitives dodge this scene?*

Nah, Colin wouldn't have recognized me if he'd seen the blonde hair and colored contacts. Maybe Colleen...but no, not druggies, surely. Worst thing Colin'd probably sampled was Georgia moonshine.

So we went, fish and all, back down the non-road a ways to a farm lane with rocks in it. And worn locust fenceposts Sherman might have spared for cookfires if he'd come this far north. Then a fine old farmhouse stood ahead, on a rise with gnarled white oaks two of us couldn't reach around.

And damn me if it wasn't a log cabin. Dogtrot, with the originally-open center space closed in with weathered clapboarding. Two-story, and a third chimney said there was a wing out back. Craig was devouring the place with his eyes, noting details I'd miss, wanting to get his hands on the wood.

And Country Colin had surely chafed here, wanting the bright lights and ice water out there when he'd had all this, right here. Well, I guess I had too, sort of.

And here we were, Wesley, Craig, Colin, and yes, Colleen, about as outback as it gets. How was she taking it, nine years later? Kids? Had she dragged this guy out into the world first? Maybe before this recession dragged them back, yeah.

Met us at the porch, still slim, with a year-old baby girl, big blues and that same red hair, just starting to grow in. Happy little grin there counterbalancing Colleen's questioning look. I'd taken off my hat, wanted to see if she'd know me. Shook out what hair I had.

Colin had the kid's grin down, and he waved to his daughter.

"Got some folks you needa meet, hon. This's Carson, and *this*," he paused, nudged me forward, "is somebody *else*." Drive the Jeep through that grin, never hit a tooth.

Colleen shifted the green eyes I remembered, from Craig to me, focused. Then she handed the baby off to Colin, stepped off that porch without a word, grabbed me and hugged me silly.

"You don't do ditzy blonde, Wes Whitestone. What, you been to Hollywood or something? And this's your leading man?"

I was babbling, Craig was looking distinguished, Colin looking like it was Christmas, and the baby laughing. Cyrano was behaving, lying where I'd told him to, eyeing us all, tail doing its thing, when a chisel-featured woman in jeans and a cable-knit sweater called down to us.

"Boy, get these folks in here 'fore dinner gets cold. Old man's here now." To the on-cue arrival of a big green tractor in the side yard. The graying driver unfolded with a third version of the family grin, and welcomed us. Mom came down the steps, took both my hands.

"I'm Lucy, and that's Angus with the cowshit on his boots. See you know Colleen, and who's this?" Head tilted toward Craig, but blue eyes still on me.

"This's Wes, Mom," Colin supplied, "an' Carson, her man." Handshakes all around, and baby Lara happy with all of us.

We were herded into the house, back to a big kitchen table and the kind of food I'd been missing. Lucy sent the fishermen to ice their catch and wash up.

Then it was a brief blessing from Angus, and ham and sweet potatoes and biscuits and black-eyed peas and turnip greens. A warm feeling washed over me like homecoming, and then my old roommate actually handed me Lara to hold.

Now, single itinerant carpenters don't often do the adoring mom-and-baby thing, and maybe this child sensed this. She regarded me with a sudden solemnity, eyes gone grave, and I felt like the accused felon before the judge. Lucy was smiling at us, and I guess it was catching: Lara just as suddenly broke into sunshine and held her arms out to me.

I melted. Damn, I *melted*. Snuggled her up like a teddy bear while her mom filled her plate. *Take your time, girl.* Then reluctantly plopped her down in her highchair with a kiss. *Gotta have me one of these.*

The catching-up talk was going nonstop. How Angus had shooed his son off to the creek after a late-night difficult calving, how Colleen had, all those years ago, gone off to D.C. while Colin had done a hitch in the Marines. How he'd come home, gone off again with a toolbelt and a pickup truck. How Colleen had eventually shoved the Beltway Blues, come back to Atlanta to find everybody she'd known all settled down or gone.

And how the recession had indeed pulled Colin back to the farm. Then, right out of a romance novel, how he'd been weekend-repairing a dock on the big electric company lake a few miles away, when this bunch of city picnickers had shown.

And there was Colleen, with another guy. Sure enough, an ad agency account exec.

Who became history.

So, our turn, and I filled them on the Rockies, Texas, the Ozarks, Pittsburg. And Virginia. Part of Virginia.

And meeting Craig, who wasn't Craig just now.

And of course, I could almost hear the un-asked question: were we or weren't we? Well, we were certainly, but okay, just how *were* were we?

Good question. Flicked a look at Craig, who I knew could/would fast-talk our way on this one.

"It'uz this way, y'see: Wes found me out in th' woods, picked th' ticks offa me, an' I follered her home. Hasn't decided whether t'keep me or not, yit."

Laughter. Tension gone. Everybody knew that was bullshit, but it also signaled *'nuff sed.* And after all, nobody'd actually asked.

After that great meal, Craig, without being asked, went out with Angus to help fix fence that a black bear had gone through. Colin headed for the cow barn, presumably to minister to the new mother. I'd done some of that with old Charlie, back in the Ozarks, yeah. I tackled those fish (no patience catching them, but like to eat 'em), while keeping up chatter with the women.

Learned that Lucy'd been a geology major at Peabody in Nashville: city girl. Ran into Angus in Atlanta while at a rock hound conference after five years out in the cruel world, and yeah, followed *him* home.

Sorta history repeating itself? Colin's construction work was an off-season thing, he obviously on track to take over this farm, whenever.

Both women were fine with the country wife thing, not feeling trapped. Not that far to the bright lights anyway, when the urge hit.

Not that bad a way/place to be. I flashed on Kelcy and Charlie, and yeah, George and Shirley Connaly, back in Arkansas. Good folks doing what good folks'd always done: keeping the world sane, God bless 'em.

Lucy was showing Colleen how to quilt, something she'd recently gotten into, and I tuned in on it. This one would be a pieced record of her and Angus' life together, in stylized shapes of rocks and cows and barns and kids. She explained this was a tradition in a lot of families, going back forever. Nice idea.

This inside hiatus was interrupted by a stint of pre-planting work in their veggie garden, which was about as big as downtown Atlanta. Colleen got on a smaller tractor with a disc behind, to slice up big clods left by the earlier plowing. Lucy monopolized baby Lara while I cleared the fence of old vines and weed stalks to be crunched and shredded by the disc. The late sun was still warm on our backs.

"I get cabin fever bad, about now," Lucy confided. "Gotta get my hands in the dirt, even this early." I could relate to that, with the smell of new earth, the moist soil promising green things and new life in the ageless cycle of the seasons. *Get me some of this too, things settle back down.*

The men came in just before dark, laughing, dusting off coats and jeans, and I thought how right this scene was. The smell of fish frying, hushpuppies bobbing, the old farmhouse welcoming its men in from the field.

Again.

So after a great evening of re-lived memories, jokes, politics (which I avoided), and a totally-enjoyed fish feast, Lucy took over.

"No way we're gonna send you off to camp out, you two. Y'got the guest room, like it or not. Just don't kick the walls down." Craig actually blushed.

And there, drifting off together, I experienced the rare and secure feeling of being taken in by strangers, far from home. But welcomed, sheltered.

Loved, even.

# Twenty

What wasn't to like about our stay with the MacNabbs? Colleen was the opposite of house-afire Shelby, but she was good to be with. Lucy could've been the mom I barely remembered, and the men were…well, what men were supposed to be.

And Lara's normal expression was delight. She only cried to tell us something wasn't right, and her mom was so *into* motherhood. Made me feel a little like I was missing out.

*Okay,* time enough for that, when and if.

No, *when.*

But of course, with their knowing my name, if not Craig's, the word could leak someway. Nobody comes into a country setting without the neighbors knowing about it, even if they aren't close. *Yeah, I heard Wes Whitestone's back f'm knockin' 'round th' country. Don't reckon all that education done her much good. Needs t'find herse'f a good ole boy, settle down. Hear she's stayin' up with th' MacNabbs…*

And somebody'd know somebody'd know somebody who knew how to get the green, or the white, and it wouldn't matter I was a blonde, with a guy sporting white hair and a new name.

Goon time again.

"So," I cornered Craig next day before he could get away to the back forty with the boys, "small world has its thorns, guy. Good fishing, good people, good country's not worth our hides. Gonna hafta roll on outta here. Webbster's surely got my home territory staked, and I guess we've pushed it too far already."

"Been thinking that, much as I hate it. Cabin up in these hills would've been great." He looked ruefully about us, at the barns, the fallow fields, the ridges rising above this creekside cove, the house with its worn edges, its secrets.

So okay, it was goodbye time again, albeit with promises to keep in touch (which wouldn't happen while we were on the run). I kissed the red fuzz on Lara's head, hugged everybody. Herded my man away, and we slipped down from this, one of Dad's favorite fishing creeks. Told the MacNabbs we were maybe headed back to Ohio. Seemed a safe dead end.

"Only thing else I wanta do here before we go to ground in New Zealand or somewhere, see the house I grew up in." Sorta mixed at that prospect, but knew I'd regret not checking it out while we were there.

The car license still said Ohio, since we'd kept it with the trade, but since nobody'd ever associated us with that state (that we knew of), we felt comparatively safe from evil ones' tracking it.

We drove around the rest of that day, ogling the mountains, avoiding lookalike major highways, and I reminisced. Yeah, here was the wide place in the road we teenagers would crowd into pickups and roar off to. Just because it was Somewhere Else and therefore hadda be different/better.

Funny how a darkened parking lot at a place with music coming out of it can seem to be a miniature cosmos, with trash talk and social levels and crushes and jealousies among smart-ass kids. Then, seen in daylight, it's just a tacky ice cream joint or roadside store, frayed, dingy, totally uncaring.

We didn't know where we wanted to go: no mysterious messages for me, so we thought about maybe staying in this general area anyway (bait the lion?), see about work. Keeping a low profile, hoping I wouldn't be I.D.'d by another local.

Atlanta itself too noisy, too big, too frenzied for both of us, and you had to stay north (or some other direction) a long way to escape it. Find a place where you could maybe find your place.

And near-poverty out in the mountain boonies there, like so many remote and lovely spots I'd found. Hillside fields you could fall out of like back in Arkansas, worn soil, old echoes of work, survival, sudden joys, clan angers, summer storms, iced-in Januarys waiting for life again.

We were searching, trying to find this place that had to be there for us, where we could hide, find work, build a nest safe from the world. But even waiting for it, I still hadn't been guided back here, as if no, Wesley wasn't supposed to go back home again.

But we tried, checking out construction sites, all of which had this scruffy look, no new trucks or shiny equipment. Maybe it was just too early in the year, too raw before things came to life again. Sort of a desultory picking at the work till the world could bloom again.

Depressing.

We thought about going further south, maybe over to the coast, down to Florida. But I'd found that too many snowbirds flocked there when winter came, and the competition'd be fierce. Nice place to visit, yeah.

I guess what iced it for me was our driving out to see the old homeplace, which wasn't a farm, but wasn't in a subdivision, either. And there were two abandoned cars in the yard, settling back to earth, surrounded by last year's stiff weed stalks. Junk stacked in Dad's shop, decaying plastic kids' toys littered the yard, and daytime television blared from somewhere out a broken window.

Hey, brother Bert had kept this place rented. What kinda people *were* these? Did he ever check up on things here?

Just then an aging minivan drove up, turned into the yard, stopped in a bare spot. A harried woman, maybe my age, pregnant, got out, glanced at us parked across the road, unstrapped a baby's car seat, herded two other dirty children toward the house. She was squinting through cigarette smoke, haranguing the kids, trying to push strands of hair the color of straw out of her eyes, also grabbing a sack of groceries and a six-pack somehow, hugging it all to her big belly.

*Dear God.*

Without a word, Craig cranked up the Jeep and drove.

~ * ~

"You were saying, back when this *déjà vu* began, that you'd like just to be able to go back to Virginia, right? Pick up where we left off." He nodded ruefully: pipe dream. But I had a scheme I'd been working on all this time. Down somewhere in the back of my mind, I guess. I said it *does* happen.

"Okay. I like that, too. Now here's the bizarre plan I've come up with: we do just that, and hide there, *in plain sight*. Back in Virginia..." I held up a hand when he started to interrupt. "Hear me out, now. We know the disguises work—Phil didn't have a clue who you were, even if he'd had a description, and Reenie wouldn't have, except she was up close and knew both of us. Just a freak thing, running into Colin, Colleen that way. And I don't mind the blonde hair thing, and I've gotten used to the contacts. Or maybe go for those Sarah Palin designer glasses—I love those. And you've got the hair and now the beard. We can be invisible, and be back in the place we wanta be.

"And here's the real deal..." I was going in for the kill. "We 'buy' your Virginia place under our new names, see. You're down that long drive; we become a little reclusive. We're a construction team, just you and me, start over where you know what's happening, where the contacts are."

"Wes..." This was just *too* fantastic. He could probably see holes all in it I hadn't picked up on, but I was hot to make my case.

"Shh, love. Now, I know people will maybe get a jolt, but not be totally fooled by your disguise, although with the beard I think it'll be enough. But they won't mine, because not that many ever saw me, outside of the crew, Sarah, and that nerdy university clique. Never at your place in the daytime for any neighbors to see. In fact, if your other girlfriends were that discreet, they're still anonymous…"

"Hey, let's don't go there." Sheepish grin.

"Couldn't resist. But okay, the clincher: you resemble the Craig everybody knew, because you're his *cousin*. Older, okay, and maybe a little more elegant—if that's possible—given to sports coats and maybe an ascot, and I swear we could pull it off."

"An *ascot?*"

"Well, maybe not go *that* far, but you could fake a pipe or something."

"You're thinking Webb would never expect us to go back." Okay, he was actually thinking about it.

"Why would he? It's been a year. The place's been for sale for about the right interval, with real estate slow like it is, so it finally sells. I'm sure he has the shreds of his little ring going there, but they won't know us. Not by that picture, not by our names. Not by anybody's tipping them."

"It'd be a risk."

"Hasn't this running and hiding been proven a risk? Three times. I mean, maybe in Australia or some other end of the earth, but I'm not into kangaroos. Back home we could have most of a life again. And I'm hoping eventually either Webb'll give up, die of old age, or the posse will get him."

"Hide in plain sight," he mused. "Got an intriguing aspect to it, all right. Let's sleep on it. We'll be out of Georgia soon, and it just happens we *are* sorta headed that way at the moment, toward Virginia."

Sleep. Yeah, we did some of that, too, in an out-of-the-way motel. But after our latest miraculously narrow escape, and now this not-old-home thing, I just curled up next to Craig and let him put those big arms around me and be good to me. I felt like we were just two vulnerable children alone out there in a world full of badasses, and we clung to each other. Really *clung*. Of course, when you're reminded of how much you really need this kind of hands-on protection, the hands *can* get sorta carried away.

~ * ~

Coming into the Virginia mountains before spring is real, in those raw, Creation-days of stark trees and forlorn fields that look dead, before anything is budding out, you can get a desolate feeling.

Or not. This was really coming home, and I don't think anything could have spoiled it. There was ridge on blue-haze ridge off forever. Then down into rounded pastures, brown now, with board fences and those stop-your-heart horses nosing around, remembering grass. The Blue Ridge on your right as you come up the Shenandoah Valley, changing colors a dozen times as the sun slips west. It'll grab you.

And to hell with Webb-Head...we *were* coming home. We were going to ground right in front of God and everyone, to become two different people, as far as the folks who used to know us were concerned.

We hoped.

And right off, back at the home place, there was a surprise. No, not another nasty one. Craig kept this shit-eating grin on as we turned off onto his woods road. Okay, glad to be home; so was I... then we came to his field, and there was a *horse* in it.

A horse I knew.

*"Walker!"* I shrieked, like a ten-year-old on her birthday. "How...when? Oh, damn, you terrific man, you!" And I hugged him so hard I thought somebody's ribs would crack. My favorite horse, and Mr. Cool here had kept him a secret all this time.

"He's been down at Alan's place until yesterday. My niece Selena rides him every chance she gets. I knew we wouldn't be gone forever."

Well. I told you I loved this man. So now I had my dog, my man, *and* my horse. Call me the queen. Just call me the luckiest damn girl alive, the watched-over, taken-care-of, queen of the whole incredible *world.*

And next day I rode him, this blonde with blue eyes, stranger in town, but same old Wes to Walker, and Cyrano'd gotten used to it. Hey, dogs don't see in color. The first time Craig had seen my disguise back in Kentucky, *he'd* gotten a jolt.

"Now this's so great," he'd said, "a strange and exciting woman in my house, and I don't even have to give up the other one." Of course, that cut both ways, now with his distinguished white hair and beard.

We settled in gingerly, not going anywhere much at first. I watched close to see if anybody recognized us when we went out, always wearing sunglasses and sunshading hats. Always had a fascination for those great hats women used to wear. Craig took to wearing a corduroy sports coat with the suede elbow patches, and looked even more like that professor. The beard had been the final touch. Still tickled, although I'd gotten used to it. But back here, where he'd virtually grown up, it would still all be pretty chancy.

He was now Donald Estes, a cousin of the Craig MacDonnell folks had known, and had bought the place from him. I was his live-in, Clarissa Steadman, given to those straw hats, a slight English accent I remembered from an obscure college play I'd been in, and an equine look.

Hot shit.

As new owners of the place, we didn't know exactly where that cousin had gone off to. And yeah, the girl who'd worked for him that time must've moved on, too: itinerate, those carpenters.

We decided it'd be fun to test our new appearances, but keep it safe, just in case. We made an appointment to see Nate Peterson at the police station. Just a friendly call. I don't even remember what the pretense was. Craig and I had dressed the parts, had these other fake names we'd invented for the occasion, and the girl at the desk, who'd known him before, didn't register a bit of recognition. When we walked into Nate's office, he glanced up from papers on his desk, rose with a slight question on his face.

"Yes, you're Mr. Ellington, I believe. And," he looked at a note, "Ms. Carraway. What can I do for you?"

*Wow, this was fun.*

"Well," Craig shut the door behind us, "we'd just like to thank you, Nate, for giving us a new life. Four times." He extended his hand, with that trademark grin. The question on the detective's face turned to astonishment, as he looked from one of us to the other.

"My God," he breathed. "It *is* you. My oldest friend, and I didn't even suspect. Sit your butts down, both of you. Wow, this is amazing. And you haven't done that much to yourselves. Wow."

"Acid test, Nate. We figured if we could fool you, we could be two other people, even here. Whattya think?"

"I think it by God worked, Craig—*Donald*, you old dog. And... Clarissa, (sure, he'd been the one who gave us our latest I.D.s) you could rob a bank looking like that and fool everybody."

"Don't give me ideas, Nate. And I second Craig's thanks, guy. You saved our asses over and over." I leaned, gave him a peck on the cheek. He actually blushed, cool cop that he was.

We talked a little about our experiences in general. Turned out he hadn't seen the house sale transfer in the paper, and had gone on worrying we'd never be able to come back. That about our buying it tickled him.

"Alan know? I haven't seen him in a while. Suppose you wanta keep it as close as possible."

"Oh, yeah. We've been in touch all along. He's solid, but I have wondered why Webb hasn't tried to find us through him."

"How would he know about Alan at all? Unless you'd told him while you were working for him."

"I'm pretty sure I didn't, no reason to. But it's worried me. A chance, but we found out being on the run can get lonely, if you can't confide in anybody. And he's the only one, besides you."

We went out of there feeling a lot more secure in our new identities. I'd heard attitude was necessary in fooling people...play the part well enough to believe it yourself, and the world will, too.

Seemed to be working, so far.

~ * ~

It was a few nights later, starry, the false smell of real spring in the air, we did a repeat of that fabulous first night together, over a year ago, now. The food, the music, the fireplace logs dancing flame. Only this time it wasn't all pins-and-needles anticipation, surprise.

Well, not exactly.

Craig had another of his grins on, but I never learn. Thought it was just remembering, like me. Then he goes down on one knee, for Crissake...

"Okay, girl, this is it. Will you?" And yeah, there *were* flowers, from somewhere...

He looked so much like a caricature, I almost giggled. Except that he meant it. And oh, God, I was so ready. Almost forgot to be flip about it. I took a long beat to answer, looking him over like yeah, a side of beef.

"Yeah, I guess. Might's well...too windy to pile rocks."

*"You!"* And he grabbed me, just like that other time. And we did this frenzied love-wrestle all over the place. Again. And again, Cyrano let us get away with it.

And it didn't matter that long-legged beasties were out there hunting us, that we were living a balancing act with our false I.D.s, makeovers, in-your-face living in the crocodile's mouth. We had each other all the way, now.

*All* the way.

'Cause marriage is still the real test of commitment, believe it. Okay, so you live with this guy for a year, you give him everything you have, are. You're both deep in love, swear your devotion. *Love like ours can never die:* Kipling.

But no matter what you say or prove, that arrangement really says, for one or both: 'I really wanta be able to toss you out with a minimum of hassle, nothing legal, nothing on paper.' Kinda an action-speaks-louder-than-words thing. And face it, that attitude, no matter how deeply buried, just ain't the way to 'as long as you both shall live.'

So yeah, we were gonna do it right. *Hallelujah.*

We tried one more identity test a few days later. We'd been to see his brother Alan and his family some before we'd had to run. And of course, now we'd have him do the wedding. So thought it'd be nice to be who we really were with the family, but have some more fun first. Didn't worry they'd blow it to anybody: Virginians are pretty private folks. And family loyalties? Stronger than steel.

Selena was my favorite. She'd be almost eighteen, a senior and accepted early-decision to the College of William and Mary. (Thank God it's a state school so we can afford it, her mother had told us on the phone.) She was a quiet, thoughtful girl who planned to study religion, we'd learned. And pretty enough for the boys to hit on...she could have it all.

The other kids were cool, too. Jason had somehow missed the awkward stage, and at fifteen was a serious prankster and a very funny kid. Had told me before that I oughta be in a Western movie, with my name (Howdy, Miss Whitestone, ma'am, you must be th' new schoolmarm...).

The twins were redheaded, just ten years old. But no way could you say they were afterthoughts. Morgan and Tegwin stole hearts with their freckles and impish grins. He was all boy, as they say of mischievous kids when they get into minor scrapes. She was all sunshine and spice, a daughter to die for.

Drove down to their place on a Saturday when we knew they'd be home, and just walked up to the door. Wife Ellen opened it, and looked at me blankly.

"Yes?" Then she looked at Craig, and I swear there wasn't a moment's hesitation...she grabbed him, hugged him, then extended an arm and included me in her embrace.

"Craig! Welcome back, brother. And Wesley, you two would fool anybody but me." Then, dropping her voice, "Oh, let's pull one on Alan. Stay right here, now." Twinkle, big smile. I'd always liked her. She went to his study, knocked. "Alan, there are some people to see you."

"Be right there," muffled, from inside. And he came to the door with his unfinished sermon in his hand, reading glasses up on his forehead. He checked us both out, puzzled.

Wow: his own *brother*.

"We'd like to talk to you about getting married," Craig began, trying to suppress that insistent grin.

"Oh. Well, yes, of course. And you are...?"

"I'm Hortense Threadneedle," I supplied, with that affected accent, "And this is my fiancé, Lord Ellesmere. We..."

Ellen couldn't hold it any longer. She let out a howl of laughter. Alan looked confused.

"Oh, Alan, you are such a *riot* to live with! You don't even know your own *brother!* Oh, I *love* this..." She whooped.

His eyes widened. He did the from-one-to-the-other bit, then his own grin, so like Craig's, began to spread. He whooped too, threw the papers aside, and hugged us both, dancing us around the living room, while Ellen just kept laughing.

Eventually the kids came in for lunch, and the parents introduced us by our new names. Selena kept looking at me more than Craig, and I knew she was close to getting it. After all, they'd been in on the secret of the house 'sale.' Knew we'd be back soon.

*But Hortense Threadneedle?*

"You're really Wesley, *aren't* you?" She still wasn't quite sure. Turning to her uncle, "And that makes you Uncle Craig, no matter what you look like." And she flew into our arms. The other kids just stared.

It was great, having family like that. Alan and Ellen were just the finest two people on the face of the earth. We caught up on everything, even our hairy escapes, which fascinated Jason and sort of scared the rest of them. He had to hear the one about the hit man and the trick tree limb several times over.

That young man also had to tell me, out of his parents' hearing, about his circle of crazies at his high school. Seems these boys had made up a list of outrageous pranks each had to play on his teachers, with points for every one he pulled off. You know, like frogs in their desk drawers, signs on the teacher's back. Top single score went for getting a restroom excuse, going outside, and walking by the classroom window in plain sight without getting caught.

Selena filled me in on her love affair with Walker, and I promised her all the rides she could stand if she'd come visit. We also talked about college, and I was suitably impressed that she'd gotten into the very popular second-oldest one in America.

The twins were so adorable, I couldn't help thinking *okay, gotta have some of that at home.*

Not that kids hadn't been in the back of my mind for a while now.

~ * ~

Along with plans for our upcoming wedding, I'd applied, on a chance, to teach lit at all four exclusive private high schools in the area, although aware this was the middle of a semester.

"Just in case one of your teachers gets sick or something, I can sub," I told them. As Clarissa Steadman, I couldn't give them my transcript, but maybe as just a substitute, I could get away with it.

What I did fall into, as a surprise, was a new construction program at the community college. Seems they had a big grant and were just now offering non-credit courses at night in carpentry, masonry, electrical, plumbing and HVAC. And get this...the very day I applied, the carpentry instructor, a retired guy, had fallen off a ladder and broken his leg.

I said call me lucky.

Call him something else.

"Can you possibly fill in, like *tonight?* the worried director of the program wanted to know. He didn't even ask for a resume. *Lucky.* And it paid fifty dollars an hour. Not that many hours, but yeah, I'd take it.

Craig ran down some leads, but with the season still not opened up for the year, things hadn't picked up yet. He did find a few short-term fix-it jobs, couple days here and there, and promises of start-ups before long. Now we had the Pierce reference in Kentucky, and felt safe clueing Mangrum in on the name change. (Hey, he *was* a lawyer, and while apparently not crooked, he knew the meaning of the word expedient). And we could refer to other vague jobs if necessary. Craig couldn't use his Class A license, but then he wasn't aiming high just yet.

Again, we could survive. I'd never asked, but Craig did have a sizeable savings account, and his own lawyer could get money to him without leaving a trail, somehow. Plus what we'd saved at those jobs we'd had. We'd eat, and reasonably well.

So, lotsa time to plan our big day, our life together, and still fish, hike, camp, before it got too busy. Ride my guy Walker, and do some more building on the place Craig had always planned. Like a horse barn, sure. My teaching was only four nights a week, three hours at a shot, two groups. Could do that without breaking a sweat.

I've never fantasized about a big wedding…all that money spent, white one-wear dress that gets in everything, dorky relatives with snotty kids. Bridesmaids checking out the groom's guys. Tears from the women; off-color jokes from the men.

So it'd be at Alan's place. His great family, although the parents wouldn't be able to make it, both homebound in Florida. Nate Peterson, wife; his lawyer, ditto; my nerdy brother, Bert, up from Atlanta with his perennial girlfriend, Hanna. Hadn't seen Bert in years, but it didn't matter: he was still a nerd, she still had her horse laugh. I liked them just fine…in Atlanta.

It'd be in Nelson County, Craig's homeplace, and sure, the record would be in the courthouse there, with our right names, but who the hell would ever make that connection? And what'd it get 'em? *Craig and Wes? Sure, they blew in here, got married, then off somewhere again. You know they sold his house…*

Selena was my maid of honor. She took over and fussed over me like a mother, and I almost cried. Teenage mother, yeah. Mine would've loved this. Dad, too. Dad maybe more. My best buddy…

I thought about that some, and a not-so new thought came: was Dad maybe my guardian angel in all this? One escape after another, too many for blind luck? Falling into great jobs every time? And now this, the biggest day of my life? Maybe so. Comforting thought. Like to produce a young version of Dad. Craig, too, of course. Yeah, two little guys…

Getting maudlin, here.

But that's what a wedding's supposed to be about, right? Laughter and tears, fears and nerves, joys and dreams. Remembrances, the rushing back of adventures and triumphs and disappointments and all you've been and done and seen, and all of it culminating in today. And the man of your dreams, if you're lucky, right there, a rock to steady you, to build the new life around and with. My guy unruffled, cool. And so damn *handsome*.

Brother Bert and his Hanna were taken aback, naturally, at my appearance. Didn't try to explain my blue-eyed-blondeness, let 'em think it was just another strange example of my being a square peg in a weird hole. Maybe I should've hung piercing dangles all over...nose, eyebrows, lip. Really freak 'em out. Nah, adolescence was a while ago...gotta decide who I was gonna be now. Old married woman? Stereotype.

We didn't write our own vows or anything that kitschy. Just whatever Alan wanted to begin with, which was of course nice and sincere. Then "Do you take..." *Yeah, forever, in whatever good and beautiful and whatever ugly and nasty and mean life and its cretinous denizens could throw at us.*

The two rings and the pronouncement that made it all legal and proper. A charge, the admonition to take strength from each other, team always against the uglies of the world...

Oh, and a very public and very sealing kiss. Great tradition, and it made my knees weak. Again.

Tickled, too.

"We'll do a honeymoon trip whenever you say," my mister told me.

"Done enough tripping for now. When we have the other thing settled, we'll do a double celebration, okay?" I tossed the bouquet, which little Tegwin caught.

"Yeah, that." Never far from our minds. He kissed me again.

# Twenty-one

"I wish you'd just forget about them, Jay," Gwen Webb declared. "It's become an obsession. They didn't put Jerry in for life, Clyde Kelly did." He was pacing. He'd finally let her in on what he'd been doing about MacDonnell and the girl.

"They helped, and I'm sure they took the money. Besides, I can't get to Clyde. Can and will get those two. If MacDonnell hadn't broken Jerry's arm, he'd have taken all three out, and we wouldn't have lost it all."

"You're saying you wouldn't fight if you knew you were about to die?" She was on her third martini. Or was it the fourth?

"You're talking like we hadn't lost our only son."

"We lost him when you got him into the whole drug thing." She was bitter.

"He was already in it. And he was a lot safer with me to keep an eye on him than out on the streets."

"Lotta good that did, wouldn't you say?"

"Oh, you're drunk. I can't talk sense to you when you're drinking. Go to bed."

"Go to bed when I'm ready. Anyway, this revenge thing's cost you two good men so far, and that other guy in Missouri. And the woman you made that deal with's inside for who knows how long. Time to cut your losses."

"Maybe more like time to quit sending boys to do a man's work. I thought Karl and Denny were pros. Wrong."

"Maybe MacDonnell's the pro. Or the girl. They seem to keep on surviving."

"Just lucky, is all. But it does make you wonder...could they have been part of the setup from the first?"

"Nah. MacDonnell's been around there forever. Just a builder. Damn, I miss that great place. Miss my horses, too."

"You never rode them much."

"Did with Wesley. She really liked that Walker. Say, I'd bet wherever they are, it's somewhere with horses."

~ * ~

In Pittsburgh, Sid Bartlett was worried. The blowup with his longtime girlfriend Cheryl Saunders had been building for a long time, yes, but he'd never expected her to walk out. Said she was tired of being manipulated, always having to do things his way. Well, whatthehell had she expected? You become half a couple, you compromise. And it'd worked for over those two years.

But then she'd gotten this idea she was giving more to the relationship than he was. And that was bullshit. Who paid for just about everything? Who put up with her quirks about wanting more than the steady, dependable arrangement they had? Hey, she hadn't had to worry about anything, so what'd set her off?

Well, a guy never knew what was in a woman's head, he guessed. So if she'd needed to get out, that was just that. But now she'd disappeared, gone off to who knew where, and that worried him. If she'd just stayed around, he knew he could've reasoned her through their differences—always had—and they could pick it up again. But not if he couldn't talk to her in the first place. *Damn.*

Or maybe it was better she was gone. He'd always suspected she wasn't 100% on board with him. And sure, he'd moved fast that time he and Phil had met her: didn't want his little brother to score right under his nose. The two of *them* might've made it together, given the chance, but no, Sid hadn't been about to let that happen.

And it hadn't. One thing about Cheryl: she was loyal. And when Wesley had been here, that had taken care of that, with Phil so wild about her. *My brother just isn't very sharp*, he smiled. *Never has been.*

So time to take another look around, he guessed. See who's out there wanting a steady guy to share a life with. Old uncle always said there was a new crop of girls every year, and that did seem to be the case. Thousands of eligible ladies in this world, so who'd miss just one?

As long as Cheryl kept her mouth shut.

~ * ~

The old carpentry instructor didn't get over his two-piece leg for a long time. Said it ached too much for the classes. So could I go on teaching them? I guessed so, yeah. I had the students, most of whom were guys, but a few women, build walls and hang windows and then take them out again. Laid out sills and joists and plates and figured framing. Did trim work, stairs. Straight stuff, but okay for now.

Most of the young studs were high-school dropouts, but there were a few older ones who just wanted to learn how to build stuff. Some, like me, had to be using their hands, so this was the first step: shut off that iPod and start swinging that hammer, dude. Of course, the first day, they'd just about all hit me with that can't-we-get-a-real-instructor roll of the eyes. But after that, it was bust your ass, kid, Miss Wesley's about a mile and a half ahead of you and gainin' fast.

Craig kept getting the short-term bits: put on an extra bedroom, convert a garage to a den. Build a porch. Kept pretty busy, and I could help when he needed me. We managed to keep ourselves from going stir crazy.

And spring had come for real, with first the crocus, then the serviceberry white on the hillsides. Then the daffodils, forsythias, redbuds, and dogwoods. Life emerging from gray winter, little green things looking around and deciding they liked all this.

And speaking of life, we'd decided it wasn't going to get any better than this. So what'd we do? We got pregnant. Really. Due by sometime in December, and both of us were ecstatic. Talk about getting some real meaning into your life. A little Craig, or a Wesley... we started the whole foolish business of picking names.

Yeah, hard-ass Wesley got so *into* the mommy thing. And Craig, who I secretly suspected had been casting himself as an old man with our May/September relationship, could toss that bit. A kid of our own wasn't gonna think his dad was old, no matter the years between them.

We started going to natural childbirth classes, looking a little like senior citizens among all those gum-chewing barely-out-of-their-teens girls and nervous boys. I reflected that the ones who really needed this guidance, the junk food high-school dropout set, would probably give birth in mama's trailer, herself only 35 or so, and the cycle would repeat itself.

Didn't matter, I guessed. World would go its lurching way, no matter whether Wes and Craig were giddy with happiness while confused dropouts with no skills became welfare statistics.

*There, but for the grace of God...*

We fixed up a spare room, of course, as the nursery. Went all the way: Craig built a crib; I built a cradle. Both of us carved wooden toys. I remembered Dad telling me I'd scorned the plastic, light-up-and-beep contraptions as a baby, for the simple wooden blocks, trucks, tractors, and animals he'd made for me. Where were those things? Didn't remember. Surely I hadn't thrown them out. Lost somehow in that lost time of losing him.

God, he'd be happy at our news.

So yeah, I can recommend it: walking among greening trees and flowers and new buds and that smell of turned earth, knowing, then later feeling the new life inside you. Something only a mother-to-be can experience. To hell with my always wanting to be a boy. Been there (sort of); done that. This was real: great life with a great husband, great place to live, great work (I was loving it), and like I said, my horse and dog, too. Somebody up there was watching out for Wesley, and I was becoming more and more aware of that whole concept...living it, actually.

~ * ~

"What I'm worried about," Barker Webb, alias Parker Goode said, "Is the way those dumb-asses I sent out to do MacDonnell and the woman left a trail. The narcs got enough out of Black's shaky wife to crack down on Baltimore, and while Denny had sense enough for fake I.D., that damn Karl didn't...too cocky. Feds tracking down more of our people, getting too close to us."

"So don't pursue this vendetta any further, duh," Gwen advised. "Maybe know when to quit."

"No, I'm thinking more along the lines of 'if you want a job done right, you have to do it yourself'."

"Oh, hell. Count me out of *that* ego trip. Where's the smart lawyer I married? Or was I fooled? Anyway, you don't have a line on where they are, so forget it."

"Oh, they'll make a mistake. Everybody does. Unless they're in Greece or somewhere."

"The Peace Corps, maybe? Building jungle huts for starving Africans? Igloos for Eskimos?"

"Wouldn't that be a bite. Well, I can wait, will wait. Something'll give sometime."

He hoped.

~ * ~

Something *was* giving, a bit at a time, Clyde Kelly reflected. Just good, solid police work, but it had pointed more and more to St. Louis as the center of an operations hub. And very probably to J. Barker Webb, late of Virginia. Who surely had another name, and it just had to be the Goode the woman in Kentucky had let slip. Clyde was still angry with himself for that tunnel escape over a year ago. And if he admitted it, he was every bit as obsessed as Webb with finishing the job he'd started and put so much time into.

The girl, Aggie Black, had unwittingly led them to middlemen in Baltimore. She'd been easy to interrogate, being a user herself, off-balance, broken up over her husband's death. And those middlemen and their associates had yielded just bits of the puzzle, but along with cop instinct, some major busts had gone down.

But no solid trace of Webb. Yet.

Better luck with the late Karl Kramer, who'd apparently scorned false papers. With what the agents already knew about some St. Louis operations, things began to link up. After all, it was clear the goons going after MacDonnell and the girl were from Webb. The Agency'd tried to get the Kentucky woman to open up, but she wasn't saying another word. Probably afraid of an inside hit, which could be entirely possible. Or just maybe she really didn't know any more about the operation, unlikely as that was.

So, with what Clyde knew of Webb, his M.O., lifestyle, even his wife's habits, he felt certain it would only be time and thorough detail work till he could uncover and nail the slippery lawyer.

The guy could continue to practice law, but only under the table and with clients who'd keep their mouths shut. Couldn't register anywhere, with no history for an assumed name. Even if he copped a dead lawyer's I.D., there'd be others who'd spot the switch. Too much risk.

So, no law practice. Probably some other cover, then. Of course, if he had enough money, he could just play the idle heir somewhere, spending his family trust fund, invisible to all but a few incurious neighbors. And Clyde was sure the man had enough money.

But he also knew Webb. The guy had an ego. He'd want to be the head of an operation. And at least twice he'd already sent the troops out after the pair, who weren't really his enemies. So he was in charge of something fairly big, with branches.

And sending that picture out to try to score so far away...this was no local cell. This was big. Maybe more and higher than Webb, sure, but you went after whoever you could, to lead on up the ladder.

Clyde paced the narrow office they'd given him. It'd almost become home, the way this whole thing was shaping up: those bits of intel coming in, the need to be on the job as much as possible. When had he taken a break, really? Didn't remember...

He did remember the girl he'd met the last time he'd slipped back into Charlottesville to see Nate Peterson. Just another attractive girl, but maybe his being on his own too much had made him receptive. Not that many women hit you between the eyes at first sight, but it'd happened. To jaded old Clyde the loner. There'd been time for just the one date before he had to get back onto the St. Louis leads Wes and Craig had provided. But he'd called her a few times since, and yeah, there was something there, all right. Have to arrange another trip to Charlottesville soon...

*But back to priorities. Can't moon over a girl when there's a top-level badass out there with my name on him.*

Webb would blunder...he was human. And angry, which would help. Lost two—no, three—guys already, but he wouldn't give up. Not Webb. Clyde remembered the not-quite-veiled arrogance that had tainted that restoration job. There'd been something just not right about that from the beginning...

Yeah, Wesley had mentioned picking up on that, too, after the Jerry collar. Woman had radar, for sure.

So she and Craig had dodged the bullet so far. Either sharper than most or lucky. That'd fuel Webb's obsession and make it more likely he'd slip. Somewhere. Sometime. Sort of surprised he'd taken it this far...they weren't really the ones got him...

*Shame we can't help those two in this,* he mused. *They're doing a good job of hiding, though, and just have to leave it at that. Nate Peterson might know where they are, and that's okay. Let 'em stay hidden. Just hope we nail Webb before he finds them. Third time that we know of: might get lucky, himself...*

"No, dummy," Clyde said aloud. "If we did know where they're hiding, that could help us with Webb. Yeah, need to know that. Because Webb's more apt to come out into the light when he finds 'em. Shouldn't, if he's smart, but he will...too obsessed."

He considered that. Would it endanger Craig and Wes if the cops knew where they were? Or would it make it easier to protect them? No again...Webb's bunch might actually have somebody in the legal loop, back in Virginia or here in St. Louis, even...

*Yeah, maybe better leave it alone, then.* Nate could reach him. If anything broke that could help the hunters, he'd be sure to pass it on.

*Like to see them, though. Like to see Cheryl again, too. Great folks, Craig and Wes. Maybe, if I'm the only one to know...*

*Let's see, he has a brother close to there...*

# Twenty-two

"He's got family!" Webb snapped his fingers. "Got to have. Now why didn't I think of that before? MacDonnell's from right around Albemarle County, Gwen. He ever mention relatives to you?"

"Not that I remember, no. Wesley said she didn't have...No, wait...she did have a brother, but I don't know where. But no, Craig never mentioned relatives. Parents maybe dead...he has to be in his forties."

"Maybe. But friends, guys he worked with. That young carpenter—what was his name?"

"The tongue-tied one? The helper?"

"No, the other one, with the mustache. Or the older one. Damn, can't remember a single name, and it's only been what, a year?"

"And a half. No, I don't remember either, but we can find out, surely. Oh, what am I saying? I want you to forget about them, Jay. Give it a rest."

"Listen, maybe I could forget, even all the money we lost. The whole Virginia plantation thing. Even having to go under cover this way. But no, I can't forget Jerry. If he could be out, here with us, yes, maybe I could 'give it a rest,' but not now.

"Not ever."

~ * ~

Summer got to be the usual muggy time, but I wasn't far along enough to be miserable. I kept hearing tales of women hugely pregnant, unable to cool off, baby whales soaking in plastic kids' pools. I rode Walker, built things, gardened. Never had a place to garden before. Nice to see stuff come up, actually growing, competing with the weeds.

And the first time the baby kicked inside me, I about lost it. Couldn't wait for Craig to get home. Cooked us a great feed—no wine for me—feeling that occasional push, stretch, whatever. Smiling like an idiot.

"Hmm. What's the occasion?" Lifting lids, just like a husband's supposed to.

"Feel this," I put his hand on my big tum.

And of course the little monster didn't move. We stood there grinning at each other, but okay, he—she—was asleep. Then, middle of the night, here it came. This time he could feel it. Both of us howled. Cyrano thought we'd gone crazy. Crazier.

My girl Selena came up to stay with us awhile, help with things, although I didn't really need her yet. As house help, that is. Loved just having her with me. Little sister. We went swimming, bicycling. She helped me roof the new horse barn, because Craig was off on a job. Hey, if the religion thing in college didn't work out, she could always go into construction. We giggled about that. We giggled a lot, Selena and I.

I was gaining weight, of course—all that fluid—but we'd learned I was to keep on with whatever I'd done before. No need to go into a Victorian "confinement," unfit to be seen in society. Selena and I had fun. I wished we had two horses so we could trail-ride the big stretch of forested land west of us toward the Blue Ridge.

She wanted to know a lot of things she probably didn't feel she could ask her mother. About pregnancy yeah, but about guys too, where to draw lines, girl stuff like that.

"Hey, your dad's a minister. I know you got a lot of guidance at home, didn't you?"

"Oh, sure. But you know, parents want you to be like, a saint, even if they weren't. And all the girls at school, daring each other, acting out. Easy to get confused."

"Not you. You got it together, girl." But she wanted advice.

"Well, I'd say, bottom line, don't ever let yourself feed some guy's ego. Stay in charge of your own life just as long as you can, but that won't be easy. The world will use you, bosses will use you, guys will use you, but only if you let it happen. You make the choices, because you're the one you have to answer to."

"And God."

"Yeah, and God. Stick with that, but you'll find most everybody else won't let God get in the way of whatever's their agenda of the moment."

"Sounds lonely."

"It can be. But believe me, when it finally happens, you'll know it's right, even if it comes on slow. And you'll be *so* sure. I was always looking for the mythical Mr. Right, in all the wrong places, getting moved on by losers, getting burned, getting tired of it all. Then here comes Craig...wrong age, outside the usual relationship circle I moved in. Not pushy, not a pushover. Just so *right*, like I said."

"You ever think it was really God who brought you two together?"

*Hey, that's the way her mind works...can't be all bad.*

"Entirely possible. Law of averages didn't, for sure." I thought of all those good things that'd happened to us, easily trumping the downers. Even with the scary stuff, we'd always come out ahead.

Way ahead.

I looked into the future. If I were carrying a girl, it'd be only a few years of toys and laughter and finger-painting till she'd be like Selena. If I were lucky. Another young woman, zipped through childhood, standing at a threshold. Life: the stream of it, going on, mother to daughter, holding the crazy world together. Yeah, maybe that *was* God, making it all happen.

Nice feeling.

I hugged Selena.

~ * ~

"Here's what I've found," a semi-excited Webb told his wife. "One of our guys checked county records in Virginia around where we were. A MacDonnell in Nelson County, south of there. Asked around, and turns out he's our man's *brother*. A preacher, of all things, lives on the old family farm. And get this, Gwen...the brother actually *married* Craig and Wesley back in the spring."

"Wow. So they breeze in from whatever end of the earth, do a family wedding, then disappear again?"

"Apparently. My guy located Craig's house—county records again—and it sold, back in the winter. So I guess they're gone from there for good. As man and wife. But I'll bet you anything the brother knows where they are..."

"No, he doesn't, Jay. That'd be stupid as hell, and so *obvious*. They know records are public. They know, after you went to all the trouble to send your goons after them, you'd think of county records. They're not *dumb*, Jay, like this whole crusade you're on. Sure, they wanted the wedding to be a family thing, but no way in hell are they gonna let bro know anything. Use your *head*, lawyer."

*Okay, okay, she's probably right. Certainly right. I'm too focused, maybe. Grasping at straws. So maybe just leave it alone for a while.*

*But...*

~ * ~

Clyde called, talked it over with Nate Peterson.

"Don't in any way wanta blow their cover, Nate. But I know Webb's not gonna back off. If we—*I*—knew where Craig and Wes are, maybe I could help head him off. Maybe not. Wanted to get your take on it. I'm afraid Webb'll find out something on them and make a move. That picture's still out there."

"Yeah, but Clyde, the picture won't help much anymore."

"Really? They're going around disguised? That's gotta be a drag. Well, might be better if I don't know, but it's nagging at me. Like to see 'em, anyway."

"Tell you what, guy. I'll get word to them. If they think it's safe, I'll be in touch. Yeah, I kinda feel that if you're gettin' close to Webb, it'd be good to know all we can, all of us…help keep 'em safe maybe, too. Craig and I go all the way back, and I like his lady a lot. I can tell you this: they got married in the spring."

"No! Wow, that's so great. Whatta pair! Nate, that's fine news. Yeah, you check with 'em. I'll keep it to myself all the way. Wow. Gotta see 'em, now."

*Yeah, and my girl Cheryl. Work something out, there.*

~ * ~

Selena had gone off, third week in August, to start her college experience. I was getting a little bigger, almost six months along. Okay, a lot bigger. Finally staying home more, putting my feet up.

I missed that girl, and company in general. So when we got the message through Alan, after Nate had discussed it with him, we talked it over and decided yeah, we'd like to see Clyde. Also maybe learn from him some of what the Webber was up to.

We called Nate.

And that weekend, our undercover wizard arrived on our doorstep, with wedding presents. When he saw me, he freaked.

"Hey, I had no idea, Wes. Boy, what a double surprise! Here I was afraid you two were cowering miserably in some desert somewhere, and no, you're right here, married, expecting, and right where you belong. Although I wouldn't have recognized either of you."

He'd brought kitchen goodies for me, and a handsome hunting knife and sheath for Craig. He kept looking intently at us, no doubt assessing whether a druggie armed with that picture could tell who we were.

"Ballsy as hell. Right here where that psychopath will never think to look. But haven't you run onto any of the old guys, Craig? Surely they'd know you. Wes, you're so natural as a blonde, nobody'd suspect you."

"We stay pretty close," Craig told him, "but you gotta know, I saw Bob last week at the supply store, and he looked right past me."

"Old Bob. Still worrying about the sky falling on him, I guess." Then, "When's the little one due, Wes?"

"Not till the end of the year. But I'm starting to feel like a cow."

"No way. You're beautiful. Right, boss?"

"You got it." Arm around me, kiss.

My guys.

Then he brought us up on what they'd found out. Seems their leads to St. Louis had pointed to Parker Goode as string-puller, but totally outta sight; nobody could I.D. him. The suspected dealers there were very, very careful about leaving trails. And that had Clyde stymied. He knew Webb was still looking for us, and the longer he was invisible, the better his chances of finding us before the Feds found him.

"Of course, if you've done everything in your new names, he should dead-end this time...picture's no good, names no good. Hope he doesn't know about your brother, Craig, but I'll bet he finds out."

Something was pecking at my mind.

"We did use our real names at the wedding, Clyde. We're on record down in Nelson County. Couldn't very well fake it with Craig's family."

"Ow. But that doesn't tell where you are now."

"Not unless he tries to sweat Alan. Or one of the family. But Alan was okay with the risk...he'd stonewall."

"But if the crazy nabbed one of the kids..." Clyde was worried. "I don't wanta think he'd do that. But he's obsessed; we know that. He's after you because he can't get to me."

Craig had been quiet, thinking.

"We need to flush him out, Clyde. Get this over with. How can we bait him out into the open?"

"Believe me, we've been working on that. Hmm. Have to be something he could use, but in no way that could possibly tell where you two are. He'd just send more goons."

"False location? If we're someplace else, you could grab his guys," I pointed out. "Maybe squeeze them hard enough."

"Hasn't worked yet. No, but try this on: only way to get Webb himself out would be to send word you wanta meet with him one-on-one, Craig, to square this once and for all, like in a corny Western. Get a promise from him to drop it, in exchange for whatever he needs. Probably wouldn't work, but he's got a giant ego. You wouldn't actually be there of course, so no danger, but he'd have backup, have checked everything out ahead. He'd handle it like a very big drug deal: no mistakes."

I didn't like this…go to the enemy? Even with all the precautions, letting Webb know *anything* scared me.

As if reading my alarm bells, Clyde went on.

"If we fed the bait up through St. Louis, there'd be no connection to here. Have to be convincing, though. Like maybe you could supply some new evidence in the Bunche case. Win a new trial for Jerry? Witness, maybe? Could say Jerry wasn't really the one did Bunche?" He thought about that for a minute. So did we. "I dunno; he's smart. Probably wouldn't go for that."

"I'd say anything to get him off our case, but he'd still stay hidden," Craig reasoned. "And any promise to leave us alone would be a lie."

"Hey, we wouldn't make a deal, just tempt him, then nail him. But you're right. He wouldn't fall for anything like that."

"Gwen might push him," I ventured. "If she even *thought* there was a chance for her baby boy, she'd jump at it. Nag the Barker long enough, he might just give in and go for it. Like you said, with lotsa precautions."

"Hmm. Maybe, but we'd have to come up with something convincing. Like one of you maybe saw Greg with someone else, say, the night he was killed, 'stead of with Jerry in his Beamer. Jerry's sworn all along he didn't do it."

"Don't they all?" Craig said. "But maybe, if we could make the right—wrong—people believe I was the only one who could bring in new evidence…But like you said, he's a lawyer…he's not dumb."

"Gwen is. Or dumb enough." I was thinking the maternal instinct thing, naturally enough, given my situation.

"Might be worth a try, all right, but it's pretty thin." He stood. "Well, enough dead-end talk. How's construction?"

"Small stuff through the spring, but okay now. Got a couple guys on board. You saw the Estes Restorations sign on the pickup. Building back up. Still had all the basic equipment here."

"That's great. Like to chuck the whole crime thing and come back in with you. But hafta keep Superwoman Wes here off the job... bad for my ego." Grin, and he squeezed my shoulder.

"Oh, no. Soon's I can, I'm putting the little one in a front pack and I'm right back on the job again."

"Have the kid warped right off. First toy would be a bevel gauge."

It was good to have Clyde around for that couple of days. He unwound, we walked and splashed in the cool creek water, talked, ate good food, talked some more. Good visit all around.

And he went into Charlottesville that night and the next on dates, he told us, both with the same girl, which I was glad of. Guy spent too much time being a do-right cop. Said her name was Cheryl. I remembered Cheryl Saunders in Pittsburgh, Sid Bartlett's girl. Like to get in touch with her again, but no, leave that one alone till things got more settled. *Don't rock that boat. Dunno what tentacles the ogres might have out.*

"Well," Clyde wrapped it as he was leaving, "We'll see if we can invent something attractive to lure Webb with, but it'd all be out in Missouri. That's where he knows you were for sure last, and maybe... Anyway, let you know anything turns up, but no—*absolutely no*—hint about your location and reality. I know you both wanta end this, more than I do, but that intel stays in here." Tap to head.

"And hey, lady, promise me you'll stay away from whatever the doc says you can't do, which I know will be hard, being who you are, even blonde. And take care of you and the bundle, y'hear?"

Hug. Neat guy, and such a switch from the loser he'd pretended to be two years before. Then I remembered that Gwen Webb had liked him.

Maybe not as dumb as I thought...

# Twenty-three

"You won't believe this, Gwen."

"Won't believe what? You're getting out of this tar pit, going back to being a mostly honest lawyer?"

"Don't be cute. No, the boys picked up on the clumsiest scheme ever invented. Some street bum—probably a police plant—passes on word that MacDonnell has some new evidence in Jerry's case..."

"New evidence? Would that help?"

"It's fake. Has to be. Jerry iced the Bunche guy. Told me he did. But according to this rumor, MacDonnell supposedly was there, saw Bunche get into a truck with some other dude the night he was killed."

"No shit?"

"I said it was fake. So the dumb-ass says MacDonnell supposedly wants to trade me the testimony for leaving him alone. Can you beat that?"

"Would new evidence get Jerry a new trial?"

"If it were real, maybe. But this is so obviously a cop setup, Gwen. They can't find me, so they're trying to bait me out. Stupid move. And MacDonnell, if that's who it really is, didn't say a word about the half million."

"A new trial. Remember, Bunche wasn't killed with Jerry's gun. The only thing that incriminated him was Clyde's testimony that he'd admitted it. Along with that couple's sworn statements."

"Gwen, he bragged about it."

"Jerry was always trying to live up to you, Jay. He'd have claimed he did it to impress you."

"You don't believe that."

"What I *believe* is that my boy is in for life, my daughter's a washout in New York, we're in hiding. And if there's a ghost of a chance for a new trial, I don't care a damn who else believes what."

"It's a trap."

"So could every delivery be a trap. You handle traps."

"The cops probably don't even know where MacDonnell is. Like I told you, they've just invented all this, fed it into the pipeline to try to get me to bite. Won't work."

"Maybe not. But maybe the cops aren't even on this. Maybe the guy's just tired of running and hiding. And the girl Wesley sure as hell must be. I am, and nobody's been shooting at me."

"Not a chance. Like he's been sitting on this all this time? Okay, just say we *could* make a judge or jury believe Jerry didn't do it, get him freed. Better lawyer might make it happen. But think about it...everybody would want to know why MacDonnell would come forward now? Why not then?"

"You were trying to kill him."

"I'm still trying to kill him."

"But they've gotten married. Maybe want to start a family. What kind of life can they have, always on the run? Okay, so he's probably just inventing the evidence. Who cares? You just stay low, get his terms. Then we can decide. What's to lose?" She spread her hands.

"I can't do anything that dumb."

*Yes, you can.*

~ * ~

October cooled down, with fall colors and chill nights. I was spending more time in the bathroom, but was fine otherwise. Craig was so attentive, so loving. You'd think nobody'd ever had a baby before. And I wallowed shamelessly in every minute of it. Christmas baby. I'd had all the tests, and little Craig/Wes was normal and healthy. Could have learned the baby's sex, but neither of us wanted to. Both okay with whatever God intended.

Yeah, God. Selena'd started me getting curious about the divine presence in things, and looking back, I could see a pattern of guidance in my life. Oh, I'd gone off on crazy tangents often enough, but I got back on track every time. Brought back? Led back? Maybe so. Maybe I was part of a Plan, somehow.

We agreed it might be good to look into the religion thing, for us and for the newcomer. Couldn't hurt. Talk with Alan about that. Liked the way his kids were turning out, in a world full of bad choices. He liked to joke about that...why are the preacher's kids so mean? 'Cause they gotta play with the elders' kids.

~ * ~

"What I do want to do is go check out MacDonnell's brother," Webb told his wife. She'd been after him to find out more about the supposed new evidence, and the intriguing possibility of a new trial for their son. Webb was firmly opposed. And he still wanted MacDonnell and the girl dead. And if possible, the chance to sweat them about the money.

"That won't get Jerry a new trial."

"Neither will that phony deal. Look, how'd a carpenter get word up the line to us? Had to be the narcs."

"Could just know a user who knows a dealer. You know how it works. Same way you got their picture out, in reverse."

"Not likely. And why this St. Louis operation? The cops might have an idea we're here, although I can't imagine how, even with that Kramer I.D. But no way a straight guy like MacDonnell could know to send word. The cops are in on it, no doubt at all."

"He was here in Missouri near Branson, last we heard. Logical path, if you ask me. A no-brainer, Jay."

He paced, then stated the decision he'd already made, as if just now coming to the conclusion. She'd seen that process hundreds of times.

*Okay, just let it come, whatever it is he's hit on this time.*

"No, I think a little road trip to Virginia might be in order. Do us good to get away. Just scope things out."

"People know us there." She'd been ready for him, but why did she always have to point out the obvious? Where was the insight he'd always had?

He countered: *next point, counselor.*

"We're tourists. Thousands of people go for the fall color. No chance in hell we'd run into a soul who knows Parker Goode. Of course, if you don't want to go, that's okay. Thought you might like to get out. Like normal people."

"Yeah, normal people. How long's it been since we were anything remotely like normal? Why you couldn't just be happy with your Baltimore practice...just greed, I guess." She was bitter.

"You know we never could have sent Samantha to acting school, set her up in New York, sent Jerry to college, bought the places in Baltimore, let alone the farm in Virginia, on just my lawyer's fees. *You* wanted it all, Gwen. *You* wanted your horses and your plantation house and your country club. Hell, I couldn't live with your bitching. *That's* why I got into the trade."

"And now I'd give everything to get out of it. Start over, really. Wouldn't you, Jay? If we could?"

"Can't. Maybe in another country, but I've built this up too well to leave it. No, we're in to our eyes, and walking away wouldn't be any better. I can't practice law anywhere, Gwen...what'd we live on? No, just got to enjoy it. And keep outwitting the cops."

"That's really it for you, isn't it? The challenge. King Jay defying the system. Well, the *system's* got our son. The system's not letting our daughter into it. The system's got us shut down. Hiding."

"But the system's not as sharp as we are. We've proved that."

~ * ~

"*...walk so heavy and know I'll have to walk heavier still before my time comes.*" I loved that character of Benet's. Melora Vilas, the wood sprite. Innocent, child of the forest, caught in a wondering web of love. I wasn't a wood sprite, but I loved walking in the tall trees along our creek (*our* creek: it's mine too, now!). Red and gold and cinnamon leaves crunching underfoot. Cyrano nosing rabbit trails, mystified by squirrels disappearing up the other sides of trees.

Feeling the life inside me a lot, now: stretching, telling me it's getting ready for whatever is outside that warm place. Hearing words: they say a newborn recognizes its mother's voice. How much does an unborn know? What currents of knowledge make their ways into its being? We know a baby cries because it can't use words to let us know what's wrong. It laughs to signal things are okay.

Selena had told me Jesus said we all must become as little children: innocent, trusting, not yet wary, cynical. Maybe I could learn from my child. Oh, I was learning already. About life, the real version, and my place in its restless, twisting stream.

I kept envisioning a sturdy little boy in overalls following his dad around, getting into everything. And then it'd be this sunny girl-child in a sea of daisies, holding out petals for me to see. I was, bottom line, a sucker for all the mom-to-be fantasies, and nobody was gonna do me out of them. So I was birthing only one baby...I felt a power, a mother-of-the-earth strength, a dominance. *Getthehell out of my way, world, I'm gonna loose a wild child onto you, ready or not.*

I found myself pitying the accidental pregnancies, the oopses, the disruptions of plans, the (ugh!) abortions. Life now was this secure, shining sphere with Craig and me and our child safe inside it.

~ * ~

"We're going." It was a flat statement, and Gwen Webb was tired of arguing. And maybe—longest of shots—if they *could* locate MacDonnell through his brother, avoiding any cop connection, they could go ahead with the deal he'd proposed. So maybe again, if she could keep Jay from going off the deep end, it could still work. If he didn't get hung up on that missing money. Hell, money was replaceable.

She didn't know, really, whether Jerry was guilty or not. There were several links in the Charlottesville drug chain, and any one of them could have killed Greg Bunche. Or it might have been a random thing: the money had already been delivered, after all. Jay insisted he hadn't ordered the junkie killed. Believed their son had done it on his own—send a message to the street.

And even if Jerry had killed the guy, there were lots of people walking around who'd done the world a favor by eliminating human scum like that Bunche. Gotten rid of the rottenest apples, you could say.

And yeah, besides that, people also reformed, started over. Cleaned up their acts, lived normal, legal lives, no matter what they'd been before.

For a moment, Gwen the mother envisioned a freed Jerry living with her, with or without Jay. They could do it, the two of them. Let her husband drown in his empire; there was still a chance for her and her son. They could...

"So, you coming?" Harsh intrusion on her fantasy.

"Oh. Yeah, I guess so. But I want your word that if we do find MacDonnell, we try to make his deal work first."

"You don't give up, do you?"

"What the hell's to lose, Jay? If it's real, we take it. If not, what've we lost by trying?"

*Okay*, he thought, wouldn't hurt to humor her. *If I don't, she won't give up, stay after me like a dog with a bone.*

"Sure, okay. You're right. We'll give that a try." He tried to sound sincere.

"Thanks, guy. I like to think you aren't all bad."

*Yeah, right.*

~ * ~

The pictures hadn't been good, those they'd been able to find. Old ones of Webb, who must've avoided photographers, Clyde mused. Later ones of Gwen, from events in Charlottesville. Bottom line: the surveillance crew couldn't I.D. Webb.

Finally, lacking other leads, they'd put a stakeout on Parker Goode's apartment, the likeliest suspected head of the St. Louis operation. And if the woman from the Kentucky incident could be believed, he'd ordered their kidnapping. At least one of the team besides Clyde felt Goode was probably Webb himself.

"Get me shots of him then, anyway you can," Clyde requested. He wasn't in charge, and had to be sure to go through channels. Turf thing, like everywhere, every organization in the world.

So it looked like a break when the team guy, Akers, called on his cell.

"Looks like they're going out of town. Suitcases. I've got a long lens on…coupla good shots. She looks like our gal, but he…well, he could be, but…"

"Disguise? This guy got hair?"

"Yeah. Can't tell from here if it's a good rug or the real thing. They're gettin' into a gray Lincoln."

"Loose tail, but don't lose 'em. Send me the pix on your laptop."

"Check that."

~ * ~

"I don't like it any better, Jay. What if somebody there recognizes us?" They were cruising east in the Lincoln, out of St. Louis.

"You worry too much. Last place anybody'd think to look, a year and half later. We'll just hide in plain sight." He reached, gave her an affectionate squeeze. Good old girl, in spite of her nagging. He'd thought of ditching Gwen a hundred times, get a younger woman. But truth was, he was smart enough to know a younger woman wouldn't stay, would waste his money, not put up with his diminished virility. Only way an older man got a young woman was to buy her, and they didn't stay bought. *No, stick with Gwen.*

Besides, she knew too much.

*Yeah, hide in plain sight. Go see the brother with some story. Can tell if he's lying about our guy. Then? Well, cross that bridge…*

*Hiding in plain sight. Whoa!* MacDonnell had dropped off the face of the earth last summer, even if that woman thought she'd found him somewhere. Then they'd married in March, then no trace. What if…*no, they sold the house. But maybe that doesn't matter. Maybe they're still close.* To the brother, to the business contacts there. *Maybe he's sharp enough to pull it off: hide in plain sight. Ballsy. The girl's brash, too; just maybe...*

He switched the turn signal to the lane that led to the other Interstate.

~ * ~

"Took the Interstate east, Clyde. From what we know, I'd say heading to Baltimore, wouldn't you?" Akers had been on his cell, following with another agent.

"Likely." Clyde was studying the digital photographs. One of Goode in sunglasses opening the car door for...yeah, that had to be Gwen Webb in that straw sun hat, or a helluva look-alike. But no, that wasn't Webb. The hair looked real...this guy was younger. Build was right, but...other pix of him carrying a briefcase, doorman with suitcases.

*What was there?* What could he recall about Webb? Always wore dark suits. This guy had on a light sports coat. Webb was left-handed, and...*where's that shot, now*...Yes, opening the car door with his left. Didn't mean anything...No, he was holding it for her, passenger side. Awkward with the left hand. So. Not much.

Phone buzzed again.

"Akers here. Goode just pulled a quick switch. In the lane to get onto I-70, then dodged to I-64 exit. Don't think he's onto us, but that ain't the way to Baltimore."

"Stay on him, but invisible. Sun should be in his eyes, this early. I can't I.D. him as Webb, but that's her, and right place, right other stuff. And...Did you say *I-64?*"

"Yeah. Trying to shake us, or changed his mind."

"Okay!" And Clyde Kelly knew where Parker Goode, lately J. Barker Webb, was headed.

And that meant he could head that way, too.

~ * ~

It would have been safer, Webb conceded, to send another team, or just one man, to sniff out MacDonnell. But the big guy up the chain had said no, again, and who knew what somebody might let slip to him. So, no.

Even after Webb had pointed out to him that losing half a million made it business. But he didn't want to risk another operative on this vendetta. The mark was either lucky or very sharp, and it just didn't add to try again, in his estimation. Veto.

And not to bring it up again.

Anyway, Webb really wanted this one himself. Face-to-face, and see the fear in the guy's eyes. Maybe hear him beg. You just didn't cross Barker Webb and walk away. Or outsmart him, either. He smiled into the Illinois sun. The big Lincoln purred, eastward. He might be wrong, but he was pretty sure he knew where MacDonnell was.

~ * ~

"You thinking of selling your place, Alan?" the woman from the Nelson County clerk's office asked. Craig's brother was well known in the little county seat town of Lovingston...the family had been there for generations.

"No, why, Arlene?" They were pushing grocery carts.

"Guy was in the office asking, couple weeks back, is all. Figured it was one of those real estate people."

"What do they do?"

"Oh, check who owns what, then go try to talk folks into listing their property. I guess one out of every so many works out for them. They call it some weird name. Think it's 'farming'."

"Odd term. Well, nobody's been out to see us. Maybe didn't like what they found in the records."

"Maybe not. How's Ellen?"

"Gettin' over that early fall flu, finally. Selena gone off to college, she's got me doing the shopping and the other kids all assigned to their household jobs. Sorta like the Army at home last few days."

"You tell her I'll get by with a casserole or somethin'. If you're doin' the cooking, I know you're tired of it."

"Thanks, Arlene. Tell 'em hi down at the courthouse."

Normally, a casual bit of non-news like that could be dismissed, but since Craig and Wesley were figuratively on the run, Alan saw a red flag. They'd all known it'd be simple for anyone to make the family connection. Even find the record of the marriage.

*So what can we expect?* he wondered. *Whoever it is has had time to look us up, if that's what this is about. I've expected someone to ask me where Craig was before now. And unless I lie, I'll have to be vague, like 'I guess I'm not my brother's keeper.'*

Drug people, though...could get rough. *I just hope they don't want Craig bad enough to come after any of my family. No justice: solid citizen like my brother runs into a bad apple, and he's— they're—being hunted a year and a half later.*

He called Craig on his cell.

"Maybe nothing but an eager beaver realtor, Dagwood. But thought I oughta give you a head's-up. Maybe those people out there're still looking for the right piece of real estate, this time in Virginia."

"Thanks, Snuffy. Expected that before now, but it shouldn't help 'em much. Unless you get a visit. That worries me...obsession."

"No reason to think I'd know anything, Dag. You buzzed in here way back when for the party, and you buzzed off again to the other end of the world. Oh, how's our girl? Getting close now."

"Should be about six weeks, give or take. You say wife's down with the flu? Everybody else doin' okay?"

"So far. And listen, don't worry about us and the realtor, probably harmless. Doubt if I'm about to get in any hot water."

"Let's hope not. Might just keep your eye on the crew a little closer, though. Lotta snakes out there. Just luck we've avoided 'em so far."

"Or God's help."

"Yeah, I'm thinking that. Thanks, Snuff."

I'd heard part of this, doing my kitchen thing. Craig filled me in.

"Makes me nervous, Craig, thinking maybe Webb's looking this close to home." Home was meaning a whole lot more to me lately.

"Yeah, but Alan's a rock, and so's his family. And he said nobody's followed up in two weeks or so."

"Well, let's hope we don't have to run again. Hate to drop the kid in the Jeep on the Interstate. You'd need to park and help."

"Wow, what a picture. I'd go to pieces."

"No, you wouldn't, wouldn't dare." I kissed him.

We got a call from good old Clyde. He was coming to see us again. Said he'd wait to tell us the situation...mysterious. But he'd land in four hours at the Charlottesville airport, which was only ten miles. Could stay over again. I planned a late supper, wondering what he'd found out.

# Twenty-four

The narcotics agents in St. Louis arranged for a second tail on Goode. One stop for gas and the first car'd lose him. This would also make it harder for him to spot them.

Then two experts gained access to his apartment, not exactly legally, and went through every paper, every stitch of clothing, every underside of every drawer, for anything they could get on him.

Clean. Parker Goode was either not the higher-up in the drug chain or he was damn thorough at hiding his tracks.

There was one piece of possible evidence: a wig stand. The nearest police artist went to work on the Goode photos, removing the hair and the sunglasses. She did it largely by computer imaging, with the agent in charge not letting her see the earlier pictures of Webb.

What emerged was, in his opinion, a likeness.

"Make him younger," he requested, giving her one of the earlier photos. She did so.

And this time the comparison looked close. He called Clyde.

"Okay, thanks. My gut told me that, but I'll read that as official. Send me the stuff on my laptop, okay? Good work."

~ * ~

"Where we stopping, Jay? I'm tired, and you've done most of the driving." Illinois, and then Indiana had been flat, boring. Kentucky wasn't much better, but then nothing was, really, from the Interstate.

"We can make Lexington, easy. Plenty time to slip on into Charlottesville by tomorrow night, or close. No hurry. Maybe take in one of those big horse farm tours in the morning before we head out. Like that?"

"Sure. Miss horses. Think we'll ever get clear enough for another country place where I can have one?"

"Why not? Missouri's got that limerock soil, good for bluegrass. Let's just wind things up first."

"Yeah, I wanta hear what MacDonnell can tell us to help Jerry."

*Will you just give it a rest? I ordered that hit; Jerry did it...*

Or just maybe he *could* tell her he'd got one of the others to do it. Maybe Denny: he was dead. No, Jerry'd have told that at the trial, he realized...save his skin. *Wish we could've been there. Damn MacDonnell...*

No, Webb reasoned, have to be something really strong for another trial, outweigh Clyde's testimony, and it just wasn't out there. *Like to get* that *guy in my sights, now. Might just leave MacDonnell and the girl alone, if I could. After all, he could just as well be the one who took my money.*

~ * ~

Clyde ate my food like he hadn't had home cooking ever, and said I was beautiful, again. I called him a liar.

He showed us all the pictures. Okay, without the hair and sunglasses, Goode was Webb. And for sure that was Gwen, with the sun hat hiding what looked like a hair dye job. With our I.D. and his, Clyde felt we were onto him.

"Okay people, that's the good news. Bad news is, they're heading east. We'd guessed Baltimore, but they switched onto I-64, and our guys are tailing them. Now I don't wanta alarm you, but I'd say he's heading back here. Now, there's no way he's picked up anything on your being here. More likely try to find one of your old crew and work it from there, or even to locate your brother, Alan, and put pressure on him to tell.”

“That fits,” and Craig told him Alan’s news. “So, can we keep him away from my brother?” He was anxious. So was I. The baby kicked me.

*Okay, you, too.*

“I’ll go down to his place tomorrow. Webb’s driving; can’t get here before tomorrow late, unless he does an all-nighter. Our guys will know.”

“Can’t you grab him now?”

“Wish we could, but got absolutely nothing on him in St. Louis. And yeah, we all heard him order the hit on you, but it didn’t happen, so not a serious enough charge. We don’t know if he actually ordered the Bunche thing. Can’t get him on possession with intent from the stash in the barn that time, because it was only the money. Jerry made the delivery. We really have to get more. Want to put him away for a long, long time.”

“And if this isn’t Webb, we got nothing.”

“What can you get after he’s here?” I was nervous about all this.

“I can bug Alan’s house, be close with help, if it gets rough. That’s just a preventive thing, though. Mostly just stick to Webb best we can, till we get him on something else. He’ll be coming here for more than the scenery. No sign of more muscle, so I’m thinking he’ll go easy. Try to get something to slip out down there at Alan’s, or from whoever, maybe one of the carpenters. But I’ll be on him; don’t worry. Just hope he doesn’t find somebody who recognizes either of you in your new getups.”

“Nobody has. We don’t go out to any place around close. Blondie here could walk up to an old boyfriend and he wouldn’t know her.”

“If I *had* an old boyfriend. No, Craig’s the stranger, Clyde. Guys he’s bought supplies from for years sell him stuff right across the counter and don’t have a clue. Looks like a country singer from Nashville.”

“Good. So you can both come out after we put Webb away.”

“I am gettin’ tired of this abusing my hair, although Craig oughta keep his...looks distinguished in white.”

"Probably *be* white when it grows in natural again, after all this," he grinned.

And Clyde was off to see his Cheryl whoever again. Both of us were glad for him. Loner no more?

~ * ~

Webb had automatically suspected he might be followed. You had to assume the enemy was one up on you if you were to survive. Never underestimate them. He hadn't even bothered to check the mirror, just assuming a narc team was back there. So they'd pull a little diversionary switch in Lexington, play it safe. He knew a guy there...

He punched the numbers on his cell.

"Sam? Parker Goode here."

"Who? Parker...Oh, yeah. Didn't pick up on the new name at first. How's it goin', big man?"

"Good. Need a favor. We'll be at the Holiday Inn Express, Downtown/University at nine tonight. Need to leave our Lincoln with you for a few days. Pull a switch. Can you get there a little after, be able to swap me some good temporary wheels?"

"You hot?"

"No, but the reason you and I both are *not* hot, now or ever, is that we always plan ahead, right?"

"You got that right. So call me back, tell me which door you'll come out, once you get the chance to scope the place out. Yeah, we'll take care of your car okay. An' don't tell me where you're goin'."

"I won't. Thanks, Sam." He punched off, smiled.

"You are so *paranoid.* So whatta we do after? Drive all night? Fall out from exhaustion? We're not young any more, Jay."

"No, we just check in somewhere else while any narcs are watching our car. No reason for them to suspect a thing, or do any motel search, till tomorrow."

"You think we're being followed?"

"Don't care. Just wanta stay a jump ahead. And we'll lose the freeway in the morning, see some scenery on back roads, totally invisible." He grinned at her.

"Okay, smart guy. Maybe we can actually afford gas for the other car, instead of this tank." She grinned back at him, reached, patted his arm.

~ * ~

Clyde had come in late and let himself in with the key we'd given him so as not to disturb us. He'd spoken softly to Cyrano, so hadn't been reduced to hamburger. Now at breakfast he had something to tell us. He looked like the cat that ate the yellow bird instead of the ham biscuits I was feeding him.

"Okay, people, I've got some weird news for you, and it has absolutely nothing to do with Webb." And he pulled a zeroxed copy of a bank deposit slip out and waved it at us. Mystery time.

"First of all, my lady Cheryl is Cheryl Saunders, Wes, the girl you knew in Pittsburgh. Never thought to mention her last name to you, being clueless about the connection. Anyway, she found out from our getting to know each other better that I'd been here a couple years ago, and asked me, on the longest of long shots, if I'd known you. You can imagine my mouth dropping open."

"Cheryl Saunders? Here? Wow, that *is* long odds. What's she doing in Charlottesville?"

"Working at an ad agency. Seems she broke up with a guy in Pittsburgh, Sid Bartlett, whose brother Phil you worked with. Controlling guy, she tells me, and that wasn't all. Anyway, she'd had it with him. So, knowing you'd come here from there, she wanted to try to find a trace of you."

"I liked her a lot. Called her a couple times, but haven't kept in touch lately, with all that's happened. And new cell number, too. You gotta know, Phil has been on my case about some missing money..."

"Yeah, all that came out. Cheryl didn't know he was after you, though. She had some serious information about just that missing money, but was afraid to reveal it to Phil. First of all, because he wouldn't have believed her."

Gears in my head started turning.

"You're heading toward his brother Sid's being the one who took the cash, aren't you, Clyde?" His eyes went wide. *Sherlock.*

"Hey, you ever need a job, lady, we got a place for you in the Agency. Yeah, seems Sid had Cheryl wait—stand watch, actually—while he ransacked Phil's apartment for something when you two were away somewhere. And that something turned out to be a bank envelope. Seems this Sid was a persuasive guy, and gave her some explanation or other for the raid. So she forgot about it.

"But after you'd left, she picked up on Sid's leaning on his brother, telling him *you'd* grabbed the cash. Nobody ever said so directly, but bits and pieces. So she puts this together and starts to get the picture."

"Cheryl's sharp. I never knew why she hung with that guy as long as she did. Hope she's got a life now."

"She's getting one." Grin. "So she gets the chance to dig out this deposit slip at Sid's place, and does a xerox. This zerox." He let us see it.

Yeah—surprise—for a hundred Gs.

"She wanted to get it to you, so you could clue Phil in. And I gotta tell you, she's afraid of Sid now, and I don't blame her.

"So, we could turn this over to the cops there, let them handle it. Or, if you wanta get hold of Phil, or send him this, that family can take care of it however they want to, among themselves. Your call." He spread his hands.

"Wow. You gotta know I was getting these calls from Phil, which were getting more accusing. Then, I guess through a mutual friend in Missouri, he actually found us in Kentucky. Didn't get a look at me, and just maybe wouldn't have recognized me as the ditzy blonde, and didn't know Craig. We faked him out anyway, and that's the last we've seen of him. But yeah, I think it'd be best if I called and sent the paper along. Don't want him knowing where we are, so I'll fax it to him from somewhere..."

"You call, and we'll fax it through police channels, okay? That'll make it more official, too." He gave us both another grin. "Looks like this might uncomplicate your lives another notch, too."

Wow, yes. I gave him a sisterly hug, and Craig gripped his hand. Did I say he was becoming our favorite person?

And what a pair if it could work: Cheryl and Clyde...

He was set to be off in his rental car with plenty of time to get set up at Alan's, knowing from checking with the tails on Webb that he hadn't left Lexington yet. And with those four men, he'd have deep backup if things got hairy. Webb could well call up troops from here: the network had to be ongoing, of course...

"I'm hopin' it's a girl," he told me. "Not enough gorgeous girls in the world." Smiled with his eyes. Nice eyes, actually, now they weren't bloodshot. I was glad for Cheryl, too.

"Maybe cross-eyed and pimply."

"Not a chance in the world, with genes from you two. Gonna be a heartbreaker, and Craig'll need to keep that old shotgun handy. I c'n hear it now: 'Just what are your intentions toward mah daughtah, young man?'"

"When are you gonna find yourself a good woman, Clyde? Or have you already?" From Craig.

"Well, maybe when I retire, put myself out to pasture. And if things could work out with Cheryl, I'm hoping I can get a shot at that soon. So maybe, if you need another carpenter—joiner—you'll get a call from me sometime."

"Make that a promise."

Afterwards, Craig called his lead man, told him he'd stay home today, Friday, so the crew could handle the job they were currently on. He wanted to be here when and if. I was glad of that, too.

And then I called Phil the Misled. Told him everything except where we and Cheryl were, and that a fax would be on its way from the cops from wherever they wanted to send it. Just give me a fax number. He was disbelieving, of course, and had tried to be angry at first, but I just talked over him.

I pointed out that I was now a married woman expecting a baby, and that while I hated burning bridges, this was a good time for us to do that. Now that we were square, which we'd really been all along.

And I didn't give a damn how he and the parents handled Sneaky Sid. Although I hoped Phil would at least beat the shit out of him. Damn guy belonged behind bars, but okay, I'd let the family handle that one.

~ * ~

When the Lincoln hadn't moved by ten a.m., the crew, who'd switched off watching ever since it'd arrived late the night before, got hold of the motel manager. They checked out the room with him, a nervous guy from India more than a little in awe of them.

Empty.

"We've been had, guys," Akers admitted. "Oh, *crap!* I can't believe I let myself fall for this one." He called in to St. Louis, got a tongue-lashing from his higher-up. He hoped that would be the worst of it. Then he called Clyde with the bad news: the dropped ball, the missed chance, the...

"We screwed up, guy. Goode slipped us, left us with a Lincoln and an empty motel room. I'm kickin' myself over it...can't *believe* I let that happen. Rookie mistake; absolutely no excuse."

"Damn. Oldest trick in the book. But hell, we let him do almost the same thing here last time. Okay, whyn't you and your partner come on over since you're on the road. Others go back. He may have muscle here, but I'm in with the local cops, too. We gotta nail him this time, even if we can't get anything more on him. The guy's a snake, and we don't know what he's up to here, but he's obviously on the way.

"And he's got some good people in his sights."

"Roger that." Akers was pissed at himself. Now he wanted in on this collar more than any other he could remember. Parker Goode/ Barker Webb owed him over this. Owed him big time.

And he *would* pay up.

# Twenty-five

Webb wasn't in a hurry. Winding along back highways through Kentucky, they visited antiques shops, historic sites, parks. And a fine horse farm. Lingered over a leisurely lunch. It had been a long time since the two of them had made time for each other, and this trip, almost free now of apprehension, was providing it.

They spent another night in West Virginia, in the towering mountains that rose straight up out of narrow, creek-cut canyons. The historic bed-and-breakfast was quaint, the nearby restaurant good, the scenery excellent. Gwen was even able to elicit a satisfactory performance between the sheets from her husband.

Next day she was pensive, reflecting on the life she—they— might have had. A simpler existence free of the frenzy of amassing wealth and spending it in a widening spiral that shut out the very things—good things—they sought. Well, that was fantasy; this was now, and they'd just have to grab what they could of happiness wherever they could, she guessed. And try to stay ahead of the game.

And yeah, the law.

~ * ~

Nothing happened Friday at our house, except that Craig and I slept in, then fed each other breakfast in bed and laughed a lot in the crumbs. You don't engage in a lot of athletic sex when you're almost eight months pregnant, but we enjoyed each other anyway. Then we walked a lot in the woods, where Cyrano re-established his domain and frightened off lions, bears, moose, and other entirely imaginary denizens. Oh, and Craig had strapped on his holster with the monster six-shooter, loaded.

Just in case.

We did a few chores, hit on a few projects, put up a little more firewood…I brushed Walker's glossy coat. Lazy day, but both of us were on pins, thinking about our still-precarious situation. Despite my recent euphoria, I didn't feel as tough and invulnerable as before, and I wanted this strong guy near all the time.

Touching distance, actually.

Clyde checked in that evening to say all was quiet at Alan's. His men from St. Louis were there, and he assured us they were on top of everything.

"Only thing bothers me," he told Craig, "is why Webb's waited this long to move. Must've finally taken the bait we planted, but why so long? He obviously smelled a trap, so that doesn't add. Makes me believe he's found out something since locating your brother those weeks ago. Could be he was just too busy selling dope to get away, but we don't wanta underestimate this guy. Made that mistake before."

Yeah, we all had.

But Craig and I settled in, doors securely locked, guard dog on his version of high alert, sound asleep on a rug. We didn't get to sleep for a while…got to talking about all that'd happened. We'd tried to make ourselves a nest, each of those other places, then finally come on back to our real one. Needed that, a lot. Each other, more. And now we were gonna have us the rest of a new life, few weeks.

Sweet.

"Just leave us the hell alone, Webb," I moaned.

Quiet night mostly, except for one medium bark from the dog. Measure of how high-strung we were, Craig slipped out of bed, down to the living area in the dark with his shotgun, waited. Cyrano sniffed a little, then licked Craig's hand and went back to sleep. Faint skunk aroma was the extent of our danger.

Morning was sunny, burning off what little chill had set in. The world looked so incredibly friendly: little fleece clouds drifting above still-colorful leaves. Saturday, a day closer to my big event. A day older. A day also closer, I hoped, to the final resolution of the Webb web that held us. My body and I needed past this anxiety... start gnawing my nails and clawing imaginary rashes soon.

I was apprehensive in spite of the day, but what else could I be, under the circumstances? And I hadn't slept well, which wasn't a surprise either. Bottom line was, though, no matter whether there was danger on the way or not, there wasn't a whole hell of a lot more we could do about it.

*So just stay calm, girl. Nobody knows where the Webbs are, and as long as they aren't here, that should be all we need.*

Not.

I ran a brush through my hair, put in the colored contacts. Hell, I looked normal to myself now, in the mirror. I'd continued with affecting that English accent, (yeah, Clarissa the Yorkshire stone-waller) to further complicate things. And Craig...he was distinguished Donald Estes, gentleman contractor, to everybody. Guess no need to worry. Even if by some insane chance Webb could find out from Alan or somebody else where we were, we weren't *we* any more. At least not from a distance. And I sure wasn't the lean, sassy athlete they'd remember, whale that I was now.

But I couldn't help thinking of Reenie Wilkes. And Phil Bartlett. Sure, they must've found out where we were from Glenn. He'd given us a recommendation that time to a guy having a job done right where we'd landed: the connection was a no-brainer. But even given the now-worthless picture that was in circulation, the creepy way those people had found us was still creepy. There could still be a crack somewhere that Webb had just found, as Clyde must have suspected.

A deadly crack.

~ * ~

"Well, lady, we're here. The scene of the crimes," Webb announced as the car crested the Blue Ridge on I-64 into Albemarle County.

"Yep, for what that's worth. You haven't told me our M.O., though. I am assuming my Sherlock husband has one."

"Well, it *was* to have been to look up MacDonnell's brother, down there to our right somewhere. Play nice, try to find the fine craftsman we'd heard about who'd done so many restorations around. So he could do one for us, see. The Parker Goodes. Hint at big bucks, restore one of those plantation houses we've heard about we're maybe looking to buy. See how that played…

"*Was* to've been?"

"Yeah. But I think there's a better, quicker way. Your shrewd lawyer husband has second-guessed the quarry."

"The suspense is killing me."

"Simple. MacDonnell is *hiding in plain sight*. Just like us. Now I could be wrong, but what you said, my dear, about his surely being tired of running, remember? I say he's right back here, maybe under another assumed name, like us, too, doing his same thing, lying low all right, but *here.*"

"People have known him all his life, Jay."

"They knew Craig MacDonnell. They don't know John and Jane Doe, who I'll bet don't look anything like they did. That's gotta be why the picture of them we sent out stopped working. Anyway, we're headed first to his old place, see if the new owners know anything about where they are.

"And just so you know, I don't believe there really *are* any new owners." He couldn't suppress a triumphant, puffed-up grin. Like he'd just found all the cookies. It took her a moment to get that.

"Wow, that'd be ballsy. How'd they do that?"

"Buy it from themselves. Simple transaction. If we'd been less freaked out, we might've done the same thing with our place."

"That'd have been a little too crazy, Jay. That'd be putting our heads in the lion's mouth." He was past making sense, she realized, too obsessed. Or was he really going crazy?

"Couldn't have practiced law here, but we could've managed it, I'll bet. Anyway, putting two and two together, I got them coming back here."

"I don't see it."

"The place sold in the winter. They got married here a little later. Now, that doesn't mean a lot...you don't have to be present for a real estate closing, but most people are. And they'd want personal stuff they couldn't grab when they left town in such a hurry that time. So I'm guessing they weren't flying in from the end of the earth both times. I think they were here all along."

"My husband Sherlock Holmes." Not without some appreciation. He went on.

"So we just happen to cruise by their place, which I know approximately where is, and check it out."

"And we just waltz in and surprise them? And if it's not them, we say we're just lost dumb tourists?"

"Something like that. But yeah, they won't exactly welcome us like long-lost cousins. So we go in prepared."

"You mean with guns out. I don't like that."

"All you have to do is back me up."

She was thinking this through. Jay wanted a confrontation; she wanted a deal. Not a shoot-out. He sensed her reluctance.

"I've another plan, Gwen. If we can't talk the deal for their testimony in a new trial for Jerry, I just want Clyde. I'm sure they've kept in touch. He's really the one who put our boy away, and most likely the one who took our money. I'm getting past wanting MacDonnell and the girl, but I need the guy I trusted, went to bat for, who robbed us, set us up." The bitterness in his voice was deadly.

She was still quiet. All this had an unreal aspect to it, like something out of a suspense movie. The rounded fields of Virginia slipped past, going to brown. The big trucks pounded I-64 until their exit. Then the road wound, past familiar stores, a school. Webb pulled over, got out a map.

"Should be up here somewhere. This road goes close, I think. We'll stop about five miles on and ask."

The first query, of a housewife unloading groceries from a minivan, turned up nothing but a shrug...they hadn't lived here long. Further on, two men, obviously carpenters, were putting a long ladder on a pickup truck rack.

"We're looking for a builder, lives around here somewhere. Craig MacDonnell?"

"I've heard of him," the older of the two admitted. He had watery blue eyes, a red face and the standard issue beer gut. "Don't know him personal. You, Ronnie?" Ronnie was impossibly tall, skinny, bent like a half-open jackknife.

"Know a guy used to work for him is all. But you go on up a coupla miles. Little store, an' they know ever'body around." Webb thanked them, drove.

And yes, the aging proprietor of the crossroads store knew MacDonnell well.

"But he left here some time ago. Place sold to some new people f'm Ohio. Been in most a year now."

"Well, we'd heard that house was really unusual, wanted to see it. We're looking for a place ourselves."

"Too late for that'n. Feller an' his wife, name Estes, got it."

"Estes. Retired folks?"

"Oh no. Mr. Estes, he's white-haired, but ain't that old. An' she's younger, I'd say thirties. B'lieve she's f'm England er somewheres."

*England?*

"Maybe they wouldn't mind if we visit. Which way is it?"

"On up 'bout five miles. Driveway to th' left after a bridge. House is way back somewheres. I've never seen it."

"The Esteses come in often, do they?"

"Oh, 'bout like most folks. Save a trip to town. They're well off, I'd say, do horse stuff around."

*Horse stuff. And English?* That didn't mean much, except that yes, that couldn't be cheap. Boy, had Webb found that out the hard way. But well off? MacDonnell hadn't seemed that, at all. Small operator, with just the crew of four...But of course, the money—his money. So they *had* been the ones...

*Well, go by anyway. Take a look.* Although this was beginning to look like a definite dead end.

They found the drive after the bridge, leading off through woods, but with a glimpse of field on the right. Well beyond, on the main road at a turnout, a dusty car was parked, with a tall man scrutinizing a road map. Lost too, obviously. They turned in, came alongside the field.

"Stop, Jay!"

"What? House is on down." But he stopped.

Gwen Webb got out, went to the board fence. Called softly. The horse that had raised his head at their car perked his ears, turned.

"Walker," she called quietly again. The horse walked over. "That's my horse, Jay. That's Walker, the one Wesley liked so much."

"Hell you say. *Okay!*"

And Webb opened the trunk of the car and retrieved two guns from their bags. Black, sinister automatics.

"Jay, let's not do it this way," she reasoned. "Let's talk. We're not in danger here. Leave the guns. They may have sold the horse to the new people...couldn't possibly have taken him with them. Think about that."

"Maybe so, but just better to be prepared. MacDonnell, if it *is* him, could freak out, put a gun on *us*. Now, put this in that big bag of yours. You know how to use it, but you won't have to. We talk to whoever's there, and if it's them, we'll try to work the deal, just the way you want. Only if they *are* actually here, and he—they—start something, will we bring out the hardware. Okay?"

"Jay, I..." She felt they were crossing a line, one they wouldn't be able to go back over. She started to protest further, hoping to salvage what might be a good chance for some other way to...

"Gwen, we paid these people a whole lot of money. Took them into our house as social equals, trusted them. Then they and Clyde Kelly put our son in prison for life. Caused us to lose everything. Not to mention stealing that half million from us. Now, you just back me up if necessary, and I assure you it won't be." He slipped the gun into her bag, handed it to her. Tucked his into his belt at his back, under his sports coat.

They got back into the car, eased on toward the house. She couldn't get past the feeling they weren't handling this the right way, were heading for something that could prove disastrous. And once again, she realized her husband had let himself go beyond good judgment, had narrowed his focus dangerously in this obsession of his.

He could lose their only chance for their son...

# Twenty-six

I was alone in the kitchen when the car drove up. Craig and Cyrano were out at the creek bank doing some guy/dog thing. At first I thought it might be Clyde the Narc again, but the car was wrong: Kentucky plates. Now, who'd we know in Kentucky? Oh, of course: Mangrum and Shelby...No, that'd be Ohio, their home address...My radar or whatever it was, was slow kicking in this time.

Because the man and the woman who got out of that car were J. Barker and Gwen Webb. Disguises just like in the digital pix.

*Oh, shit.*

I knew them, but just maybe they wouldn't...Could I fake them out? Try. *Got to give it a try.* I grabbed the Sarah Palin glasses. Answered the door.

"Yes? And whaught can I do for you?" I put the fake English lilt on it, put my voice up a few notes, only shaking *inside*.

"Oh, Mrs. Estes?" Webb was fooled. "We...that is, we..." Gwen was focused on my belly. "We may have the wrong place." Hard squint. I hoped I looked nothing like Wesley Whitestone, she of the toolbelt, boots, brown ponytail, drawl. "Is you husband home? We were referred to him by friends. He's a builder, isn't he?" The damn pickup outside said he was, in big letters on the side.

"Yes, ectually, but he's out, at the meaument." *So far, it's working. Just get the hell rid of them.*

"Well, we...Perhaps we should call back." Webb was still confused, looking at the house. Gwen was looking at me now. Hard. "But we were really trying to find the man who built this house..."

"It's *her*, Jay," Gwen said. "*Wesley.*" Then to me, with a cat/canary smirk: "Nice try, dear."

Yeah, I'd always suspected she was sharper than she seemed.

I should have been scared shitless. Here were the very people who'd hunted us for a long year and a half, right in my face. Craig was out of sight. My man-eating dog was gone somewhere. The shotgun was in another room and the damn pistol in a drawer. Again. And I was hugely pregnant.

Not exactly in fighting trim.

But for some reason, I wasn't scared at all. Some sort of self-preservation had kicked in, maybe with the baby's movement inside me. And, just in a worst-case, I'd been rehearsing this scene for months.

"Come in, Gwen, Mr. Webb. Been a long time." In my normal Georgia voice.

"You're..." Webb still wasn't sure.

"Yes, and congratulations on your detective work. Craig'll be here in a minute. What can I get you? Long drive?" I was *so cool.*

"Well, I'll be damned," Webb finally got out. "You've been *expecting* us?" For a sharp guy, he still wasn't quite on board.

"We sent you word. Of course we were."

Not.

Gwen had recovered first. Hell, she was a woman, and just so you know, we have a whole 'nuther set of perceptions, tactics.

"When are you due, Wes? Gotta be soon." *Okay, play nice, Gwen.* I could do that, too, sure.

"Five, six weeks. Feel like a baby whale."

"I know. Craig must be so proud. Why don't we sit down, wait for him." She could be cool, too. "Saw Walker in the field." That smile again.

"Craig surprised me with him. Bought him from the Feds. Now, you look like you could both use a drink. Bourbon?" Damn, I was good.

"Please. I'll help. You won't want alcohol, I know." She sized me up again, and the expression changed. "Damn, girl, you look good, despite the dumb blonde frizz." She meant it...mother time.

"And your rinse is right for your coloring. Great hairpiece too, Mr. Webb."

He ignored the compliment, still uptight.

*Okay, screw you too, scumbag.*

"So I was right," he gloated. "You're under cover right out in the open. Fellow at the store said he'd known Craig for years. Can't wait to see *his* get-up."

"Okay," Craig said, stepping into the kitchen right on cue. "Here it is."

Webb jumped up, grabbed a gun from his belt, eyes scared.

"*Stop it, Jay!*" Gwen's voice cut like an axe. "Put that thing away, you fool!"

His mouth dropped open. I bet he'd never heard her talk to him that way. He was still wide-eyed, but as Craig coolly walked in smiling, he put the piece back.

I handed the bourbon around, one for Craig, too. Got lemonade for me. *Play the hostess, yeah.*

"Now, let's talk like civilized people," Gwen went on, motioning us all to sit like it was her house. "All of us are tired of this shit, so let's resolve it. You sent us word you had evidence, Craig, that could help Jerry get another trial."

"Actually," I horned in, "I'm the one." And I launched into my role. "You see, Bunche's girlfriend Sarah Wainright was my housemate. She was a student, didn't have a car, so I'd taken her to the mall that night he was killed." I was off and running.

My mouth.

"Where you saw Bunche?"

"Yes. Sarah was inside a store and I was waiting for her. Greg drives up in his car, the sports job, doesn't see me. Goes to a white pickup truck. Some guy I don't know inside. They drive off, leaving Greg's car there." White pickup truck…anonymous. Hadda be a thousand of those around.

"You saw this?" Webb was incredulous.

"And not only that. I'd overheard Greg tell Sarah he was in deep, owed a lot of money, and some guy named Vince, new to the outfit—whatever that meant—wanted to prove himself and was out to get him. Had to be the dude in the truck.

"You may not know he got Sarah to borrow my pickup for that bank robbery, trying to get the money he owed. Somebody I.D.'d my truck, so that got the cops onto the thing. I knew Greg was using, getting Sarah hooked, but I didn't know the money was for drugs. Shoulda guessed that."

"That testimony could have saved Jerry," Gwen wasn't as nice, now. Voice cold, accusatory.

"We didn't even know when the trial was. Nate Peterson, a detective here, told us to get lost fast, and we did. I don't know what kind of an organization you're in, Mr. Webb, but it's got damn long arms. And you'll remember, you told Jerry and Clyde to kill us there in the stable. We weren't hanging around for *that* party."

"*You ordered that?*" Gwen hadn't known?

"Jerry'd let it slip he'd done Bunche. These two had tried to run, had heard too much of everything. Sure, I told Jerry he'd made the mess, so it was his to clean up." He was justifying to her.

"But that doesn't mean he actually did it. I told you he wanted to impress you, measure up…" She wanted *so much* to believe it.

He waved her to silence, totally ignoring her, stood, paced. His lawyer mind was at work despite himself.

"But if we *can* actually make some sort of a deal here, you'll have to testify, help get a new trial."

"We know that. No problem."

"Except that your whole story is a lie. Don't you think I know that?" Now the hotshot lawyer boring in on the witness. But I was that witness, and Miss Wesley wasn't about to be intimidated.

"And that won't make one damn bit of difference in court, Webb. Hey, I'm about to have a baby. I want our life back. Yeah, and we've gotta trust you in this, to leave us alone. Think we didn't beat ourselves up over this a thousand times? We came back here, made it easy to find us, but not too easy. You're a smart guy, Webb. You know my testimony will be air-tight. I could've been exactly where I said I was *when* I said, and nobody on this earth can prove I wasn't.

"And hey, maybe I *was*." I spread my hands. *I* could believe it...

"You are so damn cool, Wesley," Gwen was actually admiring the act. "We want our boy back."

"And he's gotta abide by our deal, too, once he's out."

Craig had been silent, watching Webb close. Of course he didn't trust the guy, was trying plans in his head, fallbacks. Webb had that gun. And Gwen's bag could hold a cannon. *Never underestimate that woman.*

"Okay," Webb offered, "you want Jerry on board. So, quid pro quo: we want Clyde. I want Clyde, my associates want Clyde. Give us Clyde." Queer little smile...the lawyer strikes.

Like a snake.

"Last time we saw Clyde was when we left Virginia," Craig lied smoothly. "We've stayed away from cops."

Webb sighed, and it reminded me of that night when he'd supposedly regretted having to annihilate us.

"Nice try, MacDonnell. But you've had fake I.D. at least twice. That's not easy on your own. I know you've been in with the cops all along."

"I've known Nate Peterson here in Charlottesville all my life, sure. Went to school together. He came to our wedding. And he did arrange for I.D. But Clyde? He's a Fed, narcotics, I guess. Nate never mentioned him again." Telltale bead of sweat at that cool fake-white hairline. Webb could pick up on that if he were really sharp.

"Okay, maybe. But you knew who to send word through to us. No way could you have known that without the guys who're after us. Explain that."

"All right, guy I worked with in Missouri, where your man Karl found us, was a user. Drifter. We were on this Victorian house replica job. I was lead carpenter. I caught the guy on my crew sniffing coke.

Rules were to bust him...dangerous as hell around construction equipment.

"He tried to buy me off, said he could get cash any time. So I figured he was dealing, too. Maybe not, but Wes and I'd been talking about this deal with you if we could reach you. So we gave it a shot. I'd let him off with a strict eye on him if he'd get the word up. No idea if it'd work, but we did it."

"That was over a year ago." Accusation. He wasn't buying it.

"Yeah, guess the conduit broke down. When we didn't hear from you, we sent word again. Called my old boss there, just told him to tell the boy to do a repeat. He'd know what to do. Guess it finally got through." Craig spread his hands. *Helluva'n actor, my husband. I'd have bought it.*

"What was the boy's name?"

*Trap, Craig.* But not a beat of hesitation: "Billy Epps." *Who the hell was that?* "Surprised me he was still on the job. May have cleaned up his act."

But Webb wasn't having any of that...too obsessed. Gwen seemed to like it okay. That made three of us, but it was the wrong three.

"Bullshit, MacDonnell. You're both lying. I think you've been in this with the narcs all the way." Mean dude, and we hadn't been able to derail him. I could tell this was all just about to explode in our faces. But Gwen wanted to believe it: did believe it.

"Jay, you're not being reasonable. This can work. We can make it work. What more do you want from them?"

"I want Clyde, for starters. And this is all a plot to get us out in the open. You're so blinded by the idea of springing Jerry, you can't see it, Gwen."

"Out in the open?" Craig asked. "This isn't a trap for you. No cops, no Feds, no narcs. You have it all wrong, Webb."

"I don't think so. And another thing...you people killed three of my men."

*Oh, oh, mafia revenge time.* I must've tightened up inside at that, because the baby pushed back. Didn't like these people either.

"Hey, the two in Arkansas were chasing us and just didn't make a tight curve. Never laid a hand on them. And Karl? He tried to chase Wesley off a cliff and didn't make it. She did. I wasn't even there for that one."

"Self-defense, Jay," Gwen argued. "What'd you expect them to do with your goons in their faces?" She wanted so *much* for this to work out some way. And it looked like Webb was maybe wavering.

"So, put that aside for now. But you two stole half a million dollars from me. Do you think I'll just blow that off?"

Our mouths dropped open.

"Half a million...Just what in the *hell* are you talking about, Webb?" Craig seemed totally blindsided by this. And I'd nearly forgotten it, so both of us managed to look suitably confused.

"The money Wesley took from my briefcase in the stable, when she spent all that time in there, supposedly with the horse." He said it like it was the ace in his hole. Craig looked at me.

"I don't have a clue what you're talking about, Webb. And we sure as hell wouldn't have been running broke, taking peanut jobs to stay alive if we'd had that kinda cash. You're barking up the wrong tree, for sure."

*Yeah, Barker.*

He looked from one of us to the other. Evidently saw we were telling the truth, or damn good actors...He reached some kind of conclusion there inside his warped head.

*Okay, then it had to be Clyde...*

But Webb wasn't letting us off the hook. He had his teeth in this, and after an instant's reflection, he went back on the attack. Big time.

"So forget the money. I think I know for sure where it went. But now," he said, almost softly, "I'm gonna ask you just one more time, MacDonnell, where can I find that bastard Clyde?" He reached, pulled the gun again, racked a cartridge into the chamber, pointed it at Craig.

"*Jay!*"

"Shut up, Gwen! I'm not stupid enough to buy these fairy tales!" He was losing it, yeah, big time. Going over the edge.

"Jay, please don't do this. These people can't hand you a Federal agent. Use your head!"

"I am using my head. *Where,* MacDonnell?"

"She's right, Webb. You know we got no connection there. Feds can probably bury one of their own where *nobody* can find him. Think about it...the United States government is the most powerful force on earth. They want one of their own out of sight, he's out of sight." Craig was sweating. So was I.

The baby kicked.

Again, Webb considered this. Was there a chance? Could we get through to him? Things were in a precarious balance.

Then, absolutely no warning, Webb changed tactics back to insanity. He swung the gun to *me.* Barrel looked like an open manhole. I could see the ends of those spiral things inside.

"So now you got one more chance, MacDonnell. Clyde Kelly. *Now!* Or I waste your wife."

*Holy shit, this wasn't a game anymore.* I tried to look small: no way. Damn, I could go into labor...

"You even *think* about shooting her, I'll rip your heart out, Webb, even with a dozen slugs in me." Low, quiet, menacing. Craig tensed. He'd do it, too. I'd heard that tone before. But there wasn't even a kitchen knife close this time. And we were dealing with a madman. The air became charged, explosive.

Craig shifted his weight slightly, like a coiled spring. Webb flicked his eyes back to him.

"So will I, Jay," Gwen warned. "She's *pregnant,* dammit. You'd kill her and her unborn baby? That's beyond monstrous! You can't be thinking straight: You're obsessed with this. Back off, now..."

"I said *shut up, bitch!*" His face was red, contorted with hate. He'd really lost it this time, and I knew nobody and nothing could reach him. "Ah, just get your gullible ass outta here if you got no stomach for this. *Go on, get out!*"

"*Jay!*" A wail. She'd probably never heard him call her that, either. Her tough-woman exterior crumbled. And this time, I was scared totally out of my wits, looking into that gun barrel. Couldn't move, like a bird hypnotized by a snake.

"*Out!*" he roared, and Gwen gave in, realized she couldn't reach him anymore. She seemed to shrink, stepped back, all in a sort of slow motion, it seemed. Almost reached the door, stretched out her hand for the knob.

Then all hell broke loose.

As soon as Webb shifted his eyes reflexively for an instant to Gwen, Craig lunged for him, low, hard, before he could get the gun from me to him. He fired anyway, just as Craig hit him in the stomach with a shoulder, but the gun was beyond him: shot hit nothing but wall. The gun flew off and I came alive again, started to dive for it. But somehow Webb had twisted away from Craig and fell on top of it first, grabbing with both hands.

He came up with it, fumbling it, trying to jam it toward Craig, who was just regaining his balance, couldn't reach him.

This time I *knew* it was all over. The bastard had won. No baby. No years ahead of us. No great house. No man, no horse, no dog.

No *life*.

The crash of the door slamming back all the way into the wall merged into the shot from behind me, and I didn't know just whatthehell was happening. Had Webb shot my husband? No, the scum was staggering, crumpling to the floor.

Damn, had *Gwen?*...

Then tall Nate Peterson stepped through like the U.S. Cavalry, Cyrano right behind him. Gwen ran to Webb. I held my dog off; all the anger and noise might trigger something. He came, a little reluctantly at first. But then he saw the thing that'd made all the threats did appear to be dead, so okay, no job for him. He even wagged his tail.

And I had the craziest thought: I could finally let this damn bleached hair grow out, get rid of the fake contacts...

Gwen knelt over Webb, near her bag on the floor.

"Jay! Oh, God. *Jay!*" Sob, wail. She'd loved the crazy s.o.b. And I felt sorry for her, torn up like that, in spite of her being part of the ghoul-pack.

"How the hell, Nate?" Craig couldn't believe it.

"I'd staked out your road, had the pix of these two from Clyde. Saw them drive in. Dunno how Webb figured you were here, but we were afraid…"

Nobody had been watching Gwen. She suddenly put it all together, I guess.

Clyde.

Nate.

The whole thing a setup, after all.

No hope for Jerry.

J. Barker dead there on the floor.

*And no life left for her.*

She whirled, came up from his body fast, with both hands on a gun that'd materialized from her bag.

"*Bastards!*" she spat, her face twisted, wild, hate-filled. But the gun wasn't shaking. Not a bit. The only question in that nanosecond was which one of us she'd shoot first.

Nate's reaction must've been instinctive: it was instantaneous from the hip, and dead on, literally, before she could trigger her gun. *Marshall Earp.* She shuddered, collapsed across Webb's body.

I flashed: aging, corrupt Romeo and his Juliet…

There was a prolonged space of time as it all soaked in. Then Nate made the necessary calls. Craig got me upstairs into bed, all in a sort of haze, pulled off my shoes. Afraid I'd multiply right there, I guess. Ambulance came, other cops. Even some people from somewhere to clean up, scrub the floor. I was so unwinding in relief they could've dismantled the house around me, I wouldn't have noticed.

Did have some more completely irrational, disconnected flashes from somewhere. Could look Cheryl up now, have some great girl-talk sessions. Couldn't wait to show the baby off to Selena when she came home. Look up Mangrum and Shelby again, Colleen…

*Get a life back*, I guess I was thinking.

Cyrano, my first guy, nuzzled up to me and licked my hand. Like, what was I doing in bed in the daytime? Seemed to him like a good time for a romp outside, now the badasses were down. I thought, if there'd been a way for him to get inside, he'd probably have taken Webb out all by himself.

The baby stretched. Craig leaned down and kissed me. I put his hand on my big belly and we both smiled.

# Twenty-seven

We got ourselves back to normal after the Webb massacre. I stopped abusing my hair, shelved the glasses and fake contacts, and Craig shaved, started losing the premature white. We resumed our real names, handling the house thing with another paper sale. Had to explain a few things to a few people, but it all worked itself out after a coupla weeks.

Nate was the hero of the piece, and Clyde couldn't get over his being in the wrong place at the right time. Didn't matter, we told him, nobody'd outwitted Webb on any of it, except for Nate's cautionary move.

Clyde did take some time off to romance Cheryl, and we saw a lot of them afterwards. This was gonna work out, I was sure.

Strangely, though, I couldn't seem to reach a level of closure on the whole thing. Part of it was that missing money. Clyde hadn't known about it, either. But that helped explain why Webb hadn't backed off chasing us. He was sure we'd robbed him of his ill-gotten cash stash.

I guess the months of running and hiding had keyed me up enough so it'd be a long time before I stopped looking over my shoulder for the headhunters. But I'd learned not to ignore those faint intimations of...whatever they were. Warnings? I sure as hell hoped not. Tired of beasties I hadda be warned about...

But other important matters were overshadowing the whole end-of-the-nightmare experience. I refer, of course, to the new life inside me, and the preparations for my mom-to-be adventure.

That should have overjoyed me to the extent I'd get past all the creepies, but it didn't, completely. I didn't know if my sixth sense was at work to tell me things weren't as cool as they seemed, or something else...maybe just some sort of chemical imbalance with the kid's biological makeup tipping the scale.

But the glorious Virginia fall continued, with the leaves falling like oversize painted snowflakes and the nights frosty. Incredible time of year here, and not that different from back home in the mountains north of Atlanta. Craig had lots of work he enjoyed, and his new crew was okay.

About the old cast of characters: Bob the Worried had taken a job with a government agency that remodeled low-cost housing and seemed set for life. Those assignments, I'd heard, meant you never got laid off. Good for Bob.

And Clueless Don had moved to Maryland where the pay was supposedly better, and I guess the gum-chewing girls with the tattoos were more plentiful. Helper Henry left another job to come back to work for Craig, and we were glad to have him. He'd learned a lot in our absence and was on the way to becoming a competent carpenter.

Funny how a crew will shape up to be a lot like its predecessor. Number two joiner Ike Wells was this older guy with premature wrinkles in his face like a plowed Georgia field. But he was a fine craftsman and didn't worry about the sky falling, or much of anything else. Just did his thing with mortising chisels and an unerring eye.

George Clanton was young and even good-looking, but an all-around carpenter who *didn't* spend all his time daydreaming of girls in skimpy outfits straining to break free of convention and ravish his body. At least I don't think he did.

And the new helper was a riot. Chunky, cheerful kid named Clarence, who was as happy unloading a truck as mixing mortar. Played a mean electric guitar just about every day at lunch, so much so that Craig suggested strongly that he move off an acceptable distance to reduce the decibels. Clarence was on the way to becoming a good stonemason under my (modestly) expert tutelage.

I'd finally stopped hitting the work with them and had lots of time to myself. Cyrano and I'd take long walks, free of phantom baddies in the bushes. I'd never been afraid much anyhow, with him along.

And—surprise—I'd gotten nice notes and a coupla phone calls from nerdy brother Bert and his Hannah. All excited about the new niece/nephew on the way, and yeah, they *were* my only family. Another surprise: they were finally getting married. In the spring, which would make it probably some sort of record for a long pre-commitment relationship. I said good for them, and I guess, mellowed some in my admittedly uncharitable dealings with them.

Motherhood might make me downright likable, if I let it.

~ * ~

The news had not hit her as hard as she'd have thought. Probably delayed reaction, but her first thought was, *what'll I do for money?* Both parents, in a shoot-out at those carpenters' house down in Virginia. So Dad had tracked them down, even with what had been multiple moves, fake I.D.s and disguises. Only he apparently hadn't recovered that missing money.

The cop who'd killed them both had been portrayed as some kind of hero, taking out a drug lord and his crazed wife.

Samantha Webb only slowly began to feel the shock. Her family. Her safety net. Flashbacks to childhood in Baltimore, walking with her father's hand holding hers, a tether to security in crowds. Her mother's constant fussing with her hair, her clothes, to try to make her their princess.

*Omigod, they're gone. They're <u>gone!</u>*

Then the shock progressed to rage, a blinding, impotent fury. Rage at the police, at the legal system itself, despite the fact that her father had thumbed his nose at it, outwitted it for years.

And rage toward the couple who'd come through it all without a scratch. Yeah, and with the money, too. While she, again penniless, would have to toss the whole theater non-career, find herself some sort of dead-end job just to survive. To face a future with nothing more exciting in it than an occasional community theater gig, with untalented housewives and wannabe local actors.

That shit just wouldn't cut it for her. She'd taken what she wanted long enough to know it could be done, if you just had some backup. But now that was gone, along with her whole family.

But she had to calm it. Had to think rationally. Shit happened. Even this devastating, unimaginable shit that could destroy her life. *Okay now, where is that bottle? Stiff drink. Reality check. Get onto what to do...*

All right, now she'd simply have to pull off something big, something that would set her up with a decent income. Her father had tapped into the drug pipeline...that was risky as hell, and of course that was ultimately what had taken him down.

Ditto her brother.

So, what was it to be? And could there be a way to avenge the deaths and make a big score, too? There had to be, if she could just find it...

But first she had to go down there, make funeral arrangements, see what the financial situation was. No doubt the Feds would confiscate any dollars her father'd had, but maybe her mother would be excluded, and she just might have had something of her own.

And yeah, she guessed she ought to go visit Jerry in jail.

~ * ~

"I wanna buy a gun," I told Craig, "while it's still possible with all the Fed restrictions and the bleeding hearts. I can't handle either of your cannons, and given our past scrapes, I just want to be prepared."

"Understandable. Even with the Webbs gone, nothing says we might not run onto another nest of snakes sometime. Although I hope to hell we don't. What'd you have in mind?"

"Something that won't cripple my hand, and preferably one that'll hit close to what I'm aiming at. Not a Saturday night special, though." I went on to tell him I was having a hard time putting the whole Webb nightmare behind me. "Not to borrow trouble, but I just don't ever want to find myself staring into the barrel of some crazy's gun again without firepower of my own."

In our state it was even, for now, legal to carry a concealed weapon and I found myself being glad of that. I reflected that, not counting Gwen the Insane, Karl the Crasher, Reenie or the Nordic Crazy, all of whom had waved firepower around, I'd looked down the barrel of two deranged people's guns, father and son. For entirely too long. And two was enough. You hadda remember that old third time stuff.

Not that I wanted to blast anybody away, but we'd seen just how crazy people can get when their dirty doin's are threatened.

Call me paranoid.

~ * ~

Samantha learned from Barker Webb's former law partner that yes, he'd set up a separate account for Gwen, from which she'd sent the regular checks to New York. And there was, while not much left in it, enough she could access to let her get established somewhere, doing something. Apparently the drug Feds'd had nothing on Gwen herself.

She had the parents' bodies cremated after a discussion with her brother via the visitors' phone setup at the prison. It all had an unreal feeling about it, a finality she had trouble accepting. Hell, they'd always just *been there* whenever she'd needed them, and now they weren't. And neither was her dumb-ass brother Jerry... no parole. She poured another plastic glass of bourbon in the motel room, alternating between loneliness and anger.

*So it's just me now.* At least the narcs weren't after her; not a shred of evidence to tie her to anything illegal. Hadda keep it that way, she guessed. Her dad was as sharp as they came, but his revenge obsession with those damn carpenters had unraveled it all. And the Feds'd seemed to know a lot about him anyway. Matter of time, probably.

Her mom had always insisted she stay the hell away from that whole thing, and she'd resented it. *But yeah, I'm glad, now—gotta be, way things turned out.*

*But oh my God, does it piss me off, the whole setup blown all to hell. If I could've just hung in a little longer, all the contacts, all the getting my name out there, all the free gigs, had to've paid off. Now I'm a thirty-year-old orphan, and New York doesn't care a damn about me, or about half a million others in my shoes.*

But there was no bleeding way she was just gonna take this shit. That damn Clyde Kelly was out there somewhere, about a mile deep in the system where she could never find him, but the others? Hell, you could find anybody, enough time and money. And she had no money, so okay, time.

*This was Dad's thing: hit the s.o.b.s back ten times as hard as they hit you. I guess maybe I'm meant to carry that on for him. Yeah, I was always his girl...*

She set the half-empty bottle of bourbon back on the shelf, and searched for a plan.

~ * ~

The horse trainer Roy Halpern had been pleased enough with his life: horses, girls, making money, more horses. These transplanted-to-Virginia people with all their cash liked to spend it on horse shows, hunts, hobnobbing with others like them. And a lot of that money rubbed off on him. But it was all getting a little old, at mid-thirty. A man oughta settle down, he figured, maybe even get married, have some kids. The girls he met were getting to look all alike, it seemed.

Things had always come easily for Roy. People wanted to do things for him, and what was wrong with that? Women especially all seemed to have a thing for horses, and well, a thing for him, too. With the result that he was never without money coming in, or a current girlfriend.

Problem was, how did a man choose one out of a whole herd of women who were so alike they could be sisters? Hell, with a horse you had bloodlines, but that didn't mean a thing with women.

Most often, he'd observed, the ones with the most education and connections were really the ones with the least common sense.

His daddy had told him to find one with money, but he'd seen that setup too often: man married to a dollar bill never knew when the roof over his head could get jerked away. He knew a chubby old boy married to a rich woman a dozen years older'n him, always going to hunts, shows. Guy stuffed into those white britches and red coat like a blow-up toy and everybody laughing at him behind his back. Woman ordered him around like a stable hand. And he put up with it.

Besides, Roy had a pretty good bit saved up. Not having much while growing up had made him hang onto what he earned. So no, money in a woman wasn't the answer. And the educated ones were apt to look down on a man, once the newness wore off. Like to find him one hadn't been around too much, but not dumb either.

He thought back to some of the string of girls he'd gone with, clear back to high school and Shelley Davis. He'd really wanted that girl, but she'd dropped out of school to marry the guy got her pregnant. Now she was a blimp, living in a trailer up in Greene County, yelling at four kids and her drunk of a husband. *Sure glad I got past that one.*

He pulled his big truck into yet another cobblestone-paved courtyard at yet another high-priced stable with a restored plantation house beyond on its hill. Same old stuff, but hell, horses'd never get old for him. Just the people who owned them, all with the same dumb questions, the women managing to rub up against him, the husbands doing deals in their heads, probably wishing they were somewhere else.

Roy continued to daydream as he put the horses through their dressage maneuvers, conferred with the owners, gave orders to the stable hands. Done this a million times, do it in his sleep. *Just remember to smile a lot*, like these folks were the only ones mattered in the world.

It was the few girls who'd resisted his charms he remembered most. Always easy enough to get over, with a line of them waiting, but it rubbed a man's pride a little to get turned down. Shelly'd been the first, and he'd never figured that. Guy knocked her up and married her was ugly as a mud fence. Couple of others, and yeah, that carpenter girl seemed all hot for him, then cut him off cold.

Heard she was back, married to her boss, had a kid, now. *Boy, time sure gets by, doesn't it.* Yeah, the guy...MacDonnell, had got in touch with him to track down that horse of the Webbs' back a couple years ago. Real mess, that whole Webb thing...

That got him thinking about Samantha Webb, the hot New York daughter, and that time at the housewarming party. Now that woman knew how to give a man a good time, even in a truck. But that was the night their whole setup went all to hell, and the girl'd disappeared. Brother'd killed a guy, was in for life. Then both parents killed in a shootout with a cop...big news a few months back.

He'd like to know what happened to that girl. *Prob'ly making it big up in New York.* Or not. He knew a lot of girls who'd gone up there after a couple parts in high school plays and community theater, all hot to set the place afire. Most of 'em came back broke, looked up their old high school sweethearts and forgot all about it.

Not the kind of girl to settle down with, Samantha—no way— but sure could make you feel like king of the mountain.

He almost got stepped on by a frisky horse, remembering her.

~ * ~

Yeah, I'd had the baby. Hardest few hours of my life. I understood why they called it labor. But Craig had been right there, holding my hand, mopping my brow, timing contractions, coaching my breathing. I got snappish a couple times, just like the childbirth class teacher had predicted, but he understood, and hung in there.

And finally, at one painful push no different from the last one, there was this whoosh, and then a blue-looking little boy in the doctor's hands, wrinkling up his face for his first cry. Didn't know what all this was about, but not happy. Until the nurse who took him placed him on my chest and he registered my heartbeat, my breathing, my voice.

Damn, what a beautiful boy, turning pink, quiet for a minute now, with mama again. I took my eyes off him to look at Craig and thought my guy was gonna bust with pride.

They had me out of there pretty quick, which is how they do it now if everything's okay, and it was. Kid weighed over eight pounds, and normal number of fingers, toes, stuff. I couldn't have been happier, aside from feeling like my guts had been turned inside out and maybe dosed with balsamic vinegar.

Craig couldn't do enough for me, and after a few days, here came my angel Selena, home for Christmas, to make me feel like a queen. We had ourselves some great girl-talk sessions. And we made her our child's godmother. Still teenage, but we couldn't have made a better choice.

Craig Wesley MacDonnell (why the hell not?) slept a lot, cried some, laughed early, and watched everything like he was building a legal case. *Oh no, not a lawyer, surely.* Anyway, he was the star of the piece, naturally, and even Cyrano thought he was terrific. God, when he started walking, he'd give my poor mutt hell.

Well, Christmas got over with, Selena went back home and then to campus again, and the kid and I holed up for the winter. Craig had plenty of work, enough of it inside where it was warm, and things were good. More than good. I was in busy-busy heaven with my two guys—four if you count Cyrano and Walker. Nice days, I'd put the baby in a front pack and walk a lot, just enjoying being alive with this precious part of me and Craig snuggled up and warm. We'd talk a lot to each other, his words not real words yet, but about as sweet sounds as I could imagine.

I'd read that babies need a lot of body contact, and we gave him that constantly. Breast-fed him, naturally, and that closeness was unlike anything I can describe. I really began to understand the mother's bond with her child, easily the most powerful in the world. So the little snot would probably be insufferable at thirteen...he was mine now—ours—and that was blessedly a long way off.

And just maybe we wouldn't screw up in our roles as parents, and he *wouldn't* be a monster. I had brother Alan's kids as role models in my head, and figured if we could do that well it'd all turn out.

But boy, did I miss not being able to share this little miracle with my parents. Let them spoil him rotten, love every minute of it. *Wherever you are, Mom and Dad, I hope you see what your girl's done. Know you're proud.*

Sad/glad every time I thought about that.

Now this picture of domestic bliss should have had me overflowing with joy, and it did, but yeah, there was still this nagging idea that something was lurking around under the bed, waiting to come up and bite us. Maybe just guilt at having so much? Could be. Or just holdover from all that running and hiding and nail-biting. It'd soon be two years since the shit first hit the fan, and I was ready for it to become just a bad memory. I had my life and it was better than anything I'd imagined for smart-ass Wesley.

Like I said before, wallow in it.

We did get the gun, an old but not-so-used 32-caliber long-barrel revolver that I could actually hit things with. We'd go out and practice like we'd tried to in Missouri, Craig with his Colt and me with the comparatively little Smith and Wesson. Never thought I'd enjoy that, but it was a mild high to see I'd put a close pattern in a paper plate against a stump at a respectable distance. Craig could, of course, outshoot me, but I was getting confident I could waste a badass if one lurched out of the woodwork at me and mine.

Again.

We were firm believers in the Second Amendment, of course, understanding that the words 'militia' and 'people' in it were interchangeable. (Had gone head-to-head with several over-tolerant folks on that subject before.) But Craig and I hadn't joined the NRA or any other activist group over the issue.

We weren't into politics as much as most of the people we knew, but we always voted, and hadn't so far managed to cancel each other out at the polls. The latest outrage from Washington or Richmond didn't usually rouse us to the level of howling, mouth-foaming revolution, but we kept track.

After all, things like local restrictions on building did affect us, passed by county (supposedly) public servants who'd come here from Philadelphia or Peoria. Usually clueless busybodies who wanted to do a makeover of our region to be like where they were from. And at the same time wanted to make sure nobody else could do that and spoil this rural countryside they'd discovered for themselves.

Can you say hypocrite?

Concentrating on restoration, we could take pride in our construction efforts, which didn't increase the number of houses crowding the landscape. Yeah, often we'd recycle two smaller historic houses into one, thereby actually reducing the total number of smears on the land.

We religiously avoided those cookie-cutter brick ranchers that got bigger every year. Upward mobility was the apparent goal, and I guess everywhere among the yuppies. It seemed a sort of game of one-upmanship: outdo your neighbors as if your intrinsic worth were measured in square footage.

Ambitious families must've had five-year-plans that put them into bigger McMansions with each career boost or executive bonus.

Yeah, just before the husbands' heart attacks.

# Twenty-eight

The Survival Plan, as Samantha Webb evolved it, was to nail herself a man, much as her mother had advised. But not just any man. Had to have some bucks, not be repulsive, and absolutely *had* to be pliable. That first requirement automatically cut out the theater hopefuls, even though a few did have Daddy's money behind them. She was beginning to suspect that most actors didn't really have any idea who they really were anyway, always playing somebody else.

So, young exec? They were all too arrogantly aware of the surplus of women in New York, and indeed in most of the bigger cities. So maybe a smaller place, but not stiflingly small. Even Baltimore was too big now, and encouraged that male ego she couldn't stand.

She actually got out a map and circled cities, towns.

Where were the desirable places, now? Okay, Bend, Oregon: small but full of lively people, she'd heard. Ditto Colorado towns. Missoula, Montana; Santa Fe; Carmel; Keene, New Hampshire; Chapel Hill in North Carolina. *Hmm: Charlottesville, Virginia again,* where her parents had found close to just what she was searching for now. Small, but the university pumped up things, apparently.

She hadn't visited them there much, and the recent trip hadn't let her see a lot she either liked or didn't. Besides, those damn carpenters were around there somewhere, and every time she thought of them, apparently blissful in their holier-than-thou lives, it pissed her off. And that grudge was growing instead of fading.

More so after visiting Jerry in the prison two counties away. He was understandably bitter, still insisting he hadn't wasted that scum. And he'd tried to talk her into picking up their father's vendetta against Clyde Kelly and those people. He'd even told her about a guy who could get her some hardware for the job. All she'd need was a few bucks...

She hadn't been—wasn't yet—ready for any drastic action like that, but yeah, some of his anger rubbed off on her and added to her own. Simply put, the family'd had everything going for it, and now they had absolutely nothing, with both parents dead and Jerry where he might as well be. Any way you cut it, that was the worst. But there had to be bigger priorities just now...the place to *be*, to start over, get going on the big score. She'd told him all that.

But then he'd gotten her attention.

"Okay, then. There's something you gotta know, Sam." He was sweating beyond the glassed partition. The phone set in his hand was slick with it. She tuned him in.

"The half million? *I* took it outta Dad's briefcase. While the girl carpenter was out back of the stable. Wanted to frame Clyde. Didn't want him muscling in on us the way he was. Always suspected him. Figured to tell Dad I'd seen him sneak back to the stable. Never got the chance, of course.

"Now, I want you to get those three people, Sam. I told you about the guy can fix you up with a gun. Plan it out; make it tight. You know where the carpenters are, and I bet they're in touch with Clyde. Find some way."

*Half a million dollars.*

"Where's the money, Jerry?"

"That's what you don't get to know till you take care of those three. It's safe, and you get all of it when you do the job. I'd like a little now and then, buy some favors in here, but it's all yours.

"But you gotta earn it."

He hung up the phone, stood and walked away. No begging, no pleading, no arguing. Just walked away from her.

*Wow*, she thought. Five hundred big ones, just waiting. *But my hard-ass brother won't tell me where.* And sure, she was as pissed as he was about all of this. Hated those people. But without that money, how did she get started on anything? She was right back in the same place.

She pondered the whole thing.

*Okay, gotta get back down there, for sure. And something will work out. It has to. But back to the immediate plan...*

Oh, that guy Roy was around Charlottesville, too, doing his horse thing. Her mother had told her he was *the* sought-after trainer in the region, and hinted he was raking in cash from the new-money country clubbers as well as the old horsey set. Handsome as hell, if a disappointment in bed, she remembered. And not educated either, which could be a drag. But maybe she could teach him some things...

Nah, have to be a continual act, living with somebody like that. No.

But hell, she *was* an actress, and a damn good one, too. And *he'd* actually been in a major movie, she'd heard, if only as a double. But there just might be a connection there...

*If* the guy were even still single. If she could get down there, find a job, survive long enough to snare him. Oh, she could do that...wind the clod around her little finger. Become the horsiest horse lover of all time, if it'd get her what she wanted. And yeah, being seen with a drop-dead hunk couldn't hurt, in any circles...

And the other: half a million couldn't hurt, either.

Time to blow off this damn receptionist job, anyway. Talk about an act; this required she put on a face for every loser who walked in the door. Make him feel like Jaworsky Financial couldn't survive without him, or at least his money. *Yes, sir, Mr. Jaworsky has made time for you, in spite of his commitments. Won't you have a seat? Coffee?* Always, always, the damn coffee. At least she'd learned how to make the best coffee in town. Might come in handy, if she had to work in a restaurant.

Again.

~ * ~

It was suddenly June, and my boy was six months old, and that's probably the cutest age there is. Personality spilling out all over, just starting to crawl, backwards most of the time, but about to get that straightened out. Smiling like the sun coming out. Pulling up flowers and eating them. Climbing up on sleeping Cyrano and snuggling. The damn dog loved it; wouldn't move a muscle as long as Craiglet was there, squashing him.

I'd take him up on Walker with me, and we'd ride the fields and woods paths, neglecting household chores with absolutely no shame. Selena was home again and came up often. I'd borrow another horse from a neighboring farmer and we'd leave the baby with Craig weekends and disappear up in the hills west of home for hours. She'd survived her first college year well and told me about the other eager religion majors, about her singing with a big *a cappella* group, studying hard.

"But some of the other kids don't seem very dedicated," she confided. "They party a lot off-campus. A lot of them plan on going into the ministry, but I wonder if it's real with some of them."

*Probably not.* I remembered the thunderous televangelists of a long generation before, and their behind-the-cameras lifestyles. But then there've always been exploiters, in every field. And Selena was *so* into religion. Couldn't be all bad, that.

Our nephew Jason had also visited, now a rising senior in high school and, from what I gathered, a young ladies' man. He was a handsome lad, with that mischief in his eyes and a grin you could drive a truck through. Selena loved her brother, but rolled her eyes a lot around him. He and Craig hit it off, and he would work with us that summer. Not to worry, I thought, my husband would work the boy's young ass off and turn him into a craftsman.

~ * ~

She'd resisted the Roy idea, but in the end hadn't come up with a better one, and had made the move to Charlottesville. She used her stage name, Samantha Montiel, and kept her real surname a secret. No need to muddy the water where it wasn't necessary. That wouldn't work with Roy, if she found him, but she was sure she'd be able to handle that. Of course, employment records would show her real name, but she'd keep those close.

She'd found an apartment with a struggling girl photographer, which reminded her too much of the New York scene. But okay for now. And yes, she soon had a job with another financial house, knowing the terminology, if not the details of the business.

And wonder of wonders, they hadn't asked her to make the coffee. It was so bad, though, the product of a college intern's clumsiness, that she actually volunteered her skills. And that got her brownie points she figured couldn't hurt.

Build on whatever she could, yeah. Build up to the big score.

It turned out to be easy enough to locate Roy Halpern, and yes, he was still single, still doing the horse circuit, still leaving the girls hungry-eyed. Susan Kraft, her freckled, dumpy roommate, had even photographed him for a spread in the local slick magazine.

"Didn't even notice me," she lamented. "He was all wrapped up in the horses, and I don't think he even registered all those older women hanging onto him."

"Probably immune to it by now," Samantha told her, examining the issue of the magazine. Yes, there he was, Virginia's answer to the remembered Marlboro Man, and just maybe part of her ticket to a real life.

She began listing the upcoming horse shows, races, events where she could bump into Roy, by accident, of course. She'd play stand-offish, claiming to've been a little smashed that other night and totally swept away. Yeah, she could do sincere. Get him to heel like a foxhound puppy and never suspect he wasn't in control. That one wouldn't even be a big challenge.

Coming here had caused a mixture of emotions. This was where her parents had settled, planning to enjoy the social life among the moneyed imports and the old families. It was also where their world had come apart, at the hand of a traitorous narcotics agent they'd trusted, aided by those two who'd helped him.

And it was where they'd died.

Now it was, she hoped, to be the scene of her own success, or at least the base for it. She was sure she could somehow get Roy into something better, somewhere better. Maybe Hollywood and more movies.

Why not?

But there was also a sort of tingle at knowing the two her father had hunted for so long were right there close, and that she would sooner or later run into one or both. And be in a position to take them out.

There MacDonnell Restorations was, listed in the telephone book, with the address out in the county. And some discreet inquiry revealed that yes, he'd married the girl Wesley, and they now had a child. A wave of envy laced with anger swept over her at the discovery. Life was just so goddam *unfair*.

~ * ~

It was at one of those horsey 'teas' the big money held periodically, with an open bar but no tea in sight. All it was really, was a chance for the stable owner to show off his/her latest acquisitions and one-up the other country clubbers. But Roy had been urged to attend, and hell, it was good for business.

And leading a new Thoroughbred around a corner, he almost ran into a girl photographer snapping away, and with her was...yes, by God, Samantha Webb! His mouth fell open and he came close to letting the spirited horse knock him over.

"Well, hello there, girl. Didn't expect to see *you*," was all he could come out with.

"Hello, Roy. Yes, things got pretty hairy there for a while, and then again later. But I'm here now. How've you been?"

Damn, she looked good. The photographer was busily getting pictures of them with the horse. Roy sidled a little, to get his good side to the camera.

"Oh, 'bout like always. Figured you'd stay in the big town for good, score big, but glad to see you back here." He was remembering that night, before the cops came and it'd gone all to hell.

"New York can get old for a girl who wants something more... meaningful, I guess. I'm learning why my parents came here in the first place." *Yeah, like I wasn't totally ignored there, like everybody else.*

"Oh, yeah. Sorry about them...and all. That whole business had to be pretty rough on you."

"Shock, to find out about my dad and my brother that way. Mom didn't know either, about...all the bad stuff."

Like she'd said, she could do sincere when she needed to.

"Well, what brings you to this thing?" Indicating the overdressed devotees. "Didn't know you were into horses."

"Just learning a little about them. Mom thought I'd better leave town back then, and I never got the chance to get to know horses better. Or you, either." Smile, that she knew softened her features just enough. "Oh, this's my roommate, Susan Kraft. She photographed you for *Equine* magazine, she tells me."

The freckled girl stammered an acknowledgement, face red in embarrassment. Roy thought he remembered her. Standing beside Samantha, the dowdy photographer made her even prettier.

And later, despite the distractions of the tanned older women and their eager daughters in their height-of fashion sundresses, Roy managed to spend some time with Samantha. Which resulted in the tentative renewal of their getting to know one another. She was a little embarrassed, and didn't seem, here in the July sunshine, at all the party girl who'd made it with him in his truck. He was just barely sensitive enough not to presume anything on that score. *After all, everybody'd been drinking a lot then...*

And that was just the explanation she gave him later on their first date, as if it'd been worrying her. She was just standoffish enough to tantalize him, and he interpreted that as her maybe not being as free and easy as he'd thought. But he still couldn't forget the way she'd responded to him that other time...

*Okay, just play this slow and careful then, and see where it takes us. Sure got a lot more going for her than some of these ugly horse groupies.*

She told him how tired she'd become of the endless maneuverings and deal-makings of the big city, the fierce competition in the theater world, how she'd wanted more reality in her life. So, with her parents gone, she'd come back here hoping to start over...

"Yeah, I know some of what you're talking about. I was pretty impressed with all those uptown movie people that time I did the double thing, but I guess even a lot of that would get you down."

*No, a lot of it would set me up just fine, but we'll get to that.*

"I'd have thought they'd be after you for more work after that picture. Mom told me about you in it, and I saw it again with the background features. And there you were, dressed just like whatshisname, at a shoot."

"Oh, this agent wanted me to move out to California, try for more parts. I thought about it, but had a lotta commitments here, and by the time I coulda got it together, the idea had just worn off, I guess."

*And you missed the chance of a lifetime, you redneck.*

~ * ~

"There's this girl you oughta meet," Susan told her roommate. "Works at an ad agency that has me do photo shoots for them. Real sharp, from up in Pennsylvania. I know you two would hit it off."

Samantha wasn't sure she wanted to meet another girl, but yeah, she hadn't made friends here. The local theater wannabes were so pathetically amateurish she didn't want any more to do with the ones she'd met. And although she'd let matters progress suitably with Roy Halpern these few weeks, she was finding he wasn't any more appealing, beyond his looks, than she remembered. After a few drinks, she'd been able to shove that feeling aside each time, but how would it play, long-term?

Maybe this wasn't going to work out, after all...

But okay, this Cheryl might be fun; she wasn't small-town local after all. So sure, the three of them would take in one of the music venues in town. These at least were good, she'd discovered, although Roy's taste ran more to bluegrass than the jazz she liked.

And the girl was sharp, it turned out. Had dumped a loser in Pittsburgh the year before, and now had a fairly serious relationship with some Federal employee, she said. Sort of mysterious about that, but hey, everybody to his/her own thing. They had fun together, and sure, it was good to do the girl thing. Do it again soon.

Samantha told Susan how much she'd enjoyed the evening. They'd had just a drink too much, and laughed together a lot.

"Cheryl seems like a great girl. Glad she's got herself a man."

"Yeah, she doesn't talk much about him. Don't even know his name, but he flies in from some place in the Midwest—maybe St. Louis or somewhere—once in a while. Probably marry him, and move off to wherever." Dumpy Susan was plainly envious. Of Cheryl, and now of Samantha, with to-die-for Roy. Probably never land herself a guy or have much of an existence, Samantha reflected, but hell, that's just the way life kicked some people in the gut, if you let it.

*Better you than me, girl.*

~ * ~

We got a call from our guy Clyde that he was flying in for a visit with Cheryl for a few days. I invited them out, of course. Been busier than a one-legged man at an ass-kickin' with the kid, but I'd had a couple of good girl sessions with her. She didn't make any bones about adoring our offspring, and I could sense that Crimestopper Clyde's bachelor days were maybe starting to end.

And good enough for him, too.

He'd be here for a week this time, so we set our dinner thing for Saturday night, after he and Cheryl would have each other for a day or so first. Craig swore he'd catch us a feast of smallmouth bass that morning down at his favorite fishing spot on the Moorman's River, and we'd have a fish-fry to remember. I said sure, honey, but laid in some steaks, anyway. Hell, nobody'd notified the fish their worst nightmare was after them, and they just might have plans for a party of their own.

It'd be good to see Clyde again...been several months. Cheryl had managed a couple of long weekends from her advertising job to fly out to St. Louis, but the man just hadn't had much time for a visit here before. He'd told us his agency was knocking over links in the drug chain there one at a time. Like slow-motion dominoes, but it seemed he had to be on top of it all constantly.

Time for a little R and R. And just maybe seeing our mini-Craig would tip his scales toward domesticity a little, too. The guy couldn't be too hard-boiled to resist our number one attraction.

~ * ~

Susan Kraft told her roommate Samantha she'd had lunch with Cheryl and that their friend had some good news.

"Her mystery man's coming for a whole week," she said breathlessly, "and I'll finally get to meet him."

"That's nice, yeah," Samantha was washing the second-hand car she'd bought for practically nothing down. The dealers were dying to move their stock, and it apparently hadn't mattered that she'd been at her job only a short time. This one was an anonymous flesh-color Japanese import, shaped like every other car in the world, and she'd already almost tried to get into the wrong ones twice at shopping center parking lots.

"Oh, and I finally learned his name," Susan went on.

"Great." *Maybe a good wax job would improve the looks of this drab thing.* She missed the red sportscar she'd sold when she went to New York. No way to keep a car there, where garages cost as much as apartments in small towns…

"It's Clyde Kelly."

"Clyde…*Kelly?*" No, couldn't be. Not…She tried to keep the astonishment off her face as a tide of shock, unbelief and anger surged inside her. *The* Clyde Kelly?

"Yeah, but she still won't say exactly what he does for a living. Except that Federal thing. Maybe something in government. Anyway, we should get together one night, maybe with Roy? And just maybe Roy has a friend who'd come along…"

Samantha had to get away for a minute, think this through…

"Yeah, maybe. Listen, Sue, I'm soaked. Gonna go dry off. Yeah, we'll work on that." She shut off the hose, hands shaking, managing to spray more water on herself, and went inside to her room where she sank onto the bed.

*Clyde by God Kelly.* Could it really be? Hell yes, with all that secrecy about his job. Federal narcotics agent. Undercover traitor who'd set all this disaster in motion. Had to be the same guy. So sure, they'd transferred him off somewhere so her father couldn't get to him. And while he apparently hadn't been in on the killing of her parents, he'd put Jerry away, and brought the family's world down around their ears to begin with. The son of a *bitch!* She dug out a fifth of bourbon, took a big drink directly from the bottle.

And she thought fleetingly that perhaps this coincidence, this accidental crossing of paths, might indeed have been beneath the surface of her coming back here...some sort of justice that needed to be done...

Thoughts kaleidescoped in her head: the plan to take those carpenters out and how she could do it, Jerry's plea for revenge, that money, the specter of the Feds, the entire police system embodied in the one man: Clyde Kelly.

It was a long time later that Samantha Webb, with the now half-empty bottle stowed away, made a call to the man her brother had told her about. Part of the other plan she'd spent many weeks evolving. A plan that let her believe she was really following a real-life script, taking steps already laid out for her. One her father would have put together: just as tight, just as foolproof...

# Twenty-nine

Samantha had done a complete makeup job on herself, so that here, in the little Charlottesville airport, not even a close friend could recognize her. No trick for an actress, and she mingled anonymously with the crowd of university students, professors, business people at the terminal. She'd followed Cheryl's blue Mazda here, and yes, a flight on the D.C. shuttle was due in a few minutes. Surely following the St. Louis one, she reasoned.

So she'd know for sure if there could be more than one Clyde Kelly in so small a place. She stepped behind a pillar and sipped Coke with a healthy dash of bourbon in it. *Not long, now...*

And yes, by God, just minutes after the commuter plane had touched down, that was Clyde, coming through the gate, doing a quick automatic check of the place, then holding his arms out for Cheryl, who ran to him. Samantha felt a surge of adrenaline. He was *here,* not thirty feet from her, and there was no way in hell he'd ever know her.

She smiled at an elderly man with a cane, turned and walked out of the terminal. The anger, the rage was building inside her, but she willed herself to stay calm. This operation required absolute control, and she must channel the emotions, keep herself completely in hand...

*Okay, phase one complete. They'll go to her place, for sure, and it's Friday night, so set up tomorrow, watch. They'll go somewhere, and if I hang back in my nothing car, I'll be invisible. And I won't look like anybody either of them's ever seen. So, sooner or later there'll be the chance. Just wish I could get him separated from her, but I guess that's too much to expect. She'll just have to be collateral damage, if necessary, victim of a violent robbery gone bad.*

*But no, she won't even know it's me, so yeah, leave her hysterical and disappear, long's she doesn't see my license plate.*

She knew she had to be careful, though, get Kelly before he could pull any quick cop stuff. No talk, all surprise. Shoot first, then rob. Dark parking lot maybe, Saturday night. Or if they went for a drive in the country.

Do him. Then the others.

*It'll happen. This is all planned out for me. This is a starring role, and Samantha Montiel can sure as hell play it.*

She took another drink. Through the pleasant haze of the alcohol, she didn't recognize the blindness of what had become an obsession. *Get Clyde Kelly and the others,* that was what mattered. After that, in another place, she could start over any way she chose. But this way her family would be avenged. And she'd have the money. That need had grown to huge proportions.

And now it was clear to her that this was the real reason things had come together to bring her there.

~ * ~

Our people showed up late Saturday afternoon, which got us a head start on the evening. Cheryl melted as usual at the sight of Craig Junior, and I had to tear her away. And yeah, he'd changed a lot just since she'd seen him last, the way babies do. Caught her eyeing Clyde speculatively. *Okay, okay, go for it, girl.* And Clyde held the little guy, trying not to look awkward, and got poked in the chin, best buddies right off. Then Cheryl jumped on the stuff I hadn't finished in the kitchen, and we sent the guys out to do whatever guys do while we put dinner together.

Craig *had* caught fish as promised, and swore he had not paid somebody else for them. I taught Cheryl how to make hushpuppies, and we had ourselves an estrogen party there over the hot stove.

~ * ~

Following the blue car had been ridiculously easy. The two inside were laughing, talking, totally focused on each other, never suspecting. *Some supercop Clyde is.* But of course, Samantha's own car was that zero color, like a million others on the road. She'd let a pickup truck pass her, too, so that'd be the one he'd see if he came up for air and checked behind him.

They were going out of town to the northwest, toward the mountains. She had no idea what the situation would be, but that didn't trouble her. This would play out exactly as it was supposed to...she felt almost as if her father were directing her in this part, and had set it up beforehand.

*A script, sure.*

The turn off the secondary road into a woods road had to be a dead end. She cruised on past to a turnout, made a U, parked. Not much traffic there, and that actually had to be a driveway, so she supposed surely just one house. *Okay, slip through the woods then, get a look at things.* A while before dark, and that'd be better all around, but yes, go and see what she'd be up against.

The trees were close together with some underbrush, so she took her time, the gun she'd bought tucked into her jeans in back. She'd successfully managed the recurring bursts of blinding anger that came whenever she let her mind dwell on her ruined career, life, family. Focused the rage on this cold purpose, even the score. Period. No need to think beyond that, although she'd already planned the next steps. Yeah, and she'd have the money to help carry them out.

Field, with a horse in it. Okay, skirt it, keeping to woods. House beyond, through the trees. Pickup truck, Jeep, the blue car...Wait, what was that sign on the truck? Just a little closer...

Omigod. *Omigod! It's MacDonnell Restorations. The damn carpenters! This is their place. Right here!*

So they were inside, too.

She sank back against a tree to the ground. Had to think this through. All of them, right *here. Okay, is this perfect, or what?* But wait a minute: four people, and the damn baby, too. Did she wanta waste all of them?

Have to. Couldn't leave any eyes alive.

*No, can't kill a baby. Don't want to do Cheryl either, unless no other way. So what, then? Let her go, with the kid? Can't...*

No, it'd be okay. She wouldn't know who the killer was, with this face and this hair. So okay, back to the plan. Drop Clyde Kelly before anybody knew shit, then...

*Do I really even need to kill the carpenters?* Her dad had been so obsessed about them. Couldn't get to Clyde, so he'd transferred...

*No, they jumped Jerry, broke his arm, helped the narcs nail him.* And it was that damn Wesley who'd snooped in the first place, started it all. Yeah, and Jerry'd insisted they all had to go.

Still...*Oh, shit, whatthehell difference does it make?* Kill one snake; kill 'em all. Pop Clyde, then one-two.

*Cheryl will be out of her mind and I'll be gone.* Be in the car and away before any cops could even get the location. Lose the disguise... no car I.D., no Samantha I.D. and she was home free.

Be back at work Monday, and later leave this backwater whenever she wanted, however she wanted. With Roy or without. Probably without. The dumb guy would only be dead weight really, no matter he looked like a king.

*No, no way is Roy Halpern anybody's idea of a king, in bed or out.*

So, leave Cheryl with the kid, which should be okay. She'd lose a slimeball; she'd gain a baby...*good trade all around.*

Samantha slipped back through the woods to her car. A light rain had begun to fall. Time now to wait, hour or so. Go over the plan as many times as necessary: rehearsals.

*Smooth performance on the way, folks.*

Go toward town to that close shopping center just before the hit, then again after, for some sales receipts to show where she'd been. About ten minutes to get there afterwards, tops. Nobody would notice her leave, obviously there all the time. Then afterwards, hang with Susan, maybe go catch a music thing downtown on the mall, under that big tent.

Air-tight alibi.

Not that she should need one. No way for *anyone* to connect her with any of this. But there *was* that cop who'd shot her parents. Yeah, he just might smell a link. So, the planned precautions. *Never underestimate the enemy* had been at the core of her father's M.O. And the enemy now would be the snooping small-town cops.

Who'd be totally clueless, and she'd wait to collect the cash, not spend any of it soon, or anywhere near here. Perfect plan, to be executed perfectly.

*Oh, nice choice of words.*

And yeah, her parents could rest easy after tonight, wherever they were.

*And I'll have the money.* She had another drink, thinking about what half a million dollars could do for her, spent carefully.

Waiting, she unaccountably remembered her mother's dismay at the temper tantrums she'd throw as a child. She never gave in, no matter how Gwen tried to calm her. When Samantha Webb was pissed, she stayed pissed till whatever wrong had been righted. Or until she could avenge herself on the perp, be it another arrogant child, a middle-school tormentor, or just someone who'd gotten in her way once too often.

Black moods, that's how her parents had labeled those episodes, and they'd never found out how to handle them. Neither had the psychologists they took her to. The fact was, she'd get over them in her own good time, when that suited her, and not a damn minute before. Her brother Jerry had been terrified of her those times, and that'd been sweet. No doubt who held the whip in that family.

Thinking back, she recalled all the times that stubbornness, that refusal to give in, had worked for her. And a wave of nostalgia moved over her. Long since. No family now, no one to run to when things got to be too much. No rebuilding-time at home any more. All wiped out by the system, the cops, that *goddam* Clyde Kelly, and those two...

The rage began again: black, sure, but so what?

In just a little while, that anger, the frustration, the helplessness, the shitty *unfairness* of it all would be satisfied, avenged, made right again.

~ * ~

The knock came after our leisurely dinner, while we were having a drink and listening to Clyde tell a hilarious story from his carpenter days, shop talk, after a fashion. Outside, the rain had intensified a little, a good late summer soaker.

But just who'd be out here now? I hadn't heard a car, and super-watchdog Cyrano'd been snoozing on the rug.

I opened the door to a dark-haired woman I'd never seen, folding up an umbrella. Cyrano went to her, sniffed once, then nosed past her outside. I could smell alcohol.

"Hi. I'm afraid I got my car stuck turning around in your driveway." Her eyes went from one of us to the other as she stepped inside, stopping on Clyde, who'd risen. She closed the door behind her as I was forming some reply, still with those eyes fixed on Clyde.

Then, with absolutely no warning, this woman reached into an oversize bag as if for a tissue, pulled a gun instead, and shot Clyde Kelly. The sound was deafening, the shock worse. At the sight of her stare, then her reaching into the bag, he'd reacted, turned, but he went down with a surprised grunt.

Cheryl screamed. The baby wailed from his room.

I was dumbfounded. Craig leaped up, and the gun moved toward him. Then Cheryl hurled herself onto Clyde, and the woman shifted the gun back.

*Omigod, what is this? Who is this crazy woman? And of course, my damn gun is in a drawer somewhere.*

*Again.*

"Get off him, Cheryl! Get off the bastard!" she yelled.

*She knew Cheryl?*

And Cheryl turned at her name, tear-streaked, staring at the woman.

"Who...*Samantha?* Oh my *God! What*...?" She half-rose.

It hit Craig and me the same instant. *Samantha Webb,* the last of the crazy Webbs, here in disguise, with a gun.

And we were next...

And I'm thinking, *No, dammit, we've already done this shit once.*

But this time there was no cavalry, no cop crashing the door with a cannon...

She couldn't decide who to shoot first. I could tell Craig was tensed to rush her, and so could she. Moved the gun toward him. And that move by him would be suicide without a diversion. I started to smash her gun hand with my fists (hey, it'd worked before), but she caught my shifting, screamed at me.

"*Hold it, bitch!* You move and you're dead! Get over there with him. *Now!* She waved the gun, keeping an eye on Craig, and Clyde too, who was writhing, still shielded by Cheryl, who was down on her knees.

There were just too many targets at that split-second in time, with the baby's distracting racket, too, but I knew it wouldn't stay that way; she was committed.

She'd go for Craig first, the obvious threat, and the gun started its shift away from me to him. But her eyes kept flickering, checking each of us out.

Flash of memory: those damn spirals inside that gun barrel...

I heard a scratch at the door. I was still right at it...this hadn't taken long. I made as if to move away, but twisted the knob behind me.

And the proverbial shit hit the fan.

Cyrano burst through that door like a cannonball, and launched all ninety pounds of him into the air before anyone could blink, a chilling growl almost shaking the room.

This piece of shit was threatening *mama*, and the kill instinct exploded.

He clamped those shark teeth on Samantha's gun wrist, ripping, and the scream he tore out of her raised the hair on my neck. The gun flew off and he let go, went for the throat. She fell back, the dog on top of her, and the next scream ended in a gurgle of blood.

I ran to pull him off, trying not to sound hysterical as I called his name. Teeth were flashing everywhere, and she was feebly trying to push him away with bloody hands, eyes full of terror, a wig torn off her head.

I got through to my dog finally, and he calmed. He'd wanted to finish killing the thing, but it wasn't fighting anymore, so yeah, he guessed his job was done. He came, breath heaving, still a little wild-eyed, blood and foam flecking those jaws.

Craig bent over Samantha, unconscious, eyes rolled up in her head. A gash in her neck was pulsing blood, and he pressed fingers to it. Ditto her torn wrist.

"Call nine-one-one, Wes," he instructed me, almost calmly.

And somehow I made myself do it, gave the necessary stats, while moving to check Clyde at the same time. Multi-tasking.

I pulled a sobbing Cheryl back, cut away his bloody shirt with my kitchen scissors. He was conscious, but in terrible pain. A bullet hole was in his right side, but I hoped far enough out to miss the vital stuff. I knew peritonitis could kill you in about twenty minutes if an intestine spilled stuff in there.

Cheryl and I started to get him bandaged tight to stop the flow, gave him a washcloth to bite on. He nodded toward Samantha, whose lips were frothing blood.

"Mouth-to-mouth, Craig," he gasped.

Half of my mind was saying *no, let the bitch die.* But the other half must've been a little more civilized. My husband had me hold the neck gash closed as he put his lips on that monster's mouth and pushed air into her lungs before they could become clogged. We were still at it when the ambulance arrived.

~ * ~

Our efforts saved the woman, whom I'd had this ambivalence about at the time. And I confess I still had some mixed feelings about that, even later. But okay, she was the enemy, and as Selena had said, we were supposed to love our enemies.

Guess I still had a ways to go on that one.

Then she later went through a very brief trial. Got herself put away for the attempted murder of a Federal agent, use of a firearm, (unregistered, of course) and some other illegal stuff. So that kind of took care of the last of the Webbers okay. Just have to learn to deal with my feelings, I guessed.

Clyde had emergency surgery, where they cleaned up a nicked intestine, sewed it and some major blood veins up and got the bullet out, and he survived, too. No conflicting loyalties there...celebration time as soon as he made it out of the hospital.

For his part, he was sort of down for a while about missing it with the Webbs a total of three times in a row. Just luck, we assured him, the wrong kind.

Maybe he really just wasn't cut out for this nasty job after all, he mused. Yeah, we all tactfully agreed. Besides, we—mostly Cheryl— wanted him around for a while, and law of averages...Hey, joinery could maybe sometimes be a drag, but it didn't usually get you shot at like what he'd been doing all these years.

So he thought about it for an amazingly short time, decided, then got an extended leave from it.

Then he and Cheryl got married. Repeat of the nice small wedding Craig and I'd had, with Alan officiating. Couldn't keep Clyde and Jason apart, once they started talking about cloak-and-dagger stuff. *Oh, no, not another narc in the making. Stick with carpentry, Jason.* Susan Kraft had been taking the pictures, but handed the camera to me and caught the bride's bouquet.

Then Clyde thought about his job some more, and finally said to hell with his agency and resigned.

Then to nobody's surprise, he dug out his old tools, got himself a pickup truck, but then pulled one on us: blacked out two teeth, pretended to chew tobacco, and showed up in an old duckbill cap, redneck to the core, ready to come to work with Craig and me.

But no beer gut.

*One* of the best joiners in the business, after all. Not as fast as this other one I knew yet, but damn good. Give him a few more years and who knew? I might wanta retire someday, do the mommy thing full-time.

*Nah.*

And as soon as I got done making another lady blacksmith outta Cheryl, we'd be one helluva restoration crew: wouldn't ever have to take any crap off *anyone.*

# Meet Charles McRaven

Charles McRaven is a former journalism professor, restoration contractor, current minister, stonemason, blacksmith, timberframer and log cabin builder. He and his wife Linda live in the central Virginia woods. This is his eighth novel.

## *Other Works From The Pen Of Charles McRaven*

*A Piece Of Ground* – Troubled Revolutionary War veteran Stephen Davis searches for a place to settle, is captivated by a planter's beautiful daughter, slights a gifted farm girl as criminal violence finds him. Loses both. Maybe.

*Troublesome Creek* – Sequel to *A Piece Of Ground*, as Stephen searches Kentucky Territory for the girl he lost. He encounters mastermind of criminals he'd previously destroyed, is almost killed. Rescued by girl and friend, he dispenses justice.

*A Place Of Stone* – Aging builder drops out of rat race and ruined marriage, builds tiny wilderness cabin. He finds elusive faith, possible love. Must make life choice.

*Sagebrush Treasure* – Haunted Civil War veteran rides west, befriends dying prospector, is hunted by unscrupulous land baron for rumored treasure. Taken in by quartet of orphaned, forceful ranch sisters, he finds, loses love, but the 'family' fights together to survive.

# *Letter to Our Readers*

## Enjoy this book?

## You can make a difference

As an independent publisher, Wings ePress, Inc. does not have the financial clout of the large New York Publishers. We can't afford large magazine spreads or subway posters to tell people about our quality books.

But, we do have something much more effective and powerful than ads. We have a large base of loyal readers.

Honest Reviews help bring the attention of new readers to our books.

If you enjoyed this book, we would appreciate it if you would spend a few minutes posting a review on the site where you purchased this book or on the Wings ePress, Inc. webpages at:

**https://wingsepress.com/**

*Thank You*

# Visit Our Website

*For The Full Inventory*
*Of Quality Books:*

*Wings ePress.Inc*
*https://wingsepress.com/*

*Quality trade paperbacks and downloads*
*in multiple formats,*
*in genres ranging from light romantic comedy*
*to general fiction and horror.*
*Wings has something for every reader's taste.*
*Visit the website, then bookmark it.*
**We add new titles each month!**

Wings ePress Inc.

3000 N. Rock Road

Newton, KS  67114

* 9 7 8 1 6 1 3 0 9 5 2 7 0 *